BRYANT & MAY:
PECULIAR LONDON

Bryant & May:
Peculiar London

Christopher Fowler

BANTAM

NEW YORK

Published in the United States by Bantam Books, an imprint of Random House, a division of Penguin Random House LLC, New York.

BANTAM BOOKS is a registered trademark and the B colophon is a trademark of Penguin Random House LLC.

Originally published in hardcover in Great Britain by Doubleday, an imprint of Transworld Publishers, London, in 2022.

LIBRARY OF CONGRESS CATALOGING-IN-PUBLICATION DATA
Names: Fowler, Christopher, author.
Title: Bryant & May : peculiar London / Christopher Fowler.
Other titles: Bryant and May : peculiar London
Description: New York : Bantam Books, [2022]
Identifiers: LCCN 2022030065 (print) | LCCN 2022030066 (ebook) |
ISBN 9780593356241 (hardback ; acid-free paper) | ISBN 9780593356258 (ebook)
Subjects: LCGFT: Detective and mystery fiction. | Novels.
Classification: LCC PR6056.O846 B78 2022 (print) | LCC PR6056.O846 (ebook) |
DDC 823/.914—dc23/eng/20220624
LC record available at https://lccn.loc.gov/2022030065
LC ebook record available at https://lccn.loc.gov/2022030066

Printed in Canada on acid-free paper

randomhousebooks.com

246897531

First U.S. Edition

Book design by Caroline Cunningham
Illustrations by Keith Page

For Pete

Would you know why I like London so much? Why, if the world must consist of so many fools as it does, I choose to take them in gross, and not made into separate pills, as they are prepared in the country.

—HORACE WALPOLE

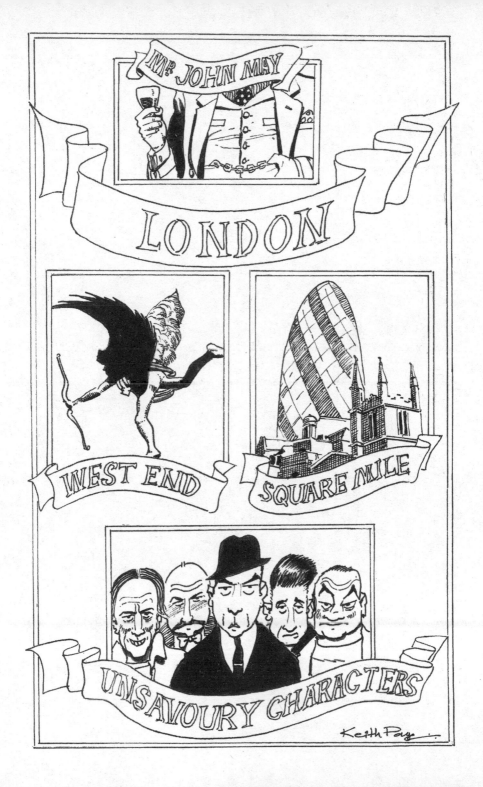

INTRODUCTION BY DCI JOHN MAY, PECULIAR CRIMES UNIT, LONDON

In all our years of crime detection in the UK capital there was only ever one main suspect: London itself.

Over the centuries the city shaped its residents, making them who they are. My partner, Arthur Bryant, knew this and used his knowledge of its sixty thousand streets to solve the unlikeliest crimes.

Before tragedy struck during our inquiry into the London Bridge murders, Mr Bryant wrote many volumes of memoirs. I wouldn't say they were popular but they were certainly different. His final volume was to be about the city in which he grew up. He treated it as an investigation, interviewing witnesses, taking testimonies from experts, gathering evidence to make his case over a number of years and finally enlisting my help to sort out the hopeless mess he'd made.

When I was clearing his medicinal herbs out of the evidence room I found a cardboard box containing the London files. Most consisted of old cassette recordings. The first challenge was finding anything that could play them. There were also some documents submitted by colleagues and friends. After cleaning them up—they were sticky, heaven knows with what—I realized that they constituted a personal, unreliable portrait of London, a tapestry with parts missing or altered, sewn together by my oldest friend.

There are new threads to be added every day. The story of London will never be finished. What follows are just a few dropped stitches.

BRYANT & MAY:
PECULIAR LONDON

The Peculiar Crimes Unit
The Old Warehouse
231 Caledonian Road
London N1 9RB

A MESSAGE FROM UNIT CHIEF RAYMOND LAND

Hello there.

As the chief of the Peculiar Crimes Unit, London's oldest specialist police division, I've been asked to say a few words about this volume. First, I'd like to point out that it's completely useless.

I thought it was some kind of guidebook but it's nothing of the kind. There's bugger all in here about what ordinary people want to do when they visit London, viz.: go to the London Eye, Big Ben and M&M'S World before sitting through the first half of *Les Mis*. Instead it's full of annoying conversations and weird historical connections no one's interested in. Half of them have no point and the other half go wandering off at a tangent, like Mr Bryant's mind. There are hundreds of perfectly acceptable London books knocking about and this isn't one of them. It's just someone randomly banging on about a lot of pointless, forgotten stuff.

Now, I respect my detectives Arthur Bryant and John May, partly because it looks bad if you're rude about old people. They've spent decades in this great metropolis solving proper crimes while the local constabulary have been busy arresting gentlemen for relaxing themselves in the neighbourhood's explicit cinemas and attacking each other with kitchen knives because the little bags they sell have been cut with Cillit Bang cleaner, but that doesn't suddenly make them experts on London. Skimming this book, it's clear that no lessons have been learned. Who cares about creepy alleyways and freezing churches? If I want to feel numb inside I'll visit my ex-wife.

Mr Bryant doesn't seem to have fact-checked half of it and there are no bloody photos. What's the point of a book about London that doesn't have a few generic copyright-free shots lifted off the internet? And all this stuff about pubs. A boozer is a place for a Scotch egg and knocking back a few pints, not trying to find out the last time Samuel Pepys was in. There are too many London 'characters,' the kind who prided themselves on being bohemian just because they got chucked out of saloons and dropped dead in Soho gutters before hitting thirty.

It's not as if Mr Bryant didn't have crimes to solve instead of running his 'Peculiar London' Walking Tours in the evenings. For some unimaginable reason people paid a few quid to follow him about in the cold, staring at brickwork and statues of blokes in silly wigs. I've seen him in action, doing all the voices and waving his hands at a group of easily duped French people as if hypnotizing them.

When people start talking about their hobbies in the office you know they're not working hard enough, a dilemma Mr Bryant solved by making work his hobby. He swears that he cracks cases by studying the history of London, which is a bit like saying you can tell the time by taking the clock to bits. What's wrong with the tried-and-tested method of arresting first and asking questions later? There's many a lad I've led up from the overnight cells with a bruise across the bridge of his nose who's ready to spill the beans on his mates, I can tell you.

Mr Bryant says who better to know about the city's dark side than a copper, but my rule of thumb is: If you know something disgusting about London, keep it to yourself and certainly don't mention it on speed dates.

I was off sick when we did history so I don't know a lot about it, but I do know that Mr Bryant's version of London's history is gibberish. He rewrites the past to incorporate his dreams or things he wishes had happened when they patently did not. And he dwells on what's not there more than what's left. I tell him, you can't live in the past, not when the rest of us are stuck in the present. It would help if he put his thoughts in some kind of order instead of behaving like the bloke who sits in the corner of the Dog and Duck telling everyone why his wife paid to have him killed.

And somehow he managed to drag his partner into this enterprise. I thought John May had more sense; he's the one who always knows which phone tariff he's on and how to split restaurant bills on an app. He's asked me to say something nice. Well, this book is not for you if you're the kind of person who likes Clarice Cliff ceramics and logging departure times at railway stations. I like detail and order and practicality. I do not enjoy whimsy, conjecture or people who call me Raymondo.

If you're still planning to read this volume of rambling conversations with half-mad friends, good luck to you. I reckon it's your last chance to dodge a bullet but what do I know, I'm only the Unit chief. You're big enough to look after yourselves. Don't come complaining to me; I live in a world of strangers where a novelty doughnut costs four quid and nothing makes sense anymore.

I suppose Mr Bryant has managed to reflect both himself and London, in that his account is annoying, all over the place, and occasionally apocryphal.

Anyway, 'enjoy the book.'

A Big Lump of Rock &
Other Stories

ARTHUR BRYANT: If history consists of what you can remember, I'm buggered.

I had my glasses in my hand a minute ago and now they've gone. And I've put a bag of chips down somewhere. I'm up in the PCU's evidence room, where we keep the impounded booze and my notes on London. I say notes. Not everything is legible. We have mice.

For years my walking tours around the capital were simply an evening job attended by retired archivists, socially awkward loners and the kind of people who shout about Jesus in public. They required me to argue with strangers, something I previously had little interest in doing if it didn't involve arresting them.

Rather than let this lot go to waste I decided to share it with you on a sort of virtual tour. I don't actually know what a 'virtual' tour is. John May tried explaining it but my attention drifted when he said 'online.' By the time he got to the metaverse I was sound asleep. He set me up on a Zoom call with Scotland Yard last week but I somehow ended up on a Welsh radio programme about knitting.

I can't compete with the kind of passionate historians who know how many double-decker buses you can fit into the Albert Hall, but I'll be making some connections that may take you by surprise. They certainly took me by surprise, not always in a good way.

Let's see if I can get this thing working. I found a cassette recorder up here that used to belong to one of the Kray twins. I erased the old tapes; you don't want to listen to some bloke screaming for two hours.

London was established by the Romans as a trading centre and that's what it still is. Almost everything else is based around ceremony and entertainment. You won't find anything here about the Little Venice Dragon Boat Pageant, the Bethnal Green Morris Dancers, the Bastille Day Waiters' Race or the Dagenham Girl Pipers, who for some unearthly reason became the punchline to many London jokes. A lot of the ceremonial events that take place in London occur in various forms around the globe, so they're not covered. The only fun thing about Trooping the Colour is waiting for guards to pass out on hot days, and you can read about Westminster Abbey anywhere (although I bet not everyone knows it's a 'Royal Peculiar,' meaning it belongs to the reigning monarch and not the Church). I'm more interested in exploring the obscure and unique. And I'm not sticking in loads of addresses. If you want those you can use the Googly-thing on your phone.

Now, your first question might be: why London?

It was the heart of the British Empire, the largest and wealthiest colonial power on the planet. There are only twenty-two countries in the world that we *didn't* invade. This expansion began in the 1600s and didn't come to a final end until 1997, when Hong Kong was handed back to China. So it makes sense to set our focus here.

The first thing you notice in Central London is the variety of buildings dating from so many different eras. When you wish to dignify a new town you first construct some municipal buildings based on classical Greek and Roman ideals. That's why there are still so many boring government offices that look like temples. Whitehall is a civil servants' Xanadu of Corinthian pillars and white stone pediments, especially when seen from across the lake in St James's Park. But grand buildings aren't enough to make you respect politicians. 'The higher the buildings the lower the morals,' said Noël Coward with some prescience. They don't build mock temples anymore. They commission global architects to design giant glass willies.

Three things transformed London: the Reformation, the Great Fire, the railways and the Blitz.

JOHN MAY: That's four things, Arthur.

ARTHUR BRYANT: You're not on yet, John. Wait for your cue.

Actually there's another thing, the revolt of the Iceni, but London as such didn't really exist that far back.

JOHN MAY: So, five things. And you have to hold both those keys down to record.

ARTHUR BRYANT: I've used a cassette player before. Believe it or not, I was once a big fan of new technology.

JOHN MAY: How am I only just hearing this? Why did you stop?

ARTHUR BRYANT: I bought the K-Tel Bottle Cutter and nearly severed my lips. Let's push on.

For me there is always a gap between what you read about a city and what you feel when you walk around it. I shall attempt to bridge that gap. I've assembled these observations with the help of my partner here, Mr John May, who took out some of the stuff that didn't exist and removed the more libellous remarks so that I wouldn't get attacked in public again.

The problem with London is its past.

Even though we often show a shocking disregard for it, it gets in the way of everything. We still build along the routes of ancient hedgerows and riverbeds, and our homes still follow Victorian principles even though the way we live has radically changed in the last seventy years. Our buildings have been repurposed, rebuilt, retouched and replaced. Look to the higher floors in Oxford Street and Tottenham Court Road and you may find a rococo plaster palace surviving above a hollowed-out discount-clothing store.

Nothing about the foundation of London is certifiably true. It's said that nine centuries before Christ, the leprous wolf-lord Bladud was the first British monarch to die in an aviation accident when his wings came off over the settlement of London. I don't entirely buy the story myself.

A better starting point for all this is the London Stone.

Until recently it sat behind a grille on Cannon Street in London's Square Mile, an unprepossessing lump of oolitic limestone about three feet wide. It had earlier been wedged somewhere on Candlewick Street, now gone, and had been blessed by Brutus himself, except that's just a legend. Brutus certainly didn't say, 'While this stone is protected London shall flourish,' because apart from the fact that he spoke Latin, why would he? It's manufactured history retrofitted for convenience, a nice little legend that adds a touch of colour.

But the London Stone did have some significance. It might have been a milestone from the Roman Forum, used to measure distances from the capital. Perhaps it was brought on a ship to symbolically found London, although it's more likely that it came from here. It was certainly mentioned in the twelfth century. Did it once exist as a Roman pillar rather than a crumb of rock? It doesn't seem to have got any smaller since. And did the rebel Jack Cade really strike his stick on it during the fifteenth century's biggest protest, Cade's Rebellion? Cade ended up being dragged through the streets and quartered, which was what happened back then if you complained about corruption in local government.

So, why have we bothered to hang on to an ugly, insignificant lump of rock of obscure origin? The truth is, we simply don't know. Over time, the London Stone became an object upon which to project our own ideas about the city. And like so much else in London, it survives unnoticed and barely commented upon.

Tenure of the Stone passed with the ownership of the land on which it stood for nearly three hundred years, the site of St Swithin's Church. Its final guardian was not Chaucer's 'parfit gentil knight' but the branch manager of WHSmith, the newsagent's shop that occupied the property. He probably let customers touch it if they bought a copy of *Razzle* and a Galaxy bar.

But there are other such objects dotted around the city. There's a huge polished stone outside University College Hospital off Tottenham Court Road that nobody venerates, yet here are sick people entering a house of healing: why don't they stroke it for luck? It's the people who decide what to honour; governments can't force us. If we think something has a bit of history behind it, just an odd anecdote, we're more likely to fight for its survival.

Yet even when I poke about in the past I can't truly know what it was like to be there. No two experiences of London are the same and any attempt to convey their fullness is doomed to failure. A timeline of Soho will take you from hunters' marshlands to rowdy coffee houses and walking its streets will give you a sense of its geography, but little can recapture its zeitgeist. The political, literary, gastronomic and artistic characters who lived there have nearly all gone, leaving behind a neighbourhood of ghosts.

| | |

I'm always surprised how little people know about the mythical foundation of London. Romulus and Remus may have founded Rome but we have two rather sinister giants, Gog and Magog, to thank for London. Early in every November there's a chance to see the wicker men themselves at the annual Lord Mayor's show.

Gog and Magog are sometimes called Gogmagog and Corineus. They're descended from a race of pagan giants. The story goes that the Roman Emperor Diocletian had thirty-three wicked daughters. He managed to find thirty-three husbands to 'curb their unruly ways'* (I love the sweeping generalizations of these myths), but the daughters were not pleased and, under the leadership of their eldest sister, Alba, they plotted to cut the throats of their husbands as they slept.

For this crime they were set adrift in a boat with half a year's rations—clearly it was a pretty big boat or they were light eaters—and following a horrible journey they arrived at the island that came to be named Albion, after the eldest. Here they stayed, and

---

* The Gigantick History of the two famous Giants, and other curiosities in Guildhall, London (volume 1), 1741.

with 'the assistance of demons'* (we're not told which ones) they populated the wild, windswept land with a race of giants. I imagine these are the same ones Beowulf tackled in his epic poem.

Some time later Brutus, the great-grandson of Aeneas, fled the fall of Troy and eventually arrived at the same islands. He also named them for himself, so we now know them as Britain. With him he brought his top champion, Corineus, who faced the leader of the giants in a massive one-on-one bundle and chucked him from a high cliff to his death.

The giant's name was Gogmagog and the rock from which he was thrown became known as Langnagog, or the 'Giant's Leap.' There's a general idea that this was at Plymouth Hoe, in the south. As a reward Corineus was given the western part of the island, which came to be called Cornwall after him. Brutus travelled to the east and founded the city of New Troy, which we know as London.

The tale slings up more questions than I can answer. When did Gogmagog switch from one creature into two separate giants? Why do they have such little legs? And why do we always venerate losers? (Boadicea, Eddie the Eagle, Boris Johnson.)

The full story can be found in Geoffrey of Monmouth's twelfth-century *Historia Regum Britanniae,* a loopy history that knits Celtic royalty into the heroic world of the Greek myth via the old Welsh legend of King Arthur.

We know it's mostly rubbish because the fall of Troy was around 1180 BCE, long before the reign of Diocletian, and the name Gogmagog is a mangled borrowing from the Old Testament.

But if that origin story doesn't suit you there are plenty of others to choose from, one involving Noah and King Albion that included a punch-up with Hercules. Why did anyone believe that

* Ibid.

Britain was founded by giants? In the fifteenth century some huge bones were unearthed and assumed to be from giants' skeletons. I suspect they were dinosaur bones.

These histories were accepted as fact for centuries. They had real importance to the medieval participants of early processions. It might simply have been that the Latins who invaded felt threatened by the British, who, like most northern races, were significantly taller than their southern counterparts.

We do know that Gog and Magog are most likely to be of Arabic origin, because they're only fleetingly in the Book of Revelation but they appear twice in the Qu'ran as Yajuj and Majuj.

If all this seems like ancient history to those in the New World, it's worth bearing in mind that merchants were busily writing out detailed receipts for goods five thousand years ago in the cradle of civilization, Iraq. It seems the Gog and Magog myths may have had an earlier life, so London might be Arabic in origin.

Which nicely complicates things.

I do hope I'm not putting you off just yet. Hang about, there's something wrong with this infernal machine. John, help me, would you?

JOHN MAY: Arthur, let me—there are yards of tape coming out, didn't you notice? Why don't you just record on your phone?

ARTHUR BRYANT: Ha ha. As if that was possible. There, I can wind it all in with a pencil.

Right, we're back. I'd just like to say—

JOHN MAY: You don't have to shout into it, you're not doing the shipping forecast.

Actually, can I say something? A bit I prepared earlier. Shall I read it?

For a city forged in fire, it's remarkable that London is two-thirds in shadow even on the brightest days. In summer there are just four hours of clammy darkness each night; in winter almost nothing but clouded gloom. Warm cities spend most of their lives asleep, but in the long winter London awakes. Its demeanour is corpse-grey and forbidding but it has the kind of temperate warmth that leaves you sweating in a raincoat. It's a city that thrives on money. Within is an ancient engorged heart that endures like a vampire feeding off willing victims.

ARTHUR BRYANT: A bit intense, John. Did you write that as a teenager, by any chance?

JOHN MAY: I did, as it happens. My first impression of London.

ARTHUR BRYANT: I do the impressions, if you don't mind. You might want to ease up on the metaphors, there's a chap.

JOHN MAY: I think you should carry on.

ARTHUR BRYANT: I was just about to. I'm old; everything takes longer. You've seen me on staircases.

This isn't a chronological history and I'm not going to drag you through every London neighbourhood, barking facts about monuments that aren't there anymore. I want you to glimpse other Londons. The good thing about this method is that you don't have to tip me and I don't have to keep you supplied with sausage rolls from Edwardian Fred's dodgy stall just because I still owe him money for a greyhound.

When you visit a new city, everything about it is exciting, with the possible exception of McDonald's. The lampposts, the food, the letter boxes: all inspire the curious. When we talk about London we often discuss it in the past tense, even though the city has a healthy disrespect for history and prefers to keep forging forward. I plan to redress the balance and wherever possible go backwards. We can talk about what's left. Much of the city is hidden from outsiders, but sometimes a door is left ajar.

You probably need a breather after all this. It gets racier as we go on, trust me. Time for a quick cuppa and a pee. Janice bought me a Tower Bridge teapot. It didn't quite find its place at home so it's downstairs in the Common Room, where we'll reconvene.

2

Going Up the Strand &
Other Stories

ARTHUR BRYANT: Like the streets themselves, London's history is contradictory and designed to trip you up. As I take you back and forth across the city, certain subjects, areas and characters will overlap. This is because many places have more than one facet to reveal, and because I tend to forget where I've been. I do know I prefer walks that aren't far from a toilet.

Unlike its rigidly planned European counterparts, London was never a regimented city. Most of its grand schemes were compromised. It was more like a disorderly natural garden, with the hardiest parts crowding out the weak and exotic new species arriving daily. It was constructed by landlords like the Duke of Bedford and builders like Thomas Cubitt, through private enterprise and public interference.

London is a city of immigrants. Hardly surprising, as the distance between England and France, using the traditional preferred measurement of London buses, is only around 2,772 bus-lengths, just over twenty miles. Immigrants built our first roads, founded Marks & Spencer, invented the Mini, the Ritz and the London Underground. Without a steady influx of global innovators the city would have died of stagnation centuries ago, and the process continues unchanged today.

I'm interested in the connections that reveal London's personality. Imagine you're on one of my walking tours. I had to give them up after an unfortunate incident. All I can say is, if you suddenly need to break wind don't slip into the royal box of the Theatre Royal, Drury Lane without first checking there's no one else in it.

Let's start this chapter in a small cul-de-sac called Rose Street, outside the Lamb & Flag public house in Covent Garden (you'd better get used to the pubs, as we'll be coming across quite a few). Back when the water of London was polluted, beer had once been recommended as a nutritional drink for children. Anyone could brew and sell it if they paid two guineas for the licence fee. By 1638 the Lamb & Flag was already an established public house, although like most London pubs of any longevity it had several other names.

Its sign is an ancient reminder of the Knights Templar, the lamb representing Christ and the flag St George. The pub is wedged into a corner of Rose Street and hemmed by Lazenby Court, connected via a narrow low-ceilinged passageway that has left many a homebound drunk with a bruised forehead. Not me, of course. I wear a hat.

In 1679 England's first Poet Laureate, John Dryden, was beaten up by three chaps in the passageway for writing an insulting satire about one of Charles II's mistresses. The assault became celebrated as the 'Rose Alley Ambuscade.' There's still an air of ambush about the place; once inside the alleyway, there is no easy way to pass someone.

The pub itself is narrow and dark, a perfect spot to set off from, like Burlington Bertie from Bow, heading along the Strand:

I'm Burlington Bertie, I rise at ten-thirty,
And saunter along like a toff.
I walk down the Strand with my gloves on my hand,
Then I walk down again with them off.

Except that this famous London music hall song is itself a parody of another earlier song, somewhat darker in tone:

Who is it that turns up, the lonely girl's friend?
Who is it that nightly his club must attend?
Who is it drinks brandy and smokes strong cheroots?
Who is it that gets into bed with his boots?
Burlington Bertie from Bow!

At the end of the original song Burlington Bertie makes up for his shady ways by offering to die for his country; not quite so jolly. You may as well get used to this; you're going to find that a lot of things are not quite how you thought they were. For now, though, let's saunter down the Strand.

As we'll see on numerous occasions, nothing in London is ever where it's supposed to be. Just as Islington's Upper Street is in fact its lower street, the Strand, one of London's grandest thoroughfares, is not a strand at all. A strand is the edge of a river, but the river in question here is the Thames. It follows a path only in the sense that you can eventually follow one end of a hurled rope to the other. The river meanders, but the Strand, its edge, does not.

This is because the Strand is not a bridle path but one of the straightest, widest roads in the capital. It was smartly paved and presented as the royal pathway to London, connecting the City's Square Mile to Westminster Abbey via the little village of Charing. It now finds itself lying inland, left high and dry because of the Victoria Embankment, which was created in 1870 by the Water Board, as the Strand was congested and London needed somewhere to site its sewage system.

Further along it is one of my favourite notorious London pubs, the Coal Hole, which turns up in my memoirs owing to its strong connection with Gilbert & Sullivan, who virtually lived their entire lives on the Strand. Although Sullivan ended up gambling his nights away in Nice, so that's not quite true. Dead at fifty-eight. Dreadful.

Gilbert & Sullivan were opposites in almost every way. William Schwenck Gilbert (words) was born just off the Strand and as a baby was kidnapped in Naples, an event which clearly influenced some of his plots. He was nervous, prickly, insular and rather posh. Arthur Sullivan (music) was lower in class, charming, expansive and likeable. Despite his constant ill health, his calm demeanour put everyone at their ease. On their opening nights at the Savoy, Gilbert would drive himself into so great a state of nervous tension that he couldn't bear to remain in the theatre. So he'd slip out and retire to the Coal Hole for a livener.

Gilbert & Sullivan are almost forgotten in their own city. Opera lovers snobbishly dismiss them as irrelevant, yet the opposite is true. Gilbert's satirical edge was enough to keep him from honours lists and Sullivan set new standards for sacred music. Theatres would have their house lights half up so that patrons could follow their librettos, but now surtitles have transformed the works and wiped away decades of horrible amateur productions by revealing how dry, witty and subtle G&S can be. They are part of the musical spirit of London.

The Coal Hole pub occupies what was once the coal cellar for the Savoy Hotel. It stands on the site of the Fountain Tavern, where the coal-heavers drank. Like many Strand venues it was a 'song and supper' club, where regulars were encouraged to sing sentimental ballads and comic songs with smutty punchlines. Gilbert & Sullivan regularly performed here after rehearsals. Well into the late twentieth century there were still pub acts parodying G&S operas.

The Shakespearean actor Edmund Kean started the Wolves' Club in the pub's basement for 'oppressed husbands forbidden to sing in the bath.' However, its real purpose involved heavy drinking and ladies of the night, most of whom worked just across the road. The cellar bar still bears the actor's name.

The theme of pale stone, dark wood and leaded windows carries into the street level bar. The ceiling is high. Black beams and hanging banners suggest something medieval, but the pub was decorated this way in 1904, a time of looking back. Beneath the beams is a marble frieze of maidens picking grapes. There's a huge fireplace decorated with a relief of vines. The gallery bar is a good vantage point, and there are dining rooms.

The pub's art nouveau décor was created in a brief interlude between the brashness of the late Victorian gin palaces and a new sentimental movement that favoured the fake Ye Olde Inne look. It's best on a rainy night, and if you venture to the rear of the pub and follow it around to the left you'll find a snug bar that can't have changed much in a century.

The Strand started the whole street-numbering thing because the official residence of the Secretary of State was here during Charles II's time and became known as '1 Strand.' There's one building with an even nicer address and that's Number One, London—Apsley House, built by Robert Adam in the 1770s, so called because it stood next to the turnpike into London. It was one of several aristocratic English townhouses on Piccadilly, but the others were demolished to widen Park Lane. It's probably the best preserved example because the 9th Duke of Wellington still lives in part of the building. It's a grand house but I've been all around the neighbourhood and couldn't find a decent tobacconist's anywhere.

I've always liked the narrow stepped ginnels that lead from the south side of the Strand down to the river. They hold hidden pubs like the Ship & Shovell, the only London pub in two halves, one bar on either side of the alley.

Its namesake, Sir Cloudesley Shovell, was Admiral of the Fleet, battling pirates and enemies of King Charles II until his ill-fated fleet was smashed on the rocks of the Scilly Isles in 1707.

Having lost his life and four of his ships in one of the greatest marine disasters in British history, Shovell was naturally commemorated on a pub sign. The disaster had spawned its own mythology; it was said that a sailor who had tried to warn the admiral that his fleet was off course had been hanged from the yardarm for inciting mutiny, and that as a result of this injustice no grass could ever grow on the admiral's grave.

There were other bizarre tales: that Shovell was still alive when he reached the shore of Scilly at Porthellick Cove but was murdered by a woman for the sake of his priceless emerald ring, and that the woman who stole it confessed on her deathbed thirty years later.

After two and a half centuries the remains of the lost fleet were discovered by a Royal Navy minesweeper. Its treasures were recovered and sold at Sotheby's. The pub survives as a monument to maritime failures. There's an elegant marble memorial to Shovell in Westminster Abbey, sculpted by Grinling Gibbons. That's what you get for being a rubbish admiral.

The Strand has a famous church in the middle of the road: St

Clement Danes, the Air Force church, surrounded by magnolia trees and traffic heading to Fleet Street. Greeting you are two statues of wartime RAF leaders, Hugh Dowding and Arthur 'Bomber' Harris.

In fact there are *two* churches right next to each other, but nobody notices the small, baroque St Mary le Strand; it's lost behind its grander sister. Charles Dickens's parents were married beneath its tiered steeple.

The Danish have long been associated with the Strand, and St Clement Danes was the centre of their settlement. The Vikings were supposedly an aggressive lot (although we don't really have a lot of information on their life in London) and had a bash at pulling down London Bridge.

Theatres were always a key part of the Strand's appeal. The Gaiety, on the Aldwych at the eastern end of the Strand, seated over two thousand patrons and sold perfumed programmes. Many theatres were built above springs, wells and waterways, partly because their impresarios wanted to incorporate water spectacles in their productions. The steam engine powering scene changes at the Palace Theatre ran (and I believe can still run) from an underground well.

On the side of the Lyceum Theatre just off the Strand three names could be seen: Terry, Stoker and Irving. Bram Stoker was the acting manager of the Lyceum. On 18 May 1897, a week before Stoker's most famous novel was published, *Dracula, or The Un-Dead* was performed at the theatre in order to secure its stage copyright. Only two members of the public paid a guinea to see it. The actor-manager Henry Irving turned down his chance to play Dracula, but then he also turned down the part of Sherlock Holmes. Bram Stoker died penniless and never saw the riches that accrued from his legacy. As for Ellen Terry, the beautiful leading lady of the late nineteenth century, she won accolades for her Shakespearian roles and moved from stage to screen. Her career spanned nearly seven decades.

The old Trafalgar Square tube station at the far end of the Strand had unique colours (brown, cream and green) so that passengers could identify it without having to read the name.

There were two other tube stations here: Embankment and Charing Cross. Strand and Trafalgar Square were too near each other to be needed. Embankment was actually Charing Cross but the Northern Line opened another Charing Cross nearer the station. You can't have two identically named stations in the same place so one became Charing Cross (Strand), then the Bakerloo opened their own Charing Cross (Strand) and the two older names sort of swapped, but there was another station called Strand at the other end of the Strand, so this became Aldwych while one Strand closed and the other became Charing Cross Embankment, and Trafalgar Square closed down and Charing Cross moved to Strand. Got it? Don't look at your friend and shake your head.

I sympathize. Like everything else in London, it's as clear as mud. God knows how visitors cope, especially after I've given them directions. If you want to know where everything is, by all means talk to a cabbie or a copper, but they'll give you different answers.

By the way, the name Charing Cross comes from Edward I's adoration of his wife, Eleanor of Castile, a successful businesswoman in her own right and an influential patron of literature; he called her his dear queen—*chère reine*. The ornate Gothic spire inconveniently stuck in the former car park outside Charing Cross Station is a Victorian replica of one of twelve monuments erected in the thirteenth century to her memory, which marked the resting places of her funeral procession. The others were at Lincoln,

Grantham, Stamford, Geddington, Northampton, Stony Stratford, Woburn, Dunstable, St Albans, Waltham and Cheapside. I'm not doing this from memory, I had Janice print them out for me.

At the other end of the Strand there's a deep and ancient holy well, underneath Australia House. It was used by the Saxons who inhabited Aldwych because they were too scared to live in the haunted Roman ruins of the City. Maybe they had a phobia about short Italians. Everyone threw their rubbish down the well and then drank out of it. Typical. But it's still there under a wooden lid, and its water is probably more potable now than it was then.

The Strand became popular with dukes and earls. The governors of the Empire headed here to purchase their fly whisks and solar topees. Dickens enjoyed the 'Roman' bath on Strand Lane, the *Strand* magazine introduced the world to Sherlock Holmes, and Strand cigarettes told smokers, 'You're never alone with a Strand.'

The Wig and Pen Club at number 230, opposite the Royal Courts of Justice, gained its name because gossip was sold to journalists from those inside the court. It's the only Strand building to survive the Great Fire of London and has now closed down, trapping the headless ghost of Oliver Cromwell inside it. The gaiety theatres and music halls, the brothels, taverns and supper clubs had nearly all vanished by the twenty-first century, unable to compete with office rents.

One end of the Strand is guarded by a legendary creature: the silver Temple Bar 'gryphon.' It marks the line where royalty is separated from commerce. Theoretically the Queen isn't allowed to go east of it without receiving a formal invitation from the Lord Mayor.

The Strand was ahead of its time. It had the first gas lamps, the first public electric lighting and the first plate-glass windows along its length. During the Second World War the plate glass was blown out and replaced with telephone directories—a decent substitute for sandbags.

But the street was also a steadfast barrier between rich and poor. While the royal family owned the land from the south side to the river, the half not under their jurisdiction was threaded with dark alleyways where mountebanks, stage-door Romeos and good-time girls loitered to smoke and flirt. A few of them are still there (the alleyways, not the good-time girls).

The Strand is full of surprises. The playwright Ben Jonson used to drink in the Palsgrave Tavern, which was turned into London's most elegant bank, Lloyds, which was covered in mosaics of beehives, fish and owls. The story goes that the dining room of Lloyds was air-conditioned by two ladies in the basement riding a tandem to power a pair of bellows. It sounds ridiculous, but when the building was renovated workmen found the bicycle and its attached airpipe.

So a bank was once a pub, and a tea shop was once a coffee house.

The Starbucks on Russell Street was a coffee house three hundred years earlier, in 1712. Back then it was called Button's, and it wasn't the first. A Greek chap had started selling Turkish coffees in London in 1652. By the beginning of the next century there were over three thousand coffee houses here. They allowed for free public discourse, bringing together ideas and discoveries. Isaac Newton once dissected a dolphin on a table in the Grecian Coffee House. The venue was frequented by members of the Royal Society and gradually became a centre of learning.

Although coffee encouraged sociability, tea remained king. Apparently 68 percent of Britons turn to tea in a dilemma, making it Britain's most common response to trouble. On Christmas mornings my old man used to put whisky in everyone's tea as part of a family tradition he had just made up. No wonder our aspidistra died.

The Twinings Tea Museum should therefore be a place of pilgrimage. It's actually a tiny shop built on the site of Tom's Coffee House in the Strand, and has been around since 1706. The tea is excellent and they have a delightful range of teapots. It's the world's oldest tea shop, a narrow canister-lined hall with a miniature 'tea museum' (actually a few cupboards) at the end. The exhibits include a wooden box with the gold-painted initials 'T.I.P.,' meaning 'To Improve Promptness.' If you wanted your beverage a bit faster you'd drop a few pence in, hence the word 'tip.'

All this recording is parching my throat. I shall be stopping at a nearby hostelry for oesophageal easement, so this part of the tour is now over. Oh, sorry, your 'virtual' tour. John, if anybody wants me I may be found in the Scottish Stores.

JOHN MAY: Your recorder is still taping.

ARTHUR BRYANT: I think it's gummed up with something. I shouldn't have gone near it with glue on my hands. Could you have a look? You're the technical one.

JOHN MAY: Only if you buy me a pint.

3

A Bent Stick
& Other Stories

ARTHUR BRYANT: I spy something beginning with beer.

Before we get too deep into my personal take on this great metropolis of nine million people, my partner John feels that as my old nickname was 'Hollow Legs' Bryant, I am the most qualified to explain why public houses occupy such an important place in London's cultural life.

Boozers became territories into which you could be invited by a landlord or landlady who had the right to favour you or bar you. They tended not to kick out the interesting ones even when they were quite mad, so pubs became places for top banter, where opposites could meet and confront each other without prejudice, on neutral territory.

That's why the landlord is referred to as the host, and why rooms in pubs were used to hold local inquests, so that the deceased could be sure of a fair and impartial verdict upon his death.

Walking into a pub alone was for many young people a rite of passage and their first act of independence. The connection between pubs and conviviality gives us a more louche attitude to drinking than, say, in America, where you have to be twenty-one years of age. Quafftide* is a cornerstone of being English.

Pubs had a profound effect on English society, acting as combined intellectual salons, psychotherapy units and hotbeds of conspiratorial rebellion. We get newspapers from coffee houses and pubs, where gossip was first written down and circulated, and they're still often owned by celebrities as a badge of pride.

Pubs are wilfully eccentric and have a complex set of social codes. Some celebrate their history with rituals or commemorative events where the patrons dress up. You never tip, but you can buy the host a pint when you order another round by saying 'Have one for yourself,' and if you feel your beer glass is not full enough, you may ask for a top-up without incurring rancour. All PCU staff have to learn the rules of a complicated coin game solely designed to trick Raymond Land into buying huge rounds. He'll be along a bit later. We can try it out on him then.

London still hosts theatre pubs, traditional pubs, readers', writers' and artists' pubs, sports pubs and a thousand places where odd societies or different professions meet. Pubs infiltrate our language; drinkers used to share the same mug, in which the level of ale was marked with a wooden peg, hence the expression 'to take you down a peg or two.' The masons who built our churches were housed at inns, hence the Masonic connections of certain pubs, and even the Knights Templar had their own drinking holes.

Pub names provided markers for all kinds of historical events and characters—Red Lion, White Hart, George & Vulture, Crown & Anchor, Royal Oak, Coach & Horses; each has its own convoluted meaning. Publicans who named their boozers after specific monarchs grew tired of repainting their signs and adopted less time-sensitive royal titles, like the more generic Rose & Crown.

* Time for drinking.

We meet our loved ones in pubs and even find our way around the city by their locations. In the late Victorian era there was one pub for every one hundred people in the country. Cultural barriers were broken down on almost every street corner. To find the real London, you need to go into the backstreets and find a corner pub.

The staff of the Peculiar Crimes Unit drink at the Scottish Stores (1901) on the Caledonian Road. When the hardboard walls of the dodgy old strip club on this site were removed a few years ago, the original Arts and Crafts décor of the earlier pub was found to have been perfectly preserved behind the panels, and the pub was restored.

We also favour the King Charles I, which has a mix of old hippies, art students and deranged barflies. It once hosted the Nude Alpine Climbing Challenge and is always either packed or closed, according to some mysterious timetable the landlord keeps in his head. There are stags' heads dotted around and a stained-glass window of someone who may or may not be one of the Everly Brothers. There was a stuffed moose above the bar billiards table but he fell to bits. The bar is tiny, yet they find room to have bands playing. The last time I went there the drinkers played themes from *Star Wars* on massed ukuleles, led by Uke Skywalker. The science fiction writer Iain Banks wandered in one evening and we got into an argument about quantum physics.

In 1867 the Trades Directory listed the top London trade as being a publican. Perusing the directory, I found a lengthy list of the mid-Victorian period's most popular pub names. In number-one place was the King's Arms (eighty-seven) and the King's Head (sixty) with the Queen's Arms and the Queen's Head following closely behind, it clearly being fashionable to spatchcock the royals into body parts.

At the last count there were twenty-six Royal Oaks, seventy-three Crowns, plus many variants thereof—Crown & Anchors, Crown & Cushions, Crown & Sceptres, Crown & Apple Trees, Crown & Anvils and Crown & Barley Mows. Then we shift down the royalty tree to include Princes Albert and Alfred and Princesses Beatrice and Alice before moving on to dukes and duchesses, oddly no barons but an assortment of lords and ladies. I do this research so that you don't have to.

There are a lot of blue things: Blue Pumps, Anchors, Lasts, Posts and one Blue-Eyed Maid in Borough High Street. Twenty-four Red Lions herald a bestiary of Dragons, Horses, Monkeys, White Harts (deer), Swans, Goats, Spread Eagles and Red Herrings. Three seems to be a lucky number: Three Tuns, Three Turks, Three Compasses, Three Spies, Three Castles, Three Horseshoes, etc. There are a lot of professions, too: Jolly Butchers, Carpenters, Skinners, Hatters, and of course a plethora of naval heroes and naval terms, like the Ship & Billet and the We Anchor In Hope. The Crooked Billet is a name that traditionally refers to a bent stick that has fallen from a tree. It dates from a time when an old boot or a stick would be hung from a tree to indicate the presence of an alehouse.

There's a steady turnover of pubs with pastiche names like the Ape & Bird, the Camel and Artichoke, the Pregnant Man, the Frog and Radiator, the Pyrotechnists Arms, John the Unicorn, the Blacksmith & the Toffeemaker, and the Racketeer, the last named after Dickensian hooligans who would make a racket on saucepans to distract a fine lady or gentleman while they were having their pockets picked.

I have a fondness for blunt names like the Dog, which was in Archway ('I'm going up the Dog for an hour'), and the Boot, one of several boozers frequented by Charles Dickens, still very much alive in Bloomsbury. Nearly every pub in London got rid of its separate bars. Only a tiny handful have retained the old screens that divided Public and Saloon. These separated the ruffians from the bank clerks, but were topped with rotating smoked-glass panels so that you could chat through them, should you wish to converse with someone from the lower orders. I'm not a fan of the class system, so in my book the removal of screens was a bloody good idea.

| | |

Now for something that's gone. You'll find I do this a lot. My only excuse is that I've lived too long and remember a great many things that aren't there anymore or were possibly never there in the first place.

A walking tour with nothing to see is depressing—'Beneath this car park was the spot where Anna May Wong performed her celebrated fan dance' and so on—but this is a book so you don't have to worry about not seeing something that isn't there. Things move about a lot in London. Right now I'm thinking about a bookshop that won't stay still.

Samuel French was a Massachusetts entrepreneur who cofounded a theatrical publishing and licensing business in 1859. He soon became the most important theatrical publisher in England. At the time of his death in 1898 almost all renowned English playwrights of the present and recent past had been represented by his Covent Garden company.

In the 1960s new theatre writing flourished, but rising labour costs forced up seat prices, which meant that theatres needed houses to stage sure-fire hits that would pay for new plays. If plays fail to enter repertoires they vanish. The shock of their experience fades, and only the scripts are left behind like phantoms. French published these phantom scripts and sold them to theatre companies. His shop was a treasure house of theatre where penniless writers and actors sat on the floor reading all day. In 2018 it found its latest home in Chelsea's Royal Court Theatre.

When you're a beat officer you see London from the pavement up. Shops are gutted and replaced at phenomenal speed. Go away for the weekend and you'll return to find that your favourite bookshop has become a Japanese bubble tea bar. I'm told they're a 'thing' now, whatever that means.

And you get to know the people who stick around. Tiny Elena Salvoni worked in the London restaurant business for more than seven decades. After the war she ran a restaurant called Bianchi's on Soho's Frith Street, and stayed there for the next thirty years. Although it was popular with Sean Connery, Maria Callas and the like, she encouraged broke actors and artists to hang out there too, knowing they would bring a certain louche, argumentative charm to the place. They would sit with their French's play scripts and bicker, and whenever it looked as though they couldn't afford to stay any longer she would stroll past the table and surreptitiously stick a bottle of cheap plonk on it so that they wouldn't leave. I blame my drinking habits on that woman, but thanks to people like her Covent Garden and Soho kept a reputation for literary and artistic gatherings. Anyone in a silly hat can be a 'character,' but Soho didn't just have characters—it had talent.

French's, Bianchi's, various basement cafés, dive bars like the Bag O' Nails, corrupted from the 'Bacchanales' (French religious festivals), did more for struggling artists than most courses in creativity. Every city needs its thinkers and dreamers, or, as Meera calls them, 'layabouts.'

While we're on the subject of London theatricals, you may wish to consider visiting Pollock's, the combined theatre shop and toy museum in Whitfield Street, just behind Charlotte Street. It was also started in Covent Garden a couple of hundred years ago by a gentleman named John Kilby Green, and continued to delight children for generations. During the Second World War a V2 rocket destroyed the building but the stock, including the beautiful printing plates used in making the toy theatres, had been moved to safety beforehand.

Painted red and green, the museum retains a strange charm in its narrow winding corridors and still sells its miniature cut-out toy theatres. If children could be encouraged to build these instead of staring at their walkie-screens the world would be a nicer place. Don't get me started before I've had one of my pills.

| | |

I need to mention the East End district of Whitechapel because it's where I was born, and thought that perhaps we could discuss it without mentioning J*ck the R*pper. But I think we'll have to brush up against his coat-tails.

For me, Whitechapel seems to exist in multiple dimensions.

Once it was the home of wealthy merchants and members of the all-devouring East India Company. It has housed French, Jewish and Bangladeshi immigrant communities, welcoming all into its teeming, pungent backstreets, and all have left their imprint. But before then, I'd like to have shown you Dorset Street (prime R*pper territory, as it housed Mary Kelly, his final victim). This was the infamous 'worst street in London,' named by George Duckworth, the investigator working for one of London's great social reformers and benefactors, Charles Booth. Dorset Street is now buried beneath blocks of squeaky clean offices.

Booth recognized the limits of philanthropy and did something about it. He pushed for the first old-age pensions and in 1889 created maps of the London poor, tabulating and grading streets, trying to understand how their residents survived.

His poverty maps show how a handful of bad families categorized as the 'vicious poor' could destroy the reputation of a whole neighbourhood. Consequently, benefactors descended upon the East End to do good works. Not all were sympathetic; the Reverend Lord Sydney Godolphin Osborne sneered in *The Times* that East Enders were 'a species of human sewage.' As far as I can tell all he ever did was write indignant letters to *The Times*.

For me Whitechapel was simply home. I was raised in a Victorian terraced house without a bathroom, a television, a fridge or a lavatory. Tell this to kids now and they look horrified. Tell them that the lavatory was outside, the food was kept cool in a tin-fronted pantry and you had to fill a tin bath in the kitchen to wash, and they'll think you're three hundred years old. Chilling food in refrigerators was a habit we adopted from America. Our produce was purchased fresh and in such a cool climate it didn't need storing just above zero.

For nearly two centuries Whitechapel became the sanctuary of paupers and those who preyed upon them, until estate agents suddenly noticed it was within walking distance of the City of London. Now developers have planted glass towers between the crumbling brick terraces. The new tenants breathe filtered air in cool grey sanctuaries while below them scarlet, azure and emerald sarees are unrolled in Indian stores.

At one edge of Whitechapel was Petticoat Lane, but in a typical London paradox there was never such a street. It's the name of the market that's still there on Sundays. Once called Hog Lane, now Middlesex Street, it remains almost as chaotic and grubby as it ever was. Some said it gained its name because the traders would steal your petticoat at one end of the market and sell it back to you at the other.

For the fashionable, Whitechapel is now filled with converted lofts and basement cocktail bars. But to those who work there it's still a ramshackle market operating from within the battered shells of the twisted old houses that line Commercial Road. Brick Lane was long known as the perfect place for a Ruby Murray* (although every Indian restaurant along it insists they're the winners of the Best Brick Lane Curry award), but now it's in decline. Office workers no longer have huge lunches and prefer to grab a bagel.

It's hardly a tourist highlight but Whitechapel has an oddity; when Wickhams department store was built in 1850 the owner failed to persuade a family of jewellers in the centre of the block to sell up. So the department store was built around the shop, leaving a bizarre gap in the middle. Eventually the jewellers outlasted the department store. It's always about the long game.

For those sensation-seekers hoping to feel a frisson of Victorian evil, Whitechapel is, for better or worse, still the home of Saucy Jack and will always be associated with the year 1888. There's less of a Gothic atmosphere about the place now, yet a few paces from busy, knocked-about Commercial Street is Whitechapel's Toynbee Hall. It was built by social reformers and on a stormy night could provide the isolated setting for a Hammer horror film. I've been to a few creepy events held there.

Whenever a film shows us Victorian London we see strumpets rolling out of inns and hansom cabs on cobbles, but what was an ordinary street like around that time?

To answer that question, let's hop across to the West End and take a look at the Tottenham Court Road of 1880. This was the artery that joined London's West End to the North. The buildings were of orange brick, grand, ornamented and freshly Gothic, surrounded by horse-drawn omnibuses and genteel squares.

The road is the crossing point of three parishes: St Maryle-

---

* Belfast singer who had five hits in the Top Twenty in a single week in 1955 and gave us rhyming slang for a curry.

bone, St Pancras and St Giles-in-the-Fields. An area coterminous with the ghosts of buildings lost. The last old wildfowl shop, one of those with gold letters on black glass, where a Christmas goose could be taken down from a rack of fifty fat birds, is long gone. The area has always been disrespectful of fine architecture; an elaborate five-floor building standing alone on Bozier's Court was demolished to 'improve the view.' Traffic grew heavy, carriages rolling in every direction.

The view changed forever as the ornate buildings fell in 1940, searchlights crossed the sky, shrapnel bounced and sparkled on the pavements and couples made frantic love in darkened doorways, fearing each night would be their last. The war changed everything, as we'll see time and again in these accounts.

The latest incarnation of Tottenham Court Road is sterile but faring better than its neighbour, poor Charing Cross Road. The old Astoria Theatre was a conversion from the Crosse & Blackwell pickle warehouse, and was torn down in 2009. Now there are blinging glass boxes, one finished in rose pink and gold for no reason other than architectural hubris. It has become a road of nothing because nobody lives here anymore.

Twenty years ago it had still been full of medics from the Middlesex Hospital, paying reduced rents to live nearby and be on call. The Middlesex was torn down in 2005 to make way for apartments, but there was a problem: hidden deep inside the old hospital was a golden Gothic Revival chapel decorated with mosaics and stained glass. It could not be destroyed without a public outcry. The Fitzrovia Chapel remains, all but forgotten within a shiny carapace of luxury lifestyle living.

Tottenham Court Road was always affectionately known as TCR—Charing Cross Road is still CXR—and was popular for its homewares. Here the rich and poor collided, to one side the used-car dealers and wide boys of Warren Street, to the other the genteel intellectuals of Bloomsbury. Now there are just a handful of shoppers, drifting between the chain stores like drowsy pollinators.

At least Heal's, the resolutely British furniture store, is still there after over two centuries of continuous service. In 1923 Dodie Smith, the author of *The Hundred and One Dalmatians*, joined Heal's and ran their toy department, as well as having an affair with Mr Heal. She sold the shop's mascot, the bronze cat on the staircase, for forty pounds and had to write to the customer to retrieve it. In Valerie Grove's book *Dear Dodie* she was described as being 'not temperamentally suited' to the job of being a floor-walker and 'once flung one of the assistants, a heavy girl, across the china department.'

| | |

There are few areas of London still associated with a smell, but one of the remaining ones is Smithfield, its old meat market. Once known as Smooth Field, it remains one of Central London's most historic and least understood spots, a strange, secular world with its own rhythms and residents. I've always liked it around there.

Smithfield has been occupied since the Bronze Age, and was favoured by the Romans. Religious orders arrived. The Priory of St Bartholomew was founded by a fool, the court jester to King Henry I, and a great hospital for the poor was built, but from worship and healing something malignant grew.

Smithfield became an execution site where Catholics and Protestants were tortured (often creatively) and burned. The area, always poor, found use as the perfect spot for resting cattle. By the eighteenth century thousands of sheep and cows were being brought to the market. By the time they had been walked to London they were thin and sickly, and needed fattening. Their waste was dumped into the Fleet waterway and eventually blocked it solid. Too much meat has a tendency to do that.

On market days the locals were in danger of being trampled or tossed by bulls. They were known to blunder through the backstreets, even barging into china shops, and I was told that's where the saying comes from. Rapine and murder took place under the blanket of night in Smithfield's mean alleyways. The alleys are still there.

London ran on meat. As the market rose it employed a great workforce and grew an immense dome above it. The airy colonnades of the underground cold stores were filled with hanging carcasses. The cellars were connected to railway lines, to speed supply and satiate the city's vast appetite.

The market porters were known as 'bummarees.' It's an eighteenth-century term still in use that feels as if it might be Indian in origin. Bummarees were initiated by being dumped in meat trolleys, stripped naked and pelted with eggs, flour and rotting offal. The tradition continues, probably without the offal part.

During the Second World War Churchill's boffins planned to take over the market's cellars and create portable aircraft landing strips from icebergs. I know it sounds like I'm making this up. When you add sawdust to water and ice you can make a shatterproof material called pykrete. The plan would have probably worked but in the end it didn't need to be actioned.

Smithfield's history is still present in its passages and alleys. It escaped the greatest conflagrations: the Great Fire and the Blitz. It remains a paradox; as its meat market operated through the night it became one of London's only twenty-four-hour neighbourhoods. Smithfield has been mostly overlooked and often appears deserted, but (as any copper knows) that's the perfect place to hide in plain sight.

I was talking to one of the butchers there and he greeted an old market friend by inviting him in to skin a rabbit. Nobody ever says that to me in Sainsbury's. By the way, providing you're not a vegetarian it's a good idea to have dinner near a meat market. I can recommend the bone-marrow salad at St. John.

The history of one building in the Smithfield complex has been almost entirely wiped away, except in the logbook of the London Fire Brigade.

In 1958, Poultry Hall, once London's second-most-recognized structure after Big Ben, burned to the ground. The building was immense—an entire city block was topped with an ornate, elegant tower. Two and a half acres of labyrinthine basement caught fire, a disaster many years in the making. The building's underground meat lockers were lined with flammable insulation made of cork affixed by tar. It was impregnated with decades of animal fat, and turned the flames into a relentless blowtorch of an inferno with only one escape channel, through the vast circular roof.

It was as if the place had been built as a giant candle lined in tallow. Firemen were sent in, and died. The underground parts were a maze that got them lost, and they were quickly cut off by the flames. The meat, fat and grease provided fuel enough to continue burning for three days. Flames eventually gutted the market floor and toppled the roof. Station Officer Jack Fort-Wells and Firefighter Dick Stocking from the Clerkenwell Fire Station died in the cold storage lockers in the early stages of the battle, which was ultimately waged by 1,700 firefighters and 389 appliances. Dozens were seriously injured.

The ornate building was replaced with a concrete shell—the largest freestanding concrete structure in Britain at the time—and it's pretty ugly, although you can get an idea of the size when you stand beneath it.

Smithfield, surrounded by colourful purple and red wrought-iron gates, remains strangely atmospheric. An area of corpses, human and animal, and of great feasts and celebration. It's a spot where the living have always danced with the dead.

And it still smells of raw flesh. The whole area is meatified.

JOHN MAY: 'Meatified' isn't a word.

ARTHUR BRYANT: I'm fairly sure it is.

JOHN MAY: No, that's a Bryantism.

ARTHUR BRYANT: Now, *that's* not a word.

JOHN MAY: It's a word we came up with at the Unit. Bryantism applies to anything you explain wrongly.

ARTHUR BRYANT: Like what?

JOHN MAY: Like 'walkie-phone' and 'internet-thingie.' You don't like jeans because they've got 'fumbly-buttons.' What did you call Raymond Land this morning?

ARTHUR BRYANT: Yoghurty-brain.

JOHN MAY: There you are. All classic examples of Bryantisms. And when you pick up the shipping forecast on your phone or get *Carry on Camping* on the video security system it's because the phone and the system have become Bryantized. When you leave us all utterly confused we know we've been Bryanted. And whenever you magnetize your waste bin or make children pass out it's because they've been subject to Bryantification.

ARTHUR BRYANT: I'm sure I don't know what you mean.

4

A Meat Pie & Other Stories

ARTHUR BRYANT: In the year 334, Jesus appeared to St Martin in a dream. Martin wasn't a saint then, just another Roman soldier. But he was canonized for having the dream and buried at the edge of Covent Garden, where Henry VIII created the parish of 'Saynt Martyns-yn-the-Ffelds' in 1536. I wish we still spelled words like that.

Henry didn't want plague victims coming anywhere near the Palace of Whitehall with their filthy germs so he had the church rebuilt. The original cockney thief and jailbreaker Jack Sheppard is buried there. William Hogarth too, and Nell Gwyn, dead at thirty-seven before her oranges had turned mouldy. She had been born in Coal Yard Alley off Drury Lane and went on stage as a man in *The Maiden Queen*. This was popular with audiences, who could see a woman's shape more clearly in men's clothes. Nell became Restoration comedy's superstar and Charles II's mistress, although everyone still thinks of her flogging fruit in Covent Garden. They never let you forget your roots.

St Martin's got grander. The church owns the adjacent alley-way so it has its own inscribed lampposts. Everyone hated the new design yet it became copied all over the world, especially in America. It's the parish church of both the royal family and the Prime Minister.

But it's an oddly unlovable building, coldly elegant within, severe without, rectangular and faced with a portico whose pediment is supported by giant Corinthian columns. It didn't improve matters much when we had to investigate a murder on its steps.

People don't talk much about London's atmospheres, but they're something I'm going to return to regularly. If you have any sensitivity at all you notice these things. St Martin's almost defies you to step inside. It feels apocalyptic somehow, much like the agoraphobia-inducing air of St Paul's. John doesn't notice it but I do, being far better attuned to such subtleties.

The crypt is welcoming and you can have lunch on top of the gravestones in there. On my mystery tours we usually stop for a cuppa and a sausage roll (with meatless option) as I have a bit of a deal going on with the cook. He's been my pal ever since I cleared his name, after he was accused of being the Smithfield Bacon Slicer.

JOHN MAY: Arthur, you know you asked me to warn you whenever you started drifting off-subject? You're doing it now.

ARTHUR BRYANT: Thanks, John. If I start doing it again, burn a feather under my nose or something.

Forget finding St Martin's in any actual fields; you're hard-pushed to locate any trees. It has always been a community church, with a history of sheltering the homeless. In both World Wars soldiers were billeted in the crypt. And check out the arched central East Window, which looks like there's some kind of space-time warp going on. I suppose it makes a nice change from shepherds and fat little cherubs tangled up in high-thread-count sheets.

St Martin's proves the point about nothing in London being where it should be. Its position in the corner at the top of the square feels wrong, but that's what happens when a city is repeatedly created and destroyed in sections over two thousand years. Trafalgar Square is much newer than the church and now dominates the area.

There are far too many churches in London for us to cover—there are nearly fifty in the Square Mile alone, and a surprising number of them have forgotten features. From somewhere holy let's go somewhere *unholy*, to the Old Bailey.

JOHN MAY: That is the worst segue I've ever heard.

ARTHUR BRYANT: Are you still here?

JOHN MAY: I think you need me here with links like that.

ARTHUR BRYANT: I'm on a learning curve.

JOHN MAY: Arthur, your learning curve flatlined about thirty years ago. If I hadn't pushed you to use a laptop you'd still be on your old Remington Portable.

ARTHUR BRYANT: How am I supposed to introduce Coatsleeve Charlie now?

JOHN MAY: Let me do it. Here to talk about the Old Bailey is Mr Cecil 'Coatsleeve' Charlie, one of London's most respected housebreakers. A bailey is another name for a city wall, and for this we need someone who knows the place from the inside.

COATSLEEVE CHARLIE: I've been sat over here listening to you for the last half-hour. I don't know what you're going on about city walls for. It all starts with an Anglo-French word, *bail,* meaning custody or charge, and also 'to hand over.' In its time the Old Bailey has handed me a few sentences I could have done without.

The Central Criminal Court of England and Wales has been housed in several buildings near this one since the sixteenth century, but the current one was only built in 1902. Anyone can visit the public gallery and sit in on a case. I love looking up and seeing you all there gawking.

Court Number One is where the nation's juiciest murders are discussed and where the most scandalous trials take place. It's good fun so long as you don't do what Mr Bryant did. He smuggled in a meat pie and surreptitiously opened it in his lap before realizing it was really hot.

ARTHUR BRYANT: I hate microwaves. I admit I shouldn't have yelled but I didn't expect to be escorted out.

COATSLEEVE CHARLIE: The twenty-two-ton golden statue on the top of the building's dome is Lady Justice. She holds the sword of retribution and the scales of justice. Contrary to popular belief she's not blindfolded, which explains a lot.

ARTHUR BRYANT: Are you saying our justice system is corrupt? You were let off.

COATSLEEVE CHARLIE: Only because they couldn't find the evidence.

ARTHUR BRYANT: I think in the interests of the legal system you should tell us what you did with two hundredweight of jellied eels at short notice. Pray continue.

COATSLEEVE CHARLIE: Inside, the courtrooms are all arranged the same way, with people like me standing in the dock facing the witness box and the judges. When it was still candlelit it must have been a pretty haunting place. The rooms were dark and shadowy, so mirrors were fixed over the bar to reflect light onto the faces of the accused. The members of the court believed that studying facial features could help you decide if a cove was innocent or guilty. I reckon if you were ugly and charged with burglary, you were more likely to be hanged.

Anyone can go to the Central Criminal Court of London without having first committed a serious crime. If you're thinking of visiting, here's what you need to know.

There are two parts to the building, old and new. The public gallery is in the old part, and Court One has seen some right notorious faces. It's where the trials of the Yorkshire Ripper and the Kray brothers took place. It's an old chamber with small seats and rotten leg room, and the jurors get restless, so judges often move to courts in the new building, which are better if you're going to be there for a long time.

Court Two is the high-security court and Court Twelve gets used for long fraud trials, which are incredibly boring unless you want to see career crims in too-tight Savile Row suits lying their faces off.

Regular punters can't go into the main body of the building, just to the public galleries to view trials. If you're lucky and get an interesting case it can be an eye-opening experience. Sometimes I've gone along just to pick up a few tips and make an afternoon of it. But you're not allowed to applaud the speeches.

The court's a public building, so anyone can go in, but you have to queue if the public gallery is full. These days so many trials have high security that it's more trouble than it's worth, and bear in mind that the bigger the case, the slower it's likely to go, so you'll be sat there for a bloody long time. It's not as much fun as going to the pictures.

In the nineteenth century, the courthouse was still part of Newgate prison. I figured out that in 1868 you could conceivably have caught the tube to see a good hanging—the first underground trains started running four years earlier. The following year Charles Dickens helped to get the practice stopped in public. Newgate was always an overpoweringly sinister place. It remained in use for over seven hundred years and didn't shut its doors until the start of the twentieth century.

There's a secret tunnel running between the Old Bailey and the church of St Sepulchre-without-Newgate, so that the chaplain could nip over and administer last rites without having to plough through the waiting crowds.

The next morning, the prisoner would be given flowers and made to listen to another prayer before getting his neck stretched. He was led along Dead Man's Walk, through a series of white brick doorways that felt as if they were becoming incrementally reduced in size.

They really were. Each doorway was smaller than the one before. It's a rare example of an architect practising psychological torture prior to the building of the Shard.

At the end of this tunnel a huge crowd would gather to chuck stones and rotten fruit at the condemned prisoner, and here they would eventually be buried. The church had a Watch House with windows facing into its graveyard so that the wardens could keep an eye out for Resurrectionists—body snatchers.

In 1670 a couple of Quakers were arrested for preaching, and the Old Bailey's jury found them innocent. The hardline judge refused to accept the verdict and locked the jurors away without food or water until they returned a guilty verdict. Instead, they got a writ of habeas corpus issued, so that juries could give verdicts according to their personal convictions. A big win for democracy. A few of our present-day leaders would do well to remember that. One of the Quakers went on to found the state of Pennsylvania.

The Old Bailey, the church and the Viaduct Tavern pub across the road look a bit stranded now. Few workers scurrying past this great court of justice appreciate its notoriety as a place of vengeful punishment. Mr B. tells me that later he's going to show you the scene from another angle. Me, I don't need to see it again. Although if I ever get to the Cayman Islands and manage to track down my defence lawyer I could be back for a murder trial.

JOHN MAY: Charlie, why is your nickname 'Coatsleeve'?

COATSLEEVE CHARLIE: It's how I was done. I caught my coat sleeve on a Jacobean drain hatch. I was still hanging there when the security arrived. I kept the hatch cover; it's a lovely bit of ironmongery.

5

A Town Named After a Drain & Other Stories

ARTHUR BRYANT: When they start calling an area 'vibrant' it means you're likely to get your pocket picked. Shoreditch is vibrant, which is to say it's loud and filthy. They say the Devil is in Shoreditch, and they're right. The ancient, ill-used parish of Shoreditch extends from Norton Folgate to Old Street, and from part of Finsbury to Bethnal Green. Originally it was a village on the old Roman northern road named Old Street by the Saxons. Old Street is still with us.

There are romantic stories about its name involving Jane Shore, the mistress of Edward IV. They're not true. But she really was beautiful and intelligent, and was forced to do public penance for 'promiscuous behaviour,' although the real reason for her punishment was far more likely to have been political.

Shoreditch is appropriately named after a shithole, Soersditch, or Sewer Ditch. It wasn't part of London until the late nineteenth century. Its death rate was four times higher than in other parts of the city, and the buildings were so poorly constructed that the mortar between bricks never fully dried out, being partly made of mud.

However, it was the home of London's first theatre, and the spot where *Romeo and Juliet* was first performed, although the audience must have had to narrow their eyes a bit to imagine themselves in fair Verona. The area was dominated by St Leonard's, the actors' church of London. Its burial register lists Henry VIII's court jester and one Thomas Cam, who died aged 207. Actors always exaggerate. Shoreditch was once known as the cradle of British drama. It was the first parish in England to have a theatre. In 1576 James Burbage built his stage—Shakespeare supposedly minded the horses there—and there's meant to be a plaque that marks the spot of the theatre, but I couldn't find it.

The nearby Geffrye Museum, now the Museum of the Home, opened its doors in 1914 to show the development of furniture. A series of full-sized living rooms like stage sets shows us how we lived across the decades. It had been built in 1714 as almshouses and is still going strong. Every Christmas they decorate the place in its different eras. Their 1950s room just looks like our sitting room. Alma and I don't collect period furniture, we just never got around to replacing the old stuff.

Having so many dodgy theatricals in one neighbourhood gave Shoreditch its first creative edge. People came here for saucy entertainment, and still do. It's had many famous residents: Richard Burbage, Christopher Marlowe, Barbara Windsor and the singing bus driver Matt Monro.

In the nineteenth century Shoreditch was an industrial powerhouse, but lost out to competing areas and declined into poverty and prostitution. Families lived eight to a room, with a bucket out on the terrace for the use of all. In the late twentieth century Shoreditch aligned itself with neighbouring Hoxton to become 'vibrant.' This meant it filled up with bare-ankled media plankton who could be tricked into purchasing poke bowls and Frida Kahlo cushions. Shoreditch is now visited by tourists looking for the creative edge and finding only mouse mats and fridge magnets.

There are still pockets of originality there, though. Last year I got a haircut that was so original I had to wear a hat just to look out of a window.

JOHN MAY: You didn't go to the Dancing Barber of Brick Lane? He's a legend.

ARTHUR BRYANT: Is that who it was? I just thought he had something wrong with him.

Have you noticed that when billionaires decide to buy houses in London because their kids liked the Paddington Bear films, the same shortlist of desirable locations always appears? Belgravia, Kensington, Holland Park, Chelsea, Notting Hill and Hampstead, hollowed-out neighbourhoods that look like film sets.

JOHN MAY: I know what you mean. I sometimes wonder if there's chipboard and scaffolding behind the house fronts.

ARTHUR BRYANT: The names of places in London's East End resonate for a different reason. Whitechapel, Limehouse, Shadwell and Bow were marshy medieval villages built around churches that became central to the lives of immigrants. From the seventeenth century onwards the French and the Irish and the Ashkenazi Jews arrived, Chinese and Italians and Germans set up shop, and then in the 1960s hard-working Bangladeshis settled in.

In Stepney one house in three was destroyed during the war. You can still see the effects; small pockets of Georgian elegance are left between the flat-packs of social housing. The area had a reputation for violence, overcrowding, poverty and political discord. Now it's quieter and more residential, with an entitled young middle class moving in to enjoy the 'vibrancy' while complaining about the noise of the market traders.

Those new residents would do well to look across at the Church of the High Seas, St Dunstan's, just off the Commercial Road. It dominated the area for many centuries. They'll see a vast graveyard with hardly any headstones. Thousands of plague victims were hastily buried here. Were no new coffins put in the ground because the sexton dared not disturb the foul soil? After all, this was an area that believed the air was so pestilential and filled with ill humours that it could only be stopped from entering wealthy London by the erection of leafy barriers.

Over the church's main door are two carvings, one showing a ship, the other St Dunstan armed with a pair of red-hot tongs. While he was a hermit, St Dunstan took up metalwork and forged the tongs, giving Lucifer's nose a hard pinch that made him fly away. It seems that whenever there's a fable involving the Devil, there's never a blacksmith far away.

Children played on the bomb sites left behind in the East End, re-creating Spitfire battles, forever being warned by their mothers not to fall through the rusty corrugated roofs of Anderson shelters. The neighbourhood kids limped home with cuts and scabs and unspent bullets that they hadn't been able to discharge despite pummelling them with bricks. Sometimes a child would bring an unexploded mortar bomb to school, which was usually good for getting half a day off.

There was a breezy carelessness about the neighbourhood, held in shape by the rigid structure of family loyalty. I look at it now and feel a lack of connection: no kids playing outside, no games, no songs, no Flash Harrys loitering on street corners. Age eventually places us at the edges of society, but it's a better way to view the whole.

JOHN MAY: When we visit some of the East End trouble spots on business, I see forgotten young men who are little more than frightened children hiding in the stairwell shadows after dark. Caught between the threats of friends and enemies, they die in attempts to claim their turf.

ARTHUR BRYANT: That's why I prefer the old films which are set there, like *Sparrows Can't Sing*, *Hue and Cry* and *It Always Rains on Sunday*. The reality of the East End's deprived kids is too much to bear.

Walking around the fancy-goods market in Spitalfields, it's all earrings and T-shirts now but still easy to imagine how such places began in London. Cheapside is a very old street that connects St Paul's Cathedral to the Bank of England. In medieval times 'cheap' meant 'market,' and markets were everywhere in this ancient part of London's Square Mile.

The streets were named after the items sold: Bread Street, Poultry, Milk Street and Honey Lane were here in all their rambunctious glory, so it's no surprise that Geoffrey Chaucer was raised among the stalls. In the markets all people were equal. The highest members of royal society passed among the lowest tradespeople.

Cheapside was described in Charles Dickens Jr's *Dickens's Dictionary of London* as 'the busiest thoroughfare in the world,' and had long been considered one of the most important streets in London. You could buy cabbages and chickens but you could also purchase gold. The city that had begun as a trading centre was on the up. Even at the end of the sixteenth century, London had become a popular shopping destination for overseas visitors. The original Royal Exchange was a veritable shopping mall of fancy goods. Our reputation as a nation of shopkeepers was already formed.

Incidentally, London's first pedestrianized street was—and

remains—resolutely Georgian. Woburn Walk in Bloomsbury is still lined with black-and-cream stucco-faced shops with bow-fronted windows, and reminds me of a box of Quality Street chocolates. Both W. B. Yeats and the modernist writer Dorothy Richardson lived here, and this odd little corner has been preserved without fuss or frippery. It's an unapologetic smidgen of Olde London.

The cockney epicentre of London is of course Cheapside's St Mary-le-Bow, a church that has always had trouble with its bells. They were so often cracked and unringable that it became a matter of national concern. The bells shook the stonework from the spire and killed a merchant in the lane below. Even so, the great bell of Bow went on to represent London. The BBC always played the peal of Bow bells at the beginning of their broadcasts to occupied Europe during the war. Bow became a symbol of the city.

After the Blitz the bells were recast, each with an inscription from the Psalms on it. The first letter of each Psalm formed the acrostic 'D Whittington.' We love word puzzles.

Cockneys are an endangered species now because the Bow bells can't be heard above the noise of traffic. Hardly anyone lives in the immediate area. The only hospital within earshot of Bow bells has no maternity ward, so there's an end to them.

JOHN MAY: Home births.

ARTHUR BRYANT: I'm sorry?

JOHN MAY: There could still be some cockneys, just born at home.

ARTHUR BRYANT: I hadn't thought of that. So there could still be a few around, sucking their teeth and saying, 'Blimey, you've 'ad some right cowboys in 'ere, luv,' as they rob pensioners blind.

Time for something more uplifting from the area. I would like to read you a selection of bawdy speeches set in Cheapside from *Henry IV, Part 1*. Anyone not wishing to be enlightened by the words of the Immortal Bard may move swiftly to the next chapter. For the rest of you, John has initiated me into the mysteries of the Zoom. I hope you can see me now because I can't.

JOHN MAY: It's just 'Zoom,' Arthur. You're running the session. You do understand that, don't you?

ARTHUR BRYANT: Of course I do. I can see some people on my walkie-phone. But I don't understand why they're all in what appear to be children's bedrooms. There's some absolutely hideous wallpaper about. Look at that one. She shouldn't be in a matching dress. She looks like a floating head.

JOHN MAY: They can hear you. I already explained how this works. You said you understood. Do you?

ARTHUR BRYANT: Absolutely. Certainly. No.

JOHN MAY: Tell you what. You go over to the Thornhill Arms and I'll look after the technical end of things here.

ARTHUR BRYANT: Thank God for that. I thought you'd never offer.

6

A Plate of Eels &
Other Stories

JOHN MAY: Before my partner beersplains to you in laborious detail about one of his favourite haunts, he's asked me to tell you about another market with an unusual history.

For seven hundred years, Bermondsey Market, just south of Tower Bridge, operated under a law that became known as the 'thieves' charter.' The market was a *marché ouvert*. The ancient ruling allowed that if an item was sold between sunset and sunrise its provenance couldn't be questioned. The law only changed its status in 1994.

Portobello Road, 'street where the history of ages is stowed,'* has never been a favourite of mine, as it mostly sells upmarket pseudo-antiques to the kind of people who keep dried lavender in enamel jugs in their kitchens. Bermondsey Market should be considered as truly the last of the great London markets, selling everything from Victorian death albums to medical skeletons and antique candelabra.

---

* 'Portobello Road' from *Bedknobs and Broomsticks*, written by Robert B. Sherman and Richard M. Sherman.

It opened at 5:00 A.M., so if you went in winter you had several hours of buying under the ancient law, which exempted buyers from prosecution so long as they did not know that the item they were purchasing was stolen.

Over the years Arthur had a lot of fun tracking down tea leaves* in this market. It tumbled from its central square into the rickety warehouses of the old dockland area, where gigantic sale items like ship's propellors, huge paintings and station clocks were housed.

When a woman called Anne White discovered that her own burgled antique carriage clock was being resold in the market, she went undercover in Britain's secondhand antique trade and found that the dodgy dealers were being aided by ancient laws which left the victims unprotected. In 1994, the *marché ouvert* was finally brought to a close.

To my knowledge the plods still have no nationwide stolen property register. Mrs White got the thieves' law revoked, and soon after property developers moved in and destroyed most of the area. The great market vanished beneath the usual conglomeration of 'luxury loft living' rabbit hutches. The stall-holders were granted a smaller space to continue in what appears to be a car park, but it's atmosphere-free and nowhere near as interesting as it had been. A few of the original dealers remain, and let's hope more of them return one day. The traders of London have a way of springing up through the cracks like buddleia.

Arthur, I thought you were going to tell us about one of your old haunts. Somewhere close to your heart.

ARTHUR BRYANT: Greenwich is not a 'haunt' for me, John, I'm not a ghost. Not quite anyway. But you're right, it's a special place. Do you mind if I have a pipe?

* 'Tea leaf' = thief.

JOHN MAY: Not that Old Mariner Tarred Rope stuff again. We couldn't get the smell out of the Unit for days.

ARTHUR BRYANT: You may find this one a little rougher.

JOHN MAY: What is it?

ARTHUR BRYANT: Fragrant Sailor's Below Deck Special Shag.

JOHN MAY: You know I don't approve, but—

ARTHUR BRYANT: Ta muchly. I'm lighting up.

JOHN MAY: God, it smells like burning bodies.

ARTHUR BRYANT: Doesn't it?

You know, considering it stood at the centre of global time, or Greenwich Mean Time, the town of Greenwich was a cut-off corner of London for most of its life. It rose at a point where the river broadens and switchbacks to create two traditionally isolated peninsulas. One displayed the leafy elegance of grand naval Greenwich, the other was a jigsaw of nineteenth-century slums and creeks overlooked by the rookeries of the Isle of Dogs.

Accessible from the centre only by one road and a foot tunnel, it was easier to reach by boat. And because it was a maritime town it kept nicely flexible pub hours. My old man always said that drinking rum before noon didn't make you an alcoholic, it made you a pirate. When he died they had to beat his liver to death with a stick.

There's a new Thames path we can follow along the southern side of the river. No longer a place of darkness and danger, the creeks, which were once silted with stinking green weed and filled with old tyres, tin baths and hawsers, have been cleaned out and filled in, the foreshore partially sanded. The narrow bridges over the waterways have gone—why waste prime real estate?

Instead of weaving your way between reeking old sailors' pubs, you'll now find yourselves in a wonderland of open-air dining opportunities and glass waterfront apartments. My poor brother and I used to dare each other to gallop across the paved alley flooded by the Thames every winter. Then we'd run beneath the swinging cranes of the terrifying junkyard that butted up against the river's edge. All gone and cleaned up, of course, and a good thing, one supposes. But what's the point of being a kid if you can't play games that risk a hundredweight of iron ore landing on you?

Opposite lies the Isle of Dogs, once called the Blackwall Levels, crisscrossed with interlocking canals and wharves. It's a drained swampland known as Stepney Marsh that the Victorians filled with warehouses and cheap terraces that regularly flooded, fatally for the inhabitants. At the end of July 1888 a month's rain fell on London overnight, overwhelming sewage pipes and drowning those trapped in the basements of the Isle of Dogs. The floodings continue to this day, with far fewer fatalities.

The London docks were mysterious because they were forbidden to outsiders. For decades the only surviving feature of the docks on the north bank of the Thames was the incredibly high brick walls that prevented dockers from throwing contraband over to their mates.

Greenwich now boasts the Big Four, branded and packaged for tourist consumption. They are the Queen's House, the Old Naval College, the Royal Observatory and, er, something else—oh yes, the formerly wonderful, now rather too kiddie-friendly Maritime Museum.

The best thing in Greenwich remains a view, from General

Gordon's statue beside the Royal Observatory, timeless and forever changing.

London is torn between the city it was, the one it is and the one it wants to be. It's filled with invisible lines dividing class and politics, real and surreal, and has meridians that provide longitude and project imaginary pathways across the city. The Greenwich Prime Meridian is the most famous—it was always fun to straddle the line that divides the East and West hemispheres. It was established by Sir George Airy in 1851 and was soon used by two-thirds of all the ships on the planet. GMT—Greenwich Mean Time—became the planet's Time Zero.

But George III's Thames Meridian had a very different purpose: to link the sacred spots that would form a paradise on earth in the Arcadian Meridian. His markers symbolized his kingdom's perfect vistas. Obelisks and paths that cut through the landscape can still be found in Richmond.

The creation of a mystical Arcadia offers us another ghostmap of London. One recent addition, the illuminated Rill water channel near Tower Bridge, was bricked up ostensibly because walkie-phone zombies kept stumbling into it. But the area is privately owned by Kuwaitis, so I doubt we'll ever know the truth.

Greenwich teeters on the edge of becoming its own parody. There are still anchors, capstans and hawsers everywhere, now purely decorative. After a disastrous fire the *Cutty Sark* tea clipper has been restored and raised up to reveal a gleaming burnished copper hull, but it no longer has the musty tar-and-tobacco smell below decks that it had when I was a nipper.

Greenwich has a couple of smart pie-and-eel shops that can't just be there for locals. They once provided cheap meals for workmen: bowls of segmented eels in herbs, vinegar and spiced gelatine. They were cheap, healthy, plentiful and tasty, and came from the Thames Estuary. Now they have to be imported from the

Netherlands. Only a handful of cafés still sell them, but they were once consumed in great quantities. A peek through the window reveals a table of exquisitely dressed Japanese girls photographing their eels. And why not? The old Greenwich market sells Chilean empanadas, bao buns and sushi—apt for a seafaring spot which once imported goods from all over the world.

As children we peered through the great iron gates at the forbidden quadrangles within the Naval College grounds, watching as Admiralty dignitaries were driven in and out. The centrepiece, the Painted Hall, has one of the most spectacular baroque interiors in Europe. The ceiling and wall decorations were conceived by Sir James Thornhill, who used a variety of techniques like *trompe l'œil* and chiaroscuro to enliven his somewhat Bisto-coloured paintings. They're filled with political allegories, astronomical symbology and Greek mythology.

The British were never top at painting, and Thornhill was ridiculed on the continent as an artist. The question was 'not in what part the artist excelled, but that in which he is less faulty.'[*] The epic scheme, dubiously known as 'Britain's Sistine Chapel,' took nineteen years and was completed in 1726. Thornhill's work earned him a knighthood and payment of £6,685. There's a pub named after him near our unit in King's Cross.

The Painted Hall has an exaggerated sense of scale. Everything is much taller than you expect, so much so that it makes a perfect film set. When Johnny Depp was shooting *Pirates of the Caribbean: On Stranger Tides* here he turned up at a local school as Jack Sparrow to help teach kids about Greenwich's past, and no doubt enjoyed a lovely bit of PR.

Originally the hall functioned as a grand dining room for impoverished naval pensioners, whom William and Mary (mostly

[*] Art critic Jean-Bernard, abbé Le Blanc in *Letters on the English and French Nations*, vol. 1, letter 23.

Mary) felt deserved to be treated as grandly as anyone else. For a hundred years from 1824 it was given over to the first National Gallery of Naval Art. The last Greenwich pensioners left the site in 1869 when it became home to the Royal Naval College, an officers' training academy. The Tudor underpinnings of the building, the museum and skittle alley are all visitable.

There's a rather good pub with a hog board (a plank filled with soldiers on horseback, Scotch eggs, hot sausage-and-fennel rolls) on the grounds, but the key thing here is that panoramic view from the Royal Observatory to the span of the Thames.

There are therefore several Greenwiches in one: the royal site of sprawling grandeur (the white stone walkways to and from the Queen's House have appeared in so many films that they've become a cliché), the gentrified Greenwich of luxurious balconied apartments and bijou nineteenth-century houses now worth a fortune, and the working-class end that nobody talks about and only locals see, with its high street of run-down takeaways and ruined terraces.

Neighbouring Deptford has strong maritime connections too, but has always been the poor relation to grandiose Greenwich. It's notable for the knighting of Sir Francis Drake by Queen Elizabeth I aboard the *Golden Hind* and for the unsolved murder of the playwright Christopher Marlowe. But as you move out of the city and the river widens, the decline of the dockyards can be felt in the high streets.

7

Hansel and Gretel &
Other Stories

ARTHUR BRYANT: I'm often told, 'Your tour is rubbish. Stuff this for a lark, I'm off to explore London with someone who can tell me how many double-decker buses you can fit inside Big Ben.'

I would suggest a simpler approach: try pushing open the odd door or two. The worst that can happen is you get arrested or they set the dogs on you. This is not North Korea or America, where touching the national flag can get you incarcerated on some kind of Devil's Island. The most that will happen is that someone apologetically asks if you can possibly come back on an open day. Dig beneath London's obvious attractions and you find another world that's better known to insiders.

Many of London's forgotten municipal and judicial buildings have been repurposed as bars and restaurants, which means sensitively adapting their interiors. Clerkenwell's Grade II listed sessions house is now a fancy eatery with a hidden entrance. Other buildings remain because they have tenacious tenants and ironclad leases. Some simply fly below the radar of property developers. Synagogues often hide in plain sight, their exteriors unornamented.

Which brings me, in a slightly back-to-front way, to this:

The Dissolution of the Monasteries meant that from the second half of the sixteenth century to the end of the eighteenth, there was no Catholic worship (or Protestant Nonconformism), so no churches. But there was an exception. If the land belonged to one of the embassies of Catholic countries, the priests were protected by diplomatic immunity. And so we are left with Our Lady of the Assumption and St Gregory in Warwick Street, Soho, one of the oddest churches I can think of and London's only surviving embassy chapel.

In order to avoid vandalism, the Catholic church's exterior was made as dowdy and un-churchlike as possible. Sealed behind thick brown bricks and steel doors, it looks like a series of residential terraced houses from the outside, but within is a richly decorated apse covered in shining stars.

And if you're wondering where the Italians are, now that they've mostly left Soho, head for St Peter's Italian Church in Clerkenwell, consecrated in 1863. It's a basilica-style church with a very beautiful pillared interior, also situated in a terrace of houses. Half shut your eyes and you could be in Naples, or that pizza joint on the Euston Road.

Equally you may find yourself thinking: If London is so multicultural, where do the Dutch hang out? There are an estimated twenty-five thousand Netherlanders living in London. Presumably they came here to get away from Dutch cuisine.

Since 1665 Dutch ships have never had to pay to unload their cargoes in the City of London. During the time of the Great Plague Holland was the only European country that continued trading with London. As a mark of gratitude all fees were waived in perpetuity.

The rather severe Nederlandse Kerk was built on the site of an Augustinian friary in 1550, and was restored after its destruction in the Blitz, making it the oldest Dutch-language Protestant church in the world. It's still Dutch-run and open to all in Austin Friars, a street in London's Square Mile. After the service you may care for a Dutch beer, so head for De Hems in Soho to be surrounded by tall blond people who seem to be stoned all the time.

London caters to everyone, so if you also think to yourself: The Dutch may be catered to, but why isn't there an art gallery dedicated to Italian futurist painting? You clearly haven't been to the Estorick Collection at Highbury Corner.

Admittedly Highbury Corner is not a place you'd ever visit willingly, unless you'd agreed to meet friends at 'Stabbies,' the Wetherspoons' pub on the corner dedicated to cheap beer and drunken physical violence. But nearby is the art collection of the white and gleaming Estorick. The Grade II listed Georgian townhouse has six galleries and an art library. The collection is known internationally for its core of Futurist works, as well as figurative art and sculpture dating from 1890 to the 1950s.

If you're looking for really invisible places, sooner or later you'll come up against a London guild. They hold a very special position in the city. There are 110 livery companies here. They were born in the thirteenth century, around the wharves where specific trades were practised, and provided financial help and schooling for craftspeople involved in those trades. Some hold beautifully crafted examples of their skills, like the Goldsmiths' Hall. Most are now only visitable by appointment. The porter at the Worshipful Company of Leathersellers in St Helen's Place told me with a roll of the eye, 'It's mostly what they call an "events space" these days. We do lots of weddings. Hindu, gay, Welsh: we've had all sorts in here. Some of them make a right bloody mess with glitter.'

Go to any of the guild buildings and push at a door. You may get no further than the lobby, but guild people are often happy to tell you about their vocations and their beautiful buildings, which are there to showcase the best of their wares. More Welshes can be found at the Welsh Centre on Gray's Inn Road. They sing a lot and have gin tastings, and host weddings too.

The places in London that don't get noticed are often those protected not just by wealth but by class. You might find yourself in an elegant street filled with architecturally fascinating houses, but the urge to hurry on is encouraged by private security guards, machine-gun towers or a look about the place that says 'You have no business here, you grubby little oik.'

The Albany (or simply 'Albany') is rather unusual. You don't find many photos of it online. There are lots of rules and regulations: 'no whistling, no noise, no publicity.' It's a three-storey 'bachelor apartment complex' built five years before the American Declaration of Independence, in plain sight right on Piccadilly, yet few people notice it. It was occupied by Prince Frederick, Duke of York and Albany (hence the confusion over the definite article; residents favour dropping it). It was subsequently turned into sixty-nine apartments or 'sets.'

The past is beguiling. The Sherlock Holmes stories transport us to a lost world of cobbled streets and hansom cabs, but it's hard to find vistas that have remained entirely unchanged in London; few buildings remain unaltered for longer than ten years. Sills and steps, roofs, chimneys, doors and windows come and go until we forget how our buildings once appeared. It's surprising to see just how bare and unadorned the East End was in old photos, or how fussy and plant-filled Leicester Square was in 1900.

From its entry off Piccadilly, the vista of the Albany that opens before you is complete and timeless, but in keeping with the period its façade is for show, like a stage set. In common with a lot of prestigious old London properties, the back of the building is unattractive. But lying to the east of the Burlington Arcade and the Royal Academy of Arts, a minute's walk from Piccadilly Circus, the Albany might as well be fifty miles away from London. It's in complete contrast to the chaos of Piccadilly Circus, yet situated right within it.

So who *can't* live there? Anyone with less than a couple of million. The sets vary in size but the smallest are very small indeed and not much of a bargain; a larger one on two floors will set you back about five million, but they're still pretty poky. You buy into Albany for the prestige, not because you want to run about the lounge. John tells me it's common to say 'lounge.' and I should say 'living room.' He also disapproves of me saying 'serviettes' instead of 'napkins' and 'toilet' instead of 'lavatory.' I remind him I'm from common stock and he's lucky that I manage to say 'toilet.'

There are no children under fourteen in the Albany. You no longer have to be a bachelor, but residents are vetted—unusually for London—by a daunting residents' committee. That means no riffraff, which in turn means it's about class more than money. The roll-call of previous occupants gives the game away. They include (and this is just a grab at the first few names I spotted) Byron, Wordsworth, Gladstone, Lord Stanley, Sir Thomas Beecham, Sir Isaiah Berlin, Dame Edith Evans, Sir Kenneth Clark, Bill Nighy, Aldous Huxley, J. B. Priestley and Terence Stamp. 'The story of Albany is largely the story of the people who have lived there,' wrote Sheila Birkenhead in *Peace in Piccadilly* in 1958.

You won't get to see interiors but as far as I can tell the sets are cramped and dark, laid out in a way that prevents any radical redesign. At least the rooms look private and quiet. Recently a New York designer, intent on ripping out the interior of her set, came up against the full might of the committee and eventually abandoned the idea.

Unlike the more raffish, bastardized Aldwych, Albany remains a secret enclave. There are many more such places dotted across the capital from Hampstead's Holly Lodge to Pimlico's Dolphin Square. We won't be going inside those, either. Rich people don't like you poking about in their things, and what you find is usually quite boring.

| | |

The time has come to talk about imaginary London. You'll notice, if any of you are still awake, that I've been skirting around the idea for a couple of chapters. In my head there's another city where every fictional character from every London book and film lives. Some fill me with happy childhood memories. Others still haunt me.

In this fictional London, the white boiler-suited droogs still maraud through concrete subways, Mrs Dalloway is off to buy flowers for her party, the sinister Professor Marcus knocks on a door in King's Cross, Fagin is training his pickpockets on Saffron Hill, hungover Netta manipulates lovesick George in darkest Earl's Court, Mr Sloane entertains himself beside the Oasis swimming pool, Pimlico's residents tear up their ration books and keep the pubs open late, and Bob Hoskins is on the Thames telling cynical Americans 'I'm a businessman and what's more, I'm a *Lundunner.*'[*] There are hundreds of other fictional characters hiding around every corner in London.

And everyone's experience is different. When he was asked

---

[*] I'm not going to list all those references for you. If you really want to know, I'm sure you'll figure them out.

about the history of London, an unnamed seventeen-year-old boy once told us, with perfect teenaged confidence, 'It begins with me. It ends with me.' And he's absolutely right. His London can never be anyone else's.

People create their own London and are very good at rebuilding it as an imaginary state. It's a tricky balance, creating a fantastical city. It's both recognizable and one step away from reality. There may be grey pigeons and grey skies, but there's also music, magic and a heartfelt London message; in a city where everyone is different, everyone can fit in.

When writers reimagine London as a tropical lagoon or make Hampstead the home of fantastical nannies, the city gets livelier and more colourful, becoming the kind of place you'd like to discover for yourself. Admiral's Walk in Hampstead even contains the house of Admiral Boom from *Mary Poppins*. It's a fantasy city many would secretly like to see, the London of Paddington Bear, the Wombles, Harry Potter and Sherlock Holmes.

If you're not sure that's true, take a walk through King's Cross Station and see people from all over the world queuing up to take selfies beside half a baggage trolley sticking out of a wall labelled Platform 9¾. There's a need to believe in the fantastical side of London because we want to create something safe and comforting.

JOHN MAY: Can I just say? In the opera *Hansel and Gretel* there's an orchestral scene that's traditionally tricky to stage, when the children are lost in the woods and protected by angels. In a production I saw, Hansel and Gretel's wood became a London park and the children were guarded by the city's postwar authority figures: constables and milkmen and lollipop ladies, who watched over them through the night. It's a charming surface nostalgia, but if I may interject further—

ARTHUR BRYANT: No, you may not.

In the first half of the twentieth century London fiction is surprisingly vivid and real, from Evelyn Waugh to Patrick Hamilton, Jean Rhys to Muriel Spark, G. K. Chesterton to Elizabeth Bowen. As you read, you need to feel you might discover something wonderful around the next corner. And sometimes—just once in a while—you do, and it makes you feel special.

To start with, there's the inverted city beneath our feet. Our relationship to the underground is complex; you would think that after numerous fires, acts of terrorism and bombs, we'd be wary of stepping below the pavements. Instead, I find the reverse to be true; it makes me feel safe and warm because it's full of people.

The London Underground is the oldest in the world, but it was once longer than it is now. The District Line used to run from Ealing Broadway all the way out to Windsor, but the line was discontinued in 1885 due to lack of passengers. And if the thought of whipping out to the Berkshire countryside to visit the castle by tube is surprising, how about this: you could once jump on a tube at, say, Blackfriars and get off in Southend-on-Sea, although why you'd want to is anyone's guess. The service ran from 1910 to 1939, the golden years of the seaside holiday.

I was born in the wrong era.

JOHN MAY: Starting in the 1980s, the unused tunnels, railway arches and offcuts of waste-ground beside railway tracks were opened up and monetized. London lost most of its underground spaces. There was a gents' toilet in Holborn where the attendant kept goldfish in the glass-sided cisterns, and we used to question suspects in funny little bars under the road in Shaftesbury Avenue and Piccadilly Circus. This would have been in the 1970s.

ARTHUR BRYANT: Mercifully I've forgotten the era of the stacked boot, John. I still remember what you wore back then. I'd seen better dressed wounds. One of the rare survivors of London's great land grab was Potters Fields, on the south side of Tower Bridge. It's another example of something that's not quite what you'd expect.

JOHN MAY: Explain, please.

ARTHUR BRYANT: Well, the term 'Potters Field' is a biblical reference to the Akeldama or 'field of blood' where Judas was paid his blood money. Then it came to mean a burial ground, presumably because the clay-rich soil was easy to dig. Naturally, such fields also housed potteries. Our particular Potters Fields (note the plural) isn't clay-rich, but it was convenient for boats arriving from Holland with clay. In 1618 an enterprising young potter founded the Pickleherring Pottery—try saying that with my teeth. It employed forty potters making English Delftware. The patterns on the pottery can be found today on the gates in Tooley Street.

Later, Potters Fields became part of the docks known as London's Larder, for the sheer amount and range of food that was unloaded there. Now it's a very pleasant park with delightful views.

There are some other left-over surprises, like the Clerkenwell House of Detention, which has gloomy catacombs with claustrophobically curved cell walls and a refectory buried deep underground. And there are more than twenty 'ghost' stations in London. Aldwych Station is often used for filming period dramas. Other forgotten spaces are being opened up. When the Crystal Palace burned down in 1936 it left behind a decorative Moorish subway from 1865 which has been rediscovered and opened to the public. The vaults at London Bridge have become fashionable nightclubs. I suppose you're the sort of person who went 'clubbing' when you were young.

JOHN MAY: Thank you, but I was always too old for such pursuits, and you don't have to put inverted commas around the word. When you're young you need a place where you can let yourself go.

ARTHUR BRYANT: I was never young and certainly never wanted to 'let myself go.' And I don't want to these days; it's far too risky, if you know what I mean. The only hip joints I care about are the ones I'm liable to break.

Londoners always loved their clubs, but not just the gentlemen's clubs of Pall Mall. There were others which were the opposite of respectable guilds and Masonic lodges. Those sought to encourage disorder, anarchy, drinking, gambling and above all promiscuity.

Historically, some were strictly for the elite—peers, military men, the gentry. The Wig Club in Edinburgh required its members to make a toast from a penis-shaped glass after donning a wig made from the pubic hair of the royal mistresses from Charles II to George IV. It was full of lice, so they all ended up infested. London clubs had their own equally bizarre rituals. The candlelit initiation rites of the Detection Club still involve swearing on a skull named Eric.

Not long ago the strip-club girls of Soho ushered punters downstairs into 'near-beer' traps that they had to pay to get out of. Old-time gangsters ran 'girlie bars' with battle-scarred hostesses who expertly parted clients from their cash. Strip clubs turned to pole dancing and became almost respectable.

Soho's gay clubs were part of the creative lifeblood of the area.

Many were gaudy little suites with red velvet curtains and names like the Rockingham and the Arts & Battledress, and were entered from alleyways up subsiding staircases. They were discreet and formal, and offered cocktails and evening newspapers in the hushed environment of a literary salon. I'm ashamed to say that in the 1970s and '80s the Soho police harassed them constantly, looking for licence infringements or anything that could shut them down.

At the time of Oscar Wilde's trial, one newspaper suggested that decent men were being driven into each other's arms because their wives were too busy being feminists and everything would go back to normal if they returned to making jam.

When Oscars, the last porn cinema in King's Cross, closed down in this century, its frontage wasn't hurriedly buried in an attempt to prove it never existed. It was lovingly installed on the wall of the pub opposite. It's this embrace, this knowingness, that characterizes London now. But it took a lot of lives lived miserably to get this far.

One of the most shocking episodes occurred at the Admiral Duncan in Old Compton Street. Few Soho pubs have boring histories, and the Duncan's is appropriately colourful; in June 1832, a chap called Dennis Collins lived there. The former sailor had a wooden leg but still got about. He was charged with high treason after chucking stones at King William IV and was sentenced to be hanged, drawn and quartered. When the court realized they were several hundred years out of date with their punishment they sent him to Australia instead.

In 1953 an extremely pissed Dylan Thomas left his only copy of *Under Milk Wood* there. Luckily his producer later found it. The play should have been called *Under a Bar Stool*.

Then in 1999 the pub was the target of a hate crime and was horrifically blown apart by a nail bomb. That night the barman was David Morley, a thirty-one-year-old who had grown up through the AIDS hysteria that saw church leaders and politicians publicly welcoming God's scourge of sin. He continued to help those less fortunate than himself and survived the horrors of that night—there's a memorial to the dead and injured set in the ceiling of the pub.

Five years later, Morley was walking home across Hungerford Bridge and was set upon by a gang of homophobic teenagers, including a fourteen-year-old girl, who beat him to death.

The attack on Morley was one of eight that the group carried out in the early hours; they had decided among themselves that they would attack people, including 'tramps, druggies or just people on the street.' In one of those coincidences that seem barely believable, Morley had survived the bomb to become the only fatality in the gang's rampage, which was caught on CCTV.

The damp, atmospheric worlds of London's hidden nightlife disappeared in the eighties' rush for property. But London rooms continued to host esoteric events. Upstairs in the Princess Louise in Holborn, the Dracula Society fell out with the Vampire Club. One lot were committed Darwinians; the others were Goths who just liked Christopher Lee.

The Handlebar Moustache Society, founded in 1947, regularly met in the Windsor Castle just off the Edgware Road. Once a month the Masons Arms in Maddox Street was filled with toy soldiers as the Society of Collectors of Model Soldiers repaired their troops. Very few pubs now play the traditional game of London skittles, but young shuffleboard players are spoilt for choice and get together regularly near London Bridge.

JOHN MAY: So there are probably clubs around for any London tribe you can name.

ARTHUR BRYANT: I can't name any.

JOHN MAY: Yet you can name every actor in *The Dam Busters*.

ARTHUR BRYANT: They can't remake that now because—

JOHN MAY: Don't say it.

ARTHUR BRYANT:—of German sensitivities in the Ruhr Valley.

8

A Big Viking & Other Stories

ARTHUR BRYANT: I was about to wrap up my potato peelings in a 'luxury lifestyle' magazine I stole from my neighbour by mistake—although why a man in a string vest wants to read about test driving the latest Maserati is beyond me; it's technically a magazine in that it has pages fastened together on one side and runs adverts for things nobody owns, like tiaras and gold-plated workout bottles—when I caught sight of an article about the former London village of Marylebone, calling it the most fashionable place to live in London.

JOHN MAY: Wait, when was this?

ARTHUR BRYANT: I believe we'd just caught the Oranges & Lemons Killer.

JOHN MAY: Who surprised us all by turning out to be—

ARTHUR BRYANT: Don't name him! Er, or her. Some people may not have read all my memoirs yet.

JOHN MAY: Hard to believe.

ARTHUR BRYANT: I know. Anyway, Marylebone. Where are my notes?

JOHN MAY: You're sitting on them.

ARTHUR BRYANT: Marylebone is an ancient area that gets its name from a church dedicated to St Mary, built on the bank of a small stream or bourne called the Tybourne, which became Tyburn. Its received pronunciation is 'MARRY-le-bon' but most Londoners say 'MAR-le-bone.' It's also a railway station. Have you noticed how everyone says 'train station' now?

Point is, the neighbourhoods around stations are always a little run-down and transient. (Throughout Europe, for some peculiar reason, there has always been a dodgy bar called the 'Why Not?' near a *railway* station.) Marylebone is also near Paddington Station and was always a little sketchy. Many of Oxford Street's shop assistants used to rent in Marylebone High Street, back when it was considered common to live above a shop.

The redbrick Georgian terraces around the high street remain intact, having missed bombings and redevelopment. I had a few rakish friends there who ate in the Indian YMCA in Fitzrovia and drank in the scruffy little corner pubs where locals sang around upright pianos. The Golden Eagle in Marylebone Lane still hosts singalong piano nights.

At some point in the 1980s something strange happened. The area started to fill with 'lifestyle' celebrities. The local fire station became the kind of restaurant that's important to people who are defined by their haircuts. Marylebone was transformed into the personification of a bijou lifestyle. But a lifestyle is something to aim for, not achieve. It's a chimera that dissolves upon arrival.

It certainly didn't stop people from desiring the Marylebone lifestyle. The cute little terraced flats started changing hands for hundreds of thousands, then millions, then multiples of millions. Soon they were being bought not by movie stars but by tycoons rinsing their dirty cash via accommodating property developers. The fickle and jejune new owners loved a nice old-fashioned English front door so long as behind it there lay a neon-lit underground concrete bunker with a twenty-five-metre pool lit by disco balls.

JOHN MAY: Your readers are going to get the impression that you're an enemy of capitalism, Arthur.

ARTHUR BRYANT: I'm not. I'm an enemy of vulgarity.

To the outward eye Marylebone continues much as before, except for the shops, listless high-end clothing chains and knick-knack souks that have hollowed out a once thriving and charming neighbourhood, the perfect place for dipsy-doodle film stars to flog their pricey woo-woo face creams.

JOHN MAY: Perhaps we ought to change the subject. The veins on your forehead are standing out.

Try to think calm thoughts.

ARTHUR BRYANT: The last time I was hypnotized, I was told to imagine a place where I'd feel calm and safe and happy.

The place I always pick is the South Bank complex, home of the National Theatre and the Royal Festival Hall. This is what was written about the formation of a national theatre, 'the property of the nation,' in 1904 by William Archer and Harley Granville-Barker, who had a major influence on drama in the early twentieth century: 'The National Theatre must bulk large in the social and intellectual life of London. It must not ever have the air of appealing to a specially literate and cultured class.'

Well, it took a while to find its place but I think the complex fulfils this brief admirably.

JOHN MAY: Totally with you on this one. There's something terribly friendly and inviting about the main building.

ARTHUR BRYANT: It was long reviled, considered to be nothing more than a collection of cubist concrete boxes. I'm glad they cancelled compromising plans to hide it under a glass dome; the space became one of London's most beloved spots. It's worn-in now, cluttered with mess and people with laptops and children and tea and wine and displays and books.

There are actually three theatres here. The largest is the Olivier, named after its first artistic director. The main auditorium is modelled on the ancient Greek theatre at Epidaurus, and has an open stage and a fan-shaped audience seating area for eleven hundred people. I'm assured that the sightlines are fantastic. This is great for audiences, but, according to director Trevor Nunn, difficult for actors, as the huge venue is hard to fill. At least that means you can nearly always get tickets. The other theatres there are the Lyttelton and the Dorfman.

Nothing goes to waste at the National. The forecourt is used for open-air performances, the terraces and foyers are available for ad hoc experimental events. The décor changes, with displays of 'outside wallpaper,' costumes, sculptures and giant bits of furniture. Everything except the auditorium interiors is open to the ticketless public, with a large bookshop, arthouse film theatres, restaurants, bars and exhibition spaces. The success of the place can be judged by looking at its common areas—every square foot is taken up with somebody doing something, young and old. There are so many people sitting on the floor that you'd be forgiven for thinking you were in Cairo Airport.

Mr May and I like heading from the north side of Waterloo Bridge to the south and seeing the building gradually appear. The building provides open decks like those of a ship and can feel oddly maritime. It's certainly the opposite of a frosty cultural temple. The South Bank walk from Westminster to Bermondsey is best in the rain when there are fewer joggers. Watch out for the man in the top hat with the flaming tuba. He busks there at the weekends.

| | |

It's funny how everything leads you back to the river. Further along there's a model of a boat sticking out of a wall. It's the first puzzle you encounter on entering St Magnus the Martyr, just across the Thames from the South Bank.

'London is like a railway junction: it has no true life of its own,' says Lucia in E. F. Benson's book *Queen Lucia*. 'There is no delicacy, no appreciation of fine shades. Individualism has no existence there; everyone gabbles together.' Well, nobody gabbles on Lower Thames Street. The area is overlooked and loved only by those who know it.

The last time I took a tour group there (two Frenches and a very annoying child who sadly missed a step in the crypt when someone thoughtlessly turned the light out), we were alone inside the church except for the vicar, who was nodding off over a book.

St Magnus the Martyr isn't just hard to find—it's hard to reach.

The arterial passage of Lower Thames Street cuts across its path, hiding it in plain sight. But here you'll find an almost perfect example of a church from the Middle Ages, long before pews became popular, when churches were still filled with food stalls and arguing tradespeople. St Magnus was at the centre of the community and was therefore rowdily overrun, especially as it was on the thoroughfare of London Bridge. It's the home of the last remaining cleric in the Church of England to use the title Cardinal— all rather high church.

Why is it the guild church of plumbers and fishmongers? The answer lies with its neighbour just up the road, the former Billingsgate Fish Market, which has a statue of Britannia on its roof. The church had to block its windows to keep out the smell of fish. Britannia is always depicted as a female warrior in a Romanesque helmet, armed with a shield and spear, and she crops up all over London. She began appearing on our coins in the second century CE, after Albion was rebranded as Britannia, and during Elizabeth I's time came to represent the nation. Her clothing and her pose have barely altered in two thousand years.

The church of St Magnus the Martyr was founded in the eleventh century but was dedicated to a number of saints, so why did it later zero in on St Magnus? The pious saint was executed on the Isle of Egilsay in Orkney in 1116, and was attached to Danish heritage and the Viking Age, which is why he's now portrayed with a massive bit of artistic licence as a Viking. There's a big statue of him inside the church looking like a character from *Game of Thrones*.

The history of St Magnus is long, dubious and ridiculously complex. The church's bells were forged in the Whitechapel Bell Foundry and were consecrated before installation. In the narthex there's an odd-looking thing: London's first fire engine, made of wood and extremely ineffective-looking. I can't imagine it was of much use in the Great Fire, but at least it could get down the narrow streets.

The Romans had built the first bridge across the Thames, London Bridge, and the original stone church was at its head. To get onto the bridge itself everyone had to pass St Magnus. Eventually London Bridge had tall houses all along it, and even had a brightly coloured castle of sorts at its centre. Outside St Magnus, strapped to a wall, there's still a section of the original Roman bridge that stood there (75 CE). Nobody even notices it. I do, of course, but then I'm the kind of copper who notices a bit of Roman timber strapped to a wall.

If you go back inside there's one more delight to discover. Within St Magnus is a large model of the old London Bridge that doesn't even warrant a mention in the church's history. Somewhere on it, I'm told, is one figure in modern dress. The model is as precarious and delicate as the bridge itself once was.

JOHN MAY: I've seen that little man on the bridge. He looks like you.

ARTHUR BRYANT: 'Precarious and delicate.' Cheers.

JOHN MAY: Actually it's the chap who built the thing. He put himself in it. I like models of buildings. There's something satisfying about looking down on the world from above.

ARTHUR BRYANT: What about looking up? There are plenty of rooftop gardens. Some of them are little more than herbaceous borders. Fen Court affords terrific views of the city. Finding the entrance is a bit of a bugger—it's at 120 Fenchurch Street, in the City's Square Mile, inside a building with rotating flowers on a circular ceiling. Take the lift to the fifteenth floor and you'll find yourself on a quirky roof with plants, a stream and a little knot garden, affording an unusual viewing angle on the city. There in the background you can see Tower Bridge. The view of the bridge from the other direction has now been wrecked by the looming 'Walkie-Talkie' building, which bisects it. As an architect told me, 'Views can be very profitable.'

JOHN MAY: Crossrail Place Roof Garden in Canary Wharf is a good size. I like the Culpeper Roof Garden in Spitalfields, and the Dalston Roof Park.

ARTHUR BRYANT: My favourite for a summer's afternoon is the Queen Elizabeth Hall Roof Garden.

JOHN MAY: That's only because they have draught beers.

ARTHUR BRYANT: They also have wildflowers and a lot of drowsy bees. Does the Barbican Conservatory count as a garden? It's the second largest in London after Kew Gardens, and is under-visited. Like the rest of the Barbican, it's a bit claustrophobic and utilitarian.

JOHN MAY: I love sitting in the Chelsea Physic Garden, tucked behind the riverfront and filled with the calming scent of herbs. We should get fresh air more often.

ARTHUR BRYANT: You'll be wanting to go to the countryside next. I wouldn't last five minutes there. If there are two words designed to bring me out in a rash they're 'Organic Market.' And another two words: 'Local Artist.' It seems to me that most rural poetry is about ploughs and flowers, whereas urban poetry is about people. William Butler Yeats said of London: 'I sometimes imagine that the souls of the lost are compelled to walk through its streets perpetually. One feels them passing like a whiff of air.'

JOHN MAY: I've smelled that whiff and it's not from lost souls, I can tell you that.

ARTHUR BRYANT: London has lost most of its smells, good, bad and very bad indeed. Hops from the West London breweries, cinnamon and nutmeg in Shad Thames, fruit in Covent Garden, coal and soot, sweat and grease. For many working-class families it was a struggle just finding clean water, hence 'the great unwashed.'

JOHN MAY: The smell of skunk in Camden Town. Dopeheads always used to lie to us, 'Honest, I'm not carrying!' And we'd say, 'We can smell you from half a mile away, you idiot.'

ARTHUR BRYANT: It's true. We know if you've had more than two beers. We know when you're lying. Or if you're an unreliable witness. We can tell whether you're unemployed or struggling or covering up for your mate or just wasting our time. But these days the biggest crimes occur in London's financial centre.

Certain things always strike me about the City's Square Mile. Charlotte Brontë found its overhanging storeys, internal courtyards and narrow alleyways deeply exciting. The population appears on the streets at one and vanishes at two. Church bells can be heard at lunchtime throughout the area. On a quiet day the bells of St Paul's can be heard for miles. There are almost no trees on the streets; it's the only part of London I can think of that doesn't have many. It does, however, have quite a few church gardens and ruins where workers can sit among the gravestones with their lunches. St Dunstan-in-the-East is a popular venue, flower-filled in summer.

It's hard to think of the Square Mile without remembering Dr Samuel Johnson and his delightful house in Gough Square. Johnson once predicted the drawbacks of aviation, you know. In his philosophical novel *The History of Rasselas, Prince of Abissinia*, he thought about the advantages of flying and concluded: 'What would be the security of the good if the bad could at pleasure invade them from the sky?'

While he was working on his dictionary he was (according to legend) entirely unaided, but old textbooks of mine say he employed six copyists at number 17, Gough Square, at twenty-three shillings a week.

The work contains 42,733 entries over 2,300 pages and remains a colossal achievement, although there are many comic touches. The word 'lexicographer' is defined as 'a harmless drudge,' and 'oats' is said to denote 'a grain, which in England is generally given to horses, but in Scotland supports the people.'

JOHN MAY: Rude of him. I thought Dr Johnson's 'dictionary attic' was bombed to pieces in the Second World War?

ARTHUR BRYANT: It was, but the rest of the house miraculously survived. Johnson paid thirty quid a year to live in his little alley off Fleet Street, and today it's pretty much as he left it. In the restoration nothing old was removed and nothing new was put in. The massive iron chain with which he would bar his door against creditors is still in place.

But there's a puzzle: in early etchings the house is completely different. Today there's a plaque that says 'Dr Johnson's house once stood upon this site.' The press baron Cecil Harmsworth opened it to the public in the early twentieth century and says he simply restored it from a state of dilapidation—but it appears notably different now. When memories fade, where does the truth lie?

Harmsworth was careful not to fill the house with 'irrelevant eighteenth-century bric-a-brac.' Items had to be connected to Johnson and appropriate for the home of an impoverished writer. Harmsworth turned down some donations, including Johnson's death mask (too gloomy) and Chippendale furniture (too fancy).

If you're looking for atmospheric alleys and courtyards, it's best to head for the area around Cornhill. You'll find the George & Vulture down there. It used to be called the George but the owner kept a live vulture tethered outside and added it to the name. There are plenty of tiny old pubs tucked in the lanes, but one of the most surprising isn't old at all.

The Counting House in St Peter's Alley was a bank founded in 1759, but only became a pub in 1998. The area burned down a lot when wig-makers' premises caught fire (wigs were huge and burned like candles, thanks to their high animal-fat content) but the buildings went back up, still following the labyrinthine street pattern, and the Counting House feels like it's been there forever.

The Square Mile is the birthplace of London, the city of trade, and has something no other area has in quite the same way: a sense of identity that no amount of remodelling can remove. The dog-leg alleys and courtyards remain in place, even though those who use them are no longer rowdy hawkers, thieves and bawds. The City has been cleaned up and brightened so much that it's good to find a few twisting lanes which are still half in shadow. If you want to get a sense of what the old city was like at night, try visiting Romania, Latvia or Lithuania. Eastern European and Baltic countries often stand in for London in period films.

9

'A Sweet and Comfortable Recreation' & Other Stories

JANICE LONGBRIGHT: The PCU must have the least amount of testosterone in it of any police unit. There's none of the racy banter you get at the Met. Even so, it's about time we had more of a woman's point of view in here. I've been working with Mr Bryant and Mr May at the PCU for as long as I can remember, although that doesn't necessarily make it a good thing.

Arthur thinks that since I spent some time as a nightclub hostess in Soho I must be an expert on everything theatrical or smutty, but when it comes to the Players' Theatre, he's not wrong. I remember it well; my mother, Gladys, performed on stage there as a little girl, singing 'The Boy in the Gallery.'

The Charing Cross Theatre is underneath the station in a gloomy railway arch. It wasn't always there. What *was* there was the Players' Theatre. Or rather, it wasn't.

ARTHUR BRYANT: If you're going to do this bit, Janice, you need to explain things clearly, like I do.

JANICE LONGBRIGHT: John just snorted his tea.

It started in Evans's Music-and-Supper Rooms at 43 King Street, Covent Garden, in the 1840s, and ran a show called *Late Joys*, named after its owner, Mr Joy. This was before the invention of the music hall. The *Late Joys* began at around 11:00 P.M. to allow the performers to get there after their own curtain calls.

Evans's may have offered a singalong and a meal but it had a darker side; its female clientele waited for gentlemen to pay for their dinners, then conducted a little business that sent them upstairs to the bedrooms. The place finally closed in 1880. It subsequently became a boxing ring.

In 1937, a Christmas programme of Victorian delights that re-created the old *Late Joys* show proved an instant success. The production became a sort of time capsule. In the theatre, change was counted out in old currencies and newspapers had Victorian headlines. Singalong song-sheets were handed out and the audience participated with call-backs through the show.

The Churchill family and Lady Violet Bonham Carter were loyal supporters. Before the war, Sarah Churchill helped out as a programme seller. With the outbreak of hostilities the theatre had to be closed because its glass roof couldn't protect the audience. So the Players' shifted to the El Morocco nightclub in Albemarle Street, in the basement of one of the few concrete buildings in London. As a result, along with the Windmill, they never closed throughout the war and became a haven for Londoners suffering the Blitz. Sandy Wilson wrote *The Boy Friend* for the venue, and the show became a smash. Maggie Smith, John Le Mesurier, Hattie Jacques and many others appeared there, often before members of parliament and the royal family.

But the theatre continued to roam London without a permanent home. Sometimes its performers turned up at old military clubs or even in members' sitting rooms. Then the owners discovered an old music hall boarded up underneath Charing Cross Station. This had been Gatti's Music Hall back in 1910. The Gatti brothers had brought ice to London via barges at King's Cross, making the first Italian ice cream in the city—their ice cave is still in the basement of the Canal Museum.

The boarded-up entrance was torn down and there it was: the complete theatre had been preserved inside. In 2002 the Players' returned and reopened there. The performers greeted the rumble of trains with the cry of 'To hell with the London, Chatham and Dover Railway—sleepers awake!' Mr Bryant says he understood all their jokes about the Crimean War. I suppose to him it was just current news, like having the BBC on.

I was very young when I first went, but I remember how amazed my mother's guests were when they entered. I think they were confused by the strangeness of stepping so completely into a past not re-created with special effects and artefacts, but through the transformed behaviour of people. Of course the shows were perversely out of time and out of step, and couldn't even be considered nostalgia, but every city needs the kind of oddities which are there purely because the residents made them stay.

ARTHUR BRYANT: Thank you, Janice. I can add another example of that phenomenon.

King's Cross was traditionally connected to the royal hunting of deer, and the connection remains when you walk around our neighbourhood and spot the number of references, either accidental or deliberate, to deer and stag horns—they adorn buildings, homes and pubs, often tucked into decorative motifs. Residents sometimes adopt them without knowing why. It seems as if psychogeography—the idea that a location is imbued with a spirit—might be a real thing after all.

In Southwark we should be looking for bears. It's here that

London's bull- and bear-baiting pits were located. The contests were not for the faint-hearted: three English mastiffs hurling themselves at a chained bull, which tossed them so far in the air that they often somersaulted into the stands. The dogs tore off the bulls' lips, eyebrows and ears while trying to avoid having their guts gored or stamped out. The betting crowd was particularly exercised when a dog got the bull by the nose and clung on while being swung about.

The bear vs dog battles were even more horrific. The bears' teeth were broken to make the fights last longer. Strong young bears were replaced by old blind ones to give the dogs more of a chance. Nobody appeared to find it cruel: in 1583 the Privy Council called it 'a sweet and comfortable recreation fitted for the solace and comfort of a peaceable people.' I find myself thinking *compared to what?* Counted as a legitimate national sport beloved by royalty, there were two baiting arenas in Bankside. Elizabeth I visited them while never managing to get to the Globe. Royals: they've never been cursed with compassion, have they?

Walking around the area now, one sees very little left of such distant past times (or pastimes), yet there are odd glimpses of the way life was lived. Maltby Street Market is a narrow alley of smoking sweetmeats where you get a distinctly timeless feeling. The secondhand stalls crowd the road from Vinegar Yard down to the river. During weekdays this area is a timber yard, but hawkers and traders always find a way in to entice the public palate.

Rounding the end of a backstreet you come to the Horseshoe Inn, Southwark, an old-school local boozer pretty typical of this area, and sure enough—there's a life-sized bear sign standing outside.

Sixty-One Nails &
Other Stories

ARTHUR BRYANT: An awful lot of obscure rituals take place in London.

The ceremony of Quit Rents is the oldest legal ceremony in England apart from the coronation. It was created in 1164 by Henry II to keep track of all that was owed to the Crown. The City of London pays rent to the Queen's Remembrancer, whose duty is to keep records of paid and unpaid taxes. Instead of coughing up hard cash, the deal was transmuted to an offering of two gifts.

The first is a pair of cutters, one sharp knife and one blunt axe, which have to be used on a hazel branch. The branch must be bent by the blunt axe and sawn through by the sharp knife. In theory, if the knife fails to cut the hazel branch the City then has to pay an actual rent.

The second gift consists of six horseshoes and sixty-one nails, payment for the use of a forge. The ceremony is performed every October in the Royal Courts of Justice, and anyone can go.

JOHN MAY: Are you making this up?

ARTHUR BRYANT: You know I enjoy a good ceremony. Another Quit Rents ceremony is the presentation of the Knollys Rose, which takes place at All Hallows-by-the-Tower every 24 June. Samuel Pepys buried his wine and his parmesan cheese for safe-keeping by the old Navy Office during the Great Fire. That's why there's a bust of Pepys at one end of the church's garden and a picture of a cheese on the wall outside. On either side of the gate were beds of red roses commemorating the date in 1381 when Sir Robert Knollys was allowed to construct a bridge across Seething Lane. The City charged him a rent of one red rose annually, and it must still be paid. The ceremony of roses is organized by the Thames Lightermen. You can go to the picking but not to the presentation.

Every month of the year brings new ceremonial events onto the London streets, many of them driven by guilds, trades and churches celebrating historical dates. Some of the most famous include the Bubble Sermon, the Fishmongers' Procession, Swan Upping, Doggett's Coat & Badge race, the Lion Sermon and various presentations of boar's heads, hats, fruit, sausages, fish, etc., once again proving that Londoners are completely East Ham, that is to say, one stop short of Barking.

THE ROYAL EPIPHANY

On 6 January the Queen and the Yeomen of the Guard hand out three purses symbolizing frankincense, gold and myrrh to the poor of the parish. The Three Wise Men's gifts represent birth, life and death. It's also the day that the Baddeley Cake is handed out. The failed actor Robert Baddeley bequeathed money to buy a Twelfth Night cake for the cast at Theatre Royal, Drury Lane—and it still happens.

THE TRIAL OF THE PYX

Who ensures that the cash in our pockets (if anyone still uses cash) is up to standard? For the last eight centuries there has been a regular trial to check on the quality of coins produced by the Royal Mint. A 'pyxis' is a small box in which money is placed. In an annual ceremony the goldsmiths examine the dosh and ensure that it has the right metallic composition, weight and size.

In 2021 the Royal Mint's H. G. Wells commemorative two-pound coin gave his *The War of the Worlds* tripod four legs instead of three. The clue should have been in the name there.

THE ORANGES & LEMONS SERVICE

In late March St Clement Danes church distributes fruit to the parish children in celebration of the rhyme, presuming it can find any children left in this area. Oh, and there's a druidical gathering on Tower Hill. You will be unsurprised to know that quite a few of my friends attend.

THE HANGING OF THE BUN

A stack of Hot Cross Buns dangles over the bar at the Widow's Son in Bromley-by-Bow. Every year a sailor adds another bun to this collection for widows, the idea being that Hot Cross Buns baked on Good Friday will never decay. Presumably the thinking lies in the power of the cross to keep faith alive.

THE BUTTERWORTH BEQUEST

This is an ancient ceremony distributing buns and sixpences to twenty-one widows in the churchyard of St Bartholomew the Great in Smithfield. Apparently there aren't any designated widows left at all now, so the money is given to children. Around the same time there's also the Harness Horse Parade and the Martyrs' Pilgrimage from Newgate to Tyburn, alas without further bun distribution.

OAK APPLE DAY

This one's on 29 May, once a formal public holiday taken to commemorate the Restoration in May 1660. It has also been known as Shick Shack Day, Oak and Nettle Day or Arbor Tree Day. Someone did try to explain the derivation of the names but the battery had fallen out of my hearing aid.

THE PEPYS SERVICE

This has connections to St Olave's church, the home of the Samuel Pepys Club. The Great Fire of London destroyed four-fifths of the city in four days, until the King decided (or Samuel Pepys and Admiral William Penn suggested to him) that blowing up buildings would create fire breaks, and that's how St Olave's escaped the conflagration. A service and a dinner are held each year.

ANNUAL SHEEP DRIVE

Every September the City's Freemen exercise their ancient right to send a bunch of woolly jumpers over the Thames and into the

City via Southwark Bridge. It was once said that you could tell how long a sheep had been grazing in Green Park just by seeing how sooty its fleece had become.

It's not just London that hosts dozens of these events—the rest of the country stages folk rituals involving bonfires, bells, ribbons, burning priests and people dressed as foxes. I suspect they'd take place whether any tourists turned up or not. If you ever wonder why the rest of the world imagines Britain to be a weird, rainy country full of eccentrics trapped in the past, you can place the blame squarely on such delightful events. I love them, although I don't usually remember getting home afterwards.

| | |

There is one ceremony that stands entirely apart from the rest.

Lutyens' Cenotaph, meaning 'empty tomb,' on Whitehall was constructed of wood and plaster for a peace parade and was only intended to be there for a week, but it quickly became such a focus for the national outpouring of grief after the First World War that in 1920 it was replaced with a permanent monument made of white Portland stone.

Since then the annual National Service of Remembrance has taken place every Armistice Day, November 11, when two minutes of silence allow us to reflect on the loss of all those who have since had their lives taken by conflict.

A Bloke with One Leg & Other Stories

JOHN MAY: Whenever someone comes up with a fun, original thing to do, it seems as if London passes a law against it. With so many people crammed into our small winding streets, I can see why hoverboards were banned, but there was a time when 1970s nightclubs held roller-skate races around traffic-filled Leicester Square for bottles of champagne. I remember them vividly because we used to patrol around there looking for the Leicester Square Vampire.* My partner went after a gang of pickpockets and might have caught them if he hadn't been wearing skates. Which he wasn't supposed to be doing.

ARTHUR BRYANT: The steps at Leicester Square tube caught me by surprise, that's all. I was younger then. I still had my ankles.

JOHN MAY: Some things are still forbidden, mainly because they haven't come off the statute books, including owning a pack of

---

* Not an actual vampire, it turned out.

cards within a mile of stores of explosives—presumably men who played cards also smoked—and standing on your window-sills to clean them.

ARTHUR BRYANT: I've got one. You're not allowed to drop dead in the Houses of Parliament. I imagine that will be a worry to the peers who still bother to turn up there.

JOHN MAY: You can't officially hire a taxi while it's moving. The London Hackney Carriages Act 1843 states even if a licensed taxi has its For Hire light turned on, the driver can only tout for trade when it's standing still.

You can't carry a plank down a pavement. Section 54 of the Metropolitan Police Act bans you from carrying ladders, hoops and wheels.

You're not supposed to get drunk in a pub if the publican knows you are doing so, but you can carry on drinking if they don't notice.

You can't eat chocolates on a bus or go to a fancy dress party as a soldier or sailor, due to the Seamen's and Soldiers' False Characters Act 1906.

Outmoded British by-laws are disregarded but still make the funny pages from time to time. The old chestnut about pregnant women being allowed to pee in coppers' helmets has no basis in law, and we've never heard of a beat copper being asked for the urgent use of his hat. I do know you can't eat a potato on Chelsea Bridge.

ARTHUR BRYANT: I've never heard that before. Why can't you, for heaven's sake?

JOHN MAY: I'm joking.

ARTHUR BRYANT: Really? I had no idea you had a sense of humour.

JOHN MAY: London by-laws and cockney slang are amusing but they're false advertising, in much the same way as Hollywood can still be referred to as 'Tinseltown.'

ARTHUR BRYANT: There were a lot of things you could do in London that you can't do now, like pet the porcupines at the London Zoo, feed the parrots and ride a fair selection of animals. You could see Lubetkin's graceful penguin pool actually filled with penguins. Or how about the chimps' tea party, where cakes were thrown by monkeys in frocks? Anthropomorphism, I know, but I recall the chimps loving it as much as us children.

At the Christmas Circus in Holborn you could see a man put his head in a lion's mouth, and wild jungle beasts tamed with a chair.

JOHN MAY: And a whip.

ARTHUR BRYANT: Look, when you're seven you can't tell a noble creature from a ragged, terrified animal with no dignity left.

There are some things London used to do jolly well but stopped doing. One was the *Daily Telegraph* information service. Started in 1948, it carried out research for people who had neither the time nor resources to find the answers themselves. You'd phone them, ask a question and they'd put it to a team of academics who'd come back to you half an hour later. And it was free.

JOHN MAY: You do know the internet does that now?

ARTHUR BRYANT: Yes, but the information service didn't give you false answers. It's still going, but now it's outsourced and really expensive.

Another useful thing was measuring the London temperature from the Air Ministry roof. With thermometers and that.

Oh, and lost property. After eighty-six years, Baker Street Lost Property Office finally moved from its historic location. Just as well, considering nearly eleven thousand umbrellas are lost in an average year on our public transport system.

When items came into the office their details were entered into a computer system called Sherlock, after the office's nearby neighbour. Each piece of lost property was tagged with a description and date, receiving a red label if it was found in a taxi, a white one if it was left on a bus or a yellow one if it ended up on a train or at a station.

And you can't get that on the inter-whatsit.

OK, next on my list is people without a full complement of legs. 'Bumper' Harris was a one-legged man supposedly employed at Earl's Court Station to ride up and down the new escalators to prove that they were safe, but was he a real person? We'll probably never know. At least one old mystery has at last been solved. Passengers on the London Underground escalators always stand on the right and tut in annoyance when anyone does the opposite, and a recently unearthed film revealed why.

JOHN MAY: Go on, then. Why?

ARTHUR BRYANT: Because unlike modern 'comb' escalators, where the end of the moving stairway is at right angles to the direction of travel, older 'shunt' escalators ended with a diagonal cut, so that the stairway ended sooner for the right foot than for the left.

The idea was to allow passengers to keep their left foot on a moving stairway as they stepped off with their right. Passengers who chose not to walk down the escalators were asked to stand on the right so that anyone wishing to overtake them at the end would be able to take advantage of the extra section of moving stairway.

JOHN MAY: That presupposes people will do what you tell them. I have a tube story for you. At Embankment tube station there's a recorded announcement of a man telling you to 'Mind the gap' when you step off the train—it's a pretty big gap. The voice belonged to a fellow named Oswald Laurence, but it was phased out and replaced with a new digital system. Mr Laurence died in 2007.

His widow, Dr Margaret McCollum, was heartbroken not to hear his voice at the station anymore, so London Transport restored it for her—and as far as I know it remains, a vocal memory on the northbound Northern Line.

ARTHUR BRYANT: The West End was very different when I was a nipper. You could stroll into any building without being body-searched. In order to get free seats in cinemas we used to walk in backwards as people were coming out. It was impossible to buy so much as a cup of tea on the Thames Embankment or anything at all on Sundays. We now experience the opposite and have to be offered thirty different types of coffee every ten feet or so. Apparently concertgoers need to be fed at fifteen-minute intervals, as if they can't concentrate on some music for an hour without stuffing their faces.

JOHN MAY: You sound as if you miss the past.

ARTHUR BRYANT: Of course I do, I remember it. Although I wouldn't want to live there. On Sundays most London cinemas showed double features. We'd see two movies and sit around to catch the beginning of the bit we missed when we arrived. It was common to come in halfway through and not think it strange that we were seeing the story told with the second half at the front.

JOHN MAY: That explains a lot about your memoirs.

ARTHUR BRYANT: In those days everyone watched and listened to the same thing. *Housewives' Choice* in the morning, *Two-Way Family Favourites* while you were washing the car on a Sunday, *The Brains Trust* on a Sunday evening, which was meant to improve the mind and did so by forcing you to turn the telly off. We watched less and spoke more. We didn't need rolling news, just a few well-written newspapers. I miss the richness and clarity of our language. If you avoid argument and offence you never develop conversational skills.

JOHN MAY: That's why you never stop talking.

ARTHUR BRYANT: I'll be happy to discuss that with you.

Language fascinated me then and still does now. When it all kicks off and people start fighting, it's known as 'the devil among the tailors.' The devil was a spinning top that knocked down pins called tailors. It came to mean a fracas when, in 1830, a benefit performance of a burlesque called *The Tailors: A Tragedy for Warm Weather* started a massive row outside the Haymarket Theatre. The tailors complained that the show was a slur on their trade. A piece of fiction caused a public riot. That doesn't happen so often now.

There are devils everywhere in London. In the reign of George II, Devil's Gap was a tenement attached to a high archway at Lincoln's Inn Fields. Its resident was a lawyer and moneylender with a reputation for ruthlessness. He fought a young rival over a rich and beautiful heiress, in the process of which the scaffolding collapsed and they both fell to their deaths, through the Devil's Gap. There are a lot of London phrases concerning death and the Devil. 'As sure as the Devil is in London' was used by visiting provincials from both sides of the Atlantic.

My father used to say that the night was 'as black as Newgate's knocker' even though Newgate Gaol was demolished in 1904, 'a right old schemozzle,' a term of Jewish origin that belonged to the nineteenth century, meaning a big argument, and 'Bob's your uncle, Fanny's your aunt,' which dates to 1887, when Prime Minister Robert Cecil invited his nephew to be the Chief Secretary for Ireland, although where the 'Fanny' comes from is unknown. There were more vulgar exclamations too, such as 'the repartee of a St Giles fair one' (a prostitute), who, when asked a question, points to her backside and says, 'Ask cheeks near Cunnyborough!'

How did Bethnal Green's notorious Blind Beggar pub get its name? From 'The Blind Beggar of Bednall Green,' obviously. This was a ballad that became several plays, about a beautiful girl with four suitors. She told them they had to obtain permission for her hand from her father, the aforesaid visually challenged knight of the road. Only one of the four, an actual knight, took up the challenge and was rewarded with a huge dowry. Her father was operating in disguise to weed out the chancers. He wasn't a beggar at all but Henry, son of Simon de Montfort. Proof that money always marries itself. There's a statue of him not far from the pub.

Speaking of beggars, the London Borough of Havering in East London forms part of Outer London and has a golden ring on its coat of arms. The story goes that King Edward the Confessor (1003–66) was approached in the area now known as Havering by a beggar asking for alms and told him, 'I have no money but I have a ring,' which he gave the beggar. This kindness gave a name to the town and is still represented on the badge.

JOHN MAY: 'I went down to the Chelsea drugstore to get your prescription filled'—you can hear Mick Jagger singing it, can't you?

ARTHUR BRYANT: I can't hear anything much, John, you know that.

JOHN MAY: The Chelsea Drugstore wasn't just a bar and discotheque in the King's Road but was also a real pharmacy modelled on a counterpart in Paris. It was immortalized in the song 'You Can't Always Get What You Want' and had a gigantic impact on swinging London, but it lasted only three years. The fusty old colonels of Chelsea complained about the noise. Like many unique and wonderful places in London the Drugstore eventually became another junk-food joint.

ARTHUR BRYANT: Conan Doyle is rhyming slang for a boil, apparently, commonly known as a 'Sir Arthur,' although who has boils anymore? Not to be confused with a 'J. Arthur,' which implies something altogether different, being connected to the J. Arthur Rank film company and the art of gentlemen's relaxation.

'I'll give you my mother for a maid' was a catchphrase heard in fashionable London circles between the 1680s and the 1740s. It means 'Not bloody likely' for the simple reason that your mother could not be a maid, i.e., a virgin.

On the subject of rhyming slang, the most complicated one I

know is 'Harris.' It comes from 'Ari,' which derives from the rhyme of 'Aristotle' and 'bottle,' then 'bottle and glass,' and finally to 'arse.' Aristotle invented logic, so it's nice to see him the subject of something so illogical.

To the discerning ear, Londoners have quite distinct accents depending on which quadrant of the city you hail from. On this subject, George Bernard Shaw wrote in *Pygmalion*, 'Men begin in Kentish Town with eighty pounds a year and end in Park Lane with a hundred thousand. They want to drop Kentish Town but they give themselves away every time they open their mouths.' 'My Fair Lady' was intended to be cockney speak for 'Mayfair Lady,' which shows you how much accents have changed.

To many Londoners certain words still hold terrible memories. 'Moorgate' refers to the Moorgate disaster which occurred on 28 February 1975, when a Northern Line train smashed into the tunnel end at full speed, killing forty-three people. The driver died and people wondered if he had planned to kill himself—except that he was buying his daughter a car that day and still had the money in his pocket. The mystery remains. The safety device introduced to prevent such a tragedy from happening again is known as a 'Moorgate Control.'

The four terrorist bombings that killed fifty-two UK residents of eighteen different nationalities in King's Cross and three other locations became known as '7/7,' but the 'King's Cross Fire' is something different. The tragedy occurred in 1987 and killed thirty-one commuters after a discarded cigarette end was dropped onto one of the wooden escalators. A tornado of flame formed that drew a blast furnace of fire up into the main ticket hall.

One more word: 'flash.' Before there were flash mobs there were flash houses* and even published guides to them. Before *that*

---

* Drinking dens of highly dubious reputation.

there were flash boys and flash girls, forerunners of the 1950s wide boys. Their fondness for shiny buttons led to the creation of the Pearly Kings and Queens. When we say that someone is flashy we mean they're unsophisticated in behaviour or loudly dressed, like my partner.

And so the recurrent theme surfaces; nothing in London is new, just a variant of the past.

| | |

When I think about dragons and devils, which is quite often, I think of St Peter-upon-Cornhill. It's the oldest church site in the City of London's Square Mile. In the nineteenth century its vicar, clearly a vindictive old bugger, noticed that plans for the building next door extended by one measly foot onto church territory, so he forced the architect to redraw his design and added three crouching, leering creatures of genuinely malevolent demeanour to the building facing Cornhill from the south. They're still there in plain sight, frightening the neighbours. So much for the kind ministrations of the church.

There are other chimerical beasties on buildings, half-and-half mythical creatures, especially gryphons, which have the body, tail and back legs of a lion, a head of spiralled curls, the wings of an eagle and an eagle's talons. The lion was traditionally the king of the beasts and the eagle the king of birds, so the gryphon was thought to be even more powerful.

Guarding Holborn Viaduct, the cast-iron bridge that crosses Farringdon, there are winged lions like gryphons in reverse, but frankly their wings don't seem large enough to get them off the ground. Dragons rampant appear on shields and roundels and on the bases of the viaduct lamps, now repainted in their original gaudy colours. The old City is protected by creatures that guard the main roads. They're boundary markers and come in two distinct designs: heraldic (silver, leaning on shields) and more naturalistic. If you can call a dragon natural.

The bronze figures atop Holborn Viaduct represent Fine Art, the Sciences, Commerce and Agriculture. All are women—the Victorians liked their representatives of higher callings to be generic females. There are many other statues dotted around the viaduct, mostly boring mayoral types, although one is Sir William Walworth, most notorious for being the killer of Wat Tyler, the hero of the Peasants' Revolt in 1381.

The flying lions and dragons are fantasies rendered into iron and stone. But I have here in my notes . . . somewhere . . . hang on . . .

JOHN MAY: Are you looking for these grubby scraps of paper?

ARTHUR BRYANT: Grubby scraps? Philosophical gems, matey.

JOHN MAY: What are these drawings meant to be? Pairs of boots?

ARTHUR BRYANT: As it happens, yes. The earliest reference we have to the legend of the Field of Forty Footsteps is from 1692, when the lands around the British Museum were still open meadow. It was always a dodgy area, full of ladies of ill repute, cut-purses and so on. Nobody knows what the 'Forty Footsteps' mean now.

JOHN MAY: I imagine you do.

ARTHUR BRYANT: Well, obviously. At the time of the Duke of Monmouth's rebellion, which was, let's see, 1685, there were supposedly two brothers in love with the same titled lady. She couldn't choose between them so they fought a duel at Southampton Fields while she watched. They were both fatally wounded.

After that it was said that the grass never grew where their bodies fell, nor where their feet had trod. The footsteps they had paced out remained through the years. The Poet Laureate Bob Southey was told about the footsteps by his friend John Walsh, whose mother had seen them ploughed up, only to mysteriously reappear.

Right through the nineteenth century playwrights produced dramas about the phantom footsteps. I'm pretty certain that they were just north of Senate House and in front of Birkbeck College, on the remains of the old Torrington Square.

JOHN MAY: Have you seen them?

ARTHUR BRYANT: I've seen a bit of bare earth where they're meant to be.

JOHN MAY: That's not very interesting.

ARTHUR BRYANT: The physical remains of legends rarely are. It's the stories you attach to the stones that excite the imagination.

JOHN MAY: What about London's ghosts and hauntings? Traditionally they've always excited the imagination.

ARTHUR BRYANT: Oh, many of them were created simply to draw attention to a building—usually to encourage the public to pay for visiting it. There are rather too many hauntings in which chambermaids are discovered kicking furniture. I like the Forty Footsteps legend because nobody gains from its existence. It simply caught the public fancy, in the same way that the Harry Potter luggage trolley did.

JOHN MAY: That's not answering the question. Give us a good London ghost story.

ARTHUR BRYANT: I can tell you how they began. England's first literary ghost story provided the template for a great many ghost stories to come. In it, a Mrs Bargrave in Canterbury was visited one noon in September 1705 by a friend she hadn't seen in two years. Mary Veal arrived on her doorstep oddly kitted in night attire and a hood, and was invited in. The two friends caught up and Mrs Bargrave opened her heart, explaining that her marriage had become untenable after her husband started drinking heavily. She agreed to carry out a few small favours for Mary and bade her farewell. Later the local undertaker confirmed that Mary had dropped dead at noon that day, and that Mrs Bargrave had spent the afternoon with Mary's freshly materialized spirit. I wonder how that came up in conversation.

Anyway, the story gradually became encrusted with detail and by the end of the next month it had reached royal circles, growing ever more complex. Like Mary Veal herself the account refused to lie down, and parties on both sides came forward to condemn or vouch for the characters.

The composer of this mysterious narrative turned out to be Daniel Defoe, who is buried alongside the mystical artist/poet William Blake in the strange little cemetery near City Road, Bunhill Fields, and who may have helped inspire Dickens to write *A Christmas Carol*. But that's another ghostly London story.

A Rooftop Swastika &
Other Stories

ARTHUR BRYANT: Berlin venerates the bullet holes in its buildings, but if you look around London you'll find very few signs of Second World War damage. There's the odd shrapnel mark here or there and that's about it. An astonishing number of buildings were condemned as unsafe and levelled, the rubble sold, conveniently for town planners who couldn't wait to whack up their Le Corbusier–influenced concrete social experiments, most of which failed disastrously.

Nobody knew that in time low-grade concrete rotted, that hasty construction would cause fatalities or that the concrete movement would give licence to so many terrible architects. The designers of one East End housing estate thought it was a good idea to have their lifts opening directly onto a busy street, which turned them into public toilets.

There was good Brutalism too, of course; look at the welcoming folds of the South Bank and the listed low-rise Alexandra Road Estate by Abbey Road. Although it suited everyone except the historian to tear down cracked church spires, bomb-bashed cinemas, damaged department stores and halves of semi-detached houses, parts were sometimes saved—but the process was serendipitous to say the least.

Prior to the war the nation had a year to prepare for bombing, and as we'd been previously exposed to its effects in the First World War we knew what to do: statues, paintings, museum collections, religious artefacts and politically sensitive materials were speedily hived off to the countryside or into underground tunnels and storage sites. The beautiful font of All Hallows-by-the-Tower was destroyed with the church, but its richly carved cover had been taken for safekeeping to St Paul's Cathedral, which was surrounded by fire-watchers (not enough of them; the high altar famously suffered a direct hit).

A great Saxon wheelhead cross once stood upon Tower Hill. The remaining pieces of it fell out of All Hallows church after eight hundred years on the same spot. Inigo Jones's stunning Barbers' Company room was blown to bits but Holbein's portrait of Henry VIII was saved. Charles I's statue was hidden for safekeeping in Lord Rosebery's estate near Edinburgh and a 'strong-point,' a concrete defence post disguised as an information bureau, was built around its plinth in preparation for invasion.

Many thought they would end up in hand-to-hand combat in the London streets, so to confuse the enemy, fakes abounded; in Parliament Square throughout the war there was a fake bookstall which was actually another defence post.

It was long thought that London was undefendable. The posts were a development of the London Defence Positions, a late-nineteenth-century plan to keep invaders from the capital via thirteen fortified bunkers.

Churches were filled with treasures that could not be moved. St Leonard's, Shoreditch was damaged by a flying bomb but its most macabre monument (to Elizabeth Benson) was saved. It shows two skeletons tearing down the Tree of Life. The Wren church of St James's, Piccadilly, was destroyed, but its beautiful Grinling Gibbons font of Adam and Eve and the serpents was saved.

As buildings were stripped and reinforced to withstand air raids, their original walls and roofs revealed surprises. When Austin Friars in the City was checked, a Roman roof was uncovered with a dog's paw prints in the clay, but the friary was totally destroyed. After the rubble had settled a profusion of wild flowers returned, along with forgotten salad ingredients like salsify and rocket.

St Anne's of Soho was gutted by bombs, leaving only its tower remaining. Under it lies the novelist Dorothy L. Sayers. Its unsafe attic currently holds the collection of the Museum of Soho, which is looking for a permanent home. But some good was done: the clapboard slums of Limehouse and Wapping were wiped out along with much that was dangerous and insanitary about the East End.

Paternoster Row, now a wasteland of chain stores beside Temple Bar, was known simply as 'the Row.' Harley Street was where one went to see a private doctor or dentist, Temple was the same for lawyers, Denmark Street was where you bought musical instruments and the Row was for the book trade. Here were published *Robinson Crusoe* and *The Boy's Own Paper*, and the Chapter House Tavern was filled with writers and editors. On the night of 29 December 1940 bombs rained down and the Row, its wooden buildings filled with dry paper, was more completely destroyed than any other thoroughfare in London.

Simpkin & Marshall, founded in 1819, was acknowledged to be the largest distributor of English books in the world and lost four million books to incendiary bombs. Their great cataloguing system, the only one of its kind anywhere, was obliterated. Yet the little street of Amen Corner, next to the Row, was untouched.

Many items mysteriously disappeared during the great post-war cleanup. A memorial window in St Clement Danes showed Samuel Johnson with Burke, Garrick, Goldsmith, Boswell, Mrs Carter and a dog. Both Johnson's pew and the stained-glass window vanished. How much of what was left was stolen? What could reasonably be saved and what could be restored? London was broke. It was not until 31 December 2006 that Great Britain made the final payment of about $83 million to the USA and discharged the last part of its war loan. By the end of the Second World War Britain had amassed a debt of £21 billion. War is expensive, especially when your ally strikes a hard bargain.

Much was lost, but what survived was returned to London. The statues of the stalwart Knights Templar were pulled from the rubble of Temple Church and reinstalled in the renovated building. In devastation there was still beauty. Just as a chunk of frieze from the Parthenon was found buried in a country garden at the turn of the twentieth century, so items put aside for safe-keeping reappeared intact. Even so, the postwar world was radically altered. Nothing would ever be the same again.

Du Cane Court in Balham (a place that those of a certain age may find themselves pronouncing as 'Bal-Ham' in an American accent; somebody please explain) has more than a touch of Albert Speer about its design. Monumental, inhuman and very tidy, it supposedly acted as a guidepost for Nazi aircraft during the Second World War. Senate House in Bloomsbury, to which it bears a distinct resemblance, was also a handy marker for approaching bombers. Hitler was meant to have spies planted within Du Cane Court and planned to live there and in Senate House after his hateful Wagnerian fantasy had reached fruition.

There was talk of giving the top of the building a shape like a swastika, but here the truth and the legends merge. Both buildings remain, unlike the tower of the Crystal Palace, which was dynamited to prevent it from being used as a navigation point.

Though they don't bear the marks of war, there's hardly an old building in London that does not have a legend attached to it. The *Daily Mail* had one of its periodic screeching fits over tennis courts made of concrete, which they became convinced were secret Nazi gun placements. They also suspected a car factory in Woolwich of manufacturing gun turrets for Nazi planes. Quite how they might get from there to Germany was never explained.

Buildings are never quite what you think they are. In the 1930s, 221B Baker Street was occupied by the Abbey National Building Society, and in 1951, as part of the Festival of Britain celebrations, their HQ was turned into a re-creation of Sherlock Holmes's home. His gaslit study was laid out with scientific apparatus, and fresh crumpets complete with bitemarks were supplied each day by a local baker (the crumpets, not the toothmarks. Perhaps they paid someone to do that).

In 1957 the Northumberland Arms was refurbished and renamed the Sherlock Holmes. They acquired the exhibition, which can be seen on the pub's first floor, and now some of you believe that this is the real home of a fictional character. Admit it.

Only one other building still incorporates designs left from the Festival of Britain and that's number 219 Oxford Street, which was the first new commercial building to be erected after the war. Along the exteriors of the higher floors are the Festival logo, the Skylon and the Dome of Discovery.

There's a Festival of Britain building that has remained from the exhibition's birth through to today—the much-loved Royal Festival Hall, a wonderful concert hall and one of the most welcoming buildings in London. As much as the city changes, this crowd-pleaser, with its boxes that look like drawers in a filing cabinet, remains an elegant joy.

JOHN MAY: One always reads that its acoustics are too 'dry.' Critics said that London no longer had a world-class hall because plans to repair the acoustically superb—and beautiful—Queen's Hall near Oxford Circus were shelved. Its wartime fire damage had been too great, and after the war there was an obsession with starting over and making everything new. In fact the Royal Festival Hall has a brilliant pure sound because the slightest mistake can be heard, so the musicians raise their game for the venue.

ARTHUR BRYANT: There was also a race to temporarily house bombed-out Londoners. One solution was the prefab, a flat-pack box cleverly engineered to stay warm and bright. With indoor toilets, fitted kitchens and wrap-around corner windows, they proved an instant hit with the public all over the country, who found a strong sense of community in them and chose not to move out when offered permanent accommodation. The best ones, on the Excalibur Estate in Catford, South London, are now listed.

Ultimately the people decided what to save and what to get rid of; councillors followed guidelines but had their personal peccadilloes. Those who wanted everything restored to its prewar state lost out to those who were planning a bright new capital. Unfortunately, many of the latter had hidden interests shaping their taste, and some went to jail for it. In 1973 architect John Poulson, who had designed some truly atrocious buildings in London including Cannon Street Station, found himself at the centre of a huge corruption scandal over the awarding of building contracts.

Janice, you know about this next bit.

JANICE LONGBRIGHT: Arthur, you can't just hand me a grubby piece of paper with a name on it—

ARTHUR BRYANT: That's the second time I've been called 'grubby.'

JANICE LONGBRIGHT: Well, it's not very clean, is it? And expect me to know— Oh, actually I do know a bit about this.

The Crossbones Graveyard in Redcross Way, Southwark, is a bit of wasteland owned by Transport for London, currently used for storage. But it's also the last resting place of over fifteen thousand people, and Londoners decided to reclaim it.

Crossbones was home to the 'outcast dead': unconsecrated ground used for the burial of prostitutes. London's graveyards present a complicated story. The ones attached to churches were for Christians but others were licensed in public grounds by private companies. If those companies failed and the grounds returned to local councils, what happened to the graves? Today it's not unusual to go into a small park in London and find the headstones stacked around the edges.

The night-ladies of Southwark were known as Winchester Geese and were licensed to ply their trade by the Bishop of Winchester within the Liberty of the Clink, an area in Southwark. The women were mostly not from London but Flanders, impoverished outsiders forced into the sex trade. The Geese couldn't be buried on hallowed land or anywhere near a parish church. The age of the burial ground isn't known, but it was mentioned in some old book—

ARTHUR BRYANT: John Stow's *A Survey of London*, published in 1598. I happen to have it here with me.

JANICE LONGBRIGHT: Of course you do. Anyway, it later became a paupers' cemetery in 1665, the year of the Great Plague, and finally closed to burials in 1853 when it was declared over-full and a risk to public health and decency.

Today the Memorial Gates are festooned with ribbons, cards and flowers—a tradition which only started in a 1998 ceremony—and small shrines have been placed on the site. The colourful, celebratory nature of these offerings adds to Crossbones' atmosphere, and if you take a closer look you'll find a statue of Mary in a grotto-like setting amongst trees, accompanied by a number of ceramic geese.

Another strange spot is Abney Park Cemetery, the Nonconformist boneyard just off Stoke Newington's main shopping area in North London. Where else do bakeries and boozers face ivy-covered Victorian angels? At its heart is a derelict non-denominational chapel that sets the Steptoe-ish tone of the place. It's mossy, damp and tumbledown, but distinctly urban—one of London's so-called Magnificent Seven sites of interment, which includes the much posher Brompton and Highgate Cemeteries.

It's atmospheric rather than picturesque. To my knowledge the cemetery has always been muddy and confusingly crossed with narrow root-filled paths that trip you up. Many of the tombs are exposed to the elements and look as if they've been got at by graverobbers.

Not many people seem to know that Edgar Allan Poe went to school nearby.

Some of Poe's work is now arcane and a bit of a struggle, but his best stories are wonderful and very influential. Stoke Newington would have been a village back then and retains the genteel leafy feeling now. It's not on the tube line and is therefore a bugger to reach, even though it's so close to the city centre.

At its heart, right on the high street, the extraordinary cemetery is passed by shoppers who seem strangely at ease with so many gloomy memorials in their main high street. I've had quite a few sardine and tomato sandwiches behind those graves, doing surveillance. I hope they never tidy the place up too much.

JOHN MAY: What about Poe?

JANICE LONGBRIGHT: The young Edgar lost both his parents early on and spent five years living in the UK. Perhaps his bust, unveiled in 2011 on Stoke Newington Church Street, would have been better placed inside eerie Abney Park. I wonder if he ever visited the cemetery, and if it influenced him? I've seen a few crows around there but never a raven.

Quite a few Victorian comedians and circus performers are buried there, including one lion tamer who had his finger bitten off, a pantomime dame and a cockney costermonger comic, the fabulously named Albert Onésime Britannicus Gwathveoyd Louis Chevalier. It's also where Amy Winehouse filmed her 'Back to Black' video, keeping the performance tradition alive. For sober balance, William Booth, the founder of the Salvation Army, is stashed near the entrance.

There's something of the night about the place—it's not a good idea to pick flowers or go mushrooming there because the arsenic from so many embalmed Victorian corpses has poisoned the soil. I took a friend from California to visit it and she had a panic attack inside its ruined church. It's hard to believe that you can get lost on your local high street.

ARTHUR BRYANT: I can get lost anywhere.

The Venice of Drains &
Other Stories

ARTHUR BRYANT: It's a disreputable name is Jack, a scallywag London name that for me conjures up a Jack the Lad in a neckerchief and a leather jerkin, selling goods down the market with a line of patter. 'Mind me foot, missus, I got a broken toe from this lot after it fell off the back of the lorry.' There are much darker Jacks, from Ripper to Spring-Heeled, but Jack Sheppard is the king of them all. As I believe I mentioned, he's buried in St Martin-in-the-Fields now, a lad who never stood a chance but went down in London history.

He was born in 1702 in Spitalfields, raised in a workhouse and apprenticed to a carpenter, then switched to robbery and was jolly good at it. In 1724 he escaped from Newgate Gaol four times, usually while drunk, and used his diminutive build to slip through bars. At one point he was weighted down with three hundred pounds of iron and put on display—it was a public relations mistake that guaranteed his legend.

When he managed to get out of leg irons riveted to the floor, he even showed his jailers how to do it. He was the original working-class hero, escaping on knotted bedsheets and through sawn-out bars, on the run in ankle-cuffs, staying one step ahead of the law and laughing about it.

It's a tragic story that has the makings of a grand myth. Jack is usually a substitute for John—I had an uncle Jack/John—and so it was with Sheppard. He was short and slender, and stuttered, but was fast and witty with it, a popular pub sprite. When he met the prostitute Elizabeth Lyon, alias Edgeworth Bess, he was moved to rebellion and the politics of Levelling—the commitment to populism, equality, suffrage and religious tolerance. At least, that's according to Daniel Defoe, who distributed Sheppard's biography at his hanging. But this may just have been an example of the usual practice of pinning a man's fall from grace on a 'bad' woman.

The Sheppard misadventures largely took place around the now-vanished Clare Market, at the back of Lincoln's Inn Fields. Sheppard inspired many biographies as well as *The Beggar's Opera* by John Gay, films like *Where's Jack?* (surprisingly good considering it starred Tommy Steele) and novels like *The Fatal Tree* by Jake Arnott, written in thieves' cant.

Sheppard's fast-forward two-year career was packed with daredevil escapes and could hardly fail to capture the public imagination. Adding to the excitement, he had the love of a not-so-good woman and was pursued by a dastardly villain, the extortionist 'Thief-Taker General' Jonathan Wild.

In the absence of any effective police force, Wild exploited a strong public demand for action during a major London crime wave. As a gang leader he became a master manipulator of legal systems, collecting the rewards offered for valuables which he had stolen himself, bribing prison guards to release his cronies and blackmailing any who crossed him. He also met a sticky end, at the age of forty-two, at the end of a rope. Defoe covered that one too.

After Edgeworth Bess was locked up in the holding prison of St Giles's Roundhouse the beadle refused to let Jack visit her, so he broke in and carried her away. On the day his death warrant was signed he escaped jail dressed in women's clothes. Sheppard's flamboyant energy and cockney charm transformed him into a folk hero.

Many signed a petition to have his sentence commuted to transportation, but of course he had made a monkey of the law and had to go. On the way to his death he stopped in the Oxford Tavern on Oxford Street for a pint, to cheering crowds of well-wishers, approximately one-third of London's population.

At Tyburn the noose slowly strangled him, but the crowds who pushed in to prevent his body from being removed and dissected accidentally blocked Jack's final escape plan; friends had arranged for him to be rushed to a nearby doctor for revival.

Even as his tumbril reached the gallows Daniel Defoe's biography of Sheppard went on sale. No wonder the public took so readily to these forerunners of the penny-bloods: magazines that mixed real and fictional monsters. Fortunes were made and legends born.

Jack's tale was adapted so quickly for the stage that it opened at the Theatre Royal, Drury Lane, just two weeks later. A huge number of artists and writers were inspired by him, from Fielding to Hogarth, from Brecht and Weill to, er, Chicory Tip. He became such a cultural phenomenon that the Lord Chamberlain banned all London plays with the words 'Jack Sheppard' in the title for forty years, fearing the young would follow in his footsteps.

Between 1770 and 1860 over seven thousand men and women

were choked to death on Tyburn's hanging tree. By the time the hemp was being fastened around their necks, their stories had already been penned and printed into pamphlets for the picnicking crowds. The facts were less important than the speed with which they could be spread.

Lately the great tale of Sheppard and Wild has fallen from public favour. I suspect that new generations have never heard of the daring street urchin who thumbed his nose at the law and paid the price.

Speaking of ruffians, Jacob's Island in Bermondsey was the roughest part of London. It's where Dickens chose to send Bill Sikes to his death, a rookery of mud and sewage that was virtually in the River Thames itself. The filthy waters in the creeks that bisected it rose and fell, leaving silt and animal carcasses, so the surrounding hovels were perpetually damp and reeking. Dickens described it somewhat unflatteringly as 'the Venice of drains.'

Overcrowded and impoverished, it lay beside the Neckinger tributary which branched into streams and reservoirs used for ablutions and washing, so sickness abounded. Worse, the industry that surrounded it was of the most antisocial kind imaginable: tanning, for which you needed leather hides and a lot of dog shit; and soap-making, which also stank abominably.

Jacob's Island was a 'Liberty,' meaning it operated beyond City of London jurisdiction, so it was the place to head for if you wished to avoid the police. All that remains of it now is a chimney and a faded marker plaque, so no selfie opportunities there, I'm afraid.

When I was very young this area and all the way along to Deptford and the Isle of Dogs was 'Venetian' only insofar as there were a huge number of humpback bridges across the inlets, all of which seemed to open and close in different ways. I associate the area with bad times, bad smells, dirty pubs and visiting an ancient toothless aunt who lived in a basement slum and kept a foul-mouthed mynah bird.

By way of contrast, a little further west is Shad Thames, where my esteemed colleague John May lives in his splendid white minimalist luxury loft prison cell.

JOHN MAY: I don't like clutter, Arthur. I couldn't live like you, in a flat that could be opened as the National Museum of Rubbish.

The warehouses of Shad Thames were once packed with orange-handed porters lugging sacks of saffron and cinnamon. Now it's squeaky clean, filled with hanging baskets and sandblasted brick, and dead except at the weekends, when tourists come to take pictures.

ARTHUR BRYANT: That's because all that's left now are flats like yours. Bermondsey Street has been poncey for years, with fussy little pretend-shops selling cupcakes and knickknacks.

JOHN MAY: What strikes me most is how incredibly prosperous this formerly poor part of London has become. A lot of it's to do with the redevelopment of London Bridge Station. Its elegant modern design resolves the old problematic space; access was always dark and overcrowded. Now all fifteen platforms can be reached from one central point, a huge improvement for everyone who has to change here twice a day.

ARTHUR BRYANT: I suppose so, but in the surrounding areas the buildings have been repurposed so many times that they're palimpsests of themselves. We're looking at historical phantoms, seeing through the airbrushed present of overlit doughnut shops to the spicy, raucous fug of the nineteenth century.

JOHN MAY: I prefer buildings and structures with useful, practical functions. Look at the Hungerford railway bridge. Of the thirty-five bridges that cross the Thames, Hungerford is probably the least noticed.

The original was named after the once-popular market at its base. It had been built by Isambard Kingdom Brunel in 1845 to take trains south from Charing Cross Station, a great lattice of riveted steel more suited to spanning New York's East River than the Thames.

A rickety boardwalk was added to one side of the rail tracks, connecting the riverbanks so that pedestrians could cross. It was claustrophobically narrow and underlit. The southern buttress still has a staircase leading to the original steamer pier underneath. It was painted by Claude Monet (in a painting—he didn't paint the bridge).

The new Hungerford is now two bridges in one. You have to select which view you'd like before boarding it. Supposedly there are still unexploded Second World War bombs in the Thames mud underneath it. And there's a skateboard graveyard where boarders abandon their broken decks. We found a body down there once.

The north bank now offers terrific views of the bridges from its restored walkways, although it's the less popular side of the river. It doesn't get evening sunlight. The whole crossing was re-named the Golden Jubilee Bridges, but we decide what to call buildings and bridges, not architects, and the name refused to stick. It remains the same as it always was, the Hungerford Bridge.

ARTHUR BRYANT: For me the biggest shock was seeing the old view of Tower Bridge ruined by the 'Walkie-Talkie' building at 20 Fenchurch Street, the winner of the Carbuncle Cup for the worst new British building and now deeply regretted by the Design Council, who had supported it only to recoil in horror when they saw the damage they'd done.

The building's top-heavy concave design caused it to focus sunlight in a 'death ray' effect that melted cars, but its main problem was its bulk. Until recently I could take you to the Angel pub in Rotherhithe and show you the sun setting at the centre of Tower Bridge, but no more; the view is blocked. As I walk along the river's edge all I see are poky flats with skeuomorphic balconies and mean little entrances. Perhaps we've swapped one kind of unacceptable housing for another. It would be interesting to know which had smaller living areas, slum houses or modern flats.

Listening to the nonsense that some of my fellow tour guides come out with, one starts to wonder just how much London history is made up. The Victorians certainly didn't help, forever embroidering facts with simpering backstories of courtly honour and medieval romance.

John May: Is it true that Trafalgar Square's empty fourth plinth was once due to hold an equestrian statue of Charles I, but when they unveiled it, it became the subject of public ridicule because his horse had no stirrups?

Arthur Bryant: Unfortunately that exact same story is told of many other empty plinths, so no. The truth is likely to be more prosaic; that a statue was planned but lost its funding. If you have to choose between history and legend, print the legend.

John May: Now the fourth plinth is used as a rotating showcase for new artists like Yinka Shonibare, whose delightful *Nelson's Ship in a Bottle* was a one-thirtieth-scale replica of Nelson's flagship *Victory* with the sails rewoven in African cottons. The piece considered British colonialism through its naval history and proved highly popular with the public.

There are some excellent traditional statues in London, too. My personal favourites are those of Dame Edith Cavell on St Martin's Lane, Dame Millicent Fawcett in Parliament Square and Sir John Betjeman in St Pancras Station.

ARTHUR BRYANT: There are some hideous ones as well. Maggi Hambling's Oscar Wilde looks like a half-plastered Medusa rising from its coffin with a lit fag. You're meant to sit on it, which places Oscar lower than you. I'd prefer to sit at the feet of a master. Her statue commemorating nineteenth-century feminist Mary Wollstonecraft, depicted as a silvery nude pin-up, is on Newington Green and has come in for a lot of stick from the outraged public.

Although it seems perverse to depict the aesthete Wilde as a lumpen swirl, that's not the worst statue in London. Unfortunately no one has managed to dynamite Paul Day's hideously tasteless St Pancras statue of snogging giants modelled on him and his missus. It's called *The Meeting Place* and looks like a three-dimensional Primark sale window.

| | |

In Deptford a giant anchor in the high street reminded locals of the town's maritime history until it was removed by the safety-obsessed council, but four years of public protest eventually brought it back.

This once-unlovely neighbourhood near where I grew up is the site of Christopher Marlowe's grave. The entrance to St Nicholas Church, where he's buried, is adorned with two skull-and-crossbones (I want to pluralize both nouns but can't bring myself to do it). To understand why this is controversial you have to take into account Deptford's location, just this side of Greenwich on the Thames.

Deptford was once the King's Yard, created by Henry VIII. Captain Cook set off from here in HMS *Resolution,* and Sir Francis Drake was knighted by Elizabeth I on the same spot.

If you were commissioned by the Royal Navy to fight for the control of our trade routes, you could work freelance and sail under the Jolly Roger skull-and-crossbones instead of a Union Jack, and surrender your booty to the Crown. The leap from privateer to pirate was a small one (and still is). So it could signify that pirates are buried in the Thameside cemetery.

But that's where the story goes wrong.

The Jolly Roger was not an international symbol of piracy. The symbol was originally Spanish and was possibly copied from the existing gates of St Nicholas for a flag made in 1687. The flag failed to show the real clue to the skulls' original symbolism, for the back of the carving reveals laurel wreaths perched on the skulls, signifying the victory of transcendence over mortal bones, not a Jolly Roger at all.

Londoners chose to go with the legend, so another myth entered history. How many other tales are told as gospel, only to be revealed as wishful thinking?

What the Butler Saw & Other Stories

ARTHUR BRYANT: The spot where Farringdon Road becomes New Bridge Street is not very interesting to look at these days, but it hides a formidable history. And for me, in an odd way, it is one of London's hearts—one of its key crossing points.

The piece of tarmac just before Blackfriars Bridge on its north side has been dug up more times than I can remember. The area surrounding the crossroads of Ludgate Circus is a long-unsettled site. But the street view offers an iconic image of London, one that has been the subject of numerous paintings and etchings. You've got the hill leading to St Paul's, plus Ludgate, the site of the westernmost gate in the wall of the old City of London.

There was also on the corner not too long ago the Old King Lud, another public house where prisoners took a beer on their way to eternity, either to Smithfield to be hanged or to Tyburn, also to be hanged. The latter seems rather a long way to go by open cart so Smithfield seems the likelier option, although the Angel in St Giles makes the same claim as a provisioner for prisoner refreshment.

Running underneath Blackfriars, the River Fleet can still be seen at low tide—it enters the Thames under the bridge. There's supposed to be an old cornerstone from Ludgate knocking around, left there after the gate was torn down in 1760 and sold for £146, and also a model lighthouse that I've never been able to find.

The charming Bridewell Theatre was once a Victorian swimming pool, and if you head for the bar you'll see the waters of the Fleet rushing beneath your feet. In 1891, the St Bride Foundation was established to provide a centre for Fleet Street's print trade and still houses a superb library of print, media and design.*

A carved head of Edward VI is all that remains of the infamous Bridewell prison. Its boundary wall once ran along the front of St Bride's vicarage, so every year the vicar had to pay the prison governors a guinea* for permission to walk over his own doorstep.

There was also a famous boxing ring nearby, just off Blackfriars Road and known simply as the Ring. It was an immense redbrick octagonal rotunda familiar to all cabbies as a landmark, but was demolished after a bombing raid.

The Congregational Memorial Hall on the site of the old Fleet Prison was built to honour the two thousand clergymen who refused to obey the 1662 Act of Uniformity. This was an act that set the order of prayer to be used in the English Book of Common Prayer. All persons had to go to church once a week or be fined a shilling, a considerable sum for the poor. The clergy who fought it were all expelled from the church in an event that became known as the Great Ejection. The imposingly Gothic hall was destroyed in 1968, so in London there's clearly a time limit on memorials.

This spot at Ludgate had also been home to Thomas Cook &

* Twenty-one shillings.

Son, the travel agency founded in 1841 by a cabinet maker who started out by arranging transport to the Great Exhibition. The company finally collapsed in 2019. There was a weathervane ship on the roof of its building and bas-reliefs featuring fifteen 'races of mankind.' The area is also associated with popinjays, both the parrots and the fops. Popinjay abbots stayed in a hostel in nearby Poppin's Court, but there are also stone versions of cormorants, swallows and other oddments—hardly any of which I can now spot. Who hives these things off and never returns them? I'm convinced there used to be statues all around Unilever House overlooking Blackfriars Bridge but can't find any photos of them. Mind you, I might just need new trifocals.

And this is the frustrating thing about looking at London now: matching the past to the present in anything other than tattered fragments has become all but impossible. Only the grandest buildings have survived the centuries. But every step of the way has a story to tell. You can turn a magnifying glass on any single detail and easily fall into a badger hole.

JOHN MAY: Rabbit hole.

ARTHUR BRYANT: Is it? Turning to a page of Arthur Mee's 1937 edition of *London: The Great City Complete,* I find details of an insurance building in Moorgate. These were once among the grandest places in the city. You want your insurance company to have a look of permanence.

Ocean House provided marine insurance, and was covered in carvings of Neptune and sea-horses, plus a working model of a lighthouse. It housed the Institute of Chartered Accountants and was designed by John Belcher, who had created the high Gothic building of number 1 Poultry. Belcher reinvented classic images and subverted them, even down to the keystones that featured women turning into leaves. He proved that revolutionary styles don't have to be ugly.

Inside was the largest frieze in London (190 feet long). Sir Hamo Thornycroft planned a parade of figures showing progress through the ages. There are miners, teachers, builders, nurses and sailors, and when the building was enlarged the frieze was extended by fifty feet.

The problem was that Sir Hamo had died by this time, and his successor found that the frieze ended in the present day, even to the point of including the current building. So in order to make it longer he had to take it backwards in time.

He sculpted figures from the Renaissance, Michelangelo stroking his beard, Palladio with his folio, Wren with a model of St Paul's, right back to the Romans, Assyrians and cave-dwellers. Lo and behold, a complete history in a single frieze. London is full of friezes, like the ones on Liberty and the Albert Memorial, but I can find nothing further about the great Ocean House frieze or what happened to it. The building is still there but its doors are closed even to me.

The lighthouse used to have a light in it, but as of the time of this writing no one has bothered to rewire it.

| | |

You used to be able to find wonderful old things lying around. Mudlarks and toshers still abound along the Thames foreshore, and a couple of years back one of them discovered an unbroken Roman lamp there. I mostly remember the foreshore being covered with worn-smooth glass, bits of pottery and car tyres, which have now gone. Once toshing was a full-time job for those at the lowest level of the British Bee Hive.

There are still plenty of costermongers selling from their handcarts, but we lost the last knife-grinders and wet-fish men in

Central London only recently, and there are no more Steptoe-like rag-and-bone men calling out as their horses clop along the streets.

Women's street work included 'knocker-upping,' shooting peas at bedroom windows to act as human alarm clocks, and selling flowers at stations. They still do the latter.

Moon-cursers were link boys who saw people to their destinations in unlit streets; they were said to damn the bright moon for putting them out of work. Now you can stand in a backstreet at night listening to songbirds who think it's day. London has no more night darkness and the link boys would have no work. If the Petticoat Lane songbird-sellers were still around they would no longer have to blind their birds to ensure they'd sing their hearts out, not knowing night from day.

Patterers shouted out the stories from the newspapers they were selling, adding as many vivid details as possible. 'Pure' finders collected dog turds for the tanning industry in an age before the plastic glove. The last professional full-time sandwich man disappeared in the eighties (Michael Bentine's 1966 film *The Sandwich Man* featured him in a morning suit and sandwich board walking around a very sunny London).

There are still some traditional street workers: chestnut-sellers, singers, food-sellers, mimes and acrobats. And there are modern street jobs for *Big Issue* magazine-sellers, freebie hander-outers, marketeers, data trawlers and the dreaded shouty evangelists I enjoy seeing off with my stick. There will always be someone on the street where the money is, but the move away from hard cash to payment by walkie-phone may well spell their end.

While I go for a throat de-parcher I'll leave you in the capable hands of Margo Brandy, a Lincoln's Inn court officer who also happens to be an expert on city entertainments because she used to be in charge of their licences. Margo?

MARGO BRANDY: Happy to help out, Arthur.

The city's raffishness once showed itself in all sorts of 'sensation' entertainment. During the Edwardian era, opposite King's Cross railway station, where Mr Bryant and his fellow officers ply their dubious trade, there once stood a wooden rollercoaster surrounded by dozens of funfair booths. Today you can still find old-fashioned amusement arcades there, and a few more scattered around the West End. Is there a reason why?

To piece together an answer you have to go back to the start of the nineteenth century, when London was awash with music halls—in 1875 there were 375 in all. Supper entertainments and other evening attractions, high- and lowbrow, were designed to lure in customers looking for brief novelties.

There were all kinds of illusions available. John Henry Pepper adapted Dickens's ghost stories for the stage, creating 'Pepper's Ghosts,' figures that mysteriously appeared via a system of angled mirrors. The 'Pepper's Ghost' is still with us in the form of the electronic teleprompter. All kinds of illusions could be created. There were artificial storms, magic displays, automata, acrobatics, vanishing acts, puppets, monsters and waxworks offering sensation in halls and early 'pop-ups.'

The paying public had a desire to see the entire world moving and miniaturized. They did so with the help of panopticons, dioramas, rotundas and magic-lantern shows. When photography appeared in 1839, the game changed in an interesting way; there were two ways of viewing the new photography—in a shared public space which all the family could visit, and in semi-privacy, looking through a viewer. The latter quickly became used to show saucy sequences featuring unclothed ladies being spied upon by naughty boys.

When the kinetoscope arrived, running a moving loop of film (not very long, around thirty seconds before it began again), its

American inventors quickly saw a way to build a business. There was no point in making a film if you couldn't screen it, so they kept the patent on the physical devices and forced the new owners to lease their films, creating the production, distribution and exhibition system that remained in use until very recently.

But the patent didn't extend overseas. A British cinema pioneer named Robert Paul had hired a team to build projectors and install them around London. Instead of being reliant on American subject matter in the leased loops, he began shooting films of local interest.

It turned out that England had something the USA did not have: history. So scenes of parades, pageants and royal ceremonies, sporting events and street activities were shot and shown in specially kitted-out buildings where other amusements were added to keep public interest from waning.

Shooting galleries and mutoscopes—those 'What the Butler Saw' machines—appeared along with phonograph sounds and games of chance at these sites. Peep shows sat beside the first Boer War footage taken in the Transvaal in these new 'biographs.' The name remained a popular choice for cinemas until the 1970s, when the Victoria Biograph, a 'gentlemen's relaxation' cinema, as Arthur would call them, brought the name into disrepute.

Another form of entertainment for the time-poor urbanite became popular: the one-hour cinemas at railway stations which showed newsreels and shorts that repeated on the hour, and were used mainly by commuters waiting for trains, although they later became sleazy. These little cinemas were still going in the late 1980s. One can be seen in the film *An American Werewolf in London*.

As the city was a place where one came for sensation and entertainment, the arcades survived, thanks to the 1950s addition of music and pinball tables, when they became gathering spots for the cashless young. They also attracted pickpockets and rent boys (although rarely female prostitutes, it seems—this was a male domain) throughout their lives, and continued to do so until the twenty-first century.

The sensations of mid-twentieth-century London were scaled down to strip clubs and burlesque bars but one nightspot stood apart from them. The Windmill Theatre was a poor man's Moulin Rouge modelled on the more famous Parisian burlesque theatre, but the principle was the same. The story that it was built upon the site of a windmill dating from the eighteenth century is dubious; Soho was marshy, not windy.

In 1909 one of London's first cinemas, the Palais de Luxe, opened. In the 1930s an elderly widow and a Jewish sock-seller took it over and put the first naked ladies on its stage. Mrs Henderson fought the Lord Chamberlain, the censor who forbade nudity, and won her battle. The ladies could appear nude so long as they did not move a muscle. As a result they staged ridiculous tableaux—Beefeaters at the Tower, Britannia and the Trafalgar Square lions—and stayed open through the war.

The idea of the sensation display continues—there were fairground-style rides in Shaftesbury Avenue's Trocadero in for years, and 'experiences' like M&M'S World, a sort of funfair for the morbidly obese, extend the tradition. The latest sensations, shiny pan-Asian videogame parlours in Chinatown and on Charing Cross Road, look very different now but cater to the thing that never changes in London: the desire to be amused.

While the idea of going out specifically to enjoy what the city had to offer didn't really take hold until after 1800, over the next century London's West End became the world's leading pleasure district, offering vulgar delights as well as highbrow entertainment.

From the shops of St James's to the bars of Fleet Street there were areas of old-fashioned maleness, but Oxford Street and Regent Street were considered resolutely feminine. Shopping, it was said, aroused the emotions amenable to the female sex. The retail industry was reliant on female labour, as it was thought that only women could sell to their own kind, but they were paid a fraction of their male counterparts' wages. So, while gentlemen bought their boots on Jermyn Street, ladies tried on bonnets in Bond Street and the sexes rarely overlapped—at least when it came to shopping.

On the corner of Charing Cross Road and Leicester Square (actually Cranbourn Street) was an overbearing and rather ugly 'sensation' venue known as the Hippodrome.

It was built at the turn of the nineteenth century, and was to be used for circus performers and variety acts. In the very first variety show Little Tich and Charlie Chaplin appeared, the first in a long line of showbiz legends, and yet the great hall never entirely worked.

Like the Palace Theatre, it was built at the end of the Victorian era, and was impractical and over-elaborate. Entry to the venue was through a bar like a ship's saloon. The performance space featured both a proscenium stage and an arena that could be submerged into a 230-foot, 100,000-gallon water tank weighing four hundred tons when full. It was used for aquatic spectacles. The tank featured eight central fountains and a further circle of fountains around the sides. Entrances at the edges of the auditorium could also be flooded and used for the entry of boats.

Equestrian acts, live elephants and polar bears were misused in spectacles (how did they get them in?) and acrobats would dive from a minstrels' gallery above a sliding roof. Cantilevered galleries removed the need for columns that obstructed views, and the whole was covered by a painted-glass retractable roof which could be illuminated at night.

Later a lift was added that could raise a car, and indeed it was used when the venue became the Talk of the Town in 1958 and Eartha Kitt appeared from a Rolls-Royce. The lift was noisy and took around three minutes to rise, so rowdy musical numbers had to be staged to cover it.

There was another venue that staged water shows in the West End. Winstanley's Mathematical Water Theatre at Hyde Park Corner appeared at the end of the seventeenth century and pumped water from the River Tyburn to prove the power of hydraulics. Mr Winstanley set up the show to raise money for the Eddystone Lighthouse off the treacherous Cornish coast, and managed to build it too. Unfortunately he was swept away in a terrible storm while inside the lighthouse.

By the 1960s Leicester Square's Hippodrome was run-down, gloomy and smelled of damp, the stage proving overcrowded and awkward. As theatrical buildings go, it was not a pleasant or welcoming venue in any way. Yet Frank Sinatra, Ella Fitzgerald, Ethel Merman, Judy Garland, Diana Ross and Stevie Wonder all performed there, along with hundreds of other stars.

But the Talk of the Town always felt like a B-list Vegas where aged performers went while they were drying out. The awful food was supplied by Trust House Forte and the location was hardly desirable. Taken over in 1983, it became festooned with thugs and gangsters.

Finally it became a gambling joint and the Hippodrome Casino was opened in 2012 by Boris Johnson, who described it as 'yet another ringing endorsement of London as a great place to invest' before beating a hasty retreat. The last time I looked it was staging a male strip show. And so avaricious councils turned a blind eye and London kept its saltier side, as it has done for a thousand years.

Leicester Square was originally common land and never lost

its common touch. In the mid-eighteenth century, brothels had started opening around the square. In 1825 the severed heads of traitors at Temple Bar could still be studied through telescopes, and the public appetite for sensation remained undimmed. Wyld's Great Globe arrived in Leicester Square in 1851. This was a sixty-foot-high planet that according to *Punch* magazine offered the public a chance to walk through 'a geographical globule which the mind can take in at one swallow.'

The surrounding area closed itself off to traffic and became an official entertainment zone with council-sanctioned jugglers and singers, a pale shadow of the knobbly-kneed fez-wearing sand dancers who once collected money outside the Empire. Today the garden square has shrunk to half its former size and features bland statues of entertainment stars, but the choice of celebrities is endearingly odd: Paddington Bear, Gene Kelly, Mary Poppins, Mr Bean and Bugs Bunny lurk in the bushes or on benches. There's one more hidden on a roof—Batman stands on top of the Odeon Leicester Square, his black costume matching the black slate building.

ARTHUR BRYANT: Thanks, Margo, that was most enlightening. I'd rather look at the severed heads on Temple Bar than a Batman film at the Odeon.

MARGO BRANDY: Of course you would, dear boy. So would all of us, really.

Underneath the Arches &
Other Stories

A RTHUR BRYANT: Whenever a television show wants us to see the full horror of Victorian poverty they shoot a sequence at the back of Somerset House, which they dress to look filthy and dangerous. That's because there's a dark stone walkway with good angles underneath the existing building. Before computer graphics it was all about finding unspoiled sightlines. Somerset House could be stuffed full of rhubarbing beggars to create an authentic atmosphere.

We still refer to the penurious in terms of Henry Mayhew, the nineteenth-century journalist and reformer whose columns brought us *London Labour and the London Poor,* an exhaustive collection of literary portraits of street people and their lives totalling around two million words (the version you can buy today is massively truncated).

It's fascinating to dip into. The lives of the working poor were enmeshed with the theatre, because successful stage performances brought punters with a little more money to spare, creating a service market. Ham-sellers stood at the doors of theatres and audiences treated themselves to fried fish, baked potatoes and coffee. It was assumed that children would turn to selling the moment their parents were away, and they did, some as young as seven years old.

There was even poverty tourism. The rookeries behind Seven Dials and the Thames Tunnel, the pay-per-visit foot tunnel under the river that fell from public popularity, were visited only by the adventurous because they became the haunt of footpads and whores. But one rookery we know little about was much more famous and troublesome at the time, mainly because of its proximity to the royal and the wealthy.

During the first half of the nineteenth century, the Adelphi Arches were a high-ceilinged network of vaults, tunnels and stables that ran underneath the Aldwych. They came to be known as the Dark Arches with good reason. Before the Thames was narrowed to make a deeper channel, there was a marshy foreshore rising to the road beyond. The building of the arches raised the Adelphi Terrace to the height of the Strand, creating a multi-level platform below the Strand to the water's edge.

The structure was gigantic and was frequently flooded with raw sewage, which brought rats scampering up into the once-elegant houses above. This is where the very poorest prostitutes worked, picking up their drunken clients above and leading them below. Hundreds of poverty-stricken people stayed here, with groups often thieving from each other.

More bizarrely, pleasure steamers used to stop there on Sundays, letting people off so that they could commit 'all manner of indecencies.' In the London of the past 'indecencies' is always code for the Anglo-Saxon word I never use, not out of prudery but because overuse has rendered it unimaginative.

In the latter part of the century the labyrinthine gloom of the Dark Arches was lifted with better lighting, but nothing stopped the gatherings. What finally got rid of this den of iniquity was the construction around 1870 of the sweeping Victoria Embankment. It removed the tumbledown chaos of the wharves and many of the steamboat landings, replacing them with a single clean road.

In 1858 a gentleman named Augustus Leopold Egg painted a corner of the scene, although he couldn't capture the vastness of the Adelphi Arches. The painting now belongs to the Tate. Gradually the last pockets of degradation were cleared from Central London. The idea that poverty was somehow picturesque began to fade in the wake of crusades from Dickens and Mayhew. A new breed of female pioneering reformers rose, like Elizabeth Garrett Anderson, Britain's first woman doctor, and Barbara Bodichon, who reformed women's iniquitous property rights.

I I I

Walbrook on the north side of London Bridge is one of twenty-five wards in the City of London. It's an interesting street. It houses the often-overlooked St Stephen Walbrook, a graceful circular church with a grand dome. Inside, there's a Henry Moore altar and a black Bakelite telephone from the early fifties on which the first Samaritans call was made.

On a grey, grimy day in 1954, some workmen were clearing a bomb site for Legal & General. On the last day of their dig they were about to go over to the pub when they saw a head poking out of the rubble. The statue was that of Mithras, recognizable by his Phrygian cap. They had discovered his temple, buried under centuries of building.

There had been Roman artefacts found around Walbrook over a long period, but this—the so-called 'Pompeii of the North'— proved to be a vast store of relics associated with the Temple of Mithras . . . and here it was in Queen Victoria Street in the centre of London, preserved thanks to the muddy banks of the underground river that once passed through it, the Walbrook.

The temple was excavated and relocated. Over the years, the site became the subject of endless disputes; it was prime City property beside the Thames, and the race was on for archaeologists to uncover as much as they could before another glass box could be dumped on top of it.

When they lost the battle and an ugly new building went in, the temple was shoved on top of a car park all on one level—it would originally have been tilted so that as you approached the altar it came into the light. Worse, they stuck a load of crazy paving around it so that it looked like someone's front garden.

Mithras was a virile young god worshipped in cave-like spaces where initiates learned of his mysteries in penumbral torchlight. The Mithraic cult had grown across the Roman Empire and the temple, appropriately enough for the City of London, was dedicated to Bacchus. Over ten thousand Roman items have been recovered from the site, including writing tablets that can give us a real taste of Roman conversation. There were marble reliefs, amulets, statues of deities, and a beautiful tiny amber model of a gladiator's helmet. In addition, whole wooden jointed houses were dug out forty feet down. It's the single most important Roman find ever made in London.

Roman remains are nothing special in London, it's a city built upon them, but Mithras touched a nerve for reasons no archaeologist has ever worked out. His cult was an early rival to Christianity and very complex, with seven levels of initiation, secret handshakes and bull sacrifices known as tauroctony.

That ugly new building was removed to make way for an even newer one and Mithras was finally moved home, back to the banks of the long-vanished Walbrook stream, underneath the headquarters of Bloomberg.

As often happens in these cases, when the temple was reassembled there was no clear idea of what to do with it. It had been built on a river to supply it with fresh water. Happily, it was reconstructed as it appeared at the end of the excavation in October 1954, reflecting its condition in 240 CE. The temple remains can be seen in the basement of the Bloomberg building. There are three floors going deep underground, the first displaying pieces found on the site, like jewellery and sandals, then an audiovisual presentation and finally the Roman temple remains themselves, arranged in a *son-et-lumière* presentation.

Speaking of stuff dug out of the soil, an item lay in the Minories near Aldgate tube station for almost two thousand years, surviving in almost perfect condition while Tudor cellars, Victorian warehouses and twentieth-century concrete pilings were punched through the earth around it. That is, until the last day of an excavation to raise a sixteen-storey hotel on the site in 2013.

It was a complete statue of a Roman eagle with a snake in its beak, carved in the first century CE, at a time when the Roman city was exploding in population and wealth. It's believed to have stood on an imposing mausoleum on the edge of a cemetery just outside the city walls. It's gone to be cared for in the Museum of London.

There are other bits of old London under the streets. The Roman amphitheatre is usually overlooked by visitors. It was uncovered in Guildhall Yard during an archaeological dig taking place in preparation for the new art gallery. In 2002, its doors opened for the first time in nearly two thousand years. It was once a coliseum used for gladiator games, animal fighting and public executions. There used to be a hairdresser's next door that had a sign in the window: 'Beards trimmed, also coliseum in basement.'

In case you were wondering, the London Coliseum on St Martin's Lane is something very different; it's the largest theatre in the West End, with an illuminated globe on top and 2,359 seats inside. It was one of the first two places in Britain to sell Coca-Cola, the other being Selfridges. I have absolutely no idea why I know that.

The Romans left their mark all over the city. There are bits of wall dotted around the Square Mile, including a large section at Cooper's Row. Beneath the church of All Hallows-by-the-Tower is a tessellated Roman floor. The western gate of an old Roman fort can still be found in the London Wall underground car park and there are several Roman bathhouses, one being under an office block on Lower Thames Street.

JOHN MAY: I thought you were going to do a bit about the British Library next.

ARTHUR BRYANT: I was just getting around to it in my own time.

JOHN MAY: When was that, 1953?

ARTHUR BRYANT: You're very rude.

The library. Once it was housed in the heart of the British Museum, a rotunda of bookish hush. Since 1997 it's been in an oddly suburban-looking building on Euston Road. It's not just a library, but *the* library.

There are no Doric columns or Roman friezes here. The British Library is designed to be low profile, to keep open views to the Gothic St Pancras, a building that was almost torn down until it was saved by the architectural campaigner Sir John Betjeman. It's friendly and almost cosy. And it's home at the last count to approximately 14 million books, 60 million patents, 8 million stamps, 6 million audio recordings and 4.5 million maps.

That makes over two hundred million titles and two billion web-page thingies kept on 388 miles of shelves spread over fourteen vast floors.

JOHN MAY: Incredible that you can remember all that and can't remember what you've done with your keys. The printed material couldn't all be stored on the Euston Road so some went to Boston Spa in West Yorkshire.

ARTHUR BRYANT: So you probably know there are sixty million newspapers, spanning three centuries, kept in low-oxygen storage chambers operated by robots. The British Library's basement goes 24.5 metres below ground, and the most valuable publications are stored in inert chambers of nitrogen, carbon dioxide and argon to protect them against fire.

The King's Library Tower houses all the books that were collected by King George III. These books are protected by a special layer of UV filter glass, in contrast to the disastrous Paris library that failed to account for its modernist glass towers ruining the books, and proved inaccessible and inhospitable. The French, you see. I'm just leaving that there.

The oldest items held in the British Library collection are ancient Chinese oracle bones that are over three thousand years old. The manuscript of *Alice's Adventures in Wonderland,* or to use its correct title *Alice's Adventures Under Ground,* is here, as are the nation's greatest political speeches and Oscar Wilde's handwritten plays. Sections of the building are dedicated to saving parchment maps and legal rolls before they disintegrate. Books and rolls are attacked by several different species of insects, mostly mites, and the race to preserve them never ends.

John, you always make fun of my overcoats. The reason why

they're so voluminous is so that I can stuff my pockets with paperbacks. In London you're never far from a bookshop. Wars, viruses and economic disasters can't keep them from springing up again, from the London Book Barge to weekly markets and monthly book fairs.

And the book-lovers come out in droves. They're a special breed: hunters, gatherers, collectors and cataloguers, moulting, dishevelled and a bit on the spectrum, lacking even rudimentary social skills—

JOHN MAY: Like someone else I know.

ARTHUR BRYANT:—but able to spot a paperback first edition by Ian Fleming from thirty yards. They are almost exclusively male and older but, boy, do they know a lot about pre-1900 commemorative hand-coloured German postcards. There are Eastern European professors, hunched elderly scholars and Indian academics—but rarely a woman in sight. They have more sense. One thing unites them all, though. A light comes into their eyes when they talk about books.

In leafy Bloomsbury, on the ground floor of the Royal National, London's least attractive postwar hotel, are a hundred dealers selling the kind of ephemera that have me reaching for my wallet. The rooms smell of damp paper, rotting bindings, mildew, unread words and overlooked lives. These are my people.

I know many of the dealers, of course, like 'Hammers' Bagneesh, the former boxing debt collector and antiquarian books expert. People like 'Hammers' spent a lifetime collecting a narrow spectrum of volumes on a subject they now realize nobody is interested in, and the asking prices are low, going ever lower.

One dealer checked the price of a book I was thinking about

buying and lowered it before I had even spoken to him. Several others said it was their last fair. 'It's a dying field,' one told me. 'Who's interested in this stuff now? We're retiring. It's not worth the effort.'

What exactly is not worth the effort? Three of the more recondite items I spotted going for a song were:

A Drawing of London's Devastation Made from a Zeppelin: a huge, elaborate foldout of how London looked after the Blitz, with every bombed-out street and building etched in great detail.

Christmas Card Samples of 1895: an immense leather volume filled with beautiful lace cards salesmen would carry about to sell into shops.

Toys & Toy Shops of Europe 1900–1950: a delightful full-colour compendium of toys, puzzles and games, and their emporia.

Obviously I had to buy them (in a manner of speaking—I borrowed the money from John). Many of the items on display at first appear desirable and attractive, until you spot that there's something about them that makes them unsaleable. For example, there's beautiful Victorian sheet music for songs you've never heard of. There are handwritten court rolls where it's impossible to figure out to what they're referring, and bundles of quill-penned letters from people writing in 1770 which are incredibly boring to read. Not everyone is Elizabeth Barrett Browning.

But there are bargains to be had in the city's continuous book sales: rare children's books featuring minor unloved characters and talking animals who never achieved popularity. Early Victorian postcards from seaside resorts featuring lurid, unappealing views. And I contemplated buying a book of cigarette filter-tip analysis cataloguing cigarettes with actual snouts installed in its fold-out pages, all neatly preserved in rows. The book is both pointless and funny-smelling.

I usually roam the rows, bumping into old friends I'm vaguely surprised to find still alive, and excitedly we show each other our wares. There's a famous photograph of Londoners browsing for books in the bombed ruins of a Charing Cross Road bookshop, unconcerned with the devastation all around them.

Chelsea Old Church in Cheyne Walk has something rare in the world of books today: a small chained reference library. It was once normal practice to attach books to chains that allowed them to be read but not taken away, and dates to a time when books were too valuable to be lost. The church itself was devastated in April 1941 by huge parachute bombs, but the little library survived.

When it comes to books about London, I feel a mix of wonder and sadness. Wonder because I always learn something I did not know. Sadness because so much has been wilfully cast aside through a combination of arrogance and greed. There's a recommended reading list at the end of this book, but steel yourself before tackling the selection. *Goodbye London* is a devastating snapshot of the year 1973, when developers put Covent Garden, the City, Soho, Camden, the docks and dozens of other areas under the wrecking ball.

London seems to get more independent bookshops with every passing year. There were nearly a thousand in the UK the last time I looked, many with extremely quirky stock that attract readers with specific interests, although I've yet to find my missing volume of *Greek Post Office Cancellation Numbers*, the annotated edition obviously.

I'm passing you over to my partner, who wants to talk to you about a picture house. I don't know if I'll use it yet. Let's see if it's any good first. John?

JOHN MAY: Arthur, a 'picture house' is the National Gallery. I'm talking about movies. For fifteen years, from 1978 to 1993, the most famous cinema in London was the notorious Scala. Its first incarnation was on Scala Street in the West End, where it showed films like *Eraserhead* that came to typify the uniqueness of the whole venture. The venue was unashamedly arthouse-meets-grindhouse: tasteless, perverse, haunting and tacky in equal measure.

When the Scala shifted to its new home in the unloveliest corner of King's Cross, just around the corner from us, the audience members had their loyalty tested. King's Cross was then a lawless border town, the workplace of an awful lot of hookers and muggers, a former royal spa that had become London's red-light rubbish dump.

Stranded behind by a confluence of railway lines, dead ends and derelict warehouses, it existed as a handful of run-down streets filled with alcoholic transients, and catered for every illegal taste. But it had its useful side; for years it was the only place in London where you could buy tomorrow's papers at midnight (they were being dropped off to the northbound trains). And as Margo pointed out, the penny arcade behind the Scala provided warmth and succour for a fleet of tracksuit-clad, acne-ridden rent boys and their Hogarthian clients. And around the back of the station the local ladies of the night, affectionately known as 'sploshers,' operated from a vacant lot nicknamed Pleasure Field.

A night out here was likely to end with someone being robbed or reduced to tears, in an area where chivalry meant holding your girlfriend's hair out of her eyes while she was sick in the gutter.

There were other repertory cinemas, like the Roxie in Wardour Street, which specialized in showing incredibly boring double bills that appealed to surfers, stoners and hippies. Films like *Crystal Voyager* and *The Valley (Obscured By Clouds)* never had plots or witty dialogue, and seemed to have been shot in slow motion. It was a rite of passage to smoke your first joint there during Frank Zappa's awful *200 Motels,* not knowing that you were meant to pass it on. All I remember about that film is that there was a dwarf dressed like Aladdin.

The Scala won Londoners' hearts. Behind the selection of films that appeared to have been chosen with a blindfold and a handful of darts, one could tell someone was trying to shine lights into the corners of the cinematic universe that most people wouldn't venture into without an attack dog and a face mask.

It was said that one of the worst things you could do in the eighties was take a date to the Scala, especially if it was a John Waters retrospective. It wasn't just the films that caused issues for prudish newbies; it was the audience. Just because you couldn't see someone doing it didn't mean they weren't. In a time when much of the sex going on in London could best be described as 'furtive,' the Scala was openly and appallingly hedonistic in a now-wipe-your-hands-on-the-curtains way.

ARTHUR BRYANT: Around the corner the locals were raising money for the striking miners at the Bell Tavern, along with film-maker Derek Jarman and his muse Tilda Swinton, so it made sense to dive into the cinema afterwards and sit through a banned East German flick or a blurry bit of experimentalism featuring someone dancing naked around their gran's kitchen.

It was possible to see classic monochrome films and world cinema being taken seriously at the National Film Theatre, but it wasn't as much fun.

The NFT is still on the South Bank, housed in a building designed to punish people for liking films. Its first meeting area looked like the bar of a German cultural collective and had an auditorium with no centre aisle, so that in order to take a bathroom break you had to squeeze past at least twenty tutting, huffing people in goatees and cardigans.

As my bladder has a tendency to go on without me I'd become paranoid about needing a wee halfway through a four-hour Hungarian meditation on goats and would barely be able to concentrate on the film. The audience generally consisted of autistic loners and art teachers on their afternoons off. John never came with me; he prefers the kind of film where young ladies fire machine guns from burning cars.

JOHN MAY: You know that's not true, Arthur. I like James Bond films as well, but not the later Roger Moores. And thanks for detailing your struggles with bladder control.

The Scala raised money for political causes and operated in the community at a grassroots level. It opposed censorship, helped to fund a broad spectrum of charities and brought together wildly different tribes through a common love of film. The Scala team recognized that a film could be appallingly made and still contain great truths.

It was an example of the kind of institution that has now all but vanished, a glue holding different sections of society together, like a perverse temperance hall. Although it inevitably followed a left-wing agenda, its only true rules were respect for others and acceptance of all. And that's a good thing.

16

A Sad Little Cross &
Other Stories

JOHN MAY: It should be apparent by now that my partner is
quite capable of losing days at a time in damp old libraries
and bookshops. He once went missing in the British Library for a
fortnight. We left trays of sardine and tomato sandwiches in the
Medieval Manuscripts section until we managed to lure him out.

I prefer to walk about and talk to people. It's important to get
a feel for your city by seeing it at different times. As an early riser,
I know that London has a surprising number of clear dawn skies
that vanish by 10:00 A.M. as aircraft contrails cross-hatch to form
cloud cover and the city starts exhaling. Of course Arthur gets up
at about 4:00 A.M. but misses everything because he doesn't get
around to looking out of the window.

ARTHUR BRYANT: I don't have time, John. I'm old and there's too
much left to do. What's your favourite view of London?

JOHN MAY: I suppose it's from the middle of Waterloo Bridge
looking east towards the City, with the London Eye behind. For

some reason the classic views of the Houses of Parliament, Big Ben and Chelsea Bridge don't speak as loudly to me. Luxury towers have been dumped beside the Thames without any thought, blocking age-old vistas. Who wants to look at those?

ARTHUR BRYANT: A few weeks ago I went for a walk through Nine Elms, that ugly no man's land connecting Vauxhall to Battersea. Do you remember, there used to be a vast cold storage facility and some factories down there? It was never fit for human habitation, although decades ago I do remember a lone waterside pub.

JOHN MAY: It's surprisingly near Westminster, though. And it's now the home of the US Embassy, in a bombproof building that looks like a 1970s Birmingham car park.

ARTHUR BRYANT: Poor doomed Battersea Power Station, unloved and forgotten, has fallen victim to rapacious planners. Walk along the river between Vauxhall and Battersea and you quickly sense that something is wrong: the new apartment buildings bulge outward, bottlenecking pedestrians and casting huge shadows. One gets an impression of walls and windows, a featureless concrete dead spot the size of Monaco.

According to the developers, such properties offer buyers the chance to 'live the complete Versace lifestyle, a fantasy turned into reality,' which presumably excludes the opportunity of being shot dead on your own doorstep. All this was touted by Boris Johnson as a brilliant vision of the future when he was London's mayor.

What throws the tragedy of Nine Elms into greater relief is the fact that on the opposite bank of the Thames stands Churchill Gardens. It's a gentle low-rise Pimlico council estate that looks more appealing than the cell blocks its absent millionaire neighbours have paid through the nose for. The postwar estate's aim was to show that the lower-incomed could be treated equally by being given access to river views. The new developments do exactly the opposite.

| | |

To see a sliver of the real old London you should take a train from Blackfriars, the city's glass-sided station, strapped across the Thames and anchored on either shore by a pair of matching ticket halls. I should hate this kind of modernism but instead I find it extraordinary. The sky blurs into the water; the dawn light is orange and pale blue. The Thames is devoid of river traffic at dawn, as becalmed as the rest of the city. There are few vehicles on the roads. The mighty London engine has yet to start turning over. The train pulls out and reveals the vista from Borough Market to London Bridge, silver-grey and brick-brown.

Here you're reminded of an unchanging London feature: meandering road patterns force the buildings into contortions that leave them facing each other at impossible angles. The foreground is grooved with the last Victorian alleyways. The slate-roofed houses have soot-stained brickwork, narrow sash windows and rows of tall red chimneypots. Behind them stand modern office buildings, their designs ordered like so many off-the-peg suits, available in two or three styles only, all of which must make their employees' hearts sink as they approach for another day in a swipe-card box.

Beyond this, lightly misted, stand the great steel-and-glass skyscrapers of New Wealth, confirming London's status as a financial services sector that manufactures nothing and seeks ownership in everything. The idea that these lanes were once crowded with watchmakers, butchers, fishmongers and tailors seems almost unimaginable. When I first visited the area it smelled of tallow, iron, smoke and spice. Now it has no smell at all. Who, I wonder, had more job satisfaction, the lanyard-wearing money-mover or the silversmith?

Even here, though, the buildings are squeezed into angular sites, and therefore bear less relation to one another than to the land itself, making them appropriate to the landscape.

At London Bridge the views are atmospheric, if not especially attractive. At one turn in the elevated track you find yourself in a Gustave Doré etching, layers of buildings tumbling away across switchback streets and cables, bridges, signage. Nine new embankment outcrops, the first public spaces to thrust out into the Thames, are being created by the need to place sewage pipes beneath them in London's new ring main, Bazalgette 2.0. The designs for the sites are all different, and could add nicely to London's piecemeal appearance. South London has always been more fragmented, and benefits from the odd scraps of space left behind.

Making sense of London's boroughs and working out how they all fit together can be a challenge. How far does London extend? Do we include Brent and Harrow? In that case, is Watling Street the farthest boundary? The first western outpost of the city starts as early as Tottenham Court Road; it gets a W1 postcode. London has slowly moved west over the centuries. The Tower of London and Buckingham Palace are at opposite ends of the city.

The western part of Central London gets overlooked by guides as there are fewer reasons to visit purely residential areas. In 1824 part of Bayswater, just along from Marble Arch tube station, was christened Tyburnia but the name refused to stick. It was a high-end development intended to be the centrepiece of Paddington, but the plans were never fully realized. To this day it's crisscrossed with beautiful little streets like Archery Close, but as you head towards Paddington Station it gets scruffier.

The roads and bridges that scar Paddington and Kilburn are bewildering.

There's more befuddlement at Paddington Station, which has two tube station entrances considerably distanced from each other, and although they look the same they go to different places. Both signposts read the same too, but if you look at the small print on them you'll see that they use the same lines going in different directions, marked 'Victoria' and 'King's Cross.' Wouldn't it have been easier to label them 'East' and 'West'?

Then there are all the odd spots you may vaguely know but couldn't point to on a map, like Lisson Grove, Royal Oak, Theydon Bois, De Beauvoir Town and Westbourne Park. Paddington Recreation Ground isn't in Paddington but in Maida Vale, and the whole area darts back and forth across its major barriers, the Westway flyover and the railway lines heading out of London to the southwest.

There's an easier east–west route through London: simply walk along the Regent's Canal, starting at Euston and passing through St John's Wood.

On a sunny Sunday the first obstacle is Camden Town, unbearably crowded and reeking of skunk. The redevelopment of the market has formalized its layout and removed its charm, but it remains popular with tourists even though all that's on sale now is the same mass-produced junk you see everywhere else. Happily you soon enter the graceful canal cut that passes through the London Zoo and Regent's Park, beneath Lord Snowden's aviary and the backs of the grand grace-and-favour houses of the park.

After this you hit the obstacle of closed pathways. Canal towpaths are not public rights of way, but are known as 'permissive paths.' The tenants of houseboats have made it as tricky as possible to walk beside the canal by co-opting the towpath as gardens. Some are completely sealed off, which means you have to go up and round. The largest closed section is at Little Venice, a picturesque spot where the canal splits around an island.

In June London is absurdly fecund. In the wealthy, quiet neighbourhoods of St John's Wood and Maida Vale the mature trees almost obscure the houses. Maida Vale appears to be full of Mediterranean villas, and even a row of shops with stepped frontages look as though they belong in Dorset or Devon rather than London. They're no longer shops, of course. This is prime real estate now.

Typically, the Prince Alfred pub is one of two with the same name in the same area. One is a listed building with partitions designed to keep the classes separate. The saloon, public, snug and private bars are divided by wood panels topped with 'snob screens.' These frosted-glass panels turned on a central spindle and allowed one to spy on the lower orders. Complicating matters is the fact that you can move from one bar to the next only by opening an extremely small door in the partition and climbing through. The Alfred has all of these intact.

Chelsea, Hampstead, Belgravia and Mayfair were affluent residential neighbourhoods housing diplomats, civil servants and bankers, plus a few wealthy artists and writers. Now they're too expensive to house Londoners at all. The West London area is also affluent but more mixed, so for grubby Kilburn there's fancy St John's Wood (the home of Sephardic Jews for two centuries) and for eclectic Paddington there's elegant Maida Vale, named—*obviously*—after a public house, the Hero of Maida inn, which used to be on Edgware Road near the canal.

Paddington Basin was elaborately regenerated, but the developers failed to turn it into— John, what do they call those places?

JOHN MAY: Destination sites.

ARTHUR BRYANT: John is my expert in corporate gibberish. The King's Cross development mixed old and new buildings, adding art colleges, recreation areas and family areas, but Paddington displaced the working-class residents and ushered in corporations.

The wards to the west remain less explored by visitors, and although there are pubs and cafés lining the waterways they attract a mainly local crowd. It's an amorphous, puzzling chunk of the city that's still worth taking more time to explore.

For me, the most interesting part of West London is Southall, home to London's largest Sikh community. Its residents arrived from the Punjab in the early 1950s. It had suffered wartime bombings and went on to survive race riots, but it thrived; 94 percent of its population is ethnic minorities. I sometimes detect a faint Welsh lilt in the voices of older Indian residents; the area was once popular with migrants from Wales who settled here. Visually it's a chaotic mess of bay-fronted houses and plastic-sign-covered shop fronts, but it certainly has life.

| | |

If London's modern buildings are hard to get excited about, you can always walk around the Victorian streets and find something you've never noticed before. The metropolis is littered with overlooked meeting halls, debating chambers and lecture theatres. The clubs and cafés where talks take place are often tucked under arches or in tunnels, but there are other spaces that have been repurposed for the changing times.

One is the Horse Hospital in Herbrand Street, Bloomsbury, an avant-garde arts space for hire. It's the kind of London building that feels out of time, and you fully expect to pass it one day and find it has disappeared. The writer Alan Moore said, 'There's not another venue like it on the planet.'

It was built by James Burton, a property developer who constructed swathes of Bloomsbury. By the end of the eighteenth century London was overcrowded with horse-drawn carriages, and when the horses that drew the hansoms fell sick they were brought here. The unusual thing is that the building looks like a normal house, not a stable at all. Stone ramps with cross-slats helped the horses to climb upstairs without slipping. Many of the building's original features are still in place—to enter it you climb the horse ramp and you come out into an adaptable space where members of the maniac community can shout poetry at you. Just opposite there's an old pub, the Friend at Hand, for those arguments about the arts that always seem to spill out after interesting events.

There are a number of corners behind Russell Square that make you feel as if you've slipped back into the past. Gower Street is the kind of poker-straight thoroughfare most people don't notice and has unbroken terraces that encourage film-makers to shoot episodes of *Sherlock* here. It doesn't take much effort to dress the sets.

Head southeast towards the Thames and you come to the Bourne Estate, not the name of a film starring Matt Damon but an Edwardian housing development in the middle of Holborn that few office workers get to see. Constructed from 1905 to 1909, it's regarded as one of London's best examples of tenement housing. Most of the blocks are listed. The design has international significance and became the model for all those elegant Viennese homes built after the First World War. The estate's arches are covered in tilework and the whole neighbourhood seems to have survived undamaged by bombs, a rarity in Central

London. It also throws up some unexpected views around corners.

It's worth recalling that the great aristocratic estates of Grosvenor, Cadogan, de Walden, Portman and Bedford, together with the Crown Estate and the City of London, have survived three hundred years and still control the lion's share of Central London. It's why the parks never lost their railings during the war; the estates simply wouldn't surrender them.

| | |

Let's keep 'walking.' Work with me here.

Over in Leather Lane they're just setting up market stalls and getting ready for the day's first customers. In Hatton Garden, the jewellery shops are not yet open. No two buildings appear the same. The mismatch is like a tea service that has had all its cups replaced over time. We're now close to 'Pudding and Pie,' the start and end points of the Great Fire of London. The Monument stood opposite the bakery.

On 2 September 1666, Thomas Farriner, the baker to King Charles II, forgot to damp down his oven. Its embers ignited some firewood and by 1:00 A.M., three hours after he went to bed, the house in Pudding Lane was up in flames. Farriner, his wife and daughter escaped from an upstairs window, but the maid became the Great Fire's first victim. Farriner signed a bill falsely accusing a simple-minded French watchmaker of starting the fire. The fact that the watchmaker had not even been in London at the time of the conflagration's outbreak cut no ice. Although no one believed he was guilty, a scapegoat was needed and he was hanged at Tyburn.

Say good morning also to the Golden Boy of Pye Corner, where Giltspur Street meets Cock Lane. The gold cherub on the wall was erected to warn against the sin of gluttony that caused our fair city to burn down. It's not the only marker for the fire's end; there's another one, a column outside Temple Church indicating where it stopped.

Although we think of the fire wiping out the city's medieval street plan it's not true; some imaginative redesigns were proposed, but London was largely reconstructed according to its old layout, which is why there are still so many narrow lanes in the Square Mile.

JOHN MAY: I always thought that Brydges Place, just off St Martin's Lane, was the narrowest street in London, as my shoulders touch both walls as I walk through it, but in Emerald Court, near the back of Red Lion Square, I failed the shoulders test and had to turn sideways to pass.

ARTHUR BRYANT: It may just be that your coat is too wide. It's certainly too loud.

I thought I must have walked through every alleyway in the city by now, usually in the pursuit of miscreants, but they still have the power to surprise. Take the one at the back of St Sepulchre-without-Newgate, i.e., outside of Newgate, where little cottages appear to have been transported from the heart of the countryside.

There are two touching items inside the church itself; the first is the executioner's bell from Newgate Prison, which was rung outside a condemned prisoner's cell at midnight before their death, just in case they were starting to come to terms with impending oblivion. And most tragic of all, a poor old cross representing the deaths of one hundred soldiers at the Battle of Loos, cobbled together by survivors. For three years it marked the spot in France where they fell and has more dignity and grace than any gold-leafed crucifix paid for by fans of the Vatican.

17

The Curse of St James's & Other Stories

ARTHUR BRYANT: I don't care, I don't like the neighbourhood, no matter how pretty it looks or how near Buckingham Palace it is.

JOHN MAY: You have to admit it's very tidy.

ARTHUR BRYANT: That's not a good thing! Belgravia may appear very desirable on film—I showed *The Fallen Idol* at the PCU film club, remember? And it's *Upstairs, Downstairs* country, full of elegant mansions and pretty little mews, but it's long been the home of dodgy Russians and bacon-faced high Tories. One half expects to see Jacob Rees-Mogg at an upstairs window sneering down at the proles. Near Hyde Park and Buckingham Palace Garden, the upscale streets are defined by posh townhouses, foreign embassies and fancy hotels.

You can usually judge the wealth of an area by looking at the width of its streets, and Belgravia's are very wide indeed. But it was once an extremely dubious area. Known as Five Fields—it was intersected by five footpaths—you crossed it at your peril, as highwaymen and footpads operated there. The same as now, I suppose, although today they're in the financial sector.

The ward of Belgravia houses a Thames tributary, the Westbourne, which was bisected by Bloody Bridge, so called because it was frequented by robbers and unsafe to cross at night. In 1728, a man's body was discovered by the bridge with half his face and five fingers removed. In 1749, even a poor muffin man could be robbed and left blind. Five Fields's distance from London also made it a popular spot for duels. Now, there's a sport they should bring back.

Belgravia takes its name from a village in Cheshire on the Eaton estate of the Grosvenor family, who own 50 percent of Mayfair and three hundred acres of Belgravia. It has some fantastic squares and gardens, including Belgrave Square, Eaton Square, Chester Square and Lowndes Square. The area featured heavily in the novels of Anthony Trollope and had a bohemian atmosphere, in this instance meaning 'a smell of inherited tax-free wealth,' and nice porticos so that it could appear in any number of period TV shows.

It's one of the most expensive places to live in the world— Russian oligarchs knocked through many of the houses to build mega-mansions, but now their assets are being seized. Our government is suddenly horrified by the exploitation of London as a haven for dirty money. And if you believe that, I have a bridge I'd like to sell you.

JOHN MAY: The Duke of Westminster was only twenty-five years old when he inherited the Grosvenor fortune in 2016.

ARTHUR BRYANT: That makes him the world's most eligible kidnap victim. I read that he threw himself a very expensive twenty-first birthday party and hired Michael McIntyre as the entertainment. So much for the spirit of youthful rebellion.

Belgravia feels like a film set. It's pompous and boring, but being able to afford to live there is a sign that you are now part of the British establishment. The National Crime Agency is investigating a list of wealthy Belgravia residents to see if they've used the UK to launder their doughnuts. The problem is that anyone can lie about their source of wealth and produce a document showing that their fortune is based on, say, playing the stock market.

So, is there any reason to visit this peculiar, soulless part of super-rich London? No, not really, unless you're an architectural student or, like my partner here, excited by really clean streets. Nothing to see; do as the security guard says and move along.

Pretty from a distance, though.

The same curse afflicts St James's. It is part of Westminster, and not an area I'd naturally stroll through unless I was carrying a brick, but it's used in a lot of films. An odd spot, formerly residential and built for the aristocracy, now entirely corporate and the home of establishment clubs and embassies.

St James's Palace is the most senior royal palace in the land, constructed on the site of a leper hospital in the 1530s. The St James's Fair was held there annually, peaking in the 1760s with boxing matches, hasty-pudding eaters, eel divers, bull-baiting and merry-go-rounds. Its most famous character was Tiddy Doll the French gingerbread man, immortalized in the names of various hostelries until very recently. He wore a white and gold suit and a huge ostrich feather, and his name came from the refrain of his song, 'Tiddy Diddy Doll, Lol, Lol, Lol!' He turns up in Hogarth's astonishing painting of Southwark Fair.*

---

* The painting now resides in the Cincinnati Art Museum. God knows what they make of it.

Lower Regent Street is officially known as 'Regent Street St James's,' and despite the Westminster ward being home to swish Jermyn Street, Pall Mall 'Clubland' and the Haymarket, it's pretty boring—except for Crown Passage, a narrow street which splits off from Pall Mall opposite Marlborough House and is home to the venerable Red Lion, one of the oldest boozers in the West End still in operation.

Like all proper mad old pubs it has a mad old pub tradition: on the last Saturday in January, Cavaliers in full costume crowd into the Red Lion to lament the death of their hero Charles I, who was executed in Whitehall on 30 January 1649.

JOHN MAY: I like the sumptuously rococo Piccadilly Arcade, although it has shops you'd never buy anything from, like the one that sells rare military medals. And I like the statue of Beau Brummell in Jermyn Street.

ARTHUR BRYANT: Of course you do. You've always been a bit of a clothes horse when it comes to fashion, haven't you?

JOHN MAY: I was briefly based in St James's Square, near where policewoman Yvonne Fletcher was shot dead by an unknown gunman in the Libyan Embassy. There's a plaque there dedicated to her memory. I remember a very old-fashioned bank opposite, all marble pillars, alabaster tiles and mahogany counters. Gone now, of course.

ARTHUR BRYANT: And the London Library, founded by Thomas Carlyle, one of the city's most exclusive and expensive private libraries.

T. S. Eliot, a long-serving president of the library, argued in 1952 in an address to members that 'whatever social changes come about, the disappearance of the London Library would be a disaster to civilization.' But you need dosh to become a monthly member. I discovered that the membership rate drops according to your age. Entering my date of birth online, I found that I could get in for almost nothing, which was depressing. If I survive much longer they'll have to pay me to join.

The streets of St James's are home to ancient bootmakers and hatmakers and wine cellars and—well, let's just say you can't get a bag of chips there. With so many moneyed clubmen coming up from the country to lounge about, an army of servants and drivers was required to wait upon them, so where did they live?

The answer is through a little archway that leads from St James's Street into Blue Ball Yard. Here, in a row of prettified little country cottages from the 1740s, lived the area's coachmen.

Another place in St James's interested me. Watching *Howards End* at a PCU film night I became fascinated with the flat that Mr Wilcox takes. I managed to track the building down; it's at 51 St James's Court, off Buckingham Gate, although the Schlegels' flat wasn't opposite. The area is not considered a separate ward of the borough anymore but it feels quite different.

If you had to choose the extreme opposite to Belgravia, what would it be?

JOHN MAY: The Barbican. Modern, egalitarian, history-free.

ARTHUR BRYANT: Do you know how it came to be there?

JOHN MAY: I have a feeling you're going to tell me.

ARTHUR BRYANT: On 29 and 30 December 1940 London was hit by an epic firestorm. The ward of Cripplegate particularly suffered from bomb devastation. (The Anglo-Saxon word 'crepel' meant a covered passage leading to a watchtower.) In its place rose a series of gigantic brutalist concrete boxes, home to two thousand residents.

I'm going to lay my cards on the table here, John. In my opinion the Barbican is not a masterpiece of postwar brutalist architecture. It is a collection of misshapen pebble-dashed water-stained concrete lumps arranged in a labyrinth of blocks and towers so confounding that for years you had to follow coloured lines set in the ground to find your way through it.

In the centre an ugly stagnant-looking pond is abutted by windswept plains of blank stone. Worst of all, along one side is a row of shadowy concrete shops with mock-Tudor referencing.

JOHN MAY: The residents of the Barbican will all tell you they love it.

ARTHUR BRYANT: Perhaps they've been implanted with electrodes that jolt them if they say anything bad, I don't know.

JOHN MAY: Even you must like the High Walk.

ARTHUR BRYANT: Enlighten me?

JOHN MAY: Starting at the Barbican and heading in the direction of Moorgate, there's a sky pavement called the High Walk that takes you above the traffic of the dual carriageway through a maze of supported pedestrian avenues.

The route had been planned immediately after the Second World War but was never completed. Instead of running for thirty miles only a tiny section was built. The problem was that the 'pedway' had never been conceived as a system; there was no drawing of the network as a whole. It had to be constructed from the separate planning consents for individual office blocks.

The serpentine paths take in bird's-eye views of the city's Roman walls and garden spaces. They're a pleasant respite from the polluted canyon below. But it doesn't really lead anywhere and hardly anyone knows the High Walk is there. Pedestrians carry mental maps based on streets, but the minute you displace that map by raising people onto walkways they get lost.

ARTHUR BRYANT: Did you know that until the Second World War there were still wooden streets all over London? I was surprised to learn that the wood blocks were hard-wearing but stank, so up they came and were burned for fuel.

There were different kinds of wood used according to usage and, inevitably, class. The smarter neighbourhoods got creosoted blocks of jarrah, an Australian hardwood that was pricey but resilient. The poorer neighbourhoods had to make do with yellow deal from Sweden, a soft wood that absorbed horse piss and sprayed it back out whenever a carriage went over them. The roads had been built for horses, not the weight of vehicles. Thank you, Sweden. There are a few small wooden sections still around if you look carefully, like the little patch near Bunhill Row off Old Street. It no longer smells of horse piss, though. I checked.

JOHN MAY: That must have given passers-by a laugh.

18

A Pair of Zebras &
Other Stories

ARTHUR BRYANT: If there's a consistent theme in these conversations, it's that London will leave you puzzled. It does me.

JOHN MAY: I didn't say anything.

ARTHUR BRYANT: Nothing is ever as it should be. Your favourite monument probably wasn't built when it says it was, and used to be somewhere else. If it's a house it's probably been pulled apart, given a false façade and rebuilt.

Eros isn't Eros, of course. Anteros is standing atop the Shaftesbury Memorial Fountain with bow stretched, about to bury his shaft in Shaftesbury Avenue. Alfred Gilbert's model was a fifteen-year-old lad from Hammersmith, Angelo Colarossi, whose father was a model for Sir Frederic Leighton and John Singer Sargent. Anteros was put away for the Second World War and returned intact, but it's made of aluminium, and in 2012 a Spanish football fan climbed his bow and broke it. I hope the repair cost was charged back to him.

Other things that aren't right about London? Turning right, for a start.

To turn right you may first need to turn left (on roundabouts), to go north you must sometimes head east (on the Underground), to travel between stations it might be quicker to walk (Leicester Square to Covent Garden) and to cross a road you must wait for the green man except when his appearance has nothing to do with the passage of pedestrians or traffic, which is most of the time. And why so many people get hit by buses.

The problem begins, as all things do, with the Thames, which meanders so much that in places the north side is further south than the south side.

The West End is in the city centre, but West London is going towards the airport. Hoxton and Shoreditch in the East End aren't in East London. And wherever you stand within sight of the London Eye, it's the wrong way around. This is because if you face the river on its north side looking south, you may actually be facing east or west. If you go 'up West' from North London you're actually going down. You go *up* Tottenham Court Road and *down* Regent Street, but there are other roads you only walk *along*, like Oxford Street and Euston Road. Why? Because we instinctively describe streets as they conform to the compass.

Then there are the hospitals, which aren't where they're supposed to be. Hammersmith's is in White City, Charing Cross's is in Hammersmith and the Chelsea & Westminster is not in Westminster—you get the idea.

Bond Street, London's most high-end shopping street, doesn't exist either; it's two streets, Old Bond Street and New Bond Street, joined together in the centre. The street's last resident, Oli Claridge, has an inherited lease on a flat once occupied by Guy Burgess of the infamous Cambridge Spy Ring. He says it's pretty lonely living there. Petty France (a corruption of *petit*) is not in

France but Westminster, while Petty Wales is in Billingsgate. Lower Thames Street and Upper Thames Street are both in the same place. For years Waterloo Station had several platforms with the same number.

JOHN MAY: What about London Underground? Is that any better?

ARTHUR BRYANT: Say you want to go from King's Cross to Embankment, which is due south. You need to change at Euston, which is actually west, but to do that you need to first take the Northern line up, which is north.

But for real mystification try Baker Street Underground; to exit the station you have to go downwards to another platform going in a different direction, then back through rising tunnels and Escher-like staircases, all of which are badly signposted, so you always end up in the wrong place. The station is full of confused tourists retracing their steps.

JOHN MAY: The tourists are presumably Sherlock Holmes fans, so at least they have a mystery to solve.

ARTHUR BRYANT: Until recently you could drive right onto the platform at Paddington Station, but now there's no parking anywhere and they've separated the rail and tube lines. Or try getting out of Waterloo Station at the right exit, or escaping from Liverpool Street, which is signposted by unfamiliar street names instead of compass points. You might as well roll a die. We once did a team-building exercise in an escape room and it was easier to get out of than Liverpool Street Station.

Tube stations have no common distance setting them apart. It's hard to untangle the lines beneath them, which is why an electrical draughtsman's radical map designed in 1933 came as such a breath of fresh air, if you can use the term in relation to the tube.

Harry Beck deliberately sacrificed accuracy for clarity in an iconic London Transport design that resembled an electrical circuit. Westminster appears to be ten minutes from the next station, especially if you believe Winston Churchill's ridiculous tube trip in that film *Darkest Hour*. You'd think the war orders to turn street signs around and confuse invading Nazis were still in place.

During the war, anti-blast walls were placed over tube station entrances, floodgates were erected in tunnels and trains had nets fixed over their windows to reduce injury from flying glass. How did passengers know where to get off? The nets had little holes cut in them so people could still read the station names.

The service ran normally despite the fact that many of the stations were modified to provide shelter. They had libraries and bunk beds, medical posts, play centres and even classrooms. And racketeers: ticket touts illegally sold sleeping spaces on the platforms. The unscrupulous are always ready to profit from war. When the fighting ended, the tube's defences were dismantled at an astonishing speed and life returned to normal very quickly. The government proved to be better at running the city's travel systems than private enterprise.

At least private companies don't compete to open stations anymore. In times past, chaos reigned, nowhere more so than at Blackfriars Station.

JOHN MAY: Your favourite station, apparently.

ARTHUR BRYANT: Yes, but it's still tricky. Blackfriars is the only station that's on both sides of the river, and it's also a main line so you could end up at the coast if you're not careful. Its trains are only half the length of the platform so you can miss it even when you're on time. You'll be standing at the wrong end and no one will bother to tell you. But it was once much worse.

The London, Chatham and Dover Railway opened Blackfriars Bridge Station in 1864 but were beaten by the South Eastern Railway, who opened another Blackfriars Station a little further away, only to close it five years later. So a new Blackfriars Station was opened in 1870 and a second bridge was opened next to the old one for the overspill, which required another tube station beside it called St Paul's. Now Blackfriars Bridge was not needed and fell to bits, leaving behind the conduit's huge red pillars and the other bridge, and St Paul's Station was renamed Blackfriars because by now there was another St Paul's Station. Got all that, John?

JOHN MAY: I think I just lost the will to live.

The most common mistakes made by tourists are not standing on the right on escalators, thinking Tower Bridge is London Bridge and muddling the Museum of London with the British Museum. And there's a lot of perplexity about where and when you can drink. It seems to many European visitors that laws are casually broken and the police don't seem to mind that much.

ARTHUR BRYANT: We do but we have more important things to be getting on with than by-law infringements.

What else do you have on that list about what visitors say? The Indian restaurant food is too spicy. It's the oldest in the world outside India, so let's assume the restaurateurs know what they're doing.

The hotels have hot and cold taps instead of mixers. Fair point.

Belisha beacons are really cute. Calling a road a circus is very unhelpful. Pubs don't make good martinis. Oh, and there should be a word for feeling that it's about to rain.

JOHN MAY: I see visitors making fundamental mistakes. They get taxis everywhere when it's faster to walk or go by tube. They eat at the restaurants we go out of our way to avoid, and they miss some of the best sights by sticking to the centre.

ARTHUR BRYANT: We also confuse visitors just by being ourselves. We place tags on our sentences like 'isn't it?' and 'didn't we?' and we ask friends if they're all right all the time. We say sorry and thank you too often. We're distant to strangers until they prove themselves proactively friendly, we laugh a lot and have an unnecessarily elaborate way of speaking. And we fail to warn them that no self-respecting Londoner has ever eaten anywhere around Leicester Square. Where was I?

JOHN MAY: Bewilderment. A subject you know a lot about.

ARTHUR BRYANT: Ah yes, did I mention the culs-de-sac, canals and railway lines that isolate whole neighbourhoods and bewilder even more? Try crossing Primrose Hill, Broadway Market, Muswell Hill, Alexandra Palace, Tufnell Park or Crouch End without hitting endless dead ends. It's like a game of Pac-Man.

How about Green Lanes, which isn't named after a green lane and is only spoken of in the plural even though it's just one very long road, or Westminster Abbey and Westminster Cathedral, which are not the same thing and not even near each other, or the streets that continue across their ends and the house numbers that alternate except when new buildings have added 'A's and 'B's?

Then there's the matter of what counts as being in London. The borders constantly change. For most of my life Croydon was in the countryside halfway to Brighton, not in town. Where do the suburbs begin now? They fluctuate across the decades. One could argue that Richmond, gateway to the Thames Valley, is just another London suburb these days. When writers use London locations they're apt to set their scenes in the most famously picturesque corners of the city, yet most of the writers who famously wrote about London lived out in the suburbs.

I once took a meeting with a group of Americans working for the FBI who arrived over an hour late because they had gone to two other streets with the same name. And this is since we've had the Googly map thing. London roads still follow the lines of their original hedgerows and streams, and all efforts to change that system have ended in failure. So I suggest to visitors that they—I mean this in the nicest possible way—get lost.

There are quite a few bits of London which are in the wrong place. Obviously we do it to annoy visitors, especially the French. One bit that I'm glad is back is Temple Bar. It was the original ceremonial gateway to the City of London, used for grand parades into the city. When London was a walled city, there were eight gates:

Aldgate, leading to Colchester and Essex

Bishopsgate, leading to Shoreditch and Cambridge

Moorgate, a Roman postern turned into a gate in 1415, leading to the Moorfields, or marshes

Cripplegate, leading to the village of Islington

Aldersgate, leading to St Barts, Smithfield Market and Charterhouse

Newgate, leading towards Oxford and the west

Ludgate, leading to Bath and the southwest

But the elaborate Temple Bar is the only one left, although it's not one of the original gates. Built by Sir Christopher Wren, it was once at the junction where Fleet Street meets the Strand. The 'bar' part first gets a mention in 1293, at which time it was probably no more than a chain slung between a couple of wooden posts. The name was transferred to the gate, named after the Temple Church.

Temple Bar once displayed the heads of traitors on spikes. Perhaps we could revive that tradition, starting with everyone who annoys me.

'Temple' is the name given to the area off Fleet Street that once belonged to the Knights Templar. Dickens recalls Temple as teeming with people because barristers used to live where they worked, in the Temple inns of court. In *Bleak House,* Chuck described Temple Bar as 'that leaden-headed old obstruction, appropriate ornament for the threshold of a leaden-headed old corporation.' There are lots of stories about people being denied entry to London, although it was noted that the gate didn't keep anyone out, as you could nip into the city from the barber shop next door.

But the gate itself is now in the wrong place. It had stood outside the London boundary (as was) for two centuries before the old road was widened. The original spot has a monument marked with one of the City's heraldic gryphons. For once, though, instead of the gate simply being bashed to bits and chucked away, it was carefully taken apart, the 2,700 pieces numbered, and stored.

And there it stayed in boxes for a decade. In 1880 Lady Meux, a former banjo-playing barmaid who married a brewery owner, tried making a name for herself in society by purchasing the gate from the city and reassembling it at their estate in Theobald's Park, Hertfordshire. She made another attempt to break through the class barrier by having her portrait painted by James McNeill Whistler but then let the side down by galloping about London in a phaeton* pulled by a pair of zebras.

Anyway, the Temple Bar Trust was established to bring back

* A kind of high open-air carriage.

the gate and it was officially returned to the revamped Paternoster Square in 2004. The Bar now welcomes you into a bleak, bare space that once housed the Square Mile's bookshops but can now only offer you a soy decaf latte.

Never mind, have one of their ghastly beverages and look at the Temple Bar from where you sit—a real piece of character in the Square Mile. Also adding atmosphere throughout the area are the narrow passages and hidden gardens that have survived fire, plague and development. There are an astonishing number of these, and in recent years they've been made more accessible as buildings have been restored and their internal spaces opened.

Near our Unit HQ in King's Cross there are courtyards and alleys that were closed off to the public for the best part of a century. Some contain new artworks and conceal odd little drinking establishments. I have outstanding bills in quite a few of them.

The average lifespan of an office is much shorter than that of a residential building. London's suburbs are still largely mid to late Victorian and Edwardian. Streets in specific areas are named after Crimean War battles (Inkerman, Alma), singers (Vera Lynn Close, Newham), activists (Steve Biko Way) and a Hungarian national hero (Kossuth Street), as well as the usual archbishops and earls.

Just up from us at the PCU is a street where the houses have Egyptian motifs, including stone obelisks. They became popular after Nelson won the Battle of the Nile against Napoleon. Soon everyone was whacking up miles of Egyptian wallpaper in celebration.

JOHN MAY: Funny how nobody did that after the Falklands.

19

A Drug Lord's Hippo &
Other Stories

ARTHUR BRYANT: For a city that's psychologically dominated by a very big grandfather clock* it's appropriate that clocks and time feature so heavily in London's past and present. After all, it was the home of time itself, with the Greenwich Observatory setting Greenwich Mean Time. But there are many other London clocks of note.

Big Ben is not the largest clock in London. That place belongs to number 80 Strand. Shell-Mex House faced a height-restriction problem when it was built in 1930, but the restriction only applied to inhabited parts of a building, so a clock tower was exempt. It has two faces, best seen from Hungerford Bridge walkway.

From the window of my office at the PCU I have two grand clocks within sight. The first is the green and white Caledonian Park Clock Tower. The park in which it stands once housed Lon-

---

* It's typical that London's most iconic tower has three names, so nobody knows what to call it: St Stephen's Tower, the Elizabeth Tower and Big Ben, the nickname for the bell, which is actually called the Great Bell.

don's largest cattle market, and the tower was supposedly built to withstand the force of a bull charge. The second is the great clock-spire of St Pancras, which looks like a Disney fairy-tale castle in silhouette.

I've always liked the art deco clock on Cambridge Circus, with four women balancing a clock like a bronze beach ball, and the grand Queen of Time double-faced clock that stands above the entrance to Selfridges, the department store that invented the concept of counting down the days to Christmas.

Fleet Street and Holborn have an array of clocks, some of them hidden. St Dunstan-in-the-West boasts a clock that was installed five years after the Great Fire and which features London's great guardians Gog and Magog hitting the central bell with hammers.

When the clock on Liberty department store chimes the hour, St George rides forth and slays the dragon. Bloomsbury's Pied Bull Yard has a mounted wall clock with two strikers, a police officer, a businessman, a bull, a mohawk-toting chap and a female jogger all chasing each other when it sounds.

The church of St George the Martyr in Southwark has a celebrated three-sided clock, with the fourth face blacked out. Legend has it that the residents of Bermondsey were not prepared to contribute to the church, so the church denied them time. Eventually they capitulated and put the clock face in, but blacked it out as a reminder that it wasn't paid for. There could be a simpler explanation. You can't see the fourth side easily, so what was the point of putting a clock face there? Part of St George's churchyard is formed by the wall of the old Marshalsea Prison, where Dickens's dad was imprisoned for debt.

Two of the most unusual modern clocks I could find were the aquatic clock in Covent Garden that used to empty water onto passers-by (it's still there but the company in the building doesn't keep it working) and the bird clock of the London Zoo which squawks and swings and automates toucans, much as the Heath Robinson–like Guinness clocks of old did.

The astronomical clock at Bracken House on Cannon Street opposite St Paul's has Winston Churchill's face at its centre because Brendan Bracken was a key ally of Churchill during the Second World War. It measures time by the heavens and is set in pink to reflect the colour of the newspaper it housed, the *Financial Times*.

The clocks are examples of the city's innate eccentricity, and quirky London clings on by its fingertips, surviving in just a few unlikely spots. Here are three such places . . .

First up there's the Model Railway Club of King's Cross, a workshop and track-building club. It's the oldest such club in the world and filled with ex-railway folk working on projects that take decades to finish. There was one woman present when I last visited, model railways apparently not appealing much to sensible females. A charming chap in a railway-club tie tried to explain about double-O gauges but soon realized that I had fallen into a coma. The club's grandest project is a vast working railway model of the area, just as it looked around sixty years ago. They'll be more than happy to see you, but if you can't make it their impressive videos are on the YouTube-thingy.

You might also try a night with the Sohemians, the Soho Bohemians who meet upstairs at the mock-Tudor Wheatsheaf pub in Rathbone Place, a rare gem of a building that only dates back to the 1930s. The Sohemians are interested in all things weird and esoteric. It's like a more shocking version of a Victorian slideshow society. Grumpy old George Orwell and the brilliant but sadly overlooked writer Julian Maclaren-Ross both drank there.

And at Viktor Wynd's Last Tuesday Society in Mare Street in Hackney, the collector houses his creepy, eclectic Museum of Curiosities and a cocktail bar. It's a part of London tourists don't often get to. The museum's exhibits include items from Cornwall's Museum of Witchcraft. Down a winding staircase, taxidermy, ephemera, skeletons, eggs of extinct birds, paintings, toys, antique dentistry, masks, historical pornography and ludicrous paperbacks fill the displays. Oh, and it also houses Pablo Escobar's gold-leafed hippopotamus head. Dominating one corner is the sequinned suit of the dandy dilettante Sebastian Horsley, always spotted in his stovepipe hat drifting about Soho until he overdosed with excitement and passed away. Wynd has a love of *Gesamtkunstwerk,* the juxtaposition of many strange objects to create a total work of art. But he also cheerfully admits that he has never wanted to have an original idea in his life, so he collects instead.

The place is a cabinet of curiosities, but its real subject is the collector himself.

Speaking of peculiar old things locked away in basements, here's Maggie Armitage, a friend of the PCU, the kind of friend who follows you around in the street shouting at you. Let her explain what she's on about.

MAGGIE ARMITAGE: As a Grand Order Grade IV White Witch of the Coven of St James the Elder, Kentish Town branch, I know how important London is to the world of magic. I've practised it so often at my home near the Arsenal that I've been requested to stop on match days for fear of adversely affecting the team's performance. I think the manager is clutching at straws there.

The main problem is that tangible evidence about magic is elusive and often unconvincing—but there's no denying that its practitioners were largely associated with London, from Merlin to Dr Dee.

One of the reasons for the annoyingly grey area around magical history is that the story of London has a great black hole in it. The so-called Dark Ages lasted from 476 to 800 CE, during which time there was no Holy Roman Emperor in the West. Most of the city was in ruins, although there was at least one grand Roman villa complete with an underground heating system and private baths still lived in, well into the late 400s. It's possible that London went under another name, 'Caer-Lundein,' and moved around the St Albans area. However, the idea that Britons became atavistic and spent four centuries grubbing about in the rubble is riddled with exceptions. For a start, most scholars believed the Earth was a globe, not flat, which puts them ahead of quite a few modern day sponge-brains.

Into this three-century vacuum fell all sorts of mythologies, including the legend of King Arthur, which was eventually repurposed by Victorians seeking to reboot London with a cod-medieval past it may not have possessed, certainly not in the romantic way they imagined. There was an obsession with neo-Tudorism which only died out after repeated fires in the wood-built buildings, and the mysticism of early times was ramped up with depictions of royal magicians, misted ruins and wafting nymphs.

London has been particularly susceptible to magical lore. Certainly when I was a little girl, our family still clung to all kinds of superstitions.

Like many others my mother believed that ginger cats were lucky. She was forever trying to stroke one and finally needed tetanus shots.

Being from a Thameside family, my father would not allow shoes on the bed because it meant death for a household member within a year. The superstition was connected with setting out clothes for the deceased.

Budgerigars were not allowed into the house for the same reason. I have my own theory about this. If you were called up as a sailor during the war, it was common to buy your wife a caged bird to keep her company. Mynah birds were popular; they talked incessantly, so that it sounded as if a man was in the house. There were stories of malevolent birds mimicking the voice of a wife's lover and repeating it back to the returning husband.

London's docks were heavily associated with the power of magic. There were sailors who cast pennies into the sea to buy wind on becalmed days, a practice that was also carried out on England's notoriously fickle-weathered east coast. A couple of years ago I heard about a Romanian woman who threw a handful of coins 'for a fair wind' into the turbine of the plane she was boarding and wrecked the engine.

The dockside areas of London were poor; rented rooms were damp, filthy and without sanitation. Day and night shifts took the same beds, spreading infestations. Water and fog brought illness, and early deaths created superstitions. It's hardly surprising that charms and amulets were worn to ward off harm.

In Acton, West London, in 1914, a schools inspector revealed that children were still wearing necklaces of blue glass beads to ward off illness. The beads—'mostly blue but occasionally yellow'—were worn underneath their clothes and were meant to act as charms against bronchitis. Their owners believed that the necklaces must never be taken off. There were over sixty shops where such amulets were still being sold.

The First World War relaunched many superstitions, including the sale of Golliwogs 'to oblige a lady,' whatever that meant, and horseshoes wrapped in red fabric and hung over beds to discourage nightmares. Edward Lovett's 1925 book, *Magic in Modern London,* recounts these findings.

The history of magic in London is complex and difficult to locate behind its usual stars. As Sherlock Holmes is to Victorian detection, so Dr Dee was to the history of magic. The Renaissance alchemist and court astronomer was a favourite of Elizabeth I, and let it be known that he conducted conversations with angels. The barrier between magic and science was considered permeable.

Dr Dee signed his letters with a pictogram of a face formed by the numerals 007, meaning for the Queen's eyes only. Ian Fleming's designation for his superspy actually came from the breaking of a German diplomatic code in the First World War. Still, Dee's version counts as a very early emoji. The magician's occult explorations got him nowhere. After he lost the Queen's support he fell out of fashion and died destitute.

In Central London there are a number of bookshops specializing in the occult and magic. Societies and talks on magical thinking are scheduled across the city, from the Swedenborg Society to the Wellcome Collection. On any given weekend you can find unexpected walks, tours, meetings and pub gatherings on all manner of esoteric subjects. Magic may be invisible but it's always in the air.

Dame Maude is a fellow witch in my coven, although she's only a Grade II at the moment and frankly won't get beyond it until she overcomes her squeamishness about toads. She and I try not to discuss the occultist Aleister Crowley. While it's true that he may once have lived in the Caledonian Road in the PCU offices, much of his story is confabulation. He has always struck me as a privileged, sleazy bohemian who used his brand of fake mysticism as a cover-up for his appalling treatment of 'acolytes' (young women). The last time I argued with a Crowleyite he tore off his shirt to reveal a gigantic tattoo of Crowley across his back, so the self-styled ceremonial magician clearly still exerts an influence over the credulous.

And that's the problem: there's no part of magical London

that has not had its history anecdotally embroidered by everyone, reputable or disreputable, who has touched it. People long to become a part of a myth.

ARTHUR BRYANT: The last time I visited you some children told me to stay away from the witch's house.

MAGGIE ARMITAGE: That was ungracious of them. I performed a ritual that saved their Jack Russell's life. You should have seen their delighted faces when he burst out of his little cardboard coffin.

ARTHUR BRYANT: He wasn't dead. Their screams could be heard in the next street.

MAGGIE ARMITAGE: I am charged with guarding the veil between life and death.

ARTHUR BRYANT: You were charged with causing a public disturbance.

Go and buy yourself a cup of ginger tea or something while I do this next bit. Here, I'll treat you.

MAGGIE ARMITAGE: This is an old sixpence, Arthur.

ARTHUR BRYANT: That's worth considerably more than a cup of tea, but I'm feeling generous. Keep the change.

London has nurtured the world's greatest writers for centuries. Hopeful artists go to Paris to paint, where the light is several degrees brighter, but you rarely hear of writers going to London to write. The occupation is associated with rural tranquillity, and calm is in short supply here.

Yet London is where scribes of all shades still meet and exchange ideas. Obviously we can take Chaucer, Dickens, Shakespeare, Virginia Woolf and Conan Doyle as read, so to speak, but that's only the uppermost tip of the talent pool. At number 8 Russell Street in Covent Garden, Boswell first met Johnson in Davies's Bookshop, now a café. The Scot was thirty years younger than the great anti-Scot, and wasn't at first impressed: 'Mr Johnson is a man of a most dreadful appearance. He is a very big man, is troubled with sore eyes, the palsy and the King's Evil.* He is very slovenly in his dress and speaks with an uncouth voice.'

But Johnson was superb company, and the pair became besties over the beef-and-port meetings that followed in the Turk's Head Tavern in Gerrard Street, Soho, the most famous literary club in London. It can be said that Johnson the man gave birth to Boswell the writer.

If you take a short walk north of Oxford Street, you'll come to a rather ordinary but pleasant enough pub at number 16 Charlotte Street. This is the Fitzroy Tavern, which gave the area of Fitzrovia its name. It became the home of creative types between the 1930s and the 1950s, where Vorticists and abstract artists drank with models, poets, criminals, music hall artistes and the kind of people who usually end up becoming our informants. Just as British artists and writers had headed (some would say absconded) to Paris in the 1910s, so they now flooded back, and often ended up at the Fitzroy. Regulars included George Orwell (again), Lawrence Durrell, Dylan Thomas and fellow poet Ruthven Todd.

Some London venues are as much a state of mind as a real place. Grub Street was real, though. It was later renamed Milton Street, then mostly demolished to make way for the Barbican.

---

* Scrofula, usually a swelling of the lymph nodes in the neck caused by tuberculosis.

Writers gathered so frequently that they had their own newspaper, the *Grub Street Journal*, in which Alexander Pope had a hand. John Foxe, the author of *Foxe's Book of Martyrs*, and the 'Water Poet' John Taylor were also based here.

George Gissing wrote *New Grub Street*, his novel about writers struggling to get published, in 1891, and re-sited his writers a little further up the road, in Clerkenwell, which was then sinking into penury at a time when 'house hackers' were subdividing properties into tenement rooms.

Farringdon Road, which runs through Clerkenwell, was the second place you went to buy books, your first stop being Paternoster Square and the third being Charing Cross Road. The wonderful Farringdon book market continued to run into the twenty-first century, when it was finally forced out to make room for shops selling fairy cakes and seventy-three types of chocolate.

Cecil Court just off Charing Cross Road is still lined with antiquarian and other independent bookshops, including the wonderful and slightly eccentric Goldsboro Books, which specializes in signed first editions. The bookshops host street parties which attract every kind of literary layabout imaginable.

Number 34 Claremont Square—smart now, ratty then—was the home of the experimental writer B. S. Johnson, who famously tested the commitment of his publishers by messing with the form of a novel, publishing loose chapters in a box for *The Unfortunates* and cutting a hole through the pages of *Albert Angelo*, which is set in the spot where he lived.

And that has always been London's strength. For every Terence Rattigan, Elizabeth Bowen or George Eliot, there's always a disreputable, struggling rebel writer seeking like-minded individuals.

But of course we can only scratch the surface here. For a full picture of literary London, read *London, City of Words* by David

Caddy and Westrow Cooper, which catalogues hundreds of writers and the landscapes they inhabited.

For a bookish chap like me, Great Britain is a paradise. John tells me that if I buy any more encyclopaedias and lug them back to our shared office at the PCU the floor is going to cave in. To combat this I've imposed a weight limit on the room and now charge Raymond Land to enter. Every time he puts on a few pounds I raise the entry price.

20

The Man on the Flying Trapeze & Other Stories

ARTHUR BRYANT: I'm handing you over to an old friend of mine, the avant-garde architect Stanhope Beaufort. Keep it clean, Stanhope, and don't start banging on about the building you designed that fell down.

STANHOPE BEAUFORT: Don't tell me how to do my job, Arthur. I don't tell you how to fit up suspects.

What do you think of when you look at London? A patchwork quilt? An unravelled ball of wool? A Byzantine empire smashed flat by bloody philistines? The more cogently constructed cities are ones that don't keep getting bombed or burned down. When disasters strike cities, the opportunists move in and vanity buildings appear.

You soon start joining up the architectural dots when you look at London from the river; the wharves, the low houses, the grander finance temples behind, the roads and buildings always rising. We tend to forget that London is on a hill, starting in

Hampstead and Highgate and dipping to the Thames. London's piecemeal quality prevents us from discerning its geography.

Paris and New York belong to specific eras and this helps to protect the fabric of their neighbourhoods. The city of Gdańsk was bombed flat and rebuilt exactly as it had been before, brick by brick. Warsaw and Berlin were reconstructed. London was left with thousands of ragged bomb holes that were filled in with little thought, care or budget. Instead of being repaired, most church steeples with cracks were simply torn down.

This was nothing new. In the eighteenth century speculative development schemes involved demolishing acres of houses and replacing them with terraces that didn't sell. The arrival of the railways severed great swathes of London, and road widening sparked a new citywide round of destruction.

The Abercrombie Plan for London of 1943 set out blueprints for the new London that would rise from the ashes of the Blitz. Monocle-wearing town planner Patrick Abercrombie was the British equivalent of New York's Robert Moses. He imagined vast transport highways cutting across the city centre, but he didn't consider the pollution danger or the damage to local communities. He was accused of destroying Plymouth rather than rebuilding it after the war. Newspaper editor Sir Simon Jenkins said he had created 'a maze of concrete blocks, ill-sited towers and ruthless road schemes.'

Each generation's architects have submitted new plans for the city. In the 1970s, a time of rampant corruption and greed, London lost more buildings than it did during the war. The framework of entire areas was dismantled, and without their signature buildings whole neighbourhoods vanished. The 1980s saw the rise of the global star architect and the arrival of 'luxury loft living,' where flats are designed around a vast picture window and a narrow balcony. They looked good in investment brochures but hid nasty surprises: outrageous annual service charges, ugly common areas, sub-standard affordable housing in the same block, no long-term maintenance plans, 'poor doors,' the risk of the holding company collapsing.

Among the most polarizing London buildings of the last few years are Renzo Piano's Central Saint Giles office blocks, each with one garish-coloured wall, built around a miserable, windswept plaza full of chain cafés. The problem here is that it's massively out of scale in a low-rise neighbourhood, dwarfing everything around it. This area was St Giles, a human-sized London neighbourhood hundreds of years old, with its own delightful character. No more.

And Piano is also responsible for the Shard, of course, a trick building that's actually just an ordinary office block with sloping sides and a hollow turret to make it pay homage—in his words, not mine—to the city of churches. You're meant to think 'steeple' when you see it. The peak flickers with coloured lights at night, sometimes recalling a Macau casino, sometimes reminding me of *The Towering Inferno*. But when its jagged, angled latticework is backlit and wreathed in steam it can conjure a terrible image of the ruined Twin Towers of 9/11.

Inside there are some restaurants that manage to be spacious yet weirdly claustrophobic, so that while you're supposed to be enjoying the insanely priced food you're actually worried about being trapped up there.

ARTHUR BRYANT: What were you doing there, anyway?

STANHOPE BEAUFORT: I'd gone to protest to the mayor of Southwark about the building of the Shard. Unfortunately I'd got the wrong day and shouted at a roomful of florists.

I could point out other London horrors, like key-lining Covent Garden's Long Acre with neon to make it look like a street of Thai brothels, and Battersea's development of millionaire glass sky-pools and dictators' lofts—it's not Monte Carlo, luv!

The good news is that fine new buildings and well-preserved old ones still act as anchors to provide grace notes in cacophonous streets and remind you that every city needs to keep its own identity. Why do we flock to other cities? To understand what makes society different and special in other cultures. History is not a dead thing to be looked back on but a key to understanding how life can evolve. Of course we need new buildings, and as the South Bank and the Gherkin show, they can be quickly adopted and loved by their users. London is for everyone, not just the rich, and you shut people out at our peril.

When I think about the multiple uses that the surviving buildings in London have had over the years it's hard not to believe in psychogeography, which you mentioned earlier, Arthur—the theory that land retains resonances from times past. But I think the reason for some changeless buildings lies less in the spirit than in the patterns of the land. Let's take four examples. I could do with some PowerPoint slides and a pointing stick.

1. THE LONDON PAVILION

On the northeast side of Piccadilly Circus, this huge building began life as a song-and-supper-room annexe to the Black Horse Inn, a home of entertainments that was turned into a music hall in 1861. There was a song sung here in 1878 during the Russo-Turkish War that gives us the word 'jingoism.'

We don't want to fight, but by Jingo if we do,
We've got the ships, we've got the men, and got the money too.

That building was demolished in 1885 and replaced with a new pavilion for C. B. Cochran's spectacular revues. Cochran was the British Ziegfeld and kept the building running until 1934, when it became a warren-like cinema. Much later it housed a sensation 'museum' called 'Ripley's Believe It or Not!' so its purpose has hardly changed in centuries. But the Pavilion is where 'entertainment London' comes to a virtual full stop, at the end of Shaftesbury Avenue, before the roads slope down to royal grounds, and it makes sense that this building would establish the invisible wall of the zone.

2. THE ALHAMBRA

Houses of entertainment had licence to be exotic; this curious building in Leicester Square began life as the Royal Panopticon in 1854. It was Moorish in style and had minarets (then fashionable) and a thirty-foot fountain, but nobody wanted to come and see the scientific equipment housed within.

What to do with it, then? The Alhambra reopened as a circus and music hall with Blondin, the man who crossed Niagara Falls on a tightrope, and Léotard, 'the daring young man on the flying trapeze' who gave us the name of the fitness garment. Things got a bit saucy after that and the place lost its licence when the dancer Wiry Sal raised her leg a few inches too high.

After reopening for proms and plays, it burned down in 1882, and was rebuilt and reopened as a music hall, where 'If You Were the Only Girl in the World' was first performed. It switched to ballet performances until 1936. It's now the art deco Odeon cinema. The square, which was until recently surrounded by cinemas, is the centre of modern tourist entertainment in London, and Leicester Square has an IMAX—the closest there's yet been to another Panopticon.

3. THE LONDON PALLADIUM

This theatre in Argyll Street was originally the Corinthian Bazaar, then a circus and after that an ice rink. In 1910 it became a very high-end music hall with box-to-box telephones and a huge granite palm court. *Peter Pan* was performed there every Christmas, the Crazy Gang appeared regularly, then it became the home of the TV show *Sunday Night at the London Palladium*, which started in 1955 and is periodically still going.

Theatres are not like pubs, which live on corners, are narrow and often have five floors, three above and two below. Theatres exist in the centres of streets because they need so few windows. These ornately designed palaces of delights are hard to repurpose and have preservation orders on their luxurious interiors. But are they still fit for use? There are roughly forty theatres in the West End, and the taste for foot-stomping over-miked musicals is bringing down the delicately plastered ceilings. Twenty-first-century audiences are taller and fatter than their Victorian counterparts, and simply can't fit into the upper circle seats.

The Palladium seats well over two thousand people and stages crowd-pleasing spectacles. With the option of drinking alcohol during performances, theatres are back to being circuses of sensation.

4. ALEXANDRA PALACE

Alexandra Palace is one of the most extraordinary and least-known buildings in London. Situated high on a hill in N22 between Muswell Hill and Haringey, the Grade II listed building has a massive glass atrium and stunning 360-degree views. Nobody I know goes there.

It was constructed in 1873 as a recreation centre for Victorian

London but was a disaster right from the start, burning down just sixteen days after it opened. A new palace opened two years later as a concert hall and theatre. Dubbed the 'People's Palace,' it was built by the team behind the Albert Hall and contained a concert hall, art galleries, a museum, a lecture hall, a theatre, a library and a banqueting hall. There was also a racecourse, a pitch-and-putt course, a Japanese village, a switchback ride and a boating lake.

Nobody went again.

During the First World War it ended up being used as a barracks, then to incarcerate German prisoners of war. In 1936 the BBC bought it and the world's first public television transmitter was built there. The singer Gracie Fields, whose voice could send a dog under a table, nicknamed it 'Ally Pally.'

It burned down *again*.

It was reopened in 1980 as an events space and staged exhibitions, and still nobody went. The grand building has never worked well. Something is wrong with its location—it feels awkward to get to (although it isn't really) and has an air of bare melancholia on the brightest days. Despite the fact that it hosts music gigs it remains North London's great white elephant. Ally Pally is supposedly undergoing regeneration yet again. The words 'exciting' and 'vibrant' crop up a lot in its brochures, along with mention of a hotel. Why does every sodding building eventually have to be turned into a bloody hotel?

| | |

Arthur's not paying me for these pearls of wisdom, by the way, so I'm passing you over to his partner.

JOHN MAY: 'You know what's weird?' my Uber driver said. 'London at Christmas. It's like the 1950s. Everyone goes inside their houses and they stay in there for days, never going out. All the transport stops. There's more going on in Romania. Christmas is when I get to perform my duties. All the essential services still have to run but no one can get to work, so I do double shifts to get them where they need to be.'

He was right. Nothing has changed in my lifetime. If anything, it's got even quieter. When I was born, towns and villages were still disconnected, hard to travel between, almost isolated. As a friend points out, to visit anywhere in England without a car you have to make very careful plans. Certain small towns are more remote than they once were—the cities leeched away the ambitious young, leaving the countryside full of pensioners and burned-out former city dwellers.

While everyone was busy stockpiling toilet rolls a couple of years back Arthur and I went walking around Piccadilly, St James's and the West End, taking advantage of the fact that the buildings could be properly seen for the first time in decades.

ARTHUR BRYANT: I think we both reached the same conclusion on this next bit, didn't we, John?

It's hard to understand how London could have lost so many beautiful buildings. East India House in Leadenhall Street was so outrageously grand that no carriage was allowed to stop in front of it. The lumpen great Doric arch at Euston was demolished and replaced with nothing, but at least its destruction jump-started an outraged conservation movement. The Coal Exchange in Lower Thames Street was a stunning cast-iron rotunda that, despite massive public protest, was demolished in order to widen a road. And so it went; the Eel Pie Island Hotel, the Egyptian Hall in Piccadilly, Old Slaughter's Coffee House in St Martin's Lane, the Holbein Gate in Whitehall, the Saracen's Head on Snow Hill, all fell and—this is the point—were not replaced by anything better.

Happily there are now, at the time of writing, twenty-three

conservation areas in London dedicated to the preservation of fine buildings in neighbourhoods of special interest.

Of course, there were many grand plans created for London that collapsed due to their spiralling expense. Londoners' desire for excess resulted in doomed projects like Watkin's Tower, also known as the 'London Stump,' an absurd Eiffel-like edifice intended to reach a height of 1,150 feet, but which only managed to reach 150 feet before being demolished to make way for Wembley Stadium. The Hyde Park Pyramid of 1903, a ludicrous design involving royal tombs and a mock Stonehenge, was replaced with the even more elaborate Imperial Monumental Halls, with a great tower that, at 550 feet, would have loomed far above Big Ben and the Houses of Parliament.

Kensington's early Jacobean country estate Holland House was wrecked by incendiary bombs in the Blitz. The Imperial Institute in South Kensington had been built to celebrate Empire but was never able to find its purpose, and was demolished by stealth despite public objections. And spectacular Northumberland House off Trafalgar Square was flattened to widen a road, although they managed to save its white stone Percy lion (which originated from the crest of the Percy family). The lion has its tail sticking straight out and can now be seen in Syon Park.

Wood Lane in West London was always a miserable spot that consisted of scrubland, farmhouses and outbuildings. But for a brief shining moment, when it hosted the Olympic Games and the Franco-British exhibition, it became a place of wonder.

In 1908 a Jewish-Hungarian entrepreneur named Imre Kiralfy created an Edwardian expo. Twenty white plaster palaces were built with colonnades, gardens and Venetian canals, around which visitors could cruise inside white swans. I've got some postcards from the time that reveal a Xanadu-like fantasy land.

Sadly it fell into disrepair and was finally pulled down to make way for the BBC television studios.

The White City was never intended to last. But at the end of the nineteenth century the new classical buildings meant to represent a kind of mock-medieval image of London were facing the forces of modernism. Out would go backward-looking ornate Gothic towers, in would come apartments with shiny hygienic bathrooms, streamlined comfort and a general reduction in living space.

It was the end of memorials to Empire and the start of monuments to capitalism. The new towers would be designed for short shelf life. Everything newly built was raised in the knowledge that it was replaceable. I cling to that hope for the Shard.

21

Post Office Pranks & Other Stories

ARTHUR BRYANT: I thought you'd gone.

MAGGIE ARMITAGE: I was in your lavatory summoning my familiar when she shut me in. Absolutely refused to release me. She's never done that before.

ARTHUR BRYANT: It wasn't your familiar; the door sticks.

MAGGIE ARMITAGE: I was about to cast a Releasing Spell when I remembered I had a can of WD-40 in my handbag.

ARTHUR BRYANT: Thank goodness for that. I wouldn't have wanted our place to get a reputation for being any more haunted.

MAGGIE ARMITAGE: I once asked Dame Maude to accompany me on a mission to create a new London myth, you know. With the aid of a stake, a plank and a length of rope we made an elaborate crop circle. We planned to tell the press that aliens had landed and were walking among us.

ARTHUR BRYANT: I dread to ask, but what happened?

MAGGIE ARMITAGE: I suppose we should have chosen to do it somewhere other than Regent's Park. The keepers arrested us. A few days later, Dame Maude began to find online reports of alien landings near the park's rose garden. I didn't read about it because I couldn't work out how to turn the internet on, but it shows that London's myths didn't stop at the end of the nineteenth century. They self-perpetuate to the present day.

One of the oddest new myths I've come across is the Thames Angel. Did you hear about this?

ARTHUR BRYANT: No. I lead a sheltered life.

MAGGIE ARMITAGE: Predictably, she was a mystical white-robed floaty lady who was said to spread calm and feelings of wellbeing. She first appeared to a sixteen-year-old student on the South Bank in 2006. The photograph taken by the student created a ready-made market for memorabilia. Suddenly the cat-lady brigade and other members of the troll community crept out in search of the so-called Angel of the Thames, hovering somewhere around Blackfriars Bridge.

The Angel's history was magically backdated to include sightings during the time of Pepys, the Great Plague, the Great Fire, the Blitz and various other flashpoints in London history. As the Angel hid its original creation story, websites, followers and an online shop appeared, because myths are there to be monetized.

Fake news sites act much as the handbills that were once sold immediately after public displays of violence or affright at Tyburn and Smithfield. It was quickly assumed that there had been sightings of angels on the same spot during both World Wars and in 1951 at the Festival of Britain, for reasons which are not apparent.

A TV show host was filmed gasping at the 'Angel' and the press ran articles with shots of wisps of smoke and a crude fake 'etching' barely worthy of the ghostbuster Harry Price's attention.* This is all reminiscent of the Angel of Mons, the mystical entity that protected British forces from the German army in 1914. If Arthur Machen's short story had been labelled fiction by the *Evening News*, who published the tale, it would never have transformed itself into fact and caused such controversy.

What was missing from this newly minted legend was the satisfaction of a historical through-line. Unlike, say, the legend of Bleeding Heart Yard or even the Tower ravens, there was no attempt to couple sightings with a royal figure or a scandal from the past. The ghosts of the Theatre Royal, Drury Lane, like the eerie presence of comics Dan Leno and Joseph Grimaldi, or the Man in Grey who patrols the upper circle after performances, were either real characters or could be kitted out with suitably imaginative backstories. So why did the Angel of the Thames have no specific identity?

There was a reason; it emerged that the Angel was a planned hoax, part of an attempted viral marketing campaign for a charity event that backfired.

And there it rests as an example of how easily the gullible transpose myths into fact. Why do some people trust belief more than science, even when faced with overwhelming proof?

London goes through phases of spirituality. After the Great

* Price was an Edwardian psychic detective who exposed fraudulent hauntings.

War the loss of so many young sons in battle manifested itself in new mystical interests. The bereaved turned to séances, mediums, clairvoyants and psychometrists as quasi-religious figures reappeared across the nation, especially in the capital.

The same thing happened at the end of the 1960s. Trusts and fellowships, chivalric orders, temples and forums opened across London, offering their services to those who sought enlightenment. One of these was the Lamplighter Movement.

The lighting of a lamp in English homes began in 1964 after the BBC ditched the recorded striking of Big Ben at 9:00 P.M. It marked the beginning of the 'Silent Minute,' a time for reflection and meditation started by the frankly loopy spiritualist Wellesley Tudor Pole.

The new idea was that a lit lamp (electric or oil) would bring an atmosphere of peaceful meditation and healing into homes, and was taken up in other countries. But the movement died out, presumably after several homes burned down.

The *Aquarian Guide to Occult, Mystical, Religious, Magical London and Around* from 1970 lists hundreds of cabalists, hypnotists, healers, witches, magicians and 'unusual contacts' available to Londoners for consultation upon the provision of a small fee and a stamped addressed envelope. Reading through these lists of exotic offerings you can't help but be struck by everyone's obsession with correct postage. Exorcisms were available from several local vicars upon receipt of details accompanied with an S.A.E., no personal callers, thank you.

ARTHUR BRYANT: Why are you still in my office? Here, you can have these seaweed biscuits back; even the cat wouldn't touch them. Why are you debunking myths anyway? They're your stock in trade.

MAGGIE ARMITAGE: As a pagan I have a healthy disregard for the manufacture of Christian myths, especially Catholic ones involving saints. When you remember that the Vatican was famously manipulated into commenting on *The Exorcist* and *The Da Vinci Code* as if they were factual, you start to wonder how they choose whom to venerate.

ARTHUR BRYANT: A fair point. We'll discuss it next time. No, take the biscuits with you.

There are so many streets and squares, alleys and wharves which are now lost to London, from Cut-Throat Lane and Pissing (now 'Passing') Lane to Breakneck Steps and Crackbrain Court. You can find London's lost addresses in *The History and Survey of London from its Foundation to the Present Time* (1756), *The Compleat Compting-House Companion* (1763) and my personal favourite, *The New Complete Guide to all Persons who have any Trade or Concern with the City and Parts Adjacent*, written by Richard Baldwin in 1783.

Virtually any gory term you can think of is in those pages coupled with 'Alley' or 'Lane.' Streets were named after the activities that took place in them, which is entirely logical, if worrying. I think we should restore the practice, so that Irving Street off Leicester Square could be called 'Pavement Pizza Lane' and Oxford Street could be renamed 'Cheap Puffa Jackets Avenue.'

Few streets now describe their occupants. But what about addresses which are deliberately obscured? We may have lost most of those wonderfully arcane descriptors, but the British public love testing the Royal Mail with finding modern addresses. For years postal workers have so prided themselves on deciphering deliberately hidden addresses that for a while in the 1980s the winners were announced on television. If you write 'The best hatters in the world' on an envelope it will be delivered to Lock &

Co., 6 St James's Street. If you write 'The best hotel in the world' it will be sent to the Savoy Hotel (which houses a world-famous cocktail bar).

Pranksters, artists and people with too much time on their hands have been testing the Post Office for years with anagrams, puzzles, drawings, crosswords and dot-to-dot pictures of their intended destinations. In the 1930s, W. Reginald Bray, the king of the autograph hunters, wrote addresses backwards, in Japanese, in mirror writing, in code, then posted, unwrapped, a bee, a carved turnip, an onion, a pipe, a bicycle pump, a clothes brush, a shirt, a drawing slate, a clump of dried seaweed—and himself. All of which got delivered to the right addresses.

I wonder if Bray was the model for Albert Haddock in the 'Misleading Cases' books, A. P. Herbert's charming tales of a man who constantly tests obscure English laws. The Royal Mail remain remarkably good-natured about such tests. A couple I know recently received a Christmas card from an old friend despite the address simply saying 'Somewhere near the sea in Suffolk.' Another couple, Antony and Sarah Wren, received post in Lowestoft from a former colleague who had lost their address. Written on the envelope was the note: 'Good luck with that, postie.' The card arrived in four days.

The rich have the easiest addresses. If you live in a 126-room castle, everyone at the nearest post office is going to know where it is. And people remember aristocrats because they're all, to some degree, as mad as old trousers.

JOHN MAY: That's a bit of a sweeping statement, Arthur.

ARTHUR BRYANT: The 14th Lord Berners used to dye the pigeons at his house different colours. Sir George Sitwell grew bored with the cows on his estate so he stencilled them with the Chinese

Willow pattern. And the Marquess of Waterford successfully sent his horseman over a five-bar gate.

JOHN MAY: I don't see what's wrong with that.

ARTHUR BRYANT: In his living room.

The gate's still on the wall there in Lowesby Hall.

Lord Hartington, before he became the 8th Duke of Devonshire, once shot a pheasant flying through a gateway on his family estate at Chatsworth. He not only managed to kill the retriever chasing it but also sprayed the dog's owner with buckshot and injured his chef. When he was asked if he regretted the shot he replied: 'Of course. If I'd killed the chef we'd have had no dinner.'

That's all I need to know about toffs. My old mate Raymond Kirkpatrick had a bit of a mouth on him, so it surprised people to find out that he was a Professor of English Language and a manuscript restorer at the British Library. Raymond was keen to give me his take on certain aspects of London life. Sadly he's now deceased, thanks to being murdered, but I found his notes inside an old copy of *Kerrang!* he left in my car, so I can bring him back from the dead, as it were. Let's see what he has on the subject. Or rather had.

RAYMOND KIRKPATRICK: Arthur, you asked me to send you something on London toffs. They're allergic to me and tend to come out in bruises if I get too close, so for my purposes we need to start at number 68 Regent Street. I'll try to keep it clean.

The Café Royal was built in 1865. It has a gorgeous main room, all gilt and mirrors. There you could find Rudyard Kipling and Oscar Wilde rubbing shoulders, Lou Reed kissing David Bowie, Aubrey Beardsley, Virginia Woolf, George Bernard Shaw and Ronald Firbank nattering away from arsehole to breakfast-time.

You can find this in any half-decent guide book, but I'm after something a little different.

'If you want to see the English people at their most English,' said Sir Herbert Tree in 1914, 'go to the Café Royal, where they are trying their hardest to be French.' As well they might have been. The 'N' in the Café Royal logo, which is slapped all over the joint inside, was presumed to stand for 'Nicols,' after Daniel Nicolas Thévenon, the French wine merchant who founded it, but it actually stands for Napoleon, so we have a small poisonous gesture of opposition nestling in the nation's most British street, which sums up British society in a bloody nutshell.

In this London, desperate socialites held court in the café's cigar-fug. It's not hard to sense the fragility behind their brittle laughter; there are plenty of drawings of hollow-eyed bohemians looking every bit as haunted as the streets they inhabited. Being an inbred toff was knackering work.

In London, café society can mean something very different to that of Vienna or Paris. There's a particular kind of working-class café on almost every London high street, and they all have the same menu. I know you asked me to cover café society, not cafeterias, but I'm a socialist, what did you bloody expect? Germany and Austria had complex royal histories, not a bunch of capering half-witted chinless wonders shagging their way across the shires. Obviously the French did, but you'd expect that.

After the Second World War diet became a political hot potato, as it were. 'Community Feeding Centres' were set up to provide the undernourished with vitamins when fresh food was in short supply and, by doing so, level the playing field between rich and poor. Three-course meals were mass produced and sold for mere pennies.

The cafés that supplied cheap hot food survived and continue in the present day. They are so ubiquitous that they're barely noticed. Around the corner from your unit they're usually Greek-Cypriot, Turkish or Italian, and always serve liver and bacon, varieties of eggs, tea in mugs and a lot of sausages. They're mainly used by workmen, seniors, students and mums. There was one behind the British Library called the Capannina Café, which led to me entering and singing, 'Pardon me, sir, is this the Capannina Café?' a joke the owners grew tired of surprisingly quickly.

Rising rents forced change upon them, so that in smart areas they've all been transmuted into coffee shops, but if you follow a builder you'll usually be led to an old-fashioned one. I suppose in Hampstead all the Polish plumbers have to make do with brioche.

In the immediate postwar years, eating out was not a priority and remained the province of the upper classes. Everyone else ate at home or at cafeterias, often supplementing meals with home-grown vegetables. In *Smallbone Deceased,* Michael Gilbert breaks down the classes according to where they lunch: the senior partners ate versions of boarding school dinners at their clubs; the lawyers enjoyed refined little restaurants around the Inns of Court; the secretaries ate at an ABC or a Lyons Corner House.

For years I thought ABC stood for Associated British Cafeterias but actually it stands for the Aerated Bread Company. They moved from cakes to tea and opened their own cafés, starting at their base in Camden Town, but their monopolistic practices were disgraceful. They paid their waitresses a pittance for a sixty-two-hour week and overcharged on their menus. Soon Lyons broke the monopoly and gave people a choice. By the late 1970s handmade cakes had become an unaffordable luxury and the era of the proletarian cafeteria ended.

Restaurants were the by-product of travel. Coaching inns had always provided fresh horses but also served fresh food. As London grew it swallowed dozens of rural villages which existed as little more than coaching stops.

Along these routes inns prepared hot meals for tired merchants, but because most passengers were male the bill of fare remained resolutely masculine. The dining rooms had dark wood panelling and mock Tudor beams. The cuisine consisted of puddings, pies and rich red meats. It wasn't until the journeys became easier and carriages became more upholstered that women, who rarely ate in public, joined the gentlemen at the table. It didn't help that quite a few restaurants refused to admit them.

When forces posted overseas complained about British food being so basic, it was for a simple reason. After five years of war and more than double that of rationing, nobody knew what to cook anymore.

Affectionately known as greasy spoons, the traditional workers' cafés had another use—they were hangover joints, the only thing that could fix a pub crawl the night before. Even local cafés now seem to have grasped the nettle and gone upmarket. Where once I'd hear a cry of 'Double EB, fried slice and a cup of Rosie,' I now hear 'Two poached, smashed avocado and kale on five-seed brown.' Some serve a better Eggs Benedict than expensive hotels do. And there's a trend toward hipster versions of traditional caffs, serving postmodern ironic fare.

The Quality Chop House in Farringdon Road has retained its now-ironic 1930s sign etched into its windows that reads 'Progressive Working Class Caterers.' The London dining scene is dominated by international sharing cuisine and fusion menus. The days of 'plated meat and two veg' are remembered only by pubs serving Sunday lunch, which for some unearthly reason must always include a manhole-sized lid of cardboard known as a Yorkshire pudding.

Sorry about the digression. Right, the upper classes.

For two hundred years the London Season lay at the core of upper-class British society.

It began before Easter and ran until Midsummer, and was the time of year when rich, well-connected families, not the kind who had made their fortunes working hard in steel or textiles but the porcine indolent type who inherited wealth, left their country houses to get away from confusing questions about raising pigs and headed to London. There they would unshutter their grand houses and get ready to throw parties. This mass movement lumped together the 'right people' in a calendar of festivities and sporting events such as regattas, horse trials and flower shows.

The key word bandied about here was 'respectable.' Family backgrounds were checked for stains on the escutcheon and nobody asked 'Who are your people?' because everyone already knew. They'd been vetting the candidates as if they were placing bets at Aintree.

In actuality, the Season was a cattle market to sell off pasty aristocratic daughters who had been trapped on country estates all winter. After having their flaws painted out of society portraits, their thyroidal eyes reduced, their goitres hidden and chins removed or added in, the girls, all seventeen and eighteen, were presented as virgins swathed in white satin. With no thought of university or a career for any of them, they were forced to rely upon marrying a property-owning member of the aristocracy. Behind each one was a family forking out a fortune in frocks and furs, anxious to survive in its social terrarium for one more generation.

The Season later ran through to around 12 August, the start of grouse-hunting, when society would retire to the country to slaughter wildfowl before coming back to London again with the spring. At the end of the Season you might be left with your unmarriageable munters and have to haul them back to the sticks for more lessons in deportment. No eligible lord was prepared to hitch up to someone who walked like a farmer unless her parents were loaded.

One of the key events of the summer was Ascot, where ladies attended to show off their elaborate, expensive Paris gowns. There would be balls, parties, proms, dinners and breakfasts, and the viewing of the Royal Academy Summer Exhibition. Women were trussed into corsets and elaborate coiffures, told not to open their mouths and were put on display for dukes and earls, who circled around picking them off. Sometimes the best they could get was a knackered old baronet.

A key element of the Season was presentation at court, but this was discontinued in 1958, when the Queen announced she would no longer have well-bred gels presented to her—even Prince Philip said the ritual was 'bloody daft.' In its heyday, girls were only allowed to be presented at Court if they were sponsored by a lady who had herself been presented. One of the reasons for the Season's demise was that the sponsors began to charge hefty fees to take girls from 'trade' backgrounds (Princess Margaret, ever succinct, declared that 'every tart in London was getting in').

Jessica Mitford, one of the Mitford sisters who wasn't completely barking, described the Season as 'a specific, upper-class version of a puberty rite,' but it became more and more of an anachronism. In 1976, Queen Charlotte's Ball folded amid rumours of drug-taking and general bad behaviour. The fact that it had survived for so long was down to its charitable works.

The London Season was the whitest event on earth. In her memoirs, Lady Dorothy Nevill recalled that during her first Season she attended fifty balls, sixty parties, thirty dinners and twenty-five breakfasts. The day started around 10:00 A.M. and often finished at 3:00 A.M., so the debutantes put in more gruelling hours than dockers.

Every now and again some chancer sets up a new society to reintroduce the London Season, with the aim of dragging Chinese millionaires into Knightsbridge in a grisly parody of what was once already a pretty dismal invention. England is very good at flogging Englishness. Check out the arse end of the thirty-two universities scattered around London and you'll find quite a few St Trinian's–style finishing schools for disinterested Arabic teens. It turns out that social snobbery is still something you can package and sell to rich mugs.

22

The Ghost in the Lift &
Other Stories

Arthur Bryant: For this bit I'm taking you to Joseph Grimaldi Park, a spot so unedifying that you could walk past it a hundred times and not realize it was there. Not that you'd want to walk down this street more than once.

It's easy to forget that London's smaller green spaces were often created by churchyards and only became public parks once the churches disappeared. Sometimes they remain but their yards are decommissioned for burials, and so one ends up with the very London sight of seeing sunbathers beside gravestones.

There's a memorial on Pentonville Road to Joseph Grimaldi (1778–1837). He's commemorated in the park where he's buried, which is also a general graveyard and a basketball court.

Grimaldi was the greatest English clown, the first whiteface clown—he designed his unique make-up in 1801. From the sixteenth century clowns had always appeared as country bumpkins, but Grimaldi created the modern look, with brightly coloured outfits. His performances made the clown character the central figure in British harlequinades. He was born in Clare Market, the son of a ballet-master and a dancer, the grandson of an Italian, Signor Joseph 'Iron Legs' Grimaldi. He appeared onstage at Drury Lane before his second birthday and trod the boards at Sadler's Wells at the age of three. He was nine when his father died of alcoholism, plunging the family into debt.

Clowns registered their unique make-up by painting them on eggs as a form of copyright, and Grimaldi's was particularly memorable. After decades of performing he became crippled and broken by his energetic stunts, and by accidents that may have been arranged by embittered stage carpenters. In his final years he was supported by benefits thrown by his old pals at the Wells. In his farewell speech he told his rapt audience: 'Like vaulting ambition, I have overleaped myself and pay the penalty in advanced old age. It is four years since I jumped my last jump, filched my last oyster, boiled my last sausage and set in for retirement.'

One corner of Joseph Grimaldi Park contains a memorial to the clown: a pair of coffin-shaped graves that ring out in different tones when you leap about on them. A perfect memorial for a man who would have loved the idea of you dancing on his grave. Charles Dickens wrote his biography.

The little park's basketball players never notice that stacked all around them are the headstones of others who were buried here. While Mexico celebrates its dead on 1 November we incorporate them into places of public recreation.

| | |

Obviously one can pass weeks exploring the more than three hundred parks and gardens in London. I've always liked the rather grand St James's Park, with its gingerbread bird-keeper's lodge and species of wildfowl, including pelicans, and the rolling meadowlands of Green Park, where you can see the beautiful gilded Canada Gate and memorial commemorating the one million Canadians who served with British forces during two World Wars.

There are parks that hide in plain sight, like the lush butterfly-dappled Queen Elizabeth Hall Roof Garden, and scruffy local ones like Finsbury Park, where I'm told Jimi Hendrix and Bob Dylan both played, just not together because that would have been horrible.

Then there are the secret parks, like Maryon Wilson Park in Charlton, South London, which was once an ancient woodland called Hanging Wood. The word 'hang' also comes from the Old English *hangra*, a wooded slope, and the park feels as if it's on a hill. It's a melancholy, slightly disconcerting area. Part of the film *Blow-Up* (1966) was shot here and still looks eerily fresh. A hedonistic photographer played by David Hemmings takes pictures of figures in the park who may have committed a murder, but realizes that you can see anything if you believe in it. The park is exactly as it was then, and just as strange when the wind starts to rise and the trees creak.

| | |

At this point I'm heading out along the south side of the Thames to the limits of London. After the Norman Conquest of 1066, the area of Lesnes in Abbey Wood passed into the possession of Bishop Odo (not a character from The Lord of the Rings). It's mentioned in the Domesday Survey as 'Loisnes.' Lesnes Abbey was founded in 1178 by Richard de Luci, the Chief Justiciar of England.

De Luci was retired to the abbey to die, possibly paying penance for being involved in the murder of Thomas Becket. The surviving stonework reveals the floor plan of the abbey, and local children still clamber on top of its ruined arches, although of course this is fun and is therefore now frowned upon. No one has ever dug down to see who else lies there, and the ancient wooded ruins, which contain prehistoric burial mounds, remain at the edge of a southeast London housing estate.

Now let me introduce Georgia Standing. She may look like a Goth but she's an archivist specializing in the study of Roman lunar symbolism and, for reasons I've never been able to fathom, an expert on London's land enclosures.

GEORGIA STANDING: Thanks, Arthur. Below Abbey Wood stands Thamesmead, a vast development built on the old Erith Marshes. It's certainly near the Thames but there isn't much of a mead about it. At the British Library we found a glamorous 1970s sales brochure illustrating it as a sunlit upland full of happy laughing families. It didn't turn out like that.

Things went wrong from day one. The pilings of the concrete homes provided insufficient support and started sinking back into the marsh. The walkways cracked and subsided. Thames water flooded back in. The project ran out of money again and again.

The problem families parachuted into this new Eden soon fell afoul of the law. How grim was it? Stanley Kubrick's film *A Clockwork Orange* was shot there without much need for set dressing.

The British National Party fascists unhelpfully planned a 'Wogs Out' campaign outside the area's rows of run-down shops. Then in the 1990s, gangs with names like the Natty Turn Outs, the Goldfish Gang, the Firm and the Woolwich Mafia patrolled the streets. Racially motivated murders were common.

This new home to some fifty thousand people became London's most notorious housing estate, the fraud capital of the UK due to its association with West African criminal gangs. One fraud prevention service pointed out that Thamesmead's SE28 postcode had the worst record for credit card fraud of any postal address in the country.

It wasn't supposed to turn out this way.

The former marshland was home to London's last wild horses. It was unenclosed common land, and therefore valuable. A local newspaper competition had been run to find a name for the urban paradise that was to be built there. 'Thamesmead' conjured a bucolic image that had nothing to do with the miles of grey concrete terraces and dank, lightless underpasses that were constructed there. Cut off by the river and a motorway, Thamesmead found itself marooned as people from outside stopped visiting. Without social interaction, the inhabitants were left to create their own social rules. Police officers would no longer patrol there.

This was what had happened for centuries across the capital from Southwark to Seven Dials. Poor families had always found themselves forced together in uninhabitable neighbourhoods where they were left to fend for themselves. But this time it was the architects' utopia, a brutalist fantasy land of an instant 'community.'

Help was on its way with a massive regeneration programme that has now transformed the area. The films being shot there got nicer, like the award-winning *Beautiful Thing*, and the public spaces were thoughtfully rebooted. Thamesmead is finally welcoming, but remains an area most Londoners have never visited. I'd like to have seen the wild horses.

ARTHUR BRYANT: Thanks, Georgia. Despite its great age, London has few old 'ordinary' houses; only the grand mansions survive. We want history to be about paupers and prostitutes, or kings and crowns. What about those merchant's families who existed in the middle?

By rights, number 49 Bankside shouldn't be there at all. It's a home that has survived floods, fires, wars and developers since 1710, but it is the location that makes its existence all the more miraculous. It faces St Paul's across the Thames in an area long known for its poverty, and the poorest areas of any city are always those ripest for cheap redevelopment.

Riverbanks are prime sites that provide European cities with a chance to display grandiose public buildings. But for a long time Bankside was barely regarded as part of the city at all. Separated from its wealthy neighbours by the Thames, it was stocked with fishponds or 'stews,' then brothels, theatres and bear pits, and so the South Bank avoided becoming part of London, remaining a low-life attraction for wealthier urbanites.

Prior to the building of 49 Bankside its site was occupied by an inn, the Cardinal's Cap. The neat little riverside house was surrounded by a colourful parade of watermen and costermongers, publicans and performers. Number 49 shows that London didn't merely consist of the wealthy and the penniless, but also a swathe of middle-class residents who fought to keep their homes cleaner than any others in Europe.

Our home-hygiene obsession started with attempts to control our sooty coal-burning hearths; coal and the spread of industry gave us the means with which to furnish our homes, so 'the dirt and the money had a common source.'* The proliferation of spas is less an indication of healthy waters than a reminder of how unhealthy London's other water supplies were. If you had money, you headed out of London to raise your children in clean air.

The Victorians invented luxurious public toilets, yet prior to this facilities were built directly over the river and later flowed straight into it. Illogically, evening strolls were partaken on bridges to ward off the ill humours of typhoid fever. The dingy

---

* *The House by the Thames: and the people who lived there* by Gillian Tindall.

urbanization that brought disease and dirt was seen by those who made money from it as desirable and gentrifying.

The house at number 49 arose from the old inn's footprint, at a time when the shapes and sizes of riverside properties were more controlled for aesthetic appeal than they are today. Watermen feared the construction of bridges would destroy their trade, as it had in Paris. Their fates became entwined with the prosperity of coal; they were killed off by the arrival of steam-driven boats.

The house has remained in private hands, passing from the poor to the prosperous, eventually housing the 1930s Hollywood actress Anna Lee. Considering centuries of historical artefacts ended up in building skips, courtesy of the corporations trusted with their preservation, we should be thankful that number 49 Bankside still survives more or less intact.

The Globe Theatre next door to the house is a triumph of revived fortunes, thanks to the American director Sam Wanamaker, who made it his life's work to rebuild it based on original plans. Due to health and safety laws it now holds 1,400 people rather than the 3,000 of old, but it replicates the experience of seeing Shakespeare in circumstances approximating those of the first Globe in 1599. Fourteen years after its original opening the theatre burned down when a cannon misfired during a performance of *Henry VIII*. One man's trousers caught fire, but the flames were doused with a bottle of beer.

There are two more buildings we should visit on this little tour. The first is a puzzler to many who see it from a distance. It looks familiar but is hard to place.

Surrounded by venerable museums, pubs and churches, Senate House in Bloomsbury is the administration centre of the University of London, and has proved a source of inspiration for British writers. Books partly set there include Graham Greene's *The Ministry of Fear* and George Orwell's *1984*—Orwell's wife, Eileen, worked inside it for the Censorship Department of the Ministry of Information, which became the Ministry of Truth in her husband's novel. It has also featured in a great many films, often when London needs to look like congressional USA.

The building has plenty of remarkable features. It feels like a piece of an American city in Central London and includes an art deco ballroom with a sprung wooden floor.

Nearby there are creatures in jars at the Hunterian Museum, the extinct Tasmanian tiger and the dodo at the Museum of Zoology and the mummified corpse of social reformer Jeremy Bentham, displayed seated at UCL's student centre on Gordon Square.

Bentham had left instructions for his preservation but his dried-out head looked a bit too macabre for display, so it was cut off and replaced with a wax head containing his own hair. Students kept nicking the real head, so it was eventually locked away.

Senate House also has a reputation for being haunted. Bloomsbury is one of the most ancient areas in London and has seen more than its fair share of murders, but that doesn't explain why a relatively modern building should house so many ghosts.

Glowing spectral figures have been seen in the library, the lift, various doorways and even in the loos. The Blue Lady is said to appear in the Senate Room, sitting in one of the booths. A lost river bubbles up beneath the building, coming through vents and drains—and as we've seen, wherever there are rivers there are always phantoms.

The eighth floor of Senate House is said to make people 'uncomfortable,' while on higher floors the lights come on by themselves, the temperature falls and something up there hurls books around. One answer as to the identity of the ghost in the lift presents itself—the Principal of the University of London, Sir Edwin Deller, was crushed to death inside the lift shaft.

JOHN MAY: Arthur, I think that one's apocryphal.

ARTHUR BRYANT: No. It just may not be true.

Of course, grand houses always attracted anecdotes of embarrassment because everyone longed to come away from a weekend invitation with a scandalous story, and there was a lot of licentiousness because . . . well, they *could*. But town was where you went if you were really planning to misbehave. In Henry James's novella *The Turn of the Screw* it's clear that Flora's uncle prefers his licentious city life to being stuck in the countryside with children.

William Douglas, the 4th Duke of Queensbury (1725–1810), kept a 'female menagerie' in his house at 138 Piccadilly, studying them through a grille and ringing a bell for the ones he liked. The ultimate sex pest, he developed an obsession with a young woman and bought the house next door to her, building a bow window that allowed him to sit and spy on her. She refused to have anything to do with him despite his humongous bank account. Londoners thought he was a revolting old fool and had a good laugh at his expense.

Meanwhile, lower houses attracted tragedy. In Fitzrovia in 1956 a woman called Nina Hamnett mysteriously fell from her bedsit window onto the spiked railings around her flat. It was a sad end for the designer, illustrator and sea shanty expert. Once she had eaten caviar with Stravinsky and taken tea with Lawrence of Arabia. Her love of partying had eventually overshadowed her talent and, like so many before her, she had become lost from view. Her last words were, 'Why won't they let me die?'

Artists, musicians and writers have always mingled with us ordinary folk in the West End's drinking holes, but Soho was preferred by serious drinkers. In the heady days of the seventies there were lunchtime discos where you could 'get down' during office hours, and one, La Valbonne in Kingly Street, featured sequined dancers in a fountain daily.

The Troy Club in Hanway Street was inappropriately named for its owner, Helen, who encouraged creative types to get drunk there, not that they needed much encouragement. It consisted of a front room with some kitchen chairs. You could have been at your nan's, if your nan smoked Capstan Full Strength and got through a bottle of gin a night.

Worse still was the Colony Room Club in Dean Street, Soho, hidden away for sixty years up a dingy staircase reeking of damp, beer and fag ash. Here a peculiar mixture of writers and artists collided, united by artistic temperament and argumentative alcoholism.

Was it a salon for creative outsiders or were they just a bunch of pissed-up old rummies sheltering from reality? I felt a few collars at the club in its heyday and it filled me with horror. Conversation was far from witty, consisting mainly of raddled soaks bellowing insults at each other before falling off their stools. The West End was full of such hellish little all-day bars because the pubs shut at 3 P.M.

There's a tendency now to over-romanticize these places as 'bohemian' but I'm not sure they were. Certainly they attracted their share of flawed intellectuals craving a little *nostalgie de la boue,* but the majority were there to get blind drunk out of hours under club rules. With the broadening of pub opening times the need for them disappeared, and as one who remembers them vividly, I'm not sure that the sight of a plastered Francis Bacon looming at the bar is much of an enticement to stay. I quite like his screaming popes, though. And I like the line in Alan Bennett's *A Question of Attribution* that if Bacon had painted Her Majesty it would have been called *The Screaming Queen.*

23

Sexy London & Other Stories

ARTHUR BRYANT: I'm handing this bit over to my right-hand officer DS Janice Longbright. She wants to tell you a bit about Soho, where she used to work as a nightclub hostess, so she says.

JANICE LONGBRIGHT: Thanks, Arthur. You make it sound like I was an ecdysiast.* I did the books. I only went on the floor when they were short-staffed at the bar or needed a greeter. I never had tassels.

You see a lot of odd sights out on the streets, and for a while Soho was indeed my manor. My hours as a hostess were 10:00 P.M. to 4:00 A.M., but there were strip clubs that opened at lunchtime to catch the pension-day brigade, who queued up outside with their Tupperware boxes of sandwiches to get the seats closest to the ladies. Our club was legit and well behaved; it had to be, as the local cops checked up on us every Sunday and took 20 per-

---

* A lady who disrobes to music for a living. 'But I'm not a stripper. At these prices I'm an ecdysiast!'—Gypsy Rose Lee.

cent of the takings. That was one of the reasons why I switched sides, to help end the corruption endemic in Soho.

When stripping was still a relatively respectable profession, the girls raced from club to club doing the same act in different sessions. Occasionally couples attended at the smarter clubs, but the audiences were mostly elderly gentlemen. The clubs were seen as a legitimate part of Soho's charm, but as the times became more permissive criminal gangs moved in.

In 2014 the MP Michael Gove was asked why so many young people poured into London, and suggested that it was for the sex, which was honest if nothing else.

But London had always been 'for the sex.' There were once 107 brothels in the immediate vicinity of Drury Lane alone. Nearly a fifth of all dwellings were houses of ill repute. The prostitutes didn't just work in the houses, but plied their trade in the theatres and circuses too. In 1817 it was noted that the more high-end ladies went from box to box in the theatre. By 1840 it was noted that on a hot summer night the whole of Waterloo Road was inhabited by prostitutes, many naked to the waist, in every window and doorway, laughing and joking.

In these reports it's interesting to observe that the women are described as the ones in charge, setting their traps for hapless males and selecting their customers with care. It's never the punter's fault that they're there, of course.

Europeans felt that it was in the English nature to be coarse and indecent, but as the Victorian era progressed this liberal attitude changed. Then two World Wars removed most young men from the streets as the nation turned its attention to bigger problems.

By the time of the Street Offences Act in 1959, business had declined to just a few red-light patches of Soho. The old brothel in Meard Street almost made it into the twenty-first century. By this time half of its 'ladies' were not ladies at all, which caused quite a few fights in public.

Nearby Haymarket was known as Hell Corner and had more ladies of the night than punters. The so-called 'Piccadilly Commandos' finished their wartime service near Eros, where they had been meeting sex-starved members of the armed forces on street corners. By the 1970s Piccadilly had become the place to find rent boys.

There were a great many dance halls where prostitutes could get nightly work, and it's not much of a shock to realize that the venerable, grand Café Royal on Regent Street was once home to so many courtesans.

ARTHUR BRYANT: Did you ever meet any of these ladies at your club?

JANICE LONGBRIGHT: The only ones I knew were wealthy and discreet, and made calls to hotels by appointment. They tended to be emotionally closed off and very private. But I think that was the nature of prostitution in England. We swung between revelling in sexual freedom and condemning it. A woman had to remain on her guard.

ARTHUR BRYANT: When it comes to decadent cities I tend to think of Berlin, if by decadence one means 'closes late and suffers no embarrassment.' Either I saw too little of Berlin or it's nowhere near as excessive as London, a city which Frank Harris described as being like a bedraggled woman you turn from in disgust, only to discover she has undreamed-of depths.

London's allure is paradoxically the engine of its repulsiveness. Social inequality is at the root, of course; the slums of Shadwell and Shoreditch's Old Nichol ('the Jago' in Arthur Morrison's novel) created overcrowding and vice, while the stifling parlours of Chelsea bred boredom and the desire to philander, so one fed the other. Those who could afford indulgences were able to use the services of those who could not. It was hardly surprising in a city where artists could wax lyrical about the shroud of smog settling on dingy backstreets while ordinary workmen died in its miasmic filth.

In London the great outdoors was virtually indoors. The Wilde set worked their way through the town's tarts, guardsmen and post-boys, and might not have been pilloried had they thought to tidy their hotel rooms, while Soho's disorderly houses provided married gentlemen with 'a sleeping room for self and lady.'

Pornography was for the posh, of course, sold through antiquarian book dealers with obscuring titles like *The Spreeish Spouter or Flash Cove's Slap-Up Reciter*. Many of the newspapers dumbed down into smut and sensationalism, and fears about the nation's binge-drinking culture greatly exercised those in authority (so no change there).

Revelry was for the rich. Gangs of drunk young men would tumble into the streets of St James's looking for trouble and attempt to barge their way into restaurants. In 1893 Aubrey Beardsley told his publisher he was planning a spree and going to go out dressed as a tart, although the slang-usage of the time probably suggests generic debauchery rather than transvestism.

Too much has been written about Wilde, Beardsley and various brothel raids, but one difference between London past and present lies in the 'quality' of those who faced exposure. Prince Albert Victor might have been sighted at the Hundred Guineas Club signing in for a night of debauchery under the name of Victoria, but the man in the street didn't care. Youth, as they say, is not an achievement, and nor is inherited wealth.

The age-old story of London was always that of the wily old lady who lifts her skirts for high-born gentlemen. If there's one thing that has changed about decadent London, it's that it is much more egalitarian now. You can go for a 'spree' whether you're from Belgravia or Essex.

It wasn't just about ladies of the night, though. We sought extremes in everything, from the intense quality of our brawling and whoring to the roughness of our entertainment, where dancers aimed their highest kicks at wealthy patrons and Victorian prostitutes openly touted for trade.

Londoners, it seems, have always been a bunch of dirty-minded beasts, never more so than when seeking a night out in the 'scented whirlwind' of the theatre. The painted women of the stage had an automatic association with sin—poor Nell Gwyn had audience members yell 'Whore!' at her. Much later, the managers of the Alhambra and the Empire Theatre in Leicester Square were happily admitting prostitutes to the promenades so long as they were smartly dressed and 'respectable.'

The most notable characteristic of the audience was the very slight attention it paid to the stage. The sensual delights of West End nights were brought to a close by a pair of puritanical American visitors who unsportingly reported their experience to the National Vigilance Association.

In the battle between manners and morals, a compromise was reached that pleased no one: A screen was erected between the Empire audience and the 'women of objectionable character,' and was promptly torn down by cheering vandals who included the young cadet Winston Churchill, up for a naughty night on the town.

London took its decadent pleasures seriously. The sumptuous Café Monico was patronized by the 'better class of foreigners,' and remained in business from 1877 right up until the end of the

1950s. Solferino's, Romano's and Kettner's were founded by Europeans who seemed quite content to bring their Frenchified ways with them, providing trysting spots for horny strangers along with champagne and fine dining. Wilde and his renters cropped up in the red-velvet salons with the depressing ubiquity of soap stars.

There was a price to pay for all this decadence; the main players nearly all died between the ages of twenty-five and their late forties. Perhaps it's the cost of living in a city where pleasure is always a business.

Until the early 1970s, pornography did thriving business in the Charing Cross Road, although it was pretty tame by today's standards. A parade of chemists' shops had gentleman's trusses in their windows and mucky European books beneath their counters. The West End owed much of its rude reputation to the sensational headlines of the Sunday papers, which gleefully reported back whenever toffs behaved poorly in nightclubs, a habit they continue to this day.

Writers like Colin MacInnes and Dylan Thomas might have been legendary in terms of their capacity for drink, but I'm not sure that tales of Soho's soaks amuse anyone now. The hard-drinking raconteurs who barely masked their desperation and the watering holes that couldn't be lively without displaying a nasty side are no longer in evidence. The smart new Youngs who inhabit Soho are a far politer tribe. What's perhaps missing from the area is the sense of two extremes, the scale of ambition that allowed the owner of Soho's Gargoyle Club to hire Henri Matisse and Edwin Lutyens to jazz up his décor.

The fabric that makes the city special to Londoners unravels and weaves itself into new shapes, but London's streets don't change their character that much from one century to the next.

Mayfair was aristocratic, Soho misbehaved, Fitzrovia was bohemian and Marylebone could only be dull. Once there were guidebooks to the sporting ladies of Covent Garden and Soho, including this from a 1788 edition concerning Miss B. at 18 Old Compton Street: 'In bed she is all the heart can wish . . . every limb is symmetry, every action under cover truly amorous; her price is two pounds two.'

Dostoevsky was disgusted by the harlots of the Haymarket, but the French whores of Maddox Street were admired by police for being brisk, clean and businesslike. London conducted a schizophrenic relationship with its rentable ladies, but Soho's gay quarter was not always so tolerant.

After a raid on the White Swan pub near Oxford Circus in 1811, six men charged with intent to enjoy male pleasure were pilloried and pelted with bricks and dead animals—not an uncommon occurrence—yet nightly the parks were full of illicit lovers.

The city's drag pubs traced their origins back to the old music halls, and were in plain sight in high streets around the city. In Camden Town there were several of particular fame; the Black Cap and the Mother Red Cap, both named after local witches, were conflated into one pub for the film *Withnail & I*. The Mother Red Cap was sold off and gutted. Like so many others, the Lemon Tree simply vanished overnight as if it had never existed. The grand old Black Cap, a veritable repository of music hall history, with its unique tiling depicting the Camden Witches in its hallway, was closed despite community protests.

Only South London's Royal Vauxhall Tavern of 1863 survives them. It looks like a Victorian coliseum, and its stage once sported a trapeze. Dancers, drag acts and low comics would race along the bar, so you had to whip your drink up pretty sharpish not to have it kicked through the window. It was never a genteel boozer but there were famous faces in the audience—Princess Diana supposedly slipped out of the palace disguised as a man to see a show with Freddie Mercury, although the story may be apocryphal. The 'RVT' had many strange and wonderful acts. John and I were on duty the night they gave a joint to every customer in order to test Lambeth's relaxed one-joint-no-arrest attitude to marijuana. Bear in mind that you're within spitting distance of the Houses of Parliament, and the thought of stoned drag queens on ceiling swings singing Gilbert & Sullivan arias takes on a strange new resonance.

If you grew up in Central London there was a good chance you'd end up in one of these polysexual innuendo-filled places with your workmates or even your parents. In his biography, the hard-man actor Ray Winstone points out that he used to go to the only remaining drag venue in the East End, Benjy's, to meet girls.

Throughout history everyone from William Blake to Jeffrey Archer has used Central London for nefarious adventures. Russians, French, Italians, Hungarians, Jews, Chinese (and Maltese gangsters) all helped to shape Soho's unique character. The area was a jumble of sex shops, strip clubs, textile wholesalers, bespoke tailors, accountants, screening rooms, record stores, live music venues, coffee bars, studios, gay bars, restaurants and one of the oldest street markets in London, Berwick Street Market, now no more than a faint shadow of itself.

Certain streets had individual temperaments: Lexington Street had artists' homes and galleries and Wardour Street housed Britain's homegrown film industry. Soho wasn't entirely savoury or safe but it was full of atmosphere, so much so that the Germans shot British *Krimi* dramas in German centred on the area, rather as Hollywood filmed its own versions of Paris and London.

Most of the buildings which have come down were not lovely;

they were barely habitable postwar eyesores. In Old Compton Street were sloping mullioned-windowed rooms that had not changed in centuries. Architecture was never the point here. What made the place was its people: the seamstresses, musicians, artists, producers, designers, writers, performers and publicans who lived in the buildings and were the heart of the area. Nearly all of them have now moved out. A junior school, Soho Parish Primary, is the last surviving school in Soho, and has long co-existed peacefully with strip joints and gay bars. Janice, you know Soho well. Tell us something we don't know.

JANICE LONGBRIGHT: I don't know what you know.

ARTHUR BRYANT: I don't know what I know either, I just know that I don't want to know what I don't know because once I know it I'll forget it so I'm better off not knowing in the first place.

JANICE LONGBRIGHT: And he's an officer of the law, ladies and gentlemen. Be afraid.

ARTHUR BRYANT: Soho, woman.

JANICE LONGBRIGHT: There was never anywhere to sit outside in Soho, ever, apart from in its mean little park squares. It was always an indoor society. Sohoites never appeared before 1:00 P.M. and shunned sunlight. Now the narrow streets are packed with outdoor salad opportunities, like it's the South of France and not a maze of sooty alleys filled with rubbish trucks.

There will always be punters looking for the 'old' Soho and finding nothing but cupcake shops. Those of us who live here can't afford to be nostalgic about London. We know we're liable to come back from a holiday and find our favourite café gone. It's just the way things work. I can't think of any city that has changed so consistently over the last sixty years.

But there's a difference between the gradual transformation of an area and its spontaneous combustion. One great loss is Soho's Star Café, run by Mario Forte. A great character rarely found without a cigar in his mouth, Mario worked there all his life, bellowing behind the counter, complaining about the staff, chivvying the customers. The décor consisted of gingham tablecloths and tin signs nailed to the walls advertising Lyons tea, Hudson's soap, Robin cigarettes and Spratt's dog biscuits.

Pop, Mario's father, had it before him, from 1933, and it remained a Soho institution throughout the twentieth century. Its menu had dishes named after the producers and agents who used the joint, and its clientele was a mix of movie celebrities and workmen. More recently, the Crossrail project wrecked its business by putting hoardings all around it, so Mario beat the odds by opening a gin pop-up in the evenings called the Star at Night. He held out for as long as he could. When he died every Sohoite paid respect, and the Soho Waiters' Race was held in his honour.

Although technically bordered by four streets, Soho is as much a state of mind as a neighbourhood. For such a tiny area it still has a complexity of zones, roughly four quadrants that include artistic, manufacturing, fashion and dining parts, along with theatres, screening rooms and churches. It once had a hat warehouse and a soup factory, a French quarter, an Italian quarter, a Spanish quarter. It had pubs like the Helvetia (used by typesetters), the Bath House, the Glass House, the Crown & Apple Tree, the Bricklayer's Arms, the George and the Intrepid Fox, all of which are now gone.

I don't know how Kettner's started—

ARTHUR BRYANT: Ah, well, I do. It was originally a series of four Georgian townhouses, and was first opened as a restaurant by Auguste Kettner, the chef to Napoleon III, in 1867. It has survived four kings, a queen and the Blitz, and was popular with Edward VII, Lillie Langtry, Agatha Christie, Bing Crosby and inevitably Oscar Wilde, who had liaisons in the private rooms. Is there any place in Central London where he didn't try to have it off?

Kettner's once hosted risqué parties and landed on its uppers in the 1980s when, despite its opulent surroundings, it became a pizza bar.

JANICE LONGBRIGHT: Perhaps the location was a problem—Romilly Street, Soho, opposite a car park—although its champagne bar was unpretentious and its waiters sang (sometimes annoyingly) right through the lunch service.

ARTHUR BRYANT: I liked that the gentlemen's urinals had plateglass panels angled over your shoes. They've now been removed. I suppose today's gentlemen can't be trusted not to kick them in.

JANICE LONGBRIGHT: Many of Soho's pubs still have a kind of scruffily intelligent charm and are very atmospheric, especially when neon reflects on the wet pavements outside. Sort of romantic. The Coach & Horses was famous for being hosted by London's rudest landlord, Norman Balon, but it also happens to be the drinking hole of the Prince Edward Theatre's scenery-shifters.

ARTHUR BRYANT: Apparently someone overheard a huge tattooed shifter at the bar telling his mate, 'I says to 'im, call yourself a bleeding Polonius? I could shit better speeches to Laertes than that.'

JANICE LONGBRIGHT: Can you verify your anecdote?

ARTHUR BRYANT: Of course not. I don't need to bother with verification.

JANICE LONGBRIGHT: Says one of the nation's top detectives.

A dwindling number of old vendors still exist in Soho—the Algerian Coffee Stores, Bar Italia, Lina Stores and Ronnie's flower stall in a market dating back to 1778—but most have now gone. There were other odd niche shops in the area like the film-props store, the window-display shop, the chef's-uniforms store and 58 Dean Street Records, which only stocked old film soundtracks. It was run by a camp old queen called Derek and a pair of young identical twins. Derek would see customers off from his store with a cheery, 'Give my love to the wife and kids!' before confiding to the customers, 'Bruce and the poodles.'

Although it's not in Soho, I have to include one more place, as it was close to my heart.

My mother loved Blustons Gowns because she felt it harked back to a time when strong corsetry and a good gusset were all you needed under a pleated skirt. She told me, 'It's so refreshing to find a trapeze dress with some give in the armpits.'

Blustons was in Kentish Town Road, and for three-quarters of a century the locals could nip in and pick up a shapeless fawn cardie with bobbles on, the kind old ladies once favoured. It had old-fashioned signs in the window like 'Pac-a-Macs for the Larger Lady' and 'Full Figure Frocks for Easter Brides.' Before Blustons I never knew what a poodle skirt was. I'm still not entirely sure I know now.

Blustons was opened in 1932 by Jane and Samuel Bluston, a Jewish couple who had both been sent as teenagers from Russia to the UK in the 1890s to escape persecution. They met in an East

End sweatshop and got married in 1902. Blustons was up and running before the First World War brought austerity and rationing that saw the shop allowed to sell only utility clothing. During the Second World War German shrapnel shattered one of the display windows. Albert, the couple's son, was born there as the war ended. Samuel remembered having to control the number of women coming into the shop on the day rationing finished.

Stepping inside the place was like going back in time. Once most high streets had a store like this with a double front and half a dozen assistants. The fact that its closure made the national papers is indicative of how rare such 'gown shops' are now. Internet shopping killed Blustons' trade. As one of the owners said just before it closed its doors, 'These days we mostly cater for older West Indian ladies and drag queens. There's not much call for a court shoe in a size twelve.'

The fascia was kept and it's now a vintage charity shop. I'm a large size and have a particular fondness for 1950s frocks, so the place fitted me like a glove (white satin, elbow length, evening).

Bottom Shields &
Other Stories

Arthur Bryant: Let's go back to early London with a friend of mine who knows a lot about walls. Say hello to Catherine Porter, a custodian at Sir John Soane's Museum and creator of its hit seedcast.

Catherine Porter: Podcast.

Arthur Bryant: Yes, that thing. I tried to locate it but couldn't find a station below Radio Luxembourg.

Catherine Porter: I keep telling you, Arthur, it's online. I love your scarf.

Arthur Bryant: Do you really? I knitted it myself. I didn't quite know when to stop.

Catherine Porter: Is it meant to have sleeves? By the way, you've still got that book I lent you.

ARTHUR BRYANT: Which one was it?

CATHERINE PORTER: *The History of Office Partitions,* the illustrated edition.

ARTHUR BRYANT: Ah, yes. I'm afraid I got curry on it.

CATHERINE PORTER: How much curry? More than last time?

ARTHUR BRYANT: Ooh, a lot more. An incredible amount, actually. I have several innovative ideas for cleaning it, though. You'd better get on with your bit, I don't want to put you off.

CATHERINE PORTER: It's easy to forget that our two-thousand-year-old metropolis was as much of a walled city as any in Spain or Poland. As it continues to expand, the edges blur ever more, but there are still sections of the original Roman wall to be seen all around.

Although the exact reason for the wall's construction is unknown, it was probably built to provide defence and security to London citizens, and represented the growing status of the city. Come inside if you want protection, stay out there and be a peasant if not.

The wall was started in the late second or early third century, around eighty years after the construction of the city's fort in 120 CE, and finished at the end of the fourth century. It was one of the last major building projects undertaken by the Romans before they got fed up with the lousy weather and headed home in 410 CE.

It was constructed of Kentish ragstone and may have been built as a reaction to the invasion of northern Britain by the Picts, who briefly overran Hadrian's Wall in the 180s. Its central fort was the home of the official guard of the Governor of Britain, and housed around a thousand men in a series of barrack blocks.

The seven gates that were added matched the Roman roads and remain in name only. The crumbling statues of King Lud and his two sons which formerly stood on Ludgate now grace the porch of St Dunstan-in-the-West on Fleet Street. At Ludgate Circus, medallions of King Lud can be found up on its roofline and over doorways.

There *is* a substantial chunk of the wall you can still see. Set immediately north of the Tower of London, right on Tower Hill, it's one of its most impressive surviving sections, if you're impressed by walls.

Today, many of the buildings which had formerly hidden it have been cleared away, and you can get a clear view of what's left. The wall remained standing through a long period when the city was largely abandoned. It was repaired in the late Anglo-Saxon period and survived to become an important feature of the city at the time of the Norman Conquest.

In about 1300 a new postern gateway through the wall was built close to the edge of the Tower of London moat; it later slid down the moat bank and can be seen at the end of the underpass under the main road.

In fact, there are plenty of pieces to explore and even those that have vanished, as at Bishopsgate, have wall plaques commemorating the sites. The odd juxtaposition of Roman wall and houses can still take you by surprise.

Aldgate was the oldest gatehouse into London, built decades before the rest of the wall that subsequently adjoined it. It was also one of the busiest gatehouses, standing on the main Roman road to Colchester. During its 1,600-year history it was rebuilt three times and finally pulled down in 1761 to improve traffic access. Geoffrey Chaucer lived in the rooms over the gate from

1374. At the time he was working as a customs official at one of the local ports.

London slowly slipped its moorings, moving from east to west, shifting away from its walled origins as rich merchants sought clean new land away from the overcrowded streets. But it always left behind traces.

ARTHUR BRYANT: Thanks for the bit on walls, Catherine, I can always edit it out. Now, what do you see from the window of a plane flying over London at night?

CATHERINE PORTER: I see darkness and light. The thoroughfares like glowing arteries, and patches of the city as black as lost pages of history.

ARTHUR BRYANT: Oh, you siren. You have won my heart.

CATHERINE PORTER: I'm not sure I want it, Arthur. I imagine it's in a bit of a state.

ARTHUR BRYANT: Then thank you for coming in, there's tea and custard creams in the corner.

Hyde Park, Green Park, Regent's Park, Battersea Park—at night they're all absent from London's map of light. North of these is the largest, darkest blank of all: Hampstead Heath.

The heath was once densely forested, home to boar-hunting prehistoric tribes. The Romans drove a road through it, and those fearing the Black Death hid on it. In 1584 a great beacon was built there to warn us if the Spanish Armada landed. An elm tree grew so huge that inside its hollow trunk was room for forty-two steps, leading to a viewing platform that held twenty.

Whenever the end of the world was predicted, Londoners

came to the heath. In 1780 the Gordon Rioters headed here, but were diverted with free beer at the Spaniards Inn. Literary clubs met, duellists fought and a court of law was transferred here under canvas during the Great Plague, creating 'Judges' Walk.' To this day, the heath still hosts bank holiday fairs—Virginia Woolf was horribly snooty about them; there's a surprise—and 'Hampsteads' is still rhyming slang for teeth. Or at least it is in my house.

It's easy to forget that England is a temperate zone and so London, at its centre, gets no real extremes of weather. You can get sunburned in Scotland and freeze to death in Devon but most Londoners are within a steady range of temperature. None of which explains our passion for open-air swimming. London has seventeen open-air pools and lidos, many very large and in beautiful surroundings.

But for over four hundred years people swam in the Thames. Famous swimmers included Charles Dickens, Stanley Spencer and the actress Margaret Rutherford. (Rutherford got about by train and was in the habit of asking the engine driver to warm her teapot.)

By the 1930s, there were bathing houses, floating baths and beaches on the river, and numerous lidos across the capital. The Thames is now deemed too dangerous to swim in downstream of Putney. The strong tides are riskier than pollution. Every year there are a few drownings. Some bright spark always decides to have a swim on New Year's Eve. They usually find the corpse somewhere around Rotherhithe.

The heyday of the lidos was the 1930s, when getting a suntan suddenly became fashionable. Before this it was something only the working classes got from manual labour. In the song 'Children of the Ritz,' Noël Coward wrote that they were 'Mentally congealed lilies of the field . . . [they] lie in flocks along the rocks because [they] have to get a tan.'

A common feature of the urban lidos was a blue jelly-mould fountain in which kids could play. Recently, paranoia over accident lawsuits has closed them off behind railings.

Even Old Street in Shoreditch used to have a 'lido' of its own, after a fashion. In the seventeenth century the area was famous for duck-hunting (as was Soho, hence the names of pubs like the Dog & Duck). The land was marshy and crisscrossed with streams, but so many people drowned in Old Street's so-called 'Perilous Pond' that it was bought in 1743 and became an open-air swimming pool. Its name changed to 'Parlous Pool,' then 'Peerless Pool.' A shilling bought your way into its swanky marble changing rooms. For the next hundred years people swam there in summer and ice-skated in winter when it froze over. The nearby Peerless Street still commemorates the site of London's early lido.

The lido on Parliament Hill probably has the most attractive sylvan setting, but the Oasis in Covent Garden is arguably London's most famous outdoor pool and featured in many films, memorably in *Entertaining Mr Sloane*.

Of course London had many more elegant Victorian pools under cover, and I spent so much time in them as a child it's a wonder I didn't succumb to chlorine poisoning.

Right, that's all I have on lidos. For this next bit I needed someone who knows about the history of theatre, but I didn't want a luvvie, I wanted someone who gets his hands dirty. This is Dudley Salterton, who has been an entertainer for about a hundred years. Dudley, you're still performing around the country, incredibly. What do you look for in your stage shows?

DUDLEY SALTERTON: Usually an armchair. I still do my variety act, ladder out of a newspaper, doves from unlikely places, red-hot poker through the arm, but I'm not allowed to saw a lass in half anymore since my prescription changed.

So you've already mentioned Harry Potter's platform and Sherlock Holmes's study, but you can add another fictional address to them: 186 Fleet Street, next to St Dunstan's Church, near the doughnut shop. It's the story of how a trashy novel became an urban legend.

I'd normally do this bit with a fez on.

Come back with me to the year 1847, when a nightmare figure sprang to life in a story titled *The String of Pearls: A Romance*, published in eighteen weekly parts. It was in Edward Lloyd's *The People's Periodical and Family Library*, probably written by a lad called James Rymer, but others helped him. Unfortunately it's not a wonderful British invention at all; it was first circulated as a supposedly true story on the streets of Paris.

The tale made its way across the Channel to London, with victims ending up around the corner from Fleet Street in Bell Yard, where a pie shop was situated. The gruesome tale of Sweeney Todd and his wife turning people into pies touched more of a nerve in London. Before the serial was even completed it had been adapted as a melodrama for the Britannia Theatre, Hoxton. From that show we get Todd's once-famous catchphrase, 'I'll polish 'im off.'

Like a lot of legends, the tale of Sweeney Todd began as a 'true' story but gradually fitted itself into history, so the pie shop and barber shop are now meant to have existed. As an entertainer I thoroughly approve of turning fiction into fact.

The complete tale was finally published in book form in 1850. Seven hundred and thirty-two pages of melodrama, and the incredible thing is that even now it's completely unreadable. An illegally pirated version appeared in America, which was a common problem for books and plays back then, and that cemented its mythological status.

By this time Todd had become a bogeyman used to terrify children. There are two reasons for this—first, there was a version of the story that had been floating around London forever, a mixture of various bogeyman ideas involving murder and cannibalism, so that shut the toddlers up. Second, the original authors put a preface to the book claiming it was all true, like the ones Dennis Wheatley used for his witchcraft novels. The play was a barnstormer and continued the illusion, warning folk that it was founded on real events. All codswallop, I suppose, but it *felt* right. It was the time of sensation journalism and the penny dreadfuls. Like the internet.

There were five film versions. The most famous was *Sweeney Todd: The Demon Barber of Fleet Street,* starring Tod Slaughter. He'd changed his name, you know—from Norman Slaughter. He carried on touring the production on stage for decades. He had some lungs on him. He'd roll his eyes and bellow his speeches right to the back of the room. He stormed through venues like the Deptford Empire, thrilling London audiences, and sometimes the play was paired with another melodrama, *Maria Marten, or The Mystery of the Red Barn.*

In the 1950s the composer Malcolm Arnold even turned the tale into a ballet. Finally the playwright Christopher Bond upended the myth in the seventies, turning Todd into an anti-hero sent into a murderous rage by the seduction of his wife. Now the tale made sense to a modern world. Then in composer Stephen Sondheim's hands it became a Grand Guignol opera.

Sweeney's makeover was complete; he joined the small group of characters who were fictional but became real, along with Sherlock Holmes, Dracula and Jack the Ripper, who did the reverse, ending up on the stage and screen.

But there's another Jack we barely remember now: Spring-Heeled Jack.

With compressed springs on his boots and claws attached to

his hands, he supposedly bounced and clawed his way around London in the autumn of 1837. He frightened young lasses in the skin of a bear or in a bat costume and breathed blue and white flames as he scaled tall walls. What fascinates me is that Jack, the 'Terror of London,' was seen attacking women by so many people and continued to do so for forty years. He was created to strike an irrational fear into hearts, like Sweeney Todd or Brexit.

Spring-Heeled Jack soon made his way into comics, books and plays . . . and there was a film too, starring—you won't believe this—Tod Slaughter. By this time, Jack was sprouting wings, hooves and a tight red superhero suit.

There were other bogeymen, like the Whipping Toms, who struck in different decades, the first in 1681 in Central London, the second in Hackney in 1712. They would dash up to women, pull up their skirts and slap their buttocks with a cry of 'Spanko!'

More disturbing was the London Monster, who supposedly jabbed more than fifty women's buttocks with a knife or needle, beginning in 1788, and was reported to have blades attached to his knees or hidden in posies of flowers. Londoners went into one of their panics—there were reports of women wearing metal bottom shields over their pantaloons—and a florist named Rhynwick Williams spent six years in jail despite being innocent. But some of the victims confessed that they hadn't really been attacked, so it's likely that the London Monster never existed at all. That didn't stop reports of copycat crimes occurring for years after. Such bouts of public hysteria often occur in troubled times.

The bogeymen of today are a bloody sight more insidious. They come from urban legends on social networks. The young don't believe my ghost stories anymore. When I was overtired I used to let Arthur do part of my act where he played—I say 'played'—an old man sitting by the fireplace, and he'd tell a ghost story called 'The Dismembered Corpse' to a small child sitting on his knee.

They don't do it now because everyone thinks *paedophile*—what's wrong with them all? Arthur had the little ones all agog and at the end he made them scream by taking his teeth out. I stopped allowing it because I couldn't afford the dry-cleaning bills.

If I catch anyone using a phone when I'm on I don't have them thrown out. I bring 'em up on stage to participate in my 'Bang a Six Inch Nail Up the Nose' trick.

25

A Sinister Briefcase &
Other Stories

ARTHUR BRYANT: I've been told to go carefully here and not upset anyone's sensibilities or I'll get stamped.

JOHN MAY: I think you mean cancelled.

ARTHUR BRYANT: That too. So, where do you go in London if you want to kill yourself?

JOHN MAY: Oh Lord.

ARTHUR BRYANT: North London's Archway Bridge became so popular that a wire cage was constructed around it. But in the last few years Number 1 Poultry in Cheapside gained an unfortunate reputation as a jumping-off spot for London's depressed number-crunchers, several of whom have taken a flying leap from the building's high buttresses.

The present structure on the site was completed in 1997 and is a postmodern mélange of forms and colours that were dated before the building was finished. The pink and yellow limestone stripes and blocks look better in rain or at night, or possibly blown up.

Who would have thought that this is one of London's very oldest addresses? There has *always* been a building on this spot, right since London began, and for that reason it's worth a visit. In fact number 1 Poultry is so old that it was nicknamed the 'Heart of the City.' It rose in the centre of the Square Mile, covering what had once been the Walbrook, the stream that had fed the ancient Roman town of Londinium, part of the ghost map that exists beneath the pavement's surface.

First a Roman market grew around it; then pig farms and wool markets were replaced by the brilliantly named church of St Benet Sherehog. It had a paupers' graveyard where the bodies had been thrust so hastily into their coffins that often the nails pierced their limbs.

Much later a hatmaker's was opened on the site, but the mercuric solution used to soften fur drove milliners mad, which is where the Lewis Carroll idea of the 'mad hatter' comes from, and the building came down. In its place rose the fabulous perpendicular elegance of the Mappin & Webb jewellery store, inset with terracotta panels showing a procession of monarchs. Reminiscent of the St Pancras Hotel, it had shops at its base in keeping with the rest of this very 'London' street. The great triangular edifice could be seen from the Bank of England, and could easily have been repurposed for the modern world.

But no; after mysteriously slipping through its preservation order, the grand building was bulldozed. For a brief period in the nineties faddist architects hated all things Victorian. Sir James Stirling was the master of big red tubes and green triangles, so the Mappin & Webb building was demolished and replaced with today's pastel toybox.

Unfortunately it was completed after the postmodernism craze had collapsed into ridicule. Now marooned by changing taste and fortune, the top floor houses a restaurant and roof garden frequented by money-shufflers. At least the site remained occupied through the centuries, and will no doubt always contain a building long after trend-chasing architects have hung up their black roll-neck jumpers.

| | |

Like most Londoners I never get around to doing the things tourists do. I've mentally ticked off the things I never want to do again, like Madame Tussauds and the mercifully moribund 'Blitz Experience,' in which you paid money to sit in a corrugated iron shed listening to a tape of being bombed.

Then there are the experiences that don't sound terribly appealing. I'd assumed that the Cabinet War Rooms would offer up a handful of grim windowless cells linked by a few concrete corridors and a gift shop flogging wartime calendars. But it's also the Churchill Museum—and it's the latter that really makes the difference to your trip. Simply, these are two of the most surprising and unique museums in London.

It's the combination of real historical artefacts and intelligent interactive technology that make the visit so enriching and enjoyable. First you descend into the War Rooms themselves, with a good audio guide that sets the scene. The rooms are atmospheric and sensitively lit, and really catch the flavour of the wartime era. Even the wax dummies of staff are placed in weirdly realistic poses—one soldier is looking in a cupboard, and others are caught in mundane tasks. It's like the PCU on a slow day.

The second half is an organic extension of the first and is packed to the rafters with intelligent information. This includes technology even I can operate, with interactive charts, footage, timelines and mementoes. There's lots of archival material, from the Churchillian sense of humour to a test that requires you to measure your opinions and preconceptions of Churchill as a leader, including his racial motivations, his political malleability (he switched from being a Liberal to a Conservative) and his beliefs.

There's a surprising section on his political radicalism—he was well ahead of the game on immigration and taxing the rich—plus sections on the Boer War, Sidney Street, Empire, India and partition, the First World War, the disastrous decisions, the wilderness years and his Second World War actions, with documentary footage and an interactive timeline that takes you through his life.

The way the museum uses these interactive tools is unusual. It's data-heavy but leavened with artistic flourishes and humour— who knew that Churchill invented the velour romper suit? It's an example of art adding something to history. There's too much to take in on one visit. By the way, Winston makes an unlikely appearance in his onesie in a mosaic set in the entrance floor of the National Gallery, illustrating the word 'Defiance.' He's taking on what appears to be a mountain lion in a multi-tiered crown. The beast is clearly standing on a chunk of Europe and Churchill is waving two fingers at him. Some things never change.

| | |

On the way to the museum one passes sights Londoners rarely stop in front of, mainly Buckingham Palace and Horse Guards Parade. If you go early in the morning there's hardly anyone in St James's Park, which is London's oldest and never shuts. Walking down from Green Park it can feel like being in an open-air zoo, with cheeky urban squirrels racing beside the odd fox and fifteen varieties of wildfowl and pelicans, which have been there since 1664. It used to be more exotic; James I once kept crocodiles in the lake.

As you continue through the long dewy grass the misted palace appears before you, white and heavy, low and rectangular, like a great block of ice.

The park is full of peaceful nooks and is a great place to come and sit if you just want to think for a while. I head there whenever Raymondo is annoying me, so I go a lot, just to look at the gleaming domes and turrets of Whitehall. From this vantage point it's hard to believe you're in the centre of a teeming metropolis.

London has more places where you can sit and feel calm than most cities. Even at Piccadilly Circus it's always possible to find a quiet seat in some nearby greenery.

The park-keeper's lodge in St James's Park looks like Hansel and Gretel might have stumbled across it. On the other side of Horse Guards Parade there's Whitehall and traffic, but hardly anyone bothers to cut through the park. You'd wind up in Victoria, and who wants to go there?

Walking to Horse Guards Parade early when there are no tourists around is a strange experience—you feel as if you're in some Balkan outpost off the easyJet map. The great vista of the parade ground is a little agoraphobia-inducing. It's very tranquil and the only people you see are police, which is when you suddenly remember that the price of freedom is eternal vigilance.

Horse Guards Parade was formerly the site of the Palace of Whitehall's tiltyard. Here jousting tournaments were held in the time of Henry VIII, and you can imagine the speed with which the horses approached one another. The parade is also the scene of annual celebrations of the birthday of our Great and Good QEII. It's been used for all kinds of reviews, parades and ceremonies since the seventeenth century, yet those who live and work in Central London probably only ever see it on television.

Now I'm passing you on to my partner John May, as he explored an infamous part of London lore that I regretfully missed due to a rather fraught chiropodist's appointment. Over to you, John.

JOHN MAY: Thanks, Arthur. It wouldn't have been fraught if you hadn't attacked him.

ARTHUR BRYANT: I knocked over a tray of scalpels, that's all. He couldn't play the cello for a fortnight but otherwise he healed very quickly.

JOHN MAY: In 1874 criminal artefacts were housed in what was known as the Black Museum. It was filled with the evidence of violent crime and comprised two back rooms in Scotland Yard which only admitted police officers. For years there had been talk of moving its contents to a permanent exhibition, but there were problems finding an appropriate space and an appropriate voice for such an endeavour. After all, criminals should not be honoured with museums. How could a museum of crime ever work in London?

The curators of the Black Museum are taking a sensitive and intelligent approach that places the crimes in their proper contexts. Created with the support of the Metropolitan Police Service and the Mayor's Office for Policing and Crime, the exhibition considers the changing nature of crime and advances in detection over the last 140 years, as well as the challenges faced in policing the capital, such as terrorism, drugs and rioting.

It's an ongoing project. There are currently two sections: first, a re-creation of the original museum, followed by a looser canter through case histories and general themes. There are all the usual suspects: Haigh, Crippen, Christie, Ellis, trunk murderers and poisoners, guns and nooses, knives and diaries, spying equipment, drugs and an umbrella gun.

They also have the Krays' execution suitcase, a neat hide attaché case fitted with clips and springs that held a hypodermic needle, which could be released by a cord to inject a dose of hydrogen cyanide through a hole in the case's side when swung against someone's leg. There's a crossbow armed with evil steel-tipped arrows too, bought at Lillywhites.

Yet to me the first surprise was how mundane and small everything appeared to be. Could this ridiculous little knife really have cut a throat? Could this tiny pistol have actually shot someone through the heart? The Victorian criminal past is revealed as a grey and deeply depressing place—and perhaps that's the point; we know that real crime is usually pathetic and makeshift, and has none of the grandeur given to it by cinema.

In the latter half of the exhibition, the cut-off date for these artefacts of crime is currently the mid-1970s, to protect those still suffering the after-effects of violence, and the focus is London-based. An exception to that deadline is made for terrorist activity; indeed, the most horrifying item on display is a reproduction of a case containing a nail-bomb. It recalls various devastating attacks in London, from the IRA, a lone fanatic and Islamist terrorists, which are all within the collective London memory. Many capitals have suffered one or two attacks but London has had to deal with them serially.

For me, two items in the collection stand out. First, Charley Peace's collapsible burglary ladder: Peace was a legendary criminal who, somewhat incredibly, appeared in a popular children's comic strip as a master burglar. And secondly the binoculars with spring-loaded spikes which later featured in the film *Horrors of the Black Museum;* I'd always assumed that they were mythical, but no, there they are, along with other objects sporting concealed blades. They still look like a cheap stage prop.

The Black Museum is now called the Crime Museum, and is filled with brief histories of sad little crimes and their faded mementoes—none of them remotely glorifying violence. Denied a more carnivalesque approach, I came away with melancholy thoughts of prosaic personal tragedies rather than the awe of shocking murder.

Now the bad news; at the time of writing, we can go and visit it, but you can't. The Black Museum (the public's preferred name) is due to be added to exhibits in the Museum of London when it finally moves to Smithfield.

26

The Avoidance of Tablecloths & Other Stories

A RTHUR BRYANT: In the course of developing this project, I found a few more notes from my old friend Raymond Kirkpatrick, the gods rest his soul. I must apologize for his opinions in advance and am told I have to supply a 'trigger warning,' whatever that is.

RAYMOND KIRKPATRICK: There's a load of toss talked about London sometimes, usually from pustular youths who come up from the Shire thinking they're the first people ever to mince along the city streets dressed like Harry Styles. After three weeks of being here they become experts on London just because they've managed to negotiate the tube system all the way from Old Street to Covent Garden. Well, when they get lippy in my classes I tell them I was born forty-seven years ago just off Piccadilly Circus and I've forgotten more than they'll ever know, so they can either piss off back to the wrong part of Kent or keep their traps shut and learn something useful.

First of all, you have to eat something—look at you. But remember this: the smarter a London restaurant looks, the dodgier it's likely to be.

All the best London restaurants are scruffy. The ones serving English cuisine may trick you into thinking you're in a carpentry shop or a foundry, but only until you get the bill. Indonesian, Korean, Chinese, Szechuan and Vietnamese gaffs that look like run-down laundromats are usually ace. The general rule of thumb is, if it's got white tablecloths and candlelight, avoid it. The Angus Steak House may look inviting but no real Londoner has ever eaten in one. We don't eat in Mayfair either. The restaurant menus are designed to drain cash from champagne-swilling oligarchs eager to spaff their laundered dosh before hitting the clubs with a noseful of chang. Expect to pay several hundred quid for a plate of hummingbird tongues sprinkled with Louis XIV gold leaf, and tiny desserts served with a vinaigrette of paupers' tears.

Poor Mayfair still wants to be posh but they never thought the bridge and tunnel brigade would arrive to Instagram their desserts and prowl for footballers. The priciest restaurants are reserved for young gentlemen from the UAE who order the most expensive dishes, then play with their phones.

At least there's no dress code anymore. The only place you'll be made to wear a jacket is in a traditional London gentleman's club, and the food in those gloom-chambers is usually a 1950s school dinner sieved through an old sock.

One thing London manages superbly is the great British breakfast. Upmarket restaurants precook their poached eggs and reheat their bacon, whereas transport cafés cook from scratch, and several are total ledges. Pubs don't look like they serve breakfast but quite a few do—I'm not counting Spoons, obviously—and the portions can weigh as much as a small child. Local office workers near me eat in a lunch place that's a sex club by night. Food halls hide cinemas, nightclubs and cabaret bars. A bicycle-repair shop may be a café. A plant nursery is also a restaurant. A restaurant may stage an opera. Theatres are in pubs. Shops are in theatres. Dance classes are in churches. My top three bookstores are hidden in a medical institute, in a library and on a barge.

Also, the things that look old aren't, and the new-looking stuff is old.

Tower Bridge began construction in 1886 and was finished not long before my granddad was born. Some of the nice modern-looking, plain houses you find in London backstreets are in fact in the early Victorian style and may predate Tower Bridge by seventy years. The Gothic Midland Grand Hotel St Pancras was finished in 1876 but looks centuries older than the sleek Savoy Hotel, which opened just over a decade after it.

Not that long ago, probably until the early 1980s, certain London areas were very dangerous. Near railway stations and the river you'd always keep an eye on your wallet.

Once the Thames was an open sewer, and mere proximity to it was enough to kill you. In 1849 campaigner Charles Kingsley was horrified by the environment of Bermondsey residents. The water beneath their windows was stagnant and full of dead fish, cats and dogs. They used it to wash in and drink from.

Arsenic was everywhere, used to dye fabrics and artificial flowers green. Painters died of lead poisoning, factory girls suffered phosphorus burns from making matches and radiation burns from coating watch dials in luminous paint. Children worked in reeking factories on the riverbanks with mercury so toxic that their skeletons turned bright green. In 2008 their poor emerald-hued bones were displayed at the Wellcome Collection on Euston Road.

Now the Thames is home to fish, swans, cormorants, geese, herons and the odd lost dolphin, and you can run its reaches without being poisoned. We'll never again name a street Shit-born Alley; we call our new housing developments 'Number One Midtown' and put in poor doors.

| | |

Londoners are not unfriendly, by the way. After you make the first move and talk to them, you won't get a bloody word in edgeways. But if you become overly friendly they'll say, 'We must get together again sometime,' which means 'You will never see me again.' If they don't want to talk to you it's because you've frightened them by being enthusiastic.

But a good London friend is someone who'll tell you things about yourself no one else would dare and will follow you around like a dog on heat. They're so polite that they'll text you before they ring to ask if it's a good time to call. And if they start asking you if you're all right, like you just got hit by a car or something, you'll know you've made a friend for life.

| | |

There's a lot of great entertainment to be had in London, but it's also where old shows and their stars go to die.

Although I prefer listening to Black Sabbath I used to like the odd play of an evening. Something a bit challenging that you could have a good argument about afterwards. Now our theatres are bunged up with crappy old musicals that have been on for centuries. Don't tell me *Mamma Mia!* and *Les Misérables* are financing the fringe because they're not. *The Book of Mormon* seems to amuse Americans and *Hamilton* will run for the next seventy years so I guess I'll never see the inside of those theatres. *Matilda* is still on; she must have left university years ago. *The Phantom of the Opera* is like a carnival boat ride with added screeching. And if you're willing to pay a couple of hundred quid to see *Harry* sodding *Potter,* you deserve to sit through it. Twice.

| | |

London has too much street furniture. Know why everyone likes the idea of our prewar streets? They weren't filled with visual clutter. Across this city we now have sticks, poles, posts, signboards, arrows, maps, warnings, directions and a million other items of metal street furniture, all rendered obsolete and pointless by GPS. Sir John Betjeman was one of the first to complain; he hated 'the present craze for erecting lampposts like concrete gibbets with corpse lights dangling off them.'

On one corner alone near the British Library, I counted fifteen redundant signs on poles. Are you listening, Mr Mayor? We don't need to be told where things are. We have phones now. We're all in the twenty-first century except Mr Bryant. It's time to simplify things.

I love London but . . . don't get me started.

Like, you open a nice little café and it does all right. You don't need to open 350 more identical branches. What made the first one great was that you cooked there every night instead of swanning about on the telly. I can't tell a compote from a compost but even I can figure that one out!

In the list of annoying things the French have done to us, number one must be the construction of London's Madame Tussauds. There are currently twenty-one such waxworks attractions in her global chain, and I hope the others are less tacky than the one near Baker Street. In 1925 the building happily burned down but a number of items made by Madame Tussaud herself survived, including her moulds for Louis XVI and Marie Antoinette. Perhaps it will burn down again and melt Kim Kardashian's bottom. Although of course that might explode because who knows what's in it. (Just along from the waxworks there used to be a shop called Mad Man Two Swords. God knows what it sold.)

London is packed with cloned attractions like M&M'S World, a place to take your child only if you hate it enough to want its teeth to fall out. And why would you eat a cardboard pizza in a London chain? New York City is the only place for pizza. In a world with fewer and fewer unique experiences, always hold out for something special.

27

A Forgotten Tragedy &
Other Stories

ARTHUR BRYANT: A city is made by its people. When moneyed Londoners grew bored they had a tendency to become mischievous, suing each other over trifles or waging silly bets.

In 1810 Theodore Hook had a wager with a mate, Sam Beazley, that he could make any house in London the most talked-about place within a week. He sent out invitations, orders and letters under the name of Mrs Tottenham at number 54 Berners Street. Suddenly it received visitors by the score. Twelve chimney sweeps, delivery men of all kinds, fishmongers and shoemakers, bakers with wedding cakes, grocers, 2,500 raspberry tarts, an organ carried by six big lads, doctors, lawyers, clergymen calling to visit 'someone dying in the house' . . .

Every officer who could be mustered was enlisted to discourage visitors and disperse the crowd. They were placed at the corners of Berners Street to prevent tradesfolk from advancing towards the house with goods. The street was not cleared until a late hour, as servants of every denomination wanting places had begun to assemble early. More letters had been written to trades-people supposedly from 'persons of quality.'

Then Hook got the rich and famous to visit. Along trotted the Duke of York, the Lord Mayor and, inevitably, the Archbishop of Canterbury. Every night huge crowds gathered around the house and fighting broke out. Eventually the streets around number 54 were brought to a standstill. Hook won his bet but then decided it would be best to vanish on a 'rest cure.' Now the house he made famous is the Sanderson Hotel.

Please welcome today's guest speaker, Fraternity DuCaine, a former PCU officer and the brother of our beloved Liberty Du-Caine, who tragically lost his life at the Unit.

FRATERNITY DUCAINE: Contrary to popular belief, Britain was not all white until the arrival of the *Empire Windrush,* the troopship that brought hundreds of Caribbean people and Polish nationals to London. Their disgraceful treatment at the hands of the authorities in subsequent years resulted in belated apologies and compensations.

Many of the passengers had arrived without developed job skills and had quite reasonably expected to be trained into useful work—after all, they had been brought over to ease our postwar labour shortage. But the reality of a freezing, unfriendly and resentful England came as a shock after the golden portrait of Albion they'd been presented with in books and magazines. The Roman Empire had been multicultural but Black Romans were assumed to be slaves until a discovery was made in York in 1901. A high-ranking woman, the so-called 'Ivory Bangle Lady,' was found buried with her bracelets, pendants and earrings. People of African origin were found at all levels of Roman society, yet when the classicist Mary Beard agreed with this she was hit with a storm of online abuse.

Black people had long lived a kind of shadow existence in Central London, living in so-called 'low society.' Many have commented on their high visibility in William Hogarth's paintings and engravings. The Black slaves who came to London were so protected by a sympathetic public that magistrates despaired of ever catching them.

Did any famous names emerge? It's easy to think of Black Londoners in the present day, but what about in the past? Try this one. Samuel Coleridge-Taylor. Already you're getting mixed messages, and I bet you're not thinking of a Black man. He was born in 1875 in London and died thirty-seven years later of stress-related pneumonia.

Samuel had been named after the poet, and seemed destined for great things. He studied at the Royal College of Music and was hailed as a genius by Edward Elgar. His *Hiawatha's Wedding Feast* from *The Song of Hiawatha* was such a matter of public popularity and personal pride that he and his wife named their son after the fictional warrior. After the full piece had been premiered at the Royal Albert Hall it became one of the most famous and frequently performed pieces of music in England. Sir Arthur Sullivan regarded it a work of brilliance. Samuel toured America and met President Roosevelt.

But despite its staggering success, the composer was broke. He was painfully lacking in confidence and had sold the rights to *Hiawatha* for fifteen guineas. After his death the family received nothing and their penury led to the establishment of the Performing Rights Society.

Too late to help Samuel. His work was staged annually at the Albert Hall before thousands but he didn't live to make a penny from it.

The story of Mary Seacole, the Jamaican nurse who went to the Crimean War, is more well known. She tended to the injured close to the front line and was commended by the British commander-in-chief, but the Crimea campaign bankrupted her and she was soon living in one room in Soho. *The Times* and *Punch* magazine fought to have her losses reimbursed and she rose again, moving in royal circles even though she was required to be the personal masseuse of the Princess of Wales.

By the end of the eighteenth century there were between five and ten thousand people of colour living in London. Still, the image of the 'noble savage' was pervasive and a lack of education kept many in place as servants, although they were by no means at the bottom of the London caste system. Some had been war heroes, some rose in the arts, some had become increasingly visible in local politics, but acceptance was still hampered by racist misconceptions. Despite the fact that London was a cosmopolitan city, few residents had ever seen a person of colour and were shocked when they did. In 1961, Jimi Hendrix was run out of Seattle for daring to be born non-Caucasian and became a star in London, where his race was less of an issue. But it had taken two hundred years to get this far.

If fear of otherness and the loss of status quo hampered the acceptance of ordinary working men and women in their newly adopted communities, it only took a scandal manufactured by the press to create a sense of *ad hominem* outrage.

In the 1920s there was one area of London where newly arrived immigrants were causing much alarmed chatter. The Chinese in Limehouse were assumed to be sinister opium addicts looking to abduct and enslave white women. They were there because laundries were needed to service the merchant ships that docked with only a short time to spare. Writers like Thomas Burke and Sax Rohmer turned the laundries into opium dens and produced feverish fantasies about sinister Chinamen. I'm sure Mr Bryant has more to tell you about that.

There's the problem of institutional indifference where other races are involved. We do our best, but justice drags its feet.

The story of the Denmark Place tragedy is not well known. The Denmark Street area was swinging London's Tin Pan Alley, where everyone from the Kinks to the Rolling Stones tried out their guitars in the shops and studios, and even David Bowie slept in a camper van on the street.

The demolition squads took out most of Denmark Place, a row of battered terraced houses off Charing Cross Road which were devoured by the Crossrail development. And so one of the worst crimes of the twentieth century has become even more forgotten.

The Spanish Rooms were also known as El Hueco ('The Hole'). In 1980 London was still full of unlicensed bars, and this one was on the top floor of 18 Denmark Place. Underneath it was another club, known as Rodo's, a place for London's Colombians to hang out.

An international crowd of more than 150 people filled the rooms on this particular hot August night, talking and dancing behind lethally boarded-up windows and locked fire escapes. This was the night that John 'The Gypsy' Thompson, a small-time Scots crook, accused the barman at the Spanish Rooms of overcharging him for a drink. There was a fight, during which Thompson was booted out. Thompson held the grudge. Hailing a taxi sometime after 2:30 A.M., he headed to an all-night petrol station in Camden Town, then returned to Denmark Place, where he emptied a can of petrol through the letterbox and lit it.

Thirty-seven people were burned alive in the ensuing fire. It moved with incredible speed—firemen found corpses right where the individuals had been standing when the flames appeared. Some of the patrons managed to smash their way into the guitar shop behind and used guitars to break out of the building. It took experts two months to identify all the victims, who came from eight countries.

The bar-room ran parallel to the street, and was long and narrow with an entrance at one end. Access was limited and the wooden staircase to it was very tight. Inside was a row of packed-together bench tables with fixed pew seating. In order to seat yourself, several people had to first slide out to admit you.

There was no doorman; when you rang the bell they would throw the keys down to you. As a drinking den it was no seedier than, say, the Colony or the Troy, and not especially gangsterish, but it had its share of theatricals, so it was lively. There were a dozen or so such clubs around it, all unlicensed.

To put the tragedy in perspective, thirty-one people died in the King's Cross Underground fire. Inquiries, services, documentaries and memorials followed, and Princess Diana unveiled a plaque. At Denmark Place there was no service. The only commemorative plaque in the area is devoted to the inventor of the diving helmet. The people who died were mostly of foreign extraction, victims of a foreseeable tragedy, but because the bar in which they drank was technically illegal there had been no safety checks on it. One disaster is remembered; the other is swept under the rug.

ARTHUR BRYANT: I remember the Denmark Place fire. Nobody in the Met was remotely interested in investigating it. Grab yourself a drink, Fraternity, they're on me. Don't go mad.

The Rowton Houses were not unlike the mean terraces of Denmark Place. These vast, ugly redbrick castles with mean little windows were, according to *Len Deighton's London Dossier*, 'grim places, filled with the coughing of defeated men': a chain of gigantic hostels built across London by an eminent Victorian philanthropist, Lord Rowton. They were intended to grant working males the dignity of decent lodgings.

Constructed from 1892 on, there were six of them, in Vauxhall, Newington Butts, Camden, Whitechapel, Hammersmith and Mount Pleasant. Sixpence a night bought you a bed, and you could wash and shave and purchase useful items. The massive King's Cross hostel on Mount Pleasant had hundreds of little windows not much bigger than portholes. About that building, one unnamed worker said:

> At this bar there are three things they sell for a farthing—milk, matches and vinegar. I bought a farthing's-worth of milk to use at breakfast this morning. For a halfpenny you can get a cup of tea, coffee or cocoa, bread, watercress, onions, marmalade, pickles and butter. The articles to be purchased for a penny are too numerous to mention, but to-day you may get a small plate of cold meat, potatoes and a salad of either cucumber or lettuce with tomatoes, the cost of which will be threepence. The working man dearly loves a salad.

Times have clearly changed. The owners remarked:

> The men cooperate in maintaining good order. It is a striking compliment for them, and at the same time to the civilizing influences of Rowton House, that neither at this House nor at its predecessor in Vauxhall has there ever been any case of a lodger defacing a table, marking a wall, destroying anything or writing any indecent expression anywhere about the buildings.

The hostel in Mount Pleasant stands on the brow of a hill and briefly became a hotel, but was then demolished. I visited it once and was struck by the gloomy narrow corridors and dark, claustrophobic rooms. It was like being trapped in a bad dream, but to many who were used to sleeping on the street it was a safe and happy place. One of the Rowton Houses remains a working hostel at the time of writing; the rather fearsome-looking Arlington House in Camden.

| | |

The missing neighbourhood of Clare Market once ran between Drury Lane and Lincoln's Inn Fields. It was the centre of a web of confusing alleys and backstreets with a reputation for prostitution (for which read female poverty) and hard drinking. In the early 1700s there were at least 107 pleasure houses within it, and William Hogarth used to meet at the Bull's Head Tavern in Clare Market, no doubt to get his best ideas for paintings. There was a chapel at the Lincoln's Inn end that was supposed to bury the dead but left the rotting corpses to pile up in the basement (although they did sell their clothes after first boiling them). In 1844, excavations revealed twelve thousand bodies while the building above was still being used as a casino and a theatre.

So what happened to Clare Market? It was gradually demolished in an effort to improve the area, but now the site is inhabited by the London School of Economics (Mick Jagger and Monica Lewinsky went there, so maybe it's still a little bit scandalous), and the LSE has largely preserved its maze of alleys, courtyards and unexpected bridges, remaining a notoriously difficult area to navigate.

Other disappearing neighbourhoods include Cripplegate, which entirely vanished in one night of the Blitz; Norton Folgate, which ran between Shoreditch and the City of London; Horselydown by Tower Bridge, once known as 'London's Larder'; Ratcliff, known as Sailortown; White City, the site of London's first Olympic park—and Limehouse, London's first Chinatown.

To expand on the point Fraternity made, the writer Thomas Burke penned the luridly racist *Limehouse Nights*. Burke said it was 'a tale of love and lovers that they tell in the low-lit Causeway that slinks from West India Dock Road to the dark waste of waters beyond.' It had a Chinese hero called 'the Chink' and revealed rather too much information about Burke's own predilections, being full of voluptuous pure young girls and corporal punishment.

Incredibly, Burke became regarded as an expert on the Chinese living in London, but his books were hysterical nonsense. The 'Yellow Peril,' an idea that lasted for decades, was built around fantasies of white women being abducted into sexual slavery, but there were just a few streets in Limehouse where the Chinese ran rather ordinary shops, grouping themselves together for protection from thuggish locals.

Thanks to Burke, and Sax Rohmer, the creator of Fu Manchu, visitors to Limehouse went on the lash looking for brothels and opium dens, and there, of course, someone was more than happy to take their money and even stage ridiculously melodramatic street fights for them.

In 1922, a restaurateur named Chen Bao Luan, AKA Brilliant Chang, was hunted down by police and arrested for supplying cocaine to Freda Kempton, a twenty-one-year-old dance hostess, who had died of an overdose. The evidence against Chang was little more than hearsay and he was found innocent after it was proven that Freda was suicidal, but racist suggestions of 'yellow peril' and 'white slavery' hung about him afterwards and the police looked for an excuse to fit him up, eventually finding some cocaine that got him deported.

Chang hadn't done himself any favours with his choice of nickname. The name 'Brilliant' was popular among Victorian toffs and the surname was slang for cocaine.

Limehouse may be gone but the idea of the long-vanished neighbourhood operating as London's home of exotic vice and white slavery has somehow managed to linger in the public mind to this day on TV shows and in novels.

| | |

Modern-day street markets are very different to how Clare Market would have been. Once such places provided a direct connection between producers and buyers, inside the city walls and without. General produce was cheaper but of variable quality, and many shopped at stalls out of necessity, especially later in the afternoon when produce was less fresh and prices fell.

In 1974 Covent Garden closed its market and moved to a less congested neighbourhood, but until then the impoverished students who lived in the surrounding streets could still buy fruit and vegetables half-price just before closing time.

Now markets like Borough and Columbia Road, Brixton Village and Spitalfields offer faux-rustic gourmand treats to middle-class browsers while those looking for food bargains do so in pristine hyperstores. The markets have a hold on the London heart but they need local residents to keep them alive.

The Street That Didn't
Exist & Other Stories

ARTHUR BRYANT: Go on, admit it. If you're over forty, right after you heard about the Hatton Garden robbery you thought of Sid James and gelignite and vans roaring out of post offices. You secretly think it's a bit cool robbing safety-deposit boxes. It's old-school drop-it-copper-and-nobody-gets-hurt thieving in the grand tradition of the Great Train Robbery.

There's a complex hidden world in the jewellery quarter of Hatton Garden that got more attention in 2015, after it became the site of the biggest heist in British history.

The humble houses of Hatton Garden attract tall stories. There's a lot of talk about abandoned railway platforms, derelict churches, wartime bunkers, old passages built by monks and the remains of London's second-largest river, the Fleet. Now, much of this needs to be taken with a pinch of salt, but we do know that in Hatton Garden itself there are over sixty retail jewellery shops and a great many small workshops that can only be accessed by those in the trade. Narrow underlit stairwells lead to tiny rooms with angled floors, and if you are recognized on the

CCTV the first of several steel doors might open, but each has to lock shut before the next can be accessed. There are heavily guarded underground vaults filled with safety-deposit boxes and stores of gold and silver. They house the output of the steel-lined workshops where specialist items are made to order.

In Hatton Garden's secure basements goldsmiths use centuries-old methods and Hasidic diamond merchants sit examining gems. Once, before the war, diamond deals were conducted openly on street corners or across tables in the little kosher cafés that existed in the area. Now the latest high-tech equipment has been installed to prevent robbery—but clearly it doesn't always work. The perpetrators of the Hatton Garden heist were senior-age robbers genuinely pulling off one last job. They were caught because they didn't know that digital cameras could read number plates.

The Mayfair smash-and-grab has long been considered a bit more gentlemanly than regular crime, even if it just involves Sid James with a brick or a complicated system of disguised postal workers unloading sacks. But robberies are on the wane. The masked robber with the bag marked 'Swag' has been defeated by high-tech security.

Here to remind you of London's place in old films is Nathan Buff, a film critic who's a lovely chap but rarely talks of anything else. You have to escape from him after half an hour. You know how some blokes get.

NATHAN BUFF: Thank you, Arthur. You have the look of Alastair Sim in *Hue and Cry*, do you know that? And that sergeant of yours, Janice Longbright: very Diana Dors, I've always thought.

The temptation to set films in the Hatton Garden area is strong. Heists have always featured in British film history, from *The Lavender Hill Mob* (sublime) to *The Great St Trinian's Train Rob-*

bery (ridiculous). Stanley Baker starred in Peter Yates's excellent *Robbery*, and more recently Jason Statham turned up in the fact-based *The Bank Job*, in which safety-deposit boxes turn out to contain evidence of a royal scandal.

The buildings in these old British films revealed much about middle-class London, from the sturdy banks, jewellery shops and the grand insurance companies of Holborn to the elegant stucco terraces of Belgravia.

ARTHUR BRYANT: I find myself watching just to study our architectural heritage.

NATHAN BUFF: Whereas I find myself watching for starlets like Liz Fraser and Sabrina. I've written a monograph on the engineering of the postwar brassiere.

As for locations, starting at the top of the social structure there's *The Crown*, with Goldsmiths' Hall and Lancaster House standing in for Buckingham Palace, *Howards End* filmed in St James's, *Wilde* shot in Mayfair and Kensington, and plenty of Sherlockian dramas filmed in Chelsea, Bloomsbury and the Thames Valley.

Somerset House was the most frequently used spot in London for period movies because of its atmospheric enclosed spaces and its unobstructed skyline—the Tower of London provided something similar until office blocks were constructed behind Tower Green. *The Elephant Man* was the last film to be shot around the warehouses of Shad Thames before most of them were torn down.

On the lower rungs of the social ladder, old Soho turns up in *Mona Lisa*, *Death Line* and many other movies featuring hookers, strippers and pimps. In *The Small World of Sammy Lee*, strip-club host Anthony Newley has five hours to pay off a debt before he gets razored, and desperately dashes through the seedy Soho streets on his fool's errand. The film was given an 'X' certificate for 'coarse language.'

In Jules Dassin's superb *Night and the City* we're in tiny Goodwin's Court just off St Martin's Lane, as second-rate conman Richard Widmark tries to save his own neck. Cockney photographer Michael York talent-spots Lynn Redgrave in Carnaby Street in *Smashing Time*, then photographs Rita Tushingham beside the Regent's Canal. And photographer David Hemmings spots glamorous Vanessa Redgrave in Savile Row in *Blow-Up*.

Suburban London turns up a lot, too. A blowsily over-the-hill Beryl Reid sucks a Zoom lolly in her 'Can you see through this?' dress in *Entertaining Mr Sloane*, filmed in Camberwell Old Cemetery in Peckham Rye. The distinctly downmarket *Carry On* films were shot out in Middlesex and Ealing because nobody could afford to travel far from the studios.

Greenwich stood in for every imaginable style and era, from nineteenth-century Russia in Ken Russell's *The Music Lovers* to the crooks' caper *Layer Cake*, *The Madness of King George* and *Sunday Bloody Sunday*.

By the time we reach the East End, the Royal Oak pub in Columbia Road features in *The Krays* and the wharves that will be replaced by Canary Wharf make a farewell appearance in *The Long Good Friday*.

Vera Drake, *Sparrows Can't Sing* and *To Sir, With Love* are issue films about backstreet abortionists, troubled teens and council-flat tenants, and are set where the spivs and tarts of Limehouse and the Isle of Dogs brawled and fell in love. It was even rumoured that the Kray twins turned up as extras in *Sparrows Can't Sing*, but I've been through it frame by frame and it's not true. The back-to-back slums went long ago and there are no more pubs where Saturday night always ends in a fight.

The further out you head, towards Beckton, Silvertown and Stratford East, you get a rougher type of thug in *Bullet Boy, Spivs* and *I Hired a Contract Killer*. Keep going and you reach the settings of gangster films like *Lock, Stock & Two Smoking Barrels* and *Love, Honour & Obey*. London's social order, layer by layer, can be reconstructed in celluloid.

A number of films feature an astonishing array of London locations, from *Genevieve* to *The Sandwich Man* and *The Horse's Mouth*. In *The Fallen Idol*, set in a Belgravia embassy, Ralph Richardson shares a secret with a lonely child, and seeing London in 1948 is a revelation; not the East End of bomb sites and cheery shopkeepers, but the unharmed quarters of mansion houses and wide empty streets that still feel oddly local, especially when Richardson espies a charlady and a chimney sweep in the street below.

It's reassuring to see your own world reflected on film. A personal favourite is the night-time South London of *Nil By Mouth*, amazingly photographed through foregrounded layers of smeary glass. I wouldn't want to live there, mind.

Arthur, I have tickets for the new Richard Curtis romantic comedy if you'd like them.

ARTHUR BRYANT: Thank you, Nathan, but I'd rather spend two hours on a kidney dialysis machine. Are there any famous fictional addresses you can think of in London films?

NATHAN BUFF: The most obvious one that springs to mind is the non-existent tube station 'Hobbs End' that features heavily in *Quatermass and the Pit*.

ARTHUR BRYANT: You could have told me earlier. I spent years looking for that station.

There are imaginary London addresses scattered throughout literature, but there's also a real street in London that never actually existed, in the sense that one minute it wasn't there, then it was, and then it was gone again. Any clues?

NATHAN BUFF: Oh, I know this. It was called Broad Streete, but I don't know where it was.

ARTHUR BRYANT: It appeared on 8 January 1684 in the most central part of the city. A great many shops opened on it. Many thousands of people visited and traders arrived. A bullring was built and there were games and displays of strength and skill. Oxen were roasted and drink was sold, and a great time was had by all along its length. Still stuck?

NATHAN BUFF: Was it built for a film?

ARTHUR BRYANT: No, that's why you can't answer the question. Broad Streete could only be built because the Thames had frozen over. It was the time of the great frost fairs. Whenever Londoners held a frost fair on the river they had skittles, booths and dancing, and the roasting of a whole sheep referred to as 'Lapland Mutton,' whose cooked flesh was sold for a shilling a slice. There were even funfair rides, with whirling chairs spun on long ropes around stakes hammered into the ice. There were streamers, flags and an immense number of signs.

NATHAN BUFF: Ah yes, I should have realized. It featured in the film version of *Orlando*.

ARTHUR BRYANT: Typographers and printers set up shop along the frozen causeway, which was also named 'City Road.' A man ate hot coals. There was a bear garden. Inevitably, the Tories erected a pamphleteering booth. Tradesmen set up every imaginable kind of business. And the ladies, slipping and sliding across the increasingly stained ice in their muffs and silken winter finery, came for the shopping. At the end of March, the resulting thaw scoured the Thames of its boats and barges, as the jagged frozen blocks smashed their way towards the estuary with the ebbing of the tide.

Between the fourteenth and nineteenth centuries the Thames froze solid more than a dozen times, partly due to the narrower arches of London Bridge holding the waters in place and partly because it was bloody cold.

John Evelyn describes the street thus: 'The Ice was now become so incredibly thick, as to beare not onely whole streets of boothes in which they roasted meate, & had divers shops of wares . . . but Coaches and horses passed over.'

The frost-street displayed traditional shop signs, such as could be seen along the Strand. According to a broadside preserved in the British Museum they sold 'all sorts of goods imaginable, namely, cloaths, plate, earthenware, meat, drink, brandy, tobacco, and a hundred sorts of other commodities.'

At times the Thames ice froze to a thickness of several feet, especially between Blackfriars and London Bridge. There are various reasons for the existence of Broad Streete. One was the 'Little Ice Age' that hit England, causing gales and dreadful famines, another was that the Thames had yet to be embanked so that it flowed more slowly.

What happened when the ice melted? Rapid thaws sometimes caused loss of life and property. In January 1789, melting ice dragged away a ship which was anchored to a riverside pub, pulling the building down and causing five people to be crushed to death. When the frosts finally thawed and split the ice, the shifting floes sometimes smashed away the stanchions of bridges. The street vanished until the next time the Thames froze.

In the pedestrian tunnel under the south bank of Southwark Bridge there's an engraving by sculptor Richard Kindersley made of slabs of grey slate, depicting a frost fair. The global climate grew milder, the river was banked and flowed faster, and that was the end of Broad Streete forever.

| | |

If you're as old as I am (which I certainly hope you are not as I wouldn't wish it on a dog), you may associate certain roads in London with things that have long vanished from them. I can't help thinking of printing presses whenever I'm in Tooley Street or photo libraries in Newman Street, and I still think of dropping my trousers in Soho. There, the Italian tailors would do on-the-spot repairs while you waited with your knobbly knees on display. The other place where trousers regularly fell off was in White-hall.

In the seventeenth century there used to be an inn called Ye Old Ship Tavern near the top of Whitehall. It was replaced by an art deco theatre in 1930, opening with *The Way to Treat a Woman* by Walter Hackett, a rubbish play by the theatre's licensee. The Whitehall Theatre became famous for 'modern' (i.e., risqué) comedies. During the Second World War it housed revues, which had become common entertainment throughout the West End; there was no place for drama when too much of it was going on around the city.

In 1942, *The Whitehall Follies* starred Phyllis Dixey, a variety-show singer who became the first stripper to perform in the West End. She was an overnight sensation. Dixey was no dumb blonde and leased the theatre so that she could stay there.

A series of Feydeau-style farces known as the Whitehall Farces were produced by Brian Rix and staged over the next twenty-two years, many of them televised or made into films. Rix, with his distinctive husky voice and knockabout comic skills, starred in a great many of them and usually ended up without trousers, falling out of a cupboard in front of a vicar.

The Whitehall Theatre became permanently associated with farce until in 1969 a nude comedy called *Pyjama Tops* took over the venue and remained for five years, after which the building was closed down. But unlike many other venues (like the late, great Astoria in nearby Charing Cross Road) it didn't die. Following refurbishment it reopened in 1986 with a hit revival of J. B. Priestley's *When We Are Married*. After a few more quality productions it slid back into the world of tat like *Puppetry of the Penis* and *Sing-a-Long-a-ABBA*. It's slightly off the main route of theatres, and Londoners, being a notoriously territorial lot, rarely walked past it.

Now it's the Trafalgar Studios, a pair of intimate venues for high-end productions, which means that a blue baffle has covered the attractive ceiling for acoustic purposes. And unlike the Donmar Warehouse it's not elitist; the Warehouse, with just 250 seats, has five levels of priority booking for those who can write their tickets off on expenses. Perhaps the Whitehall's roots as an old inn keep it for the people.

| | |

It would be perverse to finish this section without mentioning the actual Whitehall.

As the centre of government Whitehall is one of London's grandest but most frequently overlooked thoroughfares. It has eight monuments and memorials dotted along its length, including the Cenotaph, the memorial to the war dead. The name is taken from the immense Palace of Whitehall, where Henry VIII married Anne Boleyn, which once occupied the area and was destroyed by fire in 1698.

Whitehall was originally the road that led to the front of the palace. The street is reached from Trafalgar Square, passing near to Downing Street (which remained open to the public until 1989), Buckingham Palace and the Thames. So it comes as a surprise to find that several old taverns have survived along it and in the side roads. The rest of the area is still identified with government departments and venerable members' clubs. The old public buildings have survived intact; powerful people still use them.

The area of Whitehall slopes to the riverside and most of its buildings are empty at night, so it has a cooler, darker imprint than the neighbourhoods around it. As a consequence it's one of the few Central London areas where you'll still see the early-morning mists and late-night fogs of Victorian London, especially in November.

Whitehall was long considered the very edge of urban London, the spot where you boarded carriages for the countryside. The Holbein Gate, a gigantic, turreted but unfortunately narrow gateway to Whitehall was demolished to make way for traffic.

There are always regrets after somebody pulls down a spectacular building. What's the connection between Liszt, Tchaikovsky, Dvořák, Grieg and Dickens? They all performed at the sumptuous St James's Hall on Piccadilly, which opened in 1858. It had a secret orchestra entrance that could be used by visiting royals. This graceful building was demolished in 1904, and was replaced by the Piccadilly Hotel.

The Queen's Hall at the top of Regent Street was a grandly pillared venue that cost just a shilling to enter. It hosted Henry Wood's promenade concerts in 1895, bringing classical music to the masses, and although its concerts continued right through the Blitz it was eventually bombed flat. Everyone thought it should be rebuilt but there was no money around. We also lost Mrs Salmon's Waxworks on Chancery Lane, but no one was much upset by that. It featured scenes horrific, tragic and historical, as well as the deathbed of a woman who had given birth to 365 babies all at once. We'll never know why she had one for every day of the year.

There's something else that went missing from London in my lifetime: trolleybuses. Known as 'Diddlers,' they were different to trams in that they ran on wheels but were still connected to overhead cables. The London trolleybuses formed the largest system in the world. Gliding silently across the city, they were pollution-free and easy to maintain, but at the end of the 1950s electricity was more expensive, so they were sold to Spain and we replaced them with . . . diesel engines. Bit of an own goal there.

29

Club Life & Other Stories

ARTHUR BRYANT: Are there still such things as clubbable men? Indeed there are. Despite the proliferation of reinvented private clubs that chuck out the chintz in favour of thumpymusic, the traditional old clubs of London do still exist. Our coroner Giles belongs to one because his ghastly sister married into the fox-bothering classes.

The last time I visited Whitehall's National Liberal Club in the course of an investigation the doorman checked my admittedly grubby shoes and trousers with a heavy hint of disapproval before I imperiously waved my Boots card at him and forced him to admit me to this sanctum of calm, civilized gentility and extremely high ceilings.

Happily it's a gentleman's club that equally allows women, founded in 1882 by William Gladstone on firm Liberal traditions which are still in place today. The club enjoyed a reputation for radicalism. It lost its main staircase in the Blitz and was blown up during the IRA campaign of 1973, but worse was to follow.

During the 1960s and 1970s, all London clubs were in serious decline, but the Liberal Club fell into a parlous state of disrepair, its membership dwindling, its coffers losing a thousand pounds a week. In 1976 the Liberal leader Jeremy Thorpe handed the club over to Canadian businessman George Marks, who styled himself His Serene Holiness the Prince de Chabris, and turned out to be a con man.

Marks claimed to be a multi-millionaire willing to pour cash into the club, and moved his family in rent-free, running several fake businesses from the premises, paying for a sports car and his children's private school fees from the club's accounts.

He fled, owing the club sixty thousand pounds, even emptying out the cash till of the day's takings as he went. He'd also sold the club a fraudulent painting. Still worse, he flogged off the National Liberal Club's Gladstone Library (which contained the largest library of seventeenth-to-twentieth-century political material in the country, including thirty-five thousand books and over thirty thousand pamphlets) to the University of Bristol on the pretext that the club could no longer afford to pay the librarian's wages. This was the finest club library in London. The collection is still housed at Bristol today.

Having introduced a con man into the club, Jeremy Thorpe had troubles of his own, surviving an allegedly establishment-biased court case in which he was accused of hiring a hitman to shoot his male lover. The hitman missed and shot a Great Dane called Rinka.

There are many other clubs still with equally colourful histories . . .

At the time of writing, the main ones are still White's (founded 1693, the original gentleman's club to which only one woman—the Queen—has ever had entrance), Pratt's (where all the staff are called George), Brooks's, the thespian Garrick, the Carlton, Boodle's, the Reform (where Phileas Fogg began his trip), the Athenaeum, the Beefsteak (where all the staff are called Charles), Buck's, the Oxford and Cambridge, the Travellers (whose original qualification was that members had to have travelled five hundred miles in a straight line from London), the RAC and the Pall Mall.

There are now just fifty clubs left between Westminster and St James's, which once had so many that this secretive area was known as 'Clubland.' The most imposing ones hide in plain sight, occupying white Palladian buildings with blinds over the windows. White's, the most exclusive, has no outward name or address. Another seventy or so have merged, with names like Crockford's, the Eccentric and the Constitutional now all gone. The Garrick, dedicated to the arts and the theatre, was founded at a time when no women were allowed on the stage and is still opposed to allowing women in.

The Savage Club is a relative newcomer, dating from 1857. Its members must be involved in one of six categories: art, drama, law, literature, music or science. To be a member of the Reform Club, members still sign a declaration agreeing to the principles of the 1832 Reform Act. The Arts Club was founded in 1863 by, among others, Charles Dickens, Anthony Trollope and Frederic Leighton, but more recently became filled with shrieking media ninnies.

The difference between these and modern London clubs like the Soho House chain could not be more pronounced. The old oases of silence and snobbery remain at the geographical heart of London life, but are no longer a part of it.

As I left the National Liberal Club I passed a choleric old gentleman bending over some leather-bound volumes in a sadly depleted bookcase, searching for something, muttering to himself.

Another snoozed behind an immense tiled pillar, a newspaper on his lap. In such places time truly stands still, and may actually have died.

How does one join such clubs? A quick trawl around their websites reveals that you don't. You have to be asked. The sites are anonymous and filled with *froideur*. Candidates for admission have to be proposed and seconded by current members of the club who have direct personal knowledge of the candidate. In certain cases you may be considered by the electoral board.

The RAC, the Liberal Club, the Pall Mall Club, the Garrick—these old-world London clubs occupy grand terraces and have illustrious roll-calls, even as they fill with smug toffs and hedge fund managers.

But Soho always had a separate clubland of its own. There are rambunctious London nights that end in oblivion and a large number of them, it seems, have occurred in the Phoenix Artists Club. What is it about this bizarre haunt underneath the Phoenix Theatre that makes people lose their wits? Why go there? The staff are . . . well, 'stand-offish' is too kind a word. The décor is 'Elderly Actor's Attic Collides with Charity Shop.' The music – let's not even go into the album *Christmas Carols Sung By Cats*. Once heard, never forgotten. Should we check out its history, then?

Noël Coward and Gertie Lawrence used to perform here for their friends. Now there's an eclectic mix of actors, musicians, writers, celebrities and wannabes who simply happened to be shiftily hanging around outside and wondered where the stairs led.

Entry to the Phoenix was always random. Sometimes you'd be charged forty quid for a lifetime membership. You might always be told that membership is closed, as Raymond Land usually is.

Once I saw the girl on the door refuse to admit someone unless he could answer three tough questions about the London theatre scene. She then gave him two out of the three answers because she liked his smile. Closing time is uncertain. The place may be empty or packed to the gills. When the old owner Maurice died one Christmas, his coffin was placed in the bar with a silver top hat on it and everyone carried on drinking.

Things go missing and magically reappear in the Phoenix. Just before Christmas I got halfway home before I realized that I was wearing someone else's jacket (the fact that the sleeves were a foot short should have alerted me). I returned it, complete with wallet and keys, to an owner who had not even missed it. I never did find mine. You don't go to such places unless you're prepared to lose or possibly gain something. The other night I found yet another tequila glass in my pocket when I got home. A director was telling me about his new film, and I discovered he had put a copy of it in my coat. It was dreadful.

I've lost evidence and documents in that blasted club, found myself with new hats and scarves, gained books, a painting and many random objects. On certain nights there's a chance that Benedict Cumberbatch will be at the bar wondering where his gloves have gone. Sometimes an opera singer will turn up and belt out a few arias, despite the fact that nobody asked her to. Last night, my watch mysteriously shed its strap while I was standing at the bar, simply rolling off my arm and vanishing into the murk of the shadowed floor for no discernible reason. I think it must have been caused by the confluence of ley lines beneath the dishwasher.

There are plenty of other Bermuda Triangles to be found in London, and whether they become popular or doomed is entirely serendipitous. Cult status is not something that can be planned.

The last time I went to the Phoenix I was cajoled into investigating a murder over shots of something that tasted of raspberry syrup and drain cleaner. We never did find out who the killer was.

COLIN BIMSLEY: I've never been to the kind of old gits' club Mr B. is talking about. My clubbing years in the East End lasted from eighteen to twenty-one. Anything after that is undignified. Paul McCartney discovered that his cut-off date was seventy-three after being turned away from an after-party celebration. First of all, he should have been at home in bed instead of wanting to stand in a roped-off VIP corner of a hard house basement bellowing 'What?' while someone shouts in his deaf ear. Second, they don't look at him and see the most popular musician of all time, they see an old bloke with a bad haircut, so why risk humiliation? There are many things you can still do as you age, but clubbing isn't one of them.

And why would you want to now? The great London clubs like Fabric, Heaven and the Ministry of Sound belong to another era. They've gone the way of the tea strainer and the importance of having a splendid navy. Their heyday was in the early 1980s and they've been in decline ever since. We didn't have silent, booze-free discos then. The death of the London club was brought about by two things: soaring property prices and a crackdown on drugs. Real clubbers went for the music, nothing else.

The legendary Bagley's in King's Cross annually hosted a four-day Bank Holiday event which was so loud that the PCU had to go on holiday until it was over. The bass speakers made my tea mug shake like that glass of water in *Jurassic Park*. Even now I can spot who went there regularly because they're all a bit deaf and SHOUT AT YOU ALL THE TIME. And the Westlers hot dog stand that stood permanently outside the club wasn't just selling hot dogs, if you know what I mean. We nicked him so many times that he used to send us a Christmas card every year.

The simplest truth behind the decline of London's dance clubs is that they require large spaces in which to operate, and those disappeared as developers moved in, enacting modern-day versions of the Enclosure Acts.*

* From the start of the seventeenth century, these acts fenced in so-called 'waste-ground' and gave the rights to landlords.

30

Taxi Nerdery & Other Stories

ARTHUR BRYANT: Wardens and vergers love telling stories about their churches, and will trap you inside for hours if you let them. I've a friend who was arrested for doing just that. I've already mentioned All Hallows-by-the-Tower, which bills itself as London's oldest church, founded by the Abbey of Barking in 675 CE, four hundred years before the Tower of London, but is it? St Pancras Old Church goes back a further three hundred years but there's not a lot left of the original structure, and evidence is now scanty.

Let's take this one church, All Hallows, for a moment and look into it a little more. In certain ways it stands in for the history of London.

It was known as Berkyncherche (Barking Church) in the twelfth century, although Barking was in Essex and the Domesday Book listed Barking Abbey as possessing 'twenty-eight houses and half a church.' But it might have been built in the seventh century and it might have stood in Lunden-Wic, the Anglo-Saxon town in the Strand outside the Roman city of Londinium. So although it was 'without' then, the current church is inside the wall.

I draw your attention to this muddle because it gets to the root of London's problems. The parts of our history which have not been lost have often been accidentally falsified. Although the city is vast its centre is small, its layout unchanged. Given the number of churches, there should be clear records showing us how everything got here. But there aren't.

Some stories about All Hallows are certainly true. John Quincy Adams got married there, the only American president to do so in the UK, as did 'Hanging' Judge Jeffreys. It's where the annual ceremony of the Knollys Rose takes place. See elsewhere for an explanation on that. And it was the home of headless corpses. Bodies were sent there after they were separated from their ears in the Tower of London. It was also blown up. In 1650 the wardens discovered it was a bad idea to store gunpowder in the churchyard. The blast took out over fifty surrounding houses.

The crypt altar comes from the Knights Templar castle outside Haifa in Palestine. Some Roman pavement was discovered under it. The church was repaired, restored, flattened again in the war, rebuilt and rededicated.

On the way down to the crypt of All Hallows there are further oddities: first the crow's nest used by Sir Ernest Shackleton on his last Antarctic voyage (although I'm not sure why it's there); and then a strange-looking sliver of metal down a wall. During the Blitz a bomb fell through the east window of the church and the intense fire melted all the lead on the roof, causing it to run in rivers through the building and pour down into the crypt, of which this molten lead stalactite is a remnant.

Despite all its wounds, All Hallows is still a stunning church with an unusually constructed ceiling, and tunnels that contain interesting oddities. I like the plaque about the exhausting carillon of bells rung on this spot in 1818: 8,448 changes rung in five hours and twenty-four minutes—was that really possible?

Although fewer Central London churches are used for congregational worship these days, they provide a very necessary space for solace and reflection, especially for anyone stressed out by working in the city. People cared enough to save All Hallows. It endures.

| | |

Next I'm heading for a church in Shakespeare's old parish, St Andrew-by-the-Wardrobe, first mentioned in 1170, when it was part of Baynard's Castle. This too was burned down, rebuilt and rebuilt again, and now survives in a simple style that renders it a bit invisible among the buzzing city streets.

It gets its odd name from the fact that Edward III stored his wardrobe there (a wardrobe being a storehouse for royal *accoutrements,* in other words the Crown's arms, clothing and other personal royal bits and bobs. And his trainers). It has steep steps going up into it and stands behind Blackfriars Station. In a wall plaque, Shakespeare is shown kneeling before 'the final curtain.' Bit over the top, that.

The takeaway from this, as the young folk say, is that the history of a single London church is usually more eventful than fifty rural ones, and to get the full story you only need to ask a verger or the person selling postcards near the entrance.

| | |

These days I usually take a sherbet* around town. Hiring a London taxi, investigating a bloody good murder and having a glass of champagne with a bowl of jellied eels are my only extravagances.

* Sherbet Dab = cab.

It's no idle boast to reiterate that the London black cab is still the best in the world; new editions have hands-free doors and are the size of your living room inside, like TARDISes. The drivers may not wear white gloves like they do in Japan, but they're curious-minded individuals and talking to them is part of the fun of the ride.

Originally, the hackney carriage was either named after that area of London, or stems from the Spanish *jaca*, a small breed of horse perfect for pulling a carriage, or most likely from *hacquenée*, the French term for a general-purpose horse; nobody is quite sure about its roots.

For a while both horse-drawn carriages and motorized ones existed side by side. Then came the hansom cab, designed by Joseph Hansom, the difference being that this one had just two wheels. It's the one you always see in Sherlock Holmes films.

Petrol-powered taxicabs with meters arrived at the start of the twentieth century. The sexiest-looking cab, the FX3, appeared in 1948, but the most famous—and the one that remained in production for nearly forty years—was the curvaceous FX4, in 1958.

Now, I'm going to get a bit nerdy here.

JOHN MAY: You've always been nerdy, Arthur.

ARTHUR BRYANT: I most certainly have not!

JOHN MAY: How tall is the dome of St Paul's?

ARTHUR BRYANT: Three hundred and sixty-five feet, one foot for every day of the year. Everyone knows that!

JOHN MAY: What's at the top of it?

ARTHUR BRYANT: An 850-ton lantern. There's an interesting story about how it was—

JOHN MAY: I rest my case. Go back to your taxis.

ARTHUR BRYANT: Sometimes if you look at one small patch of land you can get a feeling for an area. The Caledonian Road runs from outside our unit in King's Cross to insalubrious Holloway. Opposite Pentonville Prison was a dining spot used by the prison screws called the Breakout Café, and back from that at number 345 is Cally Pets, the unchanged pet shop where Monty Python filmed their dead parrot sketch. The owner must get sick of being asked about the Norwegian Blue.

There's also an unassuming building called Knowledge Point School. It's the training arm of the taxi trade, and teaches drivers the Knowledge. It's where black-cab drivers pass their live exams after they've driven all over London by scooter with a clipboard attached to their handlebars, learning every road in the city.

I don't know if their shop still sells old-fashioned A–Z maps, but above it is a classroom where you have to show that you've learned to recognize every single street in London. It's a mammoth undertaking, which is why only three out of every ten would-be drivers who sign up ever make it to the end. The Knowledge is the world's toughest taxi test. London drivers, also known as Green Badge drivers, must learn 320 routes or 'runs,' 25,000 streets and 20,000 landmarks or places of interest within a six-mile radius of Charing Cross. How's that for nerdery, John?

It can take up to four years to pass and, once qualified, cabbies can work anywhere in the Greater London area, keeping whatever hours they want.

The tutors at the Knowledge School specialize in tripping up candidates with trick questions. Pupils also have to know names that come from Londoners rather than maps. The labyrinthine city is negotiated via odd landmarks, often the names of pubs, and drop-off points are described rather than given addresses. 'It's a left past the Black Prince' or 'Just opposite the Duke of Norfolk.' To test candidates there are so-called 'trap streets' on the map that don't exist.

The first trip after a cabbie passes his Knowledge test is free to the customer. I've never found one yet. Cabbies have to learn about public buildings as well as roads, and remember roads for their test knowledge with mnemonics. Cutting through Covent Garden is 'Wet T-Shirts'—Wellington, Tavistock, Southampton and Henrietta Streets. 'Little Apples Grow Quickly Please' helps cabbies remember the order of the theatres on Shaftesbury Avenue: Lyric, Apollo, Gielgud, Queen's and Palace. They probably changed the acronym after the Queen's changed its name to the Sondheim.

And they evolve their own slang for different bits of London. For example, 'Hot & Cold Corner' is by the Royal Geographical Society's statues of David Livingstone and Ernest Shackleton.

JOHN MAY: Why do they do it?

ARTHUR BRYANT: What do you mean?

JOHN MAY: Everyone has Google Maps now so what's the point of learning acronyms and nicknames?

ARTHUR BRYANT: Because it's traditional.

JOHN MAY: The very thing that has held this country back for centuries.

ARTHUR BRYANT: Then because they learn every shortcut in London and can drive in the bus lanes to save you time, OK?

Some more taxi nerdery. The two flip-down seats in a cab are called cricket seats.

If a cabbie isn't familiar with the road you name, he or she will ask you, 'What's that off of?' and will instantly know where it is when you answer.

New drivers are called 'butter boys and girls,' possibly because older cabbies think they're pinching their bread and butter.

A 'Churchill' is a cabbie's meal. When he was Home Secretary, Winston Churchill gave cabbies the right to turn down a fare while eating.

There are supposed to be around 21,000 black cabs in London, and twelve green cabbies' cafés dotted around the city centre. There were once an awful lot more.

The first one was built in 1875 to provide cabbies with a warm shelter where they could get a fast meal. It was against the law to leave a taxi unattended at a rank, so the cabbies couldn't easily get hot food. Cabbies had to observe strict etiquette inside the green shelters, and were encouraged to read and improve their minds.

They were originally offered coffee, tea, cocoa, bread and marge, and for a penny the attendant would cook food the cabbies brought in. Later the menus became more elaborate and some of the shelters served saveloys, faggots, pease pudding, ham and eggs. I'm still not entirely sure what pease pudding is, or what's in it.

The surviving cafés continue to be used. These days they probably cater to their area's foodies by serving saveloys in a white wine reduction, but they're still famous for stonking bacon sarnies.

The black cab remains a London icon and its most stylish way to travel—I was horrified the first time I boarded a yellow taxi in

New York and found myself sitting behind scratched plexiglass like a prisoner being taken for sentencing.

As for conversation, when we were stuck in rainy traffic on the Old Kent Road recently, my black-cab driver discoursed on politics, the National Health Service, modern art, the fastest way to Wapping, London's bat population and his favourite serial killers, listed in reverse order.

You get plenty of banter with Uber, too, although a white Toyota Prius isn't as interesting.

31

The Longest-Running Play & Other Stories

ARTHUR BRYANT: I was turning out my pockets the other day. I really must do it more often because I found some heart medication which expired in 1996 and my *Guide to Scandinavian Hospital Equipment,* 1952 edition. I also found my Miscellaneous London file. I say 'file,' it's scraps of paper with indecipherable notes on, some written in my version of Babylonic cuneiform, but it reminded me of a few London oddities I'd spotted during my walkabouts. Here are the ones I could actually read.

WHO WAS RAHERE?

Hospital wards often have personal names. Elizabeth Garrett Anderson has many named after her and rightly so, as she was the first woman to qualify in Britain as a physician and surgeon. St Bartholomew's is London's oldest hospital and has a Rahere Ward—but who was Rahere?

Behind Smithfield is the twelfth-century church of St Bart's, and in the chapel is the tomb of Rahere, a tonsured monk who entertained King Henry I as a jester. But in 1118 the King lost Matilda, his wife, and two years later his son drowned in the sinking of the *White Ship,* off Normandy. He is said to have never smiled again. So Rahere was out of a job.

The ex-jester went to Rome on a pilgrimage and contracted malaria. In his fever St Bartholomew appeared to him, telling him to return and build a hospital, so he did.

King Henry granted him a royal charter in 1123 and Rahere started work, but he died before it could be finished, so his tomb was built into an arch of the presbytery. He's lying there with a couple of canons reading his verse and the King himself presenting him with a coat of arms.

In 1866 a bit of the tomb was opened during renovations and Rahere was found to still be wearing his sandals—it being the custom to bury monks in them. One was stolen by a workman but was returned; however, it was interred without being put back on Rahere's foot, which meant the monk could no longer be at peace, so ever since his cowled form is said to haunt the building and will continue to until the sandal is replaced.

So the hospital ward is named after an unquiet ghost.

WHY IS NORTHUMBERLAND AVENUE SO DESERTED?

There's one remaining part of Central London that's truly under-visited.

Mist often rolls in from the river, creating aureoles of light around the street lamps of Northumberland Avenue. At night there are often few cars and hardly any people. Yet two streets over is a bustling, busy area full of outdoor cafés.

Welcome to Westminster, which starts at Northumberland Avenue, is bordered by the Thames on its lower side, and extends to Birdcage Walk and the Houses of Parliament. Technically it goes right up to Oxford Street, but beyond its jurisdictional geography it exists in my mind as a maze of grand classical buildings in the Palladian style.

Westminster's origin begins with a myth. In the seventh century, a fisherman possibly named Edric ferried a ragged passenger to Thorney Island, an eyot* on the Thames. It turned out his fare was St Peter, coming to consecrate the church that would eventually become Westminster Abbey. St Peter rewarded the fisherman with a great catch of salmon. So every year on 29 June the abbey is presented with a salmon by the Worshipful Company of Fishmongers.

Westminster keeps its mysteries. In autumn and winter it is often damp and gloomy, with few shops, few tourists and even fewer residents. You may not be able to buy a pipe cleaner there for love nor money but it does have plenty of atmosphere.

WHY IS HOLBORN SO BORING?

There's no getting around it, Holborn is boring. And a bit Welsh. It's part of the A40 route that goes all the way to Fishguard in Pembrokeshire. Holborn is the odd no man's land between New Oxford Street and Gray's Inn Road (the boundaries changed in 1994). In the nineteenth century it was filled with sturdy, wealthy insurance offices, law firms, accountancy, marine and travel companies, and the head offices of the Empire's manufacturing outlets.

It's an old and rather handsome area. The first mention it gets is in a charter of Westminster Abbey by King Edgar, dated at 959 CE. This speaks of 'the old wooden church of St Andrew.' The name Holborn (pronounced 'Hoe-bun') is supposed to be derived from the Middle English word *hol* for 'hollow' and

* A small island.

'bourn,' a brook, referring to the River Fleet, which runs to its east side.

Holborn was the home of the pen-pusher, where the law went hand-in-glove with insurance, law and accounting. It's the setting for *Bleak House* and feels as if it should be the setting for *A Christmas Carol*, but Scrooge's office was in an alleyway off Cornhill beside the Bank of England.

Just over the road from Staple Inn, the only surviving Inn of Chancery, is the extraordinary redbrick Gothic pile called Holborn Bars. This used to be the Prudential Assurance Building ('the Pru'). Pip from *Great Expectations* was based there, and there's a statue of Dickens inside the courtyard.

On the other side is the stunning neoclassical Pearl Assurance Building, now the Holborn Dining Room. You don't want to find out that your bank manager is a stand-up comic, and when Victorians handed insurance companies their money they wanted to be assured of dedication, permanence and solidity. Holborn buildings look like they'll still be here long after the ants have reclaimed the world, but now they're being refitted as penthouses, hotels and restaurants. Right, John and I are going for a livener at the Crown & Two Chairmen so I'm getting Dudley Salterton back to talk to you about one of his *bêtes noires*—the West End phenomenon that is *The Mousetrap*.

DUDLEY SALTERTON: I've always been a fan of popular entertainment but there's a bloody limit.

Agatha Christie's play is set in a wood-panelled Olde Worlde England, a side of the nation that, as someone from Sheffield, I have mercifully never experienced. Each of the eight actors in the play has to sign up for a minimum of forty-seven weeks. I imagine many try to make a break for it by knotting together bedsheets and going out of the dressing-room window.

It's said that during quiet performances you can hear the play creaking. That's hardly surprising; *The Mousetrap* opened in the West End in 1952 and never goes away, like tuberculosis. It has by far the longest initial run of any play in history; its twenty-five-thousandth performance took place on 18 November 2012. There's a sign in the foyer of the St Martin's Theatre that tells you what number performance this is. Tourists are photographed next to it. The St Martin's is a beautiful theatre, but most of us never get to bloody see inside it. Let me tell you this: if you've not seen the play by now you never bloody will. If you couldn't get your arse down to the theatre during the first seventy years of its run, you'll never get around to it.

Agatha Christie probably realized that her whodunnit wasn't very good because she thought that it would last eight months tops. The opening-night critics called it crude and clichéd. It began life as a short radio play broadcast on 30 May 1947 called *Three Blind Mice*, and had its origins in the real-life case of a boy, Dennis O'Neill, who died while in the foster care of a farmer and his wife in 1945.

Christie asked that the story not be published as long as it ran as a play. It has still not appeared in Great Britain but can be found in the United States, in the 1950 collection *Three Blind Mice and Other Stories*. There's an unacknowledged film version too, made in India.

Christie gave the rights to her grandson as a birthday present. One of the original stars, Richard Attenborough, invested in it and ended up partially financing his film *Gandhi* with the proceeds. In this country, only one further production could be performed annually and no film could be produced until it had been closed for at least six months.

One actor has been with the play for the whole of its run—to anyone of a certain age Deryck Guyler is the unmistakeably fruity voice you hear on the radio. The set has been slightly changed a couple of times, but the clock which sits on the mantelpiece of the fireplace is the one that was there on opening night.

Unlike *Hamlet*, the inspiration for the play's revised title, the characters are cardboard, the dialogue is arthritic and the twist is ludicrous. The manor house in which the cast find themselves is snowed in, but the detective easily manages to get there on skis. Sweating actors keep bursting through the door shaking white bits of styrofoam off their shoulders and complaining how cold it is. The audience is traditionally asked not to reveal the ending after leaving the theatre, but if you haven't worked out who did it early on you've probably had a stroke. Obviously I'm not going to tell you who the killer is here, but his occupation rhymes with 'defective.'

So why does *The Mousetrap* still stagger on in a city where anything that isn't up to scratch is whisked off within days? Contrary to popular belief, much of the audience is British. It's entry-level theatre, a rite of passage, like acne. It mythologizes a cosy vanished England that folk would love to imagine themselves in. Since it became a brand, *The Mousetrap* plays all over the world and is no longer a uniquely London event. Like *Mamma Mia!* and *The Phantom of the Opera* it's become a living dead show that will never go away.

What else was there? I had it written down somewhere. Oh, aye.

Empires rise and fall, but most of the music hall empires simply vanished. The beautiful Hackney Empire was raised at the very start of the twentieth century, a techno-marvel with central heating and electric lights. Charlie Chaplin, Stan Laurel and saucy

Marie Lloyd, a local lass, all appeared there. They were followed by Louis Armstrong, Tony Hancock and Liberace. Not on the same bill, obviously.

But by the time the Second World War ended the days of music hall—a working-class entertainment—were over. In 1956, the Hackney Empire was bought by ATV, who produced many well-loved shows there, like *Emergency Ward 10* and *Take Your Pick!* But in 1963 Mecca bought it and converted it into a bingo hall. At least it was spared the wrecking ball—many other venues were destroyed and replaced by absolutely bugger all.

I remember seeing the bulldozers plough into the Putney Hippodrome, and read about other baroque Victorian and Edwardian music halls that were smashed down by councils keen to build car parks. In the 1980s the façade of the Hackney Empire was listed, and as Mecca didn't want to spend any money on it they sold it on to a satirical touring theatre group, who made a grand go of it.

The Empire reopened on its eighty-fifth birthday in 1986 and took off once more, finding the kind of market it used to have among the working people in its neighbourhood—it's a hugely successful venue and the jewel in Hackney's crown, the home of beloved Christmas pantos and many shows involving local residents.

If other councils hadn't been so short-sighted they could all have had wonderful attractions in their boroughs. Keeping the Hippodrome or the music halls in the Old Kent Road and Camden Town would have brought money into those areas. In Camden alone there were over fifty cinemas and music halls, nearly all of which have been pulled down to make way for shops which are now failing. Hackney kept something special and it's worth a trip to see, whatever's on. And if you want an example of a London venue out of the West End that's been preserved in a pristine

fashion for over a century, try visiting the New Wimbledon Theatre.

Right, that's your lot. I'm doing pensioners' matinee today.
They're getting 'If You Were the Only Girl in the World,' Barna-
cle Bill's saucy sea shanties and mind-reading from behind a
shower curtain. With any luck most of them will be asleep before
I get to my Max Bygraves impression.

ARTHUR BRYANT: You need to update your act, Dudley.

Now, crematoriums.

Some North London towns have changed very little simply because they're awkward to reach by public transport, like Crouch
End, Stoke Newington and Muswell Hill, where the land was too
hilly for underground transport.

But there's a good chance that if you live there, or in the Finch-
ley or Barnet areas, you might choose to be cremated at the Golders Green Crematorium. Although the immediate area is famously
Jewish, its crematorium is secular and accepts all faiths and non-
believers.

Well over three hundred thousand Londoners have come to
rest there, including fourteen holders of the Victoria Cross, H. G.
Wells, Anna Pavlova, Sigmund Freud, Ray Ellington, Neville
Chamberlain, Peter Sellers, Rudyard Kipling and, er, Sid James.
There's a Communists' Corner and twelve acres of gardens with
lakes and fountains, and on a sunny day it's a very pleasant place
to wander about in (on a gloomy one it's bloody depressing).

While you're up there, you'll find a surprising number of
grand houses, many of which are open to the public, from Bruce
Castle to Forty Hall and Myddelton House. North London also
had a number of lunatic asylums, some of which have been
turned into apartments.

When telephone exchanges named areas by the first three letters of their neighbourhoods they ran into a problem with Golders Green. Its letters had the same numerical equivalent on an analogue dial as those of Holborn, HOL, and couldn't be used. The telephone staff put their heads together and came up with a typically tricky London solution: SPE.

Their reasoning was this: 'Golders Green' contains two colours, so add another . . . blue. The name of a bright blue flower that could be found in Golders Green was the 'speed you well' plant, speedwell, hence SPE.

Incidentally, do you know why more British people can remember their postcodes than their PIN? In the 1950s psychologists designed the system for maximum memorability, placing the numerical part in the middle to aid recall of the last two letters, where most mistakes occur. You can send a letter just using your door number and the postcode.

Here's a postcode for you: SW10. What comes to mind when you think of Chelsea?

It rather depends on when you were born. An astonishing number of famous people are associated with the former village: Tolkien, Turner, Jagger, Mark Twain, T. S. Eliot, Ava Gardner, Isambard Kingdom Brunel, Bob Marley, Anne of Cleves, Harold Macmillan, A. A. Milne and Mary Shelley for a start.

To the late Victorians it would have conjured the homes of painters, writers, titled ladies, progressives and classicists—and Thomas Crapper, inventor of plumbing supplies. In the 1960s it was the playground of entertainers, trust-fund children and dedicated followers of fashion. In the seventies it was punks, and today, rather than the titled, the over-entitled. The tide of time has stranded Chelsea—google it now and what comes up are about twenty pages of football club news and a ghastly reality television show, but it does have the wonderful Saatchi Gallery, which alone makes it worth visiting, and those marvellous orange and white Edwardian mansion blocks in the twisting back-streets.

The King's Road is no longer glamorous or avant-garde. It has become too expensive to be fashionable. Chelsea has always turned its back on the Thames; the foreshore view is noted for its fine painterly light but is devoid of features. And it faces a power station.

Or rather, it did.

If we think of the Thames split at Charing Cross, one half going to the Tate Modern, a former power station, and the other half going to Battersea Power Station, we get two very different images of London. The eastern half is on a human scale and thronging with pedestrian life, but in the western half we have the new American Embassy, possibly the ugliest and most forti-fied building in London, surrounded by a spectacularly misjudged series of high-rise apartments, no two designs acknowledging each other. What went wrong?

Battersea Power Station was finally completed in 1955, then decommissioned in 1975. That's not much of a shelf life for such a gigantic building. It resembled an upturned billiard table and became an iconic image of West London, featuring on record album covers and in films, its profile instantly recognizable.

Endless renovation plans fell through. Margaret Thatcher tried to flog it to a Chinese developer. It was due to become a commu-nity area, an amusement park, social housing. It has now ended up as flats and offices, but the surrounding buildings have changed the Thames shoreline forever.

The problem lay with its piecemeal development. Architects Norman Foster and Frank Gehry teamed up to create a new riv-erside destination for Londoners but have created a series of claustrophobic, overcrowded, bulbously ugly future slums. The brochures may have tried to present Battersea as the new Saint-

Tropez but the reality is closer to Dickensian rookeries. Hemmed in by roads and existing buildings, the planners failed to learn from successful waterfronts like those in Oslo, Budapest or the South Bank; the walkways are narrow, the buildings loom and the only glimmer of life survives on nearby houseboats. Locked in perpetual shadow, it looks like a seventies estate awaiting demolition—and it's not even finished.

But what would have been the alternative? Quinlan Terry's neoclassical Richmond Riverside development is hated by other architects but loved by the public. If we let the residents decide how London looks, warn the architects, we'll end up with lots of twee little houses and nothing new will ever be created, and perhaps they have a point. The London that's sold abroad is a construct of misremembered prewar images, but should we simply give the people what they want?

Londoners decide what they like best. We like the Gherkin at 30 St Mary Axe (pronounced 'Simmery Axe' according to W. S. Gilbert), but we don't like the threatening Walkie-Talkie at 20 Fenchurch Street. We like the London Eye and the Royal Festival Hall and the Lloyd's building and Granary Square, but nothing can make us like the blank, dead Shard. Perhaps it's simply about building on a human scale.

In 1969 James Mason narrated an eye-opening documentary called *The London Nobody Knows* and complained back then about the bland, mass-produced look of the city's first tall buildings. If he could have seen the Shard he'd have had a heart attack.

32

The London Jacks &
Other Stories

ARTHUR BRYANT: They were once a familiar sight in railway stations—charity-collection dogs who wore cash boxes and carried on collecting even after their deaths. The plaque in London Jack's glass display case at the Bluebell Railway Museum in East Sussex reads: 'Although dead, Jack is still on duty and solicits a continuance of your contributions in support of his good work for the Orphans.'

The black retriever spent nearly a hundred years, eight living and eighty-three as a stuffed carcass, raising money for good causes. Formerly famous for patrolling Waterloo Station, he was one of a group of celebrity dogs who raised cash for charity from the mid-Victorian era until the 1950s. He started collecting in 1923 and made more than £4,000 to help run an orphanage for railwaymen's kids.

There were others, like Chelmsford Brenda, Brighton Bob, Bruce of Swindon, Oldham's Rebel and Wimbledon Nell, who were petted by commuters and sometimes hopped trains on their own to encourage more donations from passengers. They barked, shook paws and performed tricks for money, their exploits reported in the press. They probably earned more than Amazon employees.

In 1896 a criminal gang picked up Tim, an Irish terrier who worked at Paddington Station, and held him upside down over a suitcase, shaking him to free up the coins from his collection box. When his assailants released him, he bit one of them on the leg.

Some dogs were less than honest themselves. Initially they collected coins in their mouths and gave them in, but secure boxes had to be fixed to them after the discovery in the 1860s that Brighton Bob was using some of his money to buy biscuits at a bakery.

The dogs were trained and cared for by railway staff. They were so successful that there was soon a whole line of London Jacks. The first came into service in 1894 but vanished five years later. He was found in a house in Soho where he was being held by criminals; a boy heard barking and informed the police. I know, it sounds like a Disney film.

He retired, died, was stuffed and put on display in a cabinet at Waterloo Station with a slot for coins at the front. Jack Junior took over and was said to stop and look at his late father whenever he passed by.

| | |

From dogs to dinners. It's not much of a segue but I couldn't think of anything else. I'm not a fan of alphabetical order so you'll just have to take pot luck today.

I remember there used to be two establishments called Simpson's in London. One, Simpson's of Piccadilly, was an elegant gents' outfitters, as they were still called the last time I bought a whistle.* It's the building with the 'invisible glass' frontage that became the Waterstones flagship store.

---

* A suit.

The other, Simpson's in the Strand, belongs to a different world and is at the Aldwych end of the Strand. It's rather forgotten, which is a shame, and at the time of writing is closed, but promises to reopen.

The hushed, high-end venue has been there since 1828, when it started as a coffee house and chess club. In fact, that's the reason why it's still hushed. It was to avoid disturbing the championship chess players that the idea of placing large joints of meat under silver-domed trolleys and wheeling them to guests' tables first came into being (they still do it).

The rooms are terribly grand and the cuisine is terribly English. Their dining guests have included (I quote from their bumf): 'Vincent van Gogh, Charles Dickens, George Bernard Shaw, Gladstone, Disraeli and Sherlock Holmes.' Spot the odd one out.

The success of the London Tavern in Bishopsgate, rebuilt after a fire in 1768, inspired the first properly European restaurant: La Grande Taverne de Londres, which opened in Paris in 1782.

The Covent Garden restaurant Rules (1798) has an even grander history. In the year that Napoleon began his campaign in Egypt, Thomas Rule promised his despairing family that he would say goodbye to his wayward past and settle down. After saying that, he went and opened an oyster bar in Covent Garden. To the surprise and disbelief of his family, the enterprise proved to be not only successful but lasting. Diners were soon singing the praises of Rules's porter, pies and oysters, and remarking on the 'rakes, dandies and superior intelligences who comprise its clientele.'

In over two hundred years, spanning the reigns of nine monarchs, it has been owned by only three families. Rules specializes in classic game cookery, pies, puddings and, of course, oysters. The roll-call of diners has included Clark Gable, Henry Irving, Laurence Olivier, Buster Keaton, Charlie Chaplin, H. G. Wells and Charles Dickens, who clearly never made do with a sandwich when he could accept a dinner invitation. The restaurant has also appeared in the novels of Evelyn Waugh, Graham Greene, John le Carré and Dick Francis.

JOHN MAY: Forgive me, Arthur, you know how I always like to check up on witness statements. That point about Rules being the oldest restaurant in London. Well, it's not. Simpson's Tavern in Ball Court at 38½ Cornhill was opened in 1757. Its chairman had been running a restaurant since 1723. A chairman presided over each lunch and ensured it started promptly at one. Then they would introduce the guests and measure the cheese.

ARTHUR BRYANT: What would they do that for?

JOHN MAY: I have no idea. It's probably something upper-class people do.

ARTHUR BRYANT: Colin, it's about time you did something.

COLIN BIMSLEY: Not sure how I can help you, Mr B. I can tell you about the Thames bridges. I walked across all of them for charity a couple of years back.

ARTHUR BRYANT: There you go. Everyone has something they know a lot about, even you.

COLIN BIMSLEY: For seventeen hundred years there was only one crossing over the Thames, where London Bridge is today, almost dating back to the birth of Christ. There was also a prehistoric causeway around Vauxhall, but there's no sign of it left. I thought you'd know about that one, Mr B. You probably remember it.

ARTHUR BRYANT: Cheeky sod.

COLIN BIMSLEY: Westminster Bridge was the second, in 1750, followed by Blackfriars Bridge in 1769. Vauxhall Bridge has eight enormous statues mounted on its sides, four representing industry, four the arts and crafts. Each holds something that represents their calling. One of them is holding a detailed miniature model of St Paul's Cathedral. They can only be seen properly from the river itself. Don't try leaning over the side to see them; I nearly fell in.

Likewise, Blackfriars Bridge has seabirds on its east side and freshwater birds on the west to represent the boundary between salt water and fresh in the river.

The old London Bridge had nineteen arches which turned its waters into rapids that overturned water-taxis and drowned their passengers.

The latest unusual feature on a bridge is at Blackfriars Station, which has the largest solar-powered bridge in the world.

The bridge from Bankside to St Paul's has a name but nobody can remember what it is. It's the Millennium Bridge, but most of us still call it the Wobbly Bridge because when it first opened, its glass panels started shifting about, and overnight it went from being ridiculed to being loved. Everybody loves an underdog.

Usually bridge-building across the Thames requires an Act of Parliament, but this one was granted by the Port of London Authority to speed things up. It's suspended, but from below to reduce its height, which is why it's a bit vertigo-inducing; there's nothing but sky to anchor your view.

As you head up towards the Thames source the bridges seem to get more frail, with Hammersmith virtually on life-support, driving everyone mad because it needs endless repairs. Next to

Hammersmith Bridge is Digby Mansions, a block of purpose-built turreted apartments where they shot *Theatre of Blood*. I only know that because I chose the film for a PCU film night and everyone points and yells whenever they recognize a building.

Albert Bridge is the one most featured in romantic films. It was lit up with old-fashioned lightbulbs (they're LEDs now) but was always structurally weak and still has a sign about soldiers having to break step when marching over it. Clearly the designers of the Wobbly Bridge hadn't seen that.

Waterloo Bridge was nicknamed 'the Ladies Bridge' because it was constructed mainly by female welders, stonemasons and labourers during the Second World War. The Deputy Prime Minister who opened the bridge thanked all the men who worked on it. Plonker.

Charles Dickens thought Lambeth Bridge was the ugliest one in London. It was painted red to match the leather benches in the House of Lords. Westminster Bridge was painted green to match the benches in the House of Commons.

When a Russian delegation visited Vauxhall railway station in the 1840s, they liked the word 'Vokzal' so much that it entered the Russian language as the word for a railway station.

Tower Bridge is the best example of the Victorians rewriting their past in a romantic light; it's a steel bridge clad in stone to give it a classical look. Over fifty designs were submitted. I'd love to see some of the others.

It was fashionable to take in the view from the high walkways, until the fad faded and, like everywhere else in Victorian London, the bridge became the haunt of pickpockets and prostitutes. They're always 'haunts,' aren't they?

In 1952 Tower Bridge started opening while a bus was crossing. The driver, Albert Gunter, pressed his boot to the floor and jumped the gap. I guess he asked everyone to hold on very tight, please.

Apart from the bridges there are a lot of islands in the Thames.

ARTHUR BRYANT: I've counted one hundred and eighty of them, Colin.

Many are uninhabited, like Lion Island and Black Boy Island. Some were created by flood plains and locks, some are man-made, some have hotels on, Garrick's Ait is named after the actor and many are absurdly picturesque. The residents live their lives on the water. Personally I find them a bit strange.

COLIN BIMSLEY: You find everyone outside the three-mile radius of Piccadilly Circus 'a bit strange.'

33

Riverbanks & Other Stories

ARTHUR BRYANT: Here's something I should probably have mentioned a lot earlier, considering the enormous role it plays in Londoners' lives.

Rain.

You can't see it but it sees you. It hides around a corner waiting until you're about to leave the house, watches as you prevaricate about taking an umbrella, then pelts down the moment you step outdoors without one.

Pernicious, spiteful, untrustworthy, London rain is barely visible but drenching. It's a fine mist you don't notice until the pavements start to shine. It seeps in through cracks and gaps, rising up, soaking down, darkening stone and steaming windows. It grows orange lichen on slates and green moss on pavements, and reflects the red neon in Soho gutters.

When it rains the hills that encircle London drain down to the Thames. On the canal near the PCU there's a permanent wet patch that causes cyclists to skid, a channel from an underground tributary of the River Fleet that has found its way to the surface and can't be eradicated. In King's Cross Underground Station there's a yellow plastic bucket catching water in the ticket hall that has been there for over twenty years, because nobody can figure out how the rain is getting in. Bakerloo Station has always had calcium stalactites and wet patches on its walls.

You can't fight London rain, or even divert it. When the wind blows from the east I've seen it fall upwards, burrowing into the driest corners and soaking them. Yet we are disrespectful of it. We go out without waterproof shoes or raincoats and stand about in T-shirts pretending it's not utterly miserable. We expect rain to fall during Wimbledon fortnight, summer festivals, sporting events, lawn parties, barbecues and open-air concerts, yet we're never quite prepared when it does. In any part of Southeast Asia you can automatically bag an umbrella when it's wet, but nobody's thought of providing that service in London.

Our city looks more atmospheric in a downpour when the present peels away to reveal the past, yet few films capture the way it really looks. The rainy half-light damps down colour and suggests sinister plots: watch old films like *Séance on a Wet Afternoon* or *It Always Rains on Sunday*.

London has lower annual rainfall than New York (106 rainy days a year compared to 167). Even Miami gets more rain. The difference is that London's precipitation is consistent throughout the year and it's overcast even when dry. Rain may fall and dry out a dozen times in one day. Ask any Londoner what they think about the weather—better yet, don't, because they'll tell you. At great length.

It sometimes seems as if Londoners spend half their lives trying to keep water out of their houses. There are stories of the River Tyburn turning up all over the place. The river rises at Shepherd's Well in Hampstead and flows down through Regent's Park and the West End to the Thames. It surfaces in Grays Antique Market, near South Molton Lane in Central London. The building's basement was originally under six feet of water, the reason for this supposedly being a tributary running to the Thames— the hidden River Tyburn (or more likely a sewer). As the area became built up the river was culverted, but in the basement of Grays Mews it still seems to be there in a channel that's now full of goldfish, with a camp little bridge going over it.

Before Oxford Street took its present name it was known as Tyburn Road, which led to the Tyburn hanging gallows, still marked with a plaque at the site of Marble Arch and Tyburn Lane, now Park Lane.

From the thirteenth century, the Tyburn supplied water for London through conduits made of elm trunks, which were later changed to leather pipes. Brook Street in Mayfair takes its name from the Tyburn, often referred to as Tyburn Brook. The Tyburn Estate was recorded in the Domesday Book as a manor that consisted of no more than 150 people and worth only fifty-two shillings.

There have always been underground tributaries running beneath the pavements, some of which could be seen. I still remember that when you visited the Gents' in Becky's Dive Bar, a really disgusting old bar that used to exist at the bottom of some stickily carpeted stairs in the basement of the Hop Exchange in Borough, you had to step over a running stream which was a conduit for an underground river. Becky memorably said about her horrible bar, 'My customers don't come here to drink the décor.' Clearly they didn't mind fording a river to reach the loo.

Next time you're passing, stick your head near the drain just outside the Coach & Horses in Clerkenwell and you'll be rewarded by a glimpse (and the noise) of the Fleet rushing south. Waters passing north to south are supposed to be good for the wellbeing of a building, and many Central London houses have capped wells and basement break panels to access underground streams.

You can find the course of the Fleet by walking along the Regent's Canal towpath going east from Camden and seeing where it's permanently flooded. From the marshlands of Hackney and Erith to the neighbourhoods that grew up around the wells and spas, the river and its tributaries have shaped London. They swell through the eroded channels of rock and soil to surface wherever they can. A map of the largest tributaries designed like the London Underground map shows all of the 'lines' running from top to bottom, with the Thames acting as the Central Line. It reminds me once again that the city is in a basin.

London's maritime workers used to forecast rain by bird cries. Seagulls come in from the windy estuary as the weather changes. The canals are once more filled with fish, but seagulls never dive for them. Presumably the black carp that lie in shoals are a little too urban to consume. I'm told that if you put one in a bath of running water for a day you can eat it, but I'd rather go down the chippy.

| | |

The river's south bank was always rough compared to the more refined north. Why?

For years the area was neglected—its footpath passed along the edge of a dangerous neighbourhood, beneath several dark bridges. Right into the noughties it was not the safest place to be at night.

The south bank had been slower to develop. The north bank benefited from being in the deep channel of the Thames, which encouraged ships to dock along that more prosperous side. During the Middle Ages the north grew up as a place of entertainment outside the formal regulation of the City of London. It included theatres and sporting venues, and although the south had places of entertainment too it was also an area where the lawless were safe from prosecution. By the eighteenth century the shallow banks and mud flats of the south side were smothered by industrial buildings and the riverside was cut off from public access.

When the London County Council needed a new hall (built between 1917 and 1922 on the south bank near Lower Marsh) the construction returned part of the Thames to public use. But it was the 1951 Festival of Britain that caused a large part of the area to be redeveloped.

The Festival's legacy was controversial; its buildings and exhibits were demolished to make way for the Jubilee Gardens, while the Royal Festival Hall and Queen's Walk appeared. With the addition of the Queen Elizabeth Hall, the home of the National Theatre, the NFT, the Globe Theatre, the Hayward Gallery and finally Tate Modern taking over the power station, the transformation was total.

Further along, the Greenwich Peninsula was once known as Bugsby's Marshes, and housed the largest gasworks in Europe. No wonder, then, that during the Second World War it became one of London's most protected sites. After it had been pulled down nobody wanted to live on land contaminated with toxic sludge, so the temporary-looking Millennium Dome was built there to give people the chance of seeing bands and comedians they'd assumed were dead. From above, the vast dome represents a clock, the symbol of Greenwich Mean Time, and weighs less than the air inside it. The downside of this is that it can be damaged by a storm.

There was one more addition to be made to the riverscape. The London Eye was intended to be temporary, but it was liked and therefore stayed, providing the perfect spot for New Year's Eve celebrations.

With the new buildings came a new, gentler sort of free-spiritedness. A summer festival opened with performances inside a giant upturned purple cow, along with pop-up pubs and messily overgrown gardens where punters could sit with friends. Finally comfortable in its own skin, the riverside enjoys huge popularity with Londoners, and I have been known to partake of a jar there with Mr May on a summer night.

| | |

Like many places with evocative names there's not much to see at our next Thames-side site. Staying on the north side of Tower Bridge, head east and look for Dead Man's Hole, where bodies were fished from the Thames in Victorian times. It once became a mortuary because so many corpses washed up here. You'll find it at the point on the Thames tourist trail where most people turn around and start heading back, i.e., where it starts to get most interesting.

The shoreline here is green with moss, but then so are most of London's quieter spots in winter, which still tend to be dank, mild, smoky and wet. The Thames tide rises and falls by up to twenty-four feet at Teddington Lock, and can move with surprising speed.

From the mainly deserted north embankment the foreshore is reachable by many sets of steps. They're a reminder of how crowded with boats this area once was; have a look at Stephen Croad's *Liquid History: The Thames Through Time,* which contains wonderful photographs showing the wooden buildings and ships of the Pool of London.*

* The Pool (Upper and Lower) runs from London Bridge to just past Limehouse.

When the tide is right it's possible to access much of the shore. The north shore is marked by a series of iconic pubs, from the Town of Ramsgate to the Captain Kidd, the Prospect of Whitby and the Mayflower.

Over one-tenth of all Americans will tell you their families came over on the *Mayflower*. I don't know about that but I know where they set off from. The Mayflower pub was originally the Spread Eagle. In the nineteenth century sailors wanted to let their loved ones know they were fine but had no time to waste ashore, so the Mayflower helped them out by selling British and American postage stamps. It's still the only UK boozer licensed to sell them.

The wharves and jetties on the north side may have only left behind their stanchions but you can see how maritime over-crowding led them to be built out over the water. The timbers have rotted away now and are being replaced by girders. Down below there's still a strong river atmosphere. Let's just call it an 'atmosphere.'

The Thames starts to widen rapidly going east and at certain times, at certain angles, the present falls away to reveal the past. But even though the shore's ghosts are now fading from view, the river remains, changing and unchanged.

Wilfred Owen wrote, with prescience:

I am the ghost of Shadwell Stair.
Along the wharves by the water-house,
And through the dripping slaughter-house,
I am the shadow that walks there.

Shadwell apparently did have a well which contained sulphur, vitriol, steel and antimony* and was said to cure you of anything,

---

* When powdered, it becomes kohl.

although its waters ended up being used to fix coloured inks onto calico. Probably not very good for you, then.

| | |

You'll always find Victorian clay pipes on the foreshore. They were thrown away after use, so there are thousands of them, and pottery shards chucked from factories before a second firing. The bright red and yellow pebbles with holes in are worn-down London bricks discarded from homes ruined by the Blitz. When there was no bomb insurance, the rubble was often sold.

London once had a floating police station too. The Thames River Police had a railway carriage attached to an old barge which they used as their office until the end of the 1950s. They'd been formed in 1800 to stop looting from the Pool of London ships.

For over thirty years the Thames had its own beach, although I for one wouldn't have wanted to go bathing from it.

The Tower of London beach officially opened on 23 July 1934, after King George V gave his permission for children to 'have this tidal playground as their own forever.' For many years prior to that, East End kids had played on the rocky foreshore of the Tower of London at low tide. This sometimes proved fatal and led to the Tower Hill Improvement Trust creating a safe sandy beach for the children of the local area. It proved to be extremely popular. Hundreds of thousands of visitors (some estimates suggest up to half a million) flocked to it in its first five years. Considering its limitations, this was a huge number. The river's tide was low enough for people to get on the beach for only a couple of hours a day.

Swimming must have been problematic; out in the deeper channel the current is astoundingly strong, and when the tide goes out it can drag a swimmer away at terrific speed. But we're talking about a time when kids still took shells they'd found to school, and not the seaside kind, so safety standards were a tad lower.

Excepting the war, Tower Beach remained open to the public between 1934 and 1971. It was eventually closed when the water was no longer considered safe to bathe in. Although much of the sand has washed away, a considerable amount remains. And at low tide it still looks—and smells—like the seaside.

Today the beach is only open two days a year for National Archaeology Weekend in July, when people can go down and search for items that have been washed up onto the shore.

34

Dust, the Devil &
Other Stories

ARTHUR BRYANT: The Peculiar Crimes Unit wasn't always in King's Cross, but it became our natural home. Any catalogue of faces and events associated with the area would be rich with extraordinary history. It would have to include the minting of coins, deer-hunting, spa-bathing, pagan sacrifice, clowns, the invention of ice cream, St Petersburg, Mary Wollstonecraft, Thomas Hardy, Nell Gwyn, Henry VIII, Merlin and Queen Boadicea (or Boudicca, but I prefer the other spelling).

The neighbourhood sprang up around 60 CE. At that time Prasutagus, head of the Iceni, ruled as an independent ally of Rome and left his kingdom jointly to his daughters and the Roman emperor in his will. But when he died the will was ignored (to the surprise of no one) and the kingdom was taken. His wife Boadicea was flogged, her daughters were ravished and Roman financiers called in their loans.

Boadicea didn't take this well. She led one hundred thousand men in a rebellion that caused Nero to think about leaving our troublesome country.

The area of King's Cross was once a village known as Battle Bridge, an ancient crossing of the River Fleet that's still there. The name gave rise to a belief that it was the site of a major battle between the Romans and the Iceni tribe, but there's no archaeological evidence, despite the fact that Lewis Spence's 1937 book *Boadicea: Warrior Queen of the Britons* went so far as to include a map showing the positions of the opposing armies.

There is a fantasy that she was buried between platforms 9 and 10 in King's Cross Station, but it's a twentieth-century invention. Then, before becoming London's dustbin, the area became a royal spa.

As King George IV's death approached in June 1830, the former Prince Regent became linked with the area. A sixty-foot-high statue was built at the centre of the crossroads. This was to uplift the place as part of a grand entertainment complex, the Panharmonium Royal Gardens, complete with an overhead miniature railway. Very little of it was ever completed. Henceforth the area was to be known as King's Cross. The unloved statue was removed and its base demolished in 1845 in order to widen the road. And although the Regent's Canal was nearby, the association between King's Cross and the King was forgotten.

King's Cross has been a lot of things in its two-thousand-year history, from a battleground to a sacrificial site to a spa with pleasure gardens to a rubbish heap. The Great Dustheap at Battle Bridge, where London emptied its rubbish, was not a healthy place to live near. Oh, and next to it was a smallpox hospital. In 1848 the dustheap was removed, supposedly to assist in rebuilding the city of Moscow, Russia.

Searchers and sorters used to climb the London 'dust' or debris and sift the refuse, separating organic material from bits of china pottery, bones and rags, metal and glass, just as we recycle now. It was all sold off and reused: cinders went to brickmakers, animal bones were taken by soap-makers and the rags were pounded down into paper. Road foundations were made from crushed crockery and oyster shells—one of the most popular foodstuffs of the day.

Often, such piles of waste were deemed beneficial to London's neighbourhoods. Dustheaps and dunghills were allowed to flourish. In the early nineteenth century, 'night soil'—basically human excrement—was dried out and exported to the West Indies as fertilizer. Farmers came from miles around London to bag up dung for their planting.

It will come as no surprise that the dunghills existed in the poorest areas and caused terrible bouts of disease. In Spitalfields the working-class owners of dung heaps became rich from their great steaming piles, pointing out that 'it only stinks if it's stirred.' The argument that cholera was spread from the ill humours of the air took a knock-back after John Snow found that it came from infected pump water. So strong was this belief—that the air was poisoned—that London's Victoria Park was built as a clean air 'break' to keep noxious gases away from the rich.

Dickens famously wrote about the dustheaps in *Our Mutual Friend,* in my humble opinion his most surprising novel. King's Cross's ancient reputation as a place surrounded by piles of rubbish proudly survives today outside McDonald's, the popular American junk food emporium so enthusiastically endorsed by the city's morbidly portly gentlefolk.

So it turns out that the Peculiar Crimes Unit office is built on rubbish. I always suspected it.

| | |

For most of its life London has maintained an unusually low skyline. Until the 1960s St Paul's and the surrounding church spires were the only tall buildings. Westminster's UNESCO World Heritage status is now threatened by its latest towers, which are of mediocre architectural quality and badly sited. Many show no consideration for scale and setting, and make no contribution to street-level experience.

Just as St Paul's has a number of sightlines protected, so did the Tower of London. The Tower is low-set. London rose up around it. Tower Green preserved a uniquely immersive view in that no tall building could be seen from within it. That view was lost in the 1980s when the blank glass box of Tower 42 (oh, the romance of that name) split the sky above the green. Of course London can't be preserved in aspic, but the zones for tall buildings were quickly violated.

Where can you look down on London without seeing the Shard?

There are spectacular greensward spots on Primrose Hill, Greenwich Park near General Wolfe's statue and Telegraph Hill between Nunhead and Brockley. At the top of the National Gallery you feel like you're sitting backstage in London, seeing the rear of Nelson's Column and the tops of buildings you don't normally spot. And at the Tate Modern the top-floor gallery has superb vistas over the river and St Paul's Cathedral. Plus you might get to see somebody putting their pants on.*

If you're prepared to brave the stairs at the Monument—and it's not a climb for claustrophobes, or me with my knees—you'll be rewarded with an interesting view of the City, from the place where the Great Fire began. Oh, hello.

JOHN MAY: Arthur, don't rope me in on anything, I'm not stopping, I just wanted to return your trifocals.

ARTHUR BRYANT: Thank you. Where were they?

---

* The owners of the (very) nearby glass-walled flats lost their privacy case against the Tate. The judge suggested curtains.

JOHN MAY: Inside the cat.

ARTHUR BRYANT: Not Crippen? I wondered where they'd gone.

JOHN MAY: Perhaps it wasn't the best idea to let Maggie stuff our mascot. Your glasses had disappeared up her undercarriage.

ARTHUR BRYANT: You mean she sat on them?

JOHN MAY: Not Maggie's, the cat's.

ARTHUR BRYANT: I must have a word with her. How was she looking?

JOHN MAY: A bit ratty and smelly, a few fleas.

ARTHUR BRYANT: No, I meant the cat.

JOHN MAY: She said to give you a book and hopes you enjoy it, although she didn't understand the ending. Apparently a friend of hers wrote it.

ARTHUR BRYANT: This is an *A–Z*.

I suppose she means Phyllis Pearsall, the painter who founded the Geographers' A–Z Map Company. She walked an enormous number of streets to put this little book together. She's dead, of course, but I don't suppose a little thing like that stopped Maggie from talking to her.

London was never designed with getting about in mind.

Finsbury is one of those areas that confuses everyone because it's not where it should be and there are two of them. Finsbury Park is further north but Finsbury itself is one of those London pockets that gets overlooked, even though it's so close to the Square Mile. Being sandwiched between City Road and Holborn it's a bit invisible, but there's a nice square and a guild school, the Dame Alice Owen's School, founded in 1613. When Alice was young someone shot her through the hat with an arrow and nearly killed her. She outlived three husbands, bore twelve children and founded the school in gratitude for her saved life.

Nearby Clerkenwell is unsurprisingly named after a well, probably in the early twelfth century. It was set in the wall of a nunnery but built over in 1857, then rediscovered in 1924. It could once be visited, but now it's hard to see because it's in the basement of a private Farringdon Lane office. It looks like a nondescript drainhole and you can easily miss it. I mean, you can easily miss it off your itinerary.

Clerkenwell was also the home of the Knights of St John of Jerusalem. The Priory Church of the Order of St John in St John's Square was burned down by Wat Tyler in 1381, and was most recently destroyed by the Luftwaffe. A circle of granite today marks the outline of the old nave. It's a very peaceful corner of Central London with few visitors and hardly any traffic.

The Clerkenwell House of Detention off Clerkenwell Green once held prisoners awaiting trial, and is one of the most disturbing underground buildings I've ever entered. In 1867 its exercise yard was blown up by Fenians, killing twelve and injuring 120, in what became known as the 'Clerkenwell Outrage.' Its ringleader was the last person to be publicly executed outside Newgate Prison.

The underground chambers were used as shelters during the Blitz and are occasionally open to the public. The brick cells fit together like a series of molecules and open into a huge windowless refectory. The atmosphere is intensely claustrophobic even during a brief visit.

When you follow the chain of wells from King's Cross down through Sadler's Wells and Clerkenwell to the river, it feels as if there's something concealed and secretive about the Clerkenwell streets. There are roads that simply go nowhere.

One such spot is Bleeding Heart Yard, now dominated by a pleasant restaurant. After a hasty lunch there with Simon Sartorius, the charming editor of my memoirs, who was anxious to get away as soon as possible, I learned about the legend associated with this particular cobbled courtyard. According to Dickens, who wrote about it in *Little Dorrit*, a lovelorn young lady had been imprisoned in her bedchamber by a cruel father, and had murmured a love song with the refrain 'Bleeding heart, bleeding heart, bleeding away,' until she died. Unusually for Dickens, it wasn't much of a bleeding story.

But according to older sources, a poem set in 1626 told of one Alice Hatton, the wife of Sir Christopher Hatton, whose family owned the area around Hatton Garden. Alice summoned the Devil and made a pact with him in return for wealth and social standing.

On the Eve of St John at a grand housewarming ball, a tall figure in a black cloak entered at midnight. As a violent storm broke overhead he jigged like a dervish and spirited Alice Hatton away with him, bursting up through the roof. Their *danse macabre* left the tapestries and dinner tables scorched and blackened.

The next day the horrified guests found all that remained of Lady Hatton in the courtyard outside; her heart had been pierced with silver arrows and thrown down beside a pump filled with her blood—and the heart was still bleeding.

It was said that on the night of a full moon she returned in a white gown to work at the pump, trying to wash the blood away, but it continued to gush scarlet, and the ragged hole in her ribcage could never heal, for the bleeding heart had been taken off and buried in an unchristian spot. The tale could be endlessly embellished with gory details.

Dickens pointed out that around here the smoky, drizzly sky seemed to have 'gone into mourning, one might imagine, for the death of the sun,' and there's something about the low level of light that mutes the shades of brick and concrete, especially depressing for those of us who suffer through London's purgatorial month of February.

The geography of Farringdon and Clerkenwell matches its weather, being perverse, wilful, confusing and unsettling. The dark hilly roads provide fertile ground for the planting of sinister tales.

Add to that mix the ancient stories of murders and hangings associated with Smithfield, the wooden wharves of the Thames shore and the rookeries, with their tunnels and passageways burrowed through the houses to allow thieves to escape, and you can see why Dickens made London such a character. It was all around him; all he had to do was stay curious and write it down.

35

The Most Haunted House in London & Other Stories

ARTHUR BRYANT: If you've ever wondered why there are so many theatres in London (but incredibly no theatre museum—the one in Covent Garden was closed down due to lack of funding), you have to listen to this chap. I had him in my 'Friends of the PCU' black book for years, but I can see I crossed his name out and wrote 'High Risk' above it. I wonder why.

Anyway, Maurice Weiss is here, he's the proprietor of the Rooks & Emeralds magic emporium in Hatton Garden and has himself trodden the boards a few times. Those of us who saw his bravely transgressive take on Ophelia, chucking jars of herbs into the audience, will not soon forget the sight. Or indeed be able to.

MAURICE WEISS: Thank you, Arthur. I hung up my tap shoes after a dressing-room blunder led to a hasty exit from the Theatre Royal. I still can't think of Glenda Jackson without shuddering, but we're in showbiz, we plough on.

Theatre is the lifeblood of London. To understand why it became so popular you have to go back to the King's Men, the Rose and the Globe. The leading wits of the seventeenth century gathered in London's coffee houses, and much of their satirical humour was based on the scurrilous scandal-mongering they conducted over their cups of chocolate. As their performances became more extravagant they transferred to stages, finding public audiences, and very soon they incurred the royal displeasure.

The 1737 Licensing Act halted all licentious or offensive plays, and the office of the Lord Chamberlain stepped in to vet scripts. Their powers remained in force right until the 1960s, when playwrights like Joe Orton ran afoul of the law. Mr Orton, born in Leicester in 1933, was pretty much a slum kid and constantly tested the establishment's limits of acceptability. The Lord Chamberlain was concerned with displays of immorality and blasphemy, and was horrified that the central character of Orton's farce *Loot* was a corpse that gets moved about the stage. He called the play 'repellent' and 'unpleasant in many of its details,' with 'filthy dialogue' and 'references to homosexuality.'

It seems relatively tame now, but at the time Orton had to rewrite twenty-four passages. He died at thirty-four but left us with some brilliant plays and a word, 'Ortonesque,' meaning anarchic and darkly comic.

ARTHUR BRYANT: Do you think his social class had anything to do with it?

MAURICE WEISS: Undoubtedly. The establishment did not want some jumped-up working-class chap presenting them with his version of morality, but they had it wrong: Orton's writings were born from his studies of the classics.

One odd side effect of the Licensing Act was to give William Shakespeare a fresh lease of life on the stage because so many new works couldn't be performed. Still, some plays sneaked in as free shows between other productions. John Gay's *The Beggars' Opera* shocked everyone by putting the low lives of harlots and highwaymen on stage for the first time. The film version is worth watching just to see Sir Laurence Olivier share a scene with Kenneth Williams.

ARTHUR BRYANT: I always thought Kenneth Williams was the better actor.

MAURICE WEISS: You would, Arthur. David Garrick brought naturalistic performances to the West End for the first time, instead of all that waving-the-arms-about declamatory stuff, but the theatre was still a riotous place for a night out. Audiences started arriving at 3 P.M., and your footman or coachman would keep your seat for you until you turned up, so they only ever saw the first half of anything. Nobody seemed to mind if they missed great chunks of the play. Often the chatter in the stalls drowned out the actors. In Drury Lane there were iron railings with spikes between the players and the audience.

ARTHUR BRYANT: There are still two royal boxes in the theatre now. Why is that?

MAURICE WEISS: George III and the Prince of Wales hated each other, so when the 1812 theatre was built the owners gave them their own boxes with separate entrances, so that they could sit glowering at each other across the auditorium. If you look at the box seats you'll find that one side has a monarch's crown, the other the Prince of Wales's feathers, and box audiences must enter from the King's staircase or the Prince's staircase.

The theatre gave the public the best nights out that London could offer outside of a bawdy house—it was raucous, communal, argumentative, noisy, exciting and cheap.

Back then the public always felt that it owned the players; if the performances weren't up to snuff the actors had vegetables chucked at them. What with the chandeliers on the move constantly, being raised and lowered to have their candle wicks snuffed, and the general influx and outflow of rowdy people all around, the food-sellers and drunks, there was no hushed sense of sharing a play.

Theatres were also dangerous places. There had even been a murder backstage at Drury Lane in the world's first green room, when in 1735 Charles Macklin stuck his cane through a fellow player's eye after arguing with him about a wig. The cure for such wounds at the time was thought to be urine, and as male actors often played women this resulted in the unfortunate fellow being straddled and peed on by a man in drag. You never see that sort of thing nowadays, more's the pity.

ARTHUR BRYANT: I think I'd better head you off at the pass there, Maurice. Away you go, there's a good fellow. There's a tenner on the sideboard. Don't do anything illegal on the way home.

Legal London—that's an area we haven't touched on.

Lincoln's Inn is a London anomaly.

It's one of the four Inns of Court where barristers are called to the bar, the others being Gray's Inn and Middle and Inner Temples. It looks like a Gothic college in the very centre of the city, beside London's biggest public square, Lincoln's Inn Fields, which is often deserted except for tourists photographing themselves in wedding dresses. It's used as a location for films that like to pretend London is a baroque Disneyland of talking owls and men in magical cloaks.

Speaking of which, Maggie, would you come back in here for a moment?

MAGGIE ARMITAGE: Can it not wait? I'm clearing Janice's desk.

ARTHUR BRYANT: Can't she do that herself?

MAGGIE ARMITAGE: I'm clearing its aura. There are bad vibrations in here.

ARTHUR BRYANT: That's the railway line. I thought you'd like to explain the curious connection that Lincoln's Inn has to magic.

MAGGIE ARMITAGE: Does it?

ARTHUR BRYANT: You're the one who told me about it. I made a note. Here.

MAGGIE ARMITAGE: Oh yes. Well, in 1899 someone dug up a small metal 'cursing square.' Quite a bit is known about these lead tablets. On one side you write the curse, in this case: 'That nothinge maye prosper Nor goe forward that Raufe Scrope takethe in hand,' together with the names Hasmodai, Schedbarschemoth and Schartatan, and three astrological symbols. On the other side you create a square of boxes, placing consecutive numerals in them that make each line add up to the same amount. It's a trick anyone can learn. A schoolboy with the intelligence of a moder ately engaged baboon can do it.

We know that the victim of this particular square, Raufe Scrope, worked at Lincoln's Inn from 1543 to 1572. The names were found to be those of demons. Of course, this is not the only surviving example of a lead cursing square; there was a full history in Agrippa's *Three Books of Occult Philosophy*. However, it's known that Scrope ended his days happily as one of the Lincoln's Inn governors, so the curse didn't take. And we now think we know why. Whoever carved the tablet made numerical errors (no number may be used twice) so the demons didn't appear and Scrope survived.

While we're on the subject, another way of putting curses on people involved the making and mutilating of waxen dolls. There are nineteenth-century accounts, somewhat lurid and unreliable, that mention a woman in 963 CE who placed a nail-studded doll under London Bridge and was branded a witch. She was weighted down and drowned in the Thames. It was a commonly held belief that the placing of something near the potential victim, including chalked runic marks, dead animals and 'cursed' items, would bring about their demise.

Witch bottles have been found all over London. The Museum of London's collection includes several seventeenth-century stoneware pots and glass bottles found buried in sites across the city. They contain heart-shaped pieces of felt studded with pins, metal nails, locks of hair and urine, and were used to ward off curses or heal the owner. Some were created to contain witches or demons. The most recent one found on the Thames foreshore dates from 1982 and contained coins, human teeth and clove oil, a sign that the bearer wished to cure a toothache.

ARTHUR BRYANT: On the north side of Lincoln's Inn Fields stands an extraordinary London treasure house filled with esoteric items. Sir John Soane's Museum at Lincoln's Inn Fields is the world's most complete house-museum, and its most eclectic.

Soane was born in 1753, the son of a bricklayer, and had a long and distinguished architectural career; he rebuilt the Bank of

England, designed Pitzhanger Manor in Ealing and created the Dulwich Picture Gallery, the first purpose-built art gallery in England. But many of his commissions were later demolished, in that cavalier manner London councils so often had with classical buildings.

The narrow-passaged house at 12 Lincoln's Inn Fields became the setting for Soane's antiquities and works of art. Every square inch of it is filled with mouldings, pediments, busts, statues, bronzes, urns, mosaics, vases, hieroglyphs, *objets trouvés*, paintings by Watteau, Canaletto and Reynolds, and thirty thousand architectural drawings. The highlights are the Egyptian sarcophagus of Seti I, which set Soane back two grand, and—best of all—the Picture Room, with its theatrical reveal of unfolding hidden walls. There you'll find Hogarth's series *A Rake's Progress* and his *Election* paintings but you'll need a book to decode all the secret messages tucked into the pictures.

Despite London's grey skies, the building virtually lights itself. The dome in the breakfast room concentrates light on the centre, and a series of hidden mirrors can angle sunlight down through the shadowy building.

After the death of his wife Soane lived there alone, constantly adding to and rearranging his collections. Having been disappointed by the conduct of his two wastrel sons, he decided to establish the house as a museum to which amateurs and students should have access. It is better known now than it once was but still flies a little under the sightseeing radar. Just as well; there's a limit on the number of visitors that can be allowed in.

Once I've visited the Inns I like to sit in the Fields—these days a neat little park—and fantasize about poisoning the pigeons. In Berkeley Square I remember seeing the annual migration of caterpillars, wherein every inch of the square from railings to gazebo was covered in peristaltic green wrigglers, dropping from the trees down the back of your neck. Chattering starlings in the branches of the plane trees in Leicester Square would suddenly soar above the treeline in vast flocks to form sweeping, folding patterns in the sky. Neither of these events seem to have occurred again since the nineties.

You often see foxes padding across the busiest parts of the city, though, even in Piccadilly Circus. There are swans in the royal parks, pelicans in St James's, herons, cormorants and cranes near almost any watery space, but no longer many house sparrows, which used to be on every rooftop. Where did they all go? The most likely explanation seems to be that sparrow chicks require insect food for their survival, especially for the first few days after hatching. When their parents aren't able to find insects, the population decreases. They're grain-eaters, but can adapt to urban waste so long as they reach maturity first.

Nor will you find the thirty-five-thousand-odd pigeons of Trafalgar Square, thanks to the hawk and two kestrels that now keep them away. Bird-feeders used to sell us packets of seed until 2001, but they were booted out after a health and safety panic in Whitehall. When someone suggests that we're seeing more green parakeets in London, you can point out that they've been here for a couple of centuries and may have been included in Henry VIII's royal menagerie. Parakeets are faster and more sociable than many British birds but they're not at war with each other, unlike the red and grey squirrels.

From 1986 onwards, attempts to reintroduce the native red squirrel over the North American grey have met with limited success, i.e., the reds got biffed. The greys spread the squirrelpox virus, to which they're immune, but the reds are not. The return of red squirrels leads to the sound of birdsong returning. While grey squirrels eat young birds, reds do not. Unfortunately the greys are the bullies of the squizzer world and easily dominate the reds.

Contrary to popular belief, hardly any house in London has rats. They live outside our homes, but can sometimes be found inside factories or warehouses. That leaves the tube mice, which you can see from almost any London Underground platform, which are related to field mice and very attractive, even though they sometimes unnerve visitors. There are plenty of bats, geese, ducks and probably more bees in London than outside the capital, where the growing of rapeseed has created a demand for pollination that our bee population can't currently handle.

And no longer are sheep trotted down Piccadilly (although it still happened in the 1940s). Nor are cattle driven from Islington's Caledonian Market to Smithfield. However, London has a fine bestiary of non-living animals.

THE LIONS

New York is your go-to city for gargoyles, but if it's lions you're after there are approximately ten thousand of them dotted around London. Some have wings, some are on Britannia's helmet, some are sleeping or sad, and some hold shields or wear crowns. Some are roaring; many are on pubs. There's one on the newly refurbished Holborn Viaduct (and a similar one on Devonshire House, Piccadilly) that has a ball. And there are lions, dragons and something that looks like a dog creeping all over the parapets of Westminster Abbey.

The monumental fountain known as the Victoria Memorial in front of Buckingham Palace is guarded by great lions on leashes. In summer it's surrounded by geraniums to reflect the colour of guardsmen's uniforms. Frank J. Manheim's wonderful book *Lion Hunting in London* features every great beast to be found in the capital, although as the volume was published in the 1970s I imagine most of them have since been turned into one-bed apartments.

Except for the best lions of all, Sir Edwin Landseer's great bronze lions around Nelson's column in Trafalgar Square, which have come to represent London and always look as if they're about to come to life.

THE GRASSHOPPER

There have been 168 hanging signs over the Square Mile's Lombard Street across the years, but the golden Gresham grasshopper at number 68 is the most famous. There's a story about the Greshams. As a baby, the patriarch, Roger de Gresham, was supposedly dumped, Moses-like, in the Norfolk reeds and discovered there by a woman who followed the sound of a grasshopper, although why she'd do that is anyone's guess. Surely she wasn't just hanging around in the marshes listening out for distress calls issued by insects. The grasshopper was part of the Gresham heraldic symbol, but surely you wouldn't pick it as a symbol for a company; the grasshopper, if you remember your Aesop's Fables, is a symbol of laziness.

THE CAMELS

There are quite a few camels around, including a panel of pack camels on Peek House in Eastcheap, but I like the ones holding up the Thames-side benches along the Embankment best. I think they were made in the 1870s by Z. D. Berry & Son to go with the Egyptian sphinxes and Cleopatra's Needle.

THE ELEPHANT, TIGER, SHARK & GORILLA

They're all recent and lived above the doorway of Allington House, Victoria Street. The Endangered Species Triptych was sculpted by Barry Baldwin in the 1980s, but the endangered species themselves became endangered when their home was knocked down and they were handed back to the sculptor.

THE REALLY UGLY FISH

He's fantastical and possibly from the depths of the ocean, and lately seems to have lost his gilt finish, but he lives on top of the former Billingsgate Fish Market building on Lower Thames Street, now an 'events space,' where he's surrounded by fishy friends. Unsurprisingly, there are plenty of fish around London, from the Embankment's lamppost sturgeons to ones in ceramic tiles outside the few remaining original fish shops. Many of the fish seem to be presented upside down, for reasons I can't begin to fathom. But then I don't know the reason for 90 percent of what goes on around me at these days.

Sculptor David Wynne's twee children riding dolphins can be found near Tower Bridge and on Chelsea Embankment opposite the Albert Bridge. Call me a curmudgeon, but although they have an airy lightness they have none of the grace of Alfred Gilbert's statuary. Gilbert, the genius sculptor of Piccadilly's 'Eros,' is an interesting character. Commissions for his statuary eventually brought on a nervous breakdown, but he was his own worst enemy. Forever tangled in lawsuits and the destruction of his work (and his reputation), he was eventually knighted and went on to illustrate Sherlock Holmes stories in the *Strand* magazine.

Janice has just pointed out to me that a dolphin is a mammal and doesn't belong in the 'fish' section. Thank you for that, Janice.

THE UNICORNS

Wherever there's a London lion there's often a unicorn nearby. Together they represent the English–Scottish union. There's a particularly ferocious, startled-looking unicorn on the top of St George's, Bloomsbury, and another on the gates of Buckingham Palace. But the Queen Elizabeth Gate at Hyde Park has the worst, a sort of flattened *faux-naïf* biscuit-tin lid with the lion and the unicorn commemorating the Queen Mother's ninetieth birthday in 1990, also by David Wynne.

| | |

There are plenty of other London animals, from mythical chimeras all over the Square Mile to the various insects (including a gold louse and a gold bedbug) that adorn the London School of Hygiene and Tropical Medicine building on Gower Street.

The best eagle has to be the magnificent Royal Air Force Memorial (1923) on Victoria Embankment. There's an antelope in Trafalgar Square, sheep in Paternoster Square, a big feral-looking rabbit painted on Hackney Road and—for some unearthly reason—a spindly dancing hare at Admiralty Arch, but I'm not recommending that you head there, as half of them are likely to have hopped off by the time this pamphlet comes out.

Animals were often symbols of outlying parts of the British Empire, like those on George Gilbert Scott's Albert Memorial in South Kensington, which was to include a lion representing Britain, but after some genius pointed out that it wasn't native to these shores it was changed to a bull. There's a similar, simpler

Albert Memorial in Manchester too, and they got theirs in 1865, seven years ahead of London.

Not many people know that London's Albert Memorial has a basement. It's an undercroft and supports the immensely heavy monument. There are 868 arches surrounding the central column, and the brickwork is in far better nick than in most people's houses. Sadly, it's not open to the public. The area of museums and educational institutions in South Kensington was known as Albertopolis, by the way.

More recently horses have started appearing all over London, like Park Lane's evocative memorial to animal war heroes, sculpted by David Backhouse. Eight million horses died in the First World War. Many were transporting ammunition and supplies to the front. More than two hundred thousand pigeons were pressed into service in the Second World War and saved many soldiers' lives carrying messages. There were also a great many wartime dogs and mules (famously heroic), but no cats, presumably because they couldn't be arsed to help out in the war and stayed home by the fire.

There are a huge number of carved dray horses in Camden Market, very much associated with the area. The galloping fountain horses at the top of the Haymarket feel more random, but look up to the roof and you'll see three golden ladies swan-diving off it; it's the other half of the sculpture, apparently, something to do with Helios, the personification of the sun, because London is known as the Sunshine City, obviously.

36

Witches & Other Stories

ARTHUR BRYANT: I've been asked about London ghosts. I wasn't planning to cover hauntings because they're nearly all the same: scared housemaid, weird old man in blurry photo, pale figure loitering in the stalls, etc., so I'm handing you back to Maggie. This is more her sort of thing. If you get bored you can wander off and make a cup of tea while she's talking; she won't notice.

MAGGIE ARMITAGE: At the last séance Dame Maude and I conducted in my front parlour we conjured a spirit so powerful that I couldn't get him to leave for weeks. Most of the time he sat in the living room watching *Judge Judy* but I managed to lure him into the garden and Dame Maude dispatched him with a revenant's spell, five pounds of rock salt and a spade.

The problem with most ghosts is that they don't actually exist. The case of number 50 Berkeley Square, Mayfair, is typical. It first came to public attention in *Notes and Queries*, November 1872,[*]

[*] A scholarly journal publishing articles related to the English language and literature.

when someone asked about the rumours surrounding the house. It was said to be haunted by Bloody Bones, a sixteenth-century bogeyman.

No two stories about the house are alike, but they did not go away. By 1880 a brainless bishop waded in with a tale of sisters encountering a ghost lying in the bed of a housemaid who died of fright. A quick bit of research (i.e., to which hospital was the dead housemaid admitted?) showed the tale to be nonsense. And by the 1930s there was a connection to a recently published ghost story with the same circumstances written by Elliot O'Donnell, a tall-tale teller who claimed to have been strangled by a dead man in Dublin, presumably without lasting effects. O'Donnell happily added new elements, including a 'horrible shape' and a sailor dead from fright. As we have seen, fact and fiction have a tendency to collide and rub off on one another. So long as a country is at war with someone or the infant mortality rate is high, ghost tales are told.

Any empty London house attracted stories; stories would be told of screams in the night and bloody murder, but they were ridiculously easy to disprove. But what's interesting about number 50 Berkeley Square is that further embellishments accumulated in the form of a jilted bride, madness, suicides and servants who kept a room permanently locked—all classic tropes of the haunted house story.

Lord Edward Bulwer-Lytton, he of the dreadful purple prose, wrote *The Haunted and the Haunters,* which also appeared to be about the house. Berkeley Square gained its 'most haunted' title from Peter Underwood, the President of the Ghost Club, the world's oldest psychical research organization, which is still going strong.

The end of the 1930s brought to a close the craze for haunted houses, possibly coinciding with an improvement in photography, most certainly affected by the more real horrors of another approaching World War.

Through sixty years of the Mayfair haunted-house saga, no coroners' reports or police statements back up any of the details in these 'hauntings.' Folklorist Steve Roud calls this 'reversal of causation': The house is not empty because it is haunted, but is haunted because it is empty. So manifestations appear because the psychological conditions are right.

If we apply the 'reversal of causation' theory to other hauntings, from the spectres of Hallam Street to those of the Cock Lane ghost, the Man in Grey at Drury Lane, the Tower ghosts and so on, spooks arise in eerie atmospheres and legends accrete to them as others claim authorship.

ARTHUR BRYANT: I thought you of all people would believe in hauntings, Maggie.

MAGGIE ARMITAGE: Do I think they really saw ghosts? I believe in what people believe, because I understand *why* they believe. Today some believe that more likes on social media will improve their wellbeing, a modern-day phantasm. You have to remember that London was a dark place filled with unseen terrors.

ARTHUR BRYANT: I know that the first building to be lit with electricity was the Savoy Theatre in 1881. Suddenly everyone could see how dirty the ceiling was. Even until the 1960s the whole of London was blackened and dark.

Is there a spot that gives you chills?

MAGGIE ARMITAGE: I don't like the Theatre Royal, Drury Lane. It's a great shadowy mausoleum of a building, chilly and depressing even in bright sunshine. There are tunnels and corridors everywhere, and at least four ghosts, including a couple of old music hall stars and the powdered and tricorned Man in Grey, whose remains were found in a walled-up passage in 1848. The actor Charles Macklin—

ARTHUR BRYANT: The chap who stabbed his fellow actor through the eye and killed him.

MAGGIE ARMITAGE: He's supposed to haunt the theatre, but it's the way in which he does it that gives me the creeps. He stands just behind actors and whispers their lines in their ears.

ARTHUR BRYANT: You still didn't tell me if you believe in ghosts.

MAGGIE ARMITAGE: If I tell people I'm a white witch someone will always ask that question. It's a bit like asking a surgeon if they're also a plumber. What I do is much subtler. It involves the dissection of the soul.

ARTHUR BRYANT: Sounds messy. And vaguely illegal. When did you stop being persecuted in the UK?

MAGGIE ARMITAGE: You mean witches? Take a guess.

ARTHUR BRYANT: I don't know . . . 1820?

MAGGIE ARMITAGE: 1944. Jane Rebecca Yorke was working as a medium in South London when she was arrested under the Witchcraft Act of 1735 for spreading disinformation and exploiting fears during a time of war. She was found guilty at the Central Criminal Court, but since she was seventy-two at the time of her conviction the judge went lightly on her. She was sentenced to three years of good behaviour and fined five pounds.

ARTHUR BRYANT: So she wasn't imprisoned.

MAGGIE ARMITAGE: No, that honour belongs to 'Hellish Nell,' Helen Duncan, also in 1944, but her case was much more serious. She was accused of being a traitor and tried at the Old Bailey.

ARTHUR BRYANT: That's a charge which used to carry a death sentence. What did she do to earn it?

MAGGIE ARMITAGE: In 1941 she told the audience at one of her séances that HMS *Barham* had sunk. She conjured up the spirit of a sailor who was one of over eight hundred who had died in the torpedo attack. She upset quite a few people and drew the attention of the authorities, because it wasn't public knowledge that the *Barham* had been destroyed; only the direct relatives of the dead had been told. Duncan had picked up the gossip and weaponized it. She had even made a fake HMS *Barham* hatband to produce as an artefact, but she didn't realize that the navy had stopped putting the names of ships on them two years earlier for security reasons.

They couldn't think how to prosecute her. She was arrested under the Vagrancy Act, but then it was remembered that the Witchcraft Act covered fraudulent spiritualism. She was convicted and went to the pokey for nine months. One of the rules of her release was that she could not conduct any more séances, but of course she was arrested for doing it again some years later.

The psychical researcher Harry Price conducted a battery of tests on her and concluded, 'Could anything be more infantile than a group of grown-up men wasting time, money and energy on the antics of a fat female crook.'

The funny thing is that she'd been proven to be a fake, over and over, regurgitating bits of egg white and cheesecloth and passing them off as ectoplasm, but her followers continued to support her even after her death.

ARTHUR BRYANT: I guess belief is sometimes stronger than science, even when it's completely dunderheaded.

37

Mayfair Ladies &
Other Stories

ARTHUR BRYANT: Most Londoners tend to think of Mayfair as the home of embassies and billionaires and leave it well alone. The only time I ever cross it is when I've been to the annual Police Federation Ball, so I'm not really studying the houses. I'm trying to negotiate the pavement using each eyeball alternately.

Besides, what is there to see? Park Lane, of course, but nobody hangs around those dated hotels and hideous car showrooms. I thought I'd better get someone who's more of a toff than me, i.e., anybody else, to answer this question.

Giles Kershaw is the St Pancras coroner and has some dead posh connections. You sense this when you first meet him because he always looks like he just came off a tennis court. Whereas I look like I just came out of a police court.

GILES KERSHAW: I'm actually not posh, Mr Bryant. Upper-class people don't buy their own furniture. I shop at IKEA. You just think I'm posh because I use Received Pronunciation.

ARTHUR BRYANT: How do I sound, then?

GILES KERSHAW: Like a greengrocer trying to impress a girl.

We're right to find something slightly sinister about those perfect Mayfair façades with their polished brass knockers, mysterious nameplates and shielded windows.

I did a bit of homework. Mayfair is a roughly square area bordered by Park Lane, Oxford Street, Regent Street and Piccadilly. It was named after the fortnight-long May fair that took place on the site in the seventeenth and eighteenth centuries. Like most British revelries it tended to get a bit out of control, and in 1764 it was banned due to over-boisterous behaviour. The Mayfair residents didn't want the lower classes coming in.

The Queen was born on Bruton Street; Churchill, Disraeli, Henry James and Frideric Handel all lived there. Many of the shops hold a royal warrant.

The grand mansions of Mayfair stood in their own grounds, but most were destroyed and rebuilt on a smaller scale, although the Saudi Arabian Embassy still inhabits an elegant survivor, Crewe House. It's impossible to take a picture of anymore, as it's now surrounded by British officers with machine guns.

Mayfair is where Keith Moon and Mama Cass both died in the same room, in a flat owned by Harry Nilsson. It's where Jeffrey Archer met a lady friend and lied about it, and where Bertie Wooster lived in a bubble of languid luxury with his faithful butler. It's the home of the oldest object in London, an Egyptian sculpture above the door of Sotheby's that dates to before 1600 BCE.

There are supposed to be all kinds of passageways underneath Mayfair. Some buildings have shared facilities, with linked cellars on either side of the street. The wine merchants Berry Bros. &

Rudd and the perfumiers Penhaligon's are connected by tunnels that also head off in other directions.

Mayfair was a place in which to publicly display your wealth. In the last few years it has become somewhere to hide it. The neighbourhood's nefarious activities have continued in a more covert manner into the present day in the form of fake international companies, with certain Mayfair houses existing purely to launder suspect money. The government's desire to serve Putin's oligarchs became so strong that our fair city was openly referred to as 'Londongrad.' Eventually the government was shamed into cleaning it up a little, but it has become an impossible task.

At the very heart of Mayfair is a square developed in 1735–46 by Edward Shepherd— now known as Shepherd Market. The narrow backstreets off the square always had a scandalous reputation. I'm sure Mr Bryant remembers those dark roads in the 1970s, or possibly the 1870s, when they were still full of expensive prostitutes.

ARTHUR BRYANT: I suppose it's having no one but dead people to talk to all day that makes you so rude. You're right about the ladies, though. While the vice unit regularly raided Soho houses, they kept away from Mayfair. Too many senior politicians and members of the upper classes used them.

GILES KERSHAW: It was the home of 'Skittles,' London's last real courtesan. Mrs Catherine Walters really didn't care what society thought of her. She lived at 15 South Street from 1872 to 1920 and was the mistress of the Duke of Devonshire, among many others.

She drove better carriages and wore finer clothes than any of her clients' wives, and she swore like a navvy. In old age she was pushed through Hyde Park in her wheelchair by Lord Kitchener, and, although disreputable, she was awarded the highest of honours: a blue plaque that can still be seen outside her house.

ARTHUR BRYANT: Second-highest. The highest is having a pub named after you.

GILES KERSHAW: There were plenty of drinking establishments in Mayfair too. The illicit basement bars gradually withered away, with one of the most famous, the rather disreputably glamorous Embassy Club, the last to leave. Annabel's is still there, of course, but these days it's associated with—

ARTHUR BRYANT: I'm going to head you off there, Giles, before you commit a libel that gets us all in trouble.

GILES KERSHAW: You mean slander, not libel. I'm speaking it.

ARTHUR BRYANT: If the book gets published it comes under 'wide dissemination' and counts as libel.

GILES KERSHAW: It's a book? You never mentioned that. Am I getting paid?

ARTHUR BRYANT: Absolutely adorable to see you again, Giles, we must do this more often. Help yourself to tea and take a biscuit from the barrel.

| | |

I don't mix in posh circles but I did once meet the mayor. Every November he puts on a show which is now eight centuries old. A big attraction is always the golden State Coach of the Lord Mayor, built in 1757 and the oldest ceremonial vehicle in regular use in the world. It's covered in allegorical paintings, weighs nearly three tons and has had over a hundred coats of paint.

The head of the procession leaves Mansion House at 11 A.M. and close to the front you'll find the wicker figures of Gog and Magog. Behind them the procession is gradually zipped together from three moving streams to create a single broad parade that takes over an hour to pass.

The State Coach leaves Guildhall and trundles round to Mansion House to pick up the new Lord Mayor. It joins the procession near the back—over an hour behind the first float—and goes with it to St Paul's, where the Lord Mayor and his officials receive a blessing. It continues down Ludgate Hill and Fleet Street to the Royal Courts.

While the new Lord Mayor makes an oath of loyalty to the Crown, the Pageant Master squashes the procession into the side streets around Aldwych while taking care of hundreds of horses. The coach finally returns the Lord Mayor to Mansion House some time before 2:30 P.M.

After the procession there are free guided tours of the City's more strange and wonderful corners, then in the evening the Lord Mayor's fireworks light up the sky over the river.

The Lord Mayor's Show has long been considered the longest, grandest, most meticulously organized procession in the world. There is no way to rehearse a three-mile procession in the middle of the City of London, so it's all put together on the day.

One other thing can always be relied upon at the Lord Mayor's Show; it will absolutely piss down.

38

A Torture Chair &
Other Stories

Around London in Thirty Objects with Arthur Bryant

THE OTHER ELEPHANT

We remember the Elephant & Castle (or Newington, as it was) for the density of its traffic, its appallingly ugly shopping precinct and the general air of despair on people's faces as they tried to get across the vast, miserable roundabout. No more, for it has all been demolished to make way for a bright new future where we all visit each other's luxury apartments in jet packs.

'Elephant and Castle' was supposed to be a corruption of 'La Infanta de Castilla,' referring to the Queen Consort of Edward I, but she has nothing to do with it, because the area was named after a pub. On the roof of the Elephant & Castle boozer was a large elephant, sometimes painted pink, with a castle on its back. It stood on top of one of the roughest pubs the Met ever had to police. Weirdly it was also where the comic Lily Savage started out. Quite how it became London's dodgiest drag pub remains a mystery. The spot where nightly fights once broke out and se-quins were scattered across the pavement is now a dreary coffee chain. But the last time I looked, the elephant was still on its roof.

There's another elephant nearby on the South Bank, opposite Big Ben: Salvador Dalí's unsettling giraffe-legged mammal appears to stride above the Houses of Parliament on the facing side of the river.

THE TWELFTH NIGHT CAKE

Twelfth Night is the only one of Shakespeare's plays we can truly date. It was first performed for Elizabeth I on 6 January 1601. Twelfth Night marked the end of a winter festival that started on Hallowe'en. Robert Baddeley (1733–94) was a pastry chef who became a comic actor. To raise money for 'an asylum for decayed actors' he bequeathed a traditional Twelfth Night cake and ale to the performers, to be cut in the green room of the Theatre Royal, Drury Lane on Twelfth Night in perpetuity. It's still handed out every year. Similar ceremonies are conducted around the country, and there are all kinds of recipes for Twelfth Night cakes online. So I'm told. I don't go online as I keep accidentally ordering things. I still have to find a way of sending back one hundred jars of gherkins. I thought they were expensive.

A WILLOW STICK

London is a city of villages, boroughs and wards, all marked with boundaries. Every third Ascension Day (no, I don't know when that is either) choirboys go around the boundaries of the Tower of London with the Yeoman Warder, beating the pavements with willow wands. They are no longer laughed at. Wands have new-found respectability since Harry Potter.

This ancient custom is about protecting what's yours. It's carried out during Rogationtide, the fifth week after Easter, and requires parishes to mark out their jurisdiction. It involves a band of community members led by the parish priest and church officials who walk the boundaries of the parish and pray for protection, blessing the land. In London, boundaries may lie in the Thames, so part of the ritual involves thrashing the river too.

Before the Reformation these days were known as Gang-Days. The territorial marking is also conducted in some parts of America. Apparently 'Beating of the Bounds' is still conducted in the kind of English towns that try to prevent Starbucks from opening where the old wool shop used to be—you know, next to where that lovely cake shop was that's now a tandoori restaurant.

DICK WHITTINGTON'S CAT

This malevolent little bugger is made of stone and sits on Dick's marker on Highgate Hill. It marks the spot where Dick heard the Bow bells telling him to 'Turn again, Whittington, thrice Lord Mayor of London.' You can see him right near the entrance to the Whittington Hospital. It's likely that Dick Whittington didn't have a cat at all. A 'cat' was a nickname for a coal-barge. Whittington made his fortune in coal.

Thanks to him the principal boy in the eponymous pantomime can still slap her thigh and cry, 'Two hundred miles from London and still no sign of Dick.' Which always got a laugh from my old dad.

THE FISH IN THE PAVEMENT

On London's Marchmont Street there are a number of odd tokens embedded in concrete paving stones, including a pineapple, a fish and a key. In 2007 an artist created them to symbolize the items left behind by impoverished mothers who needed to identify their babies. The children were left in the Foundling Hospital at Coram's Fields, to await collection when their mothers were better-off, although few ever were.

The saddest item left around a baby's neck in the collection has to be a label from a gin bottle. The practice only lasted about fifteen years after its initiation in 1741. Illegitimacy was such a stigma that the abandoning of babies proved all too successful; admission rates soared to four thousand a year. But that's another story.

THE BOLAN SWANS

Forget Freddie Mercury; the real hero of the glam-rock movement was the less remembered Marc Bolan, born Mark Feld, whose band T. Rex strode like a colossus over Britain in the early seventies. Bolan had a lifelong fear of cars and never got behind the wheel of one, but was killed in a car driven by Gloria Jones, his partner, who was charged with being unfit to drive but fled back to America before the trial. In the meantime their home was looted by fans. Fellow band member Steve Currie was killed in a car crash four years later.

The swans aren't official epitaphs, but in Golders Green Crematorium a number of them are regularly placed by fans to mark his death, after his signature song 'Ride a White Swan.' At his memorial statue in Barnes, where the accident happened, swan-feather wreaths and china swans are still left by fans.

THE CABLE STREET MURAL

'They Shall Not Pass!' was the war-cry. The Battle of Cable Street took place on Sunday, 4 October 1936 in East London's Cable Street, a clash between the police and protestors. The cops were overseeing a march by the British Union of Fascists led by Oswald Mosley, who were faced down by local people, including Jewish, Socialist and Communist groups.

Mosley planned to send thousands of marchers dressed in uniforms styled on Mussolini's blackshirts through the East End, which had a large Jewish population. The mural has long been controversial because it asks whether the arts should fund political statements, but it has been restored and survives as a symbol of freedom.

THE EUSTON ROAD TORTURE CHAIR

There's a Chinese torture chair in the Wellcome Trust's museum in Euston Road that's at least a couple of hundred years old. It features the heads of mythological sea monsters called *makara* and is covered in razor-sharp steel blades. However, it could never have actually been used for torture as it would have killed its sitter too quickly. It was probably used to frighten prisoners into talking. It's so lethal-looking that we wouldn't even try to trick Raymondo into sitting on it. There are probably a few authoritarian nations that would like to get their hands on one, but as a psychological torture device it did the job.

THE LED ZEPPELIN TOWER

It's hard to believe that such a tower house is in London, but it's at 29 Melbury Road, Kensington, and looks like something out of a horror film. It contains an astrology hall and extraordinarily elaborate mock-medieval frescoes, mosaics and fireplaces, in a late-Victorian style that manages to be fussy and ornate without being remotely attractive. Oh, and it's been the home of the actor Richard Harris, and Jimmy Page from Led Zeppelin. What is it about old rebels wanting to live like baronial lords? The experimental film-maker Kenneth Anger (né Anglemyer) once lived in its basement. Fans make pilgrimages there, which must be annoying when Jimmy Page is looking out of the window doing the washing-up. No lift, but there's probably a stairway to heaven.

THE PLAGUE BELL

Who would have thought that a seventeenth-century London device would take on new resonance in the twenty-first century? Plague bells were simply made from a stick attached to a ring of metal with a clapper, and were rung for three-quarters of an hour at burials to remind everyone of the rules surrounding prevention of the 1665 plague, which wiped out 15 percent of London's population. The Museum of London has one.

THE BUCKET OF SAND

You used to see them in theatres by the back wall—primitive forms of fire prevention—and at railway stations. People stubbed their fag ends into them. But they also gave their name to the announcements you still sometimes hear in stations: 'Calling Inspector Sands.' It was originally theatre code for fire, but is now used by public transport controllers to alert staff to a potential emergency such as a fire, a bomb scare or a McFlurry spill without exercising the public and creating panic.

THE SOHO SQUARE COIN TUBE

The House of St Barnabas on the corner of Soho Square and Greek Street was for many years a hostel. Whenever I parked outside, an old dear from there always accused me of stealing her car and would try to thump me. Dickens featured the house as Dr Manette's home in *A Tale of Two Cities*. The building was always designated a House of Charity (there had been a property on this site from 1679 onwards) and it still holds charity status, although it is now a private club, the appeal being its listed rooms and its secret garden.

Attesting to its status as a charitable institution, there was for over a century a coin tube that went from street level to the basement for charitable donations. Such tubes were quite common around London; our local toy shop had one when I was a child— you dropped in a penny and an elaborate train set came to life. The St Barnabas tube may still be there for all I know. I don't drive into Soho anymore, the parking's a nightmare, or at least it is when I park.

THE GOLDEN FIREBALL

If you've ever wondered what that gold thing was on the top of the Monument, the tower designed by Christopher Wren in 1671 to commemorate the Great Fire of London, it's a finial made of gilt copper intended to represent a ball of flame. It was set to be a phoenix but councillors decided that no one would know what it was. It looked like a starved chicken.

THE SNUFFER

You can still see these set to one side of doorways outside certain houses in Bloomsbury and in the oldest parts of London. There's one at number 9 St James's Square. They're snuffers, which link boys used to put out their flaming tar-covered sticks after escorting visitors through unlit streets for a few pence. People went to restaurants preceded by link boys, lighting the dark and scaring off would-be thieves.

THE BEATRIX POTTER TOMBSTONES

It turns out that Beatrix Potter's characters were real after all. The celebrated children's author used to take walks in Brompton Cemetery, and noted down the names on the tombstones she saw all around her. These include Mr Nutkins, Peter Rabbett, Mr Mc-Gregor and Jeremiah Fisher.

THE PINEAPPLE OF ABUNDANCE

If you look at the top of the dome of St Paul's Cathedral, you'll find a golden pineapple. In fact, they're all over the place, on tops of railings, on the obelisks at Lambeth Bridge, on Sir John Soane's tomb, and all over the Pineapple Pub, Kentish Town. Because they were so scarce, pineapples were an exotic symbol of wealth. But they weren't eaten; in the eighteenth century they could be rented as centrepieces for dinner parties.

Acorns abounded almost as much and can still be seen on many London railings. Dozens of regilded acorns around Devonshire Street remind me of our debt to the Romans in London— these are symbols of hospitality that welcome you into buildings.

THE MUMMY CATS

Dirty Dicks started out as the Old Jerusalem, and is the only example I can think of where a pub has chosen a new identity that makes it sound less salubrious.

You can blame health and safety for a lot of things, but perhaps getting rid of the very dusty mummified cats which until the 1980s graced the ceiling of Dirty Dicks in the East End wasn't an altogether bad thing. I remember going there as a child and being delighted by them. Nathaniel Bentley, the owner, lived in notoriously unclean conditions for decades, supposedly mourning the death of his fiancée and in the process inspiring Dickens to create Miss Havisham's wedding-feast table in *Great Expectations*.

Like most London stories it's probably hogwash built around a grain of truth, but that's how I like my mythology. We do know that Bentley's property became so filthy that he was considered 'a Celebrity of Dirt.' He became so famous for his lack of cleanliness that letters intended for him would be addressed to 'The Dirty Warehouse, London.' He died in 1809, probably from long-term germ exposure.

THE PEARLY KING COSTUME

Henry Croft (1862–1930) was a costermonger* and was very short, so he made his own clothes. He performed charitable works for children, and it's said that when a shipment of pearly buttons came in he made himself a suit. It was eventually taken up by others who sold fruit, fish and veg in the East End, and until the late nineties the Pearly King costume could be found on

---

* We've had this word a lot so I should probably have told you sooner. It just means someone who sells fruit and veg from a handcart.

his statue, atop his tomb in St Pancras Cemetery. Vandals repeatedly damaged it, and finally the statue was taken away to St Martin-in-the-Fields. The Pearly Kings and Queens still raise money for charity.

THE BOWLER HAT

It's part of a fantasy London of umbrellas and cockneys. I have only ever seen a handful of people wearing a bowler hat, and one of them was David Tomlinson in *Mary Poppins*. Old photographs of chaps pouring into the Square Mile in bowler hats look as if they're a hundred years old, but banking types were still wearing them in the 1960s.

It wasn't called a bowler hat originally. It was a Coke (pronounced Cook) hat, after a man called Coke entered Lock & Co., the St James's Street hatters, and asked them to design a hat for his gamekeepers that would not get snagged on branches. It needed to be strong, too, and Coke jumped on the finished hat to test its strength. But it was a company called Bowler that produced the hat in large numbers and gave it the name that stuck. Soon, the City of London businessmen were all wearing them. But at Lock's, to this day, you must never call it a bowler.

The bowler hat was exported, too. The story goes that one consignment was intended for railway engineers working in Bolivia, but when a tradesman discovered that the hats received in the shipment were too small he flogged them to the local ladies, who took a fancy to them and made them part of their traditional costume.

Bowler hats are once again undergoing a resurgence as designer lights inspired by the Magritte painting *The Son of Man*.

THE TUDOR BANANA

It was found in 1999 in a former fish pond in Southwark along with other Tudor objects: tools, pewter spoons, armour, a bowling ball and more than four hundred shoes, all in very good nick. Modern forensic testing shows us it was thrown onto the south bank of the Thames around 1560. The banana is an anomaly among the other objects. It's almost a century older than any previously recorded banana in Britain, and dates to a full three centuries before the first regular banana imports.

The earliest recorded bananas in Britain were a bunch imported in 1633 from Bermuda and hung up in Thomas Johnson's herbalist shop on Snow Hill. It's now thought that bananas were more common in Tudor England than we realized, but they were eaten overripe due to the transport time from Africa. Their black spotting and forever changing skins prevented them from being featured in paintings.

The banana turned up where it was least expected, but items from the past are all around if you know where to look. All over London you'll find bollards made of upturned cannon barrels, or modelled on them.

THE LONDON SWASTIKA

London had quite a few Nazi symbols that were either removed or painted over during the war. At Carlton House Terrace there's an interior staircase with marble supplied by Mussolini, although it looks rather ordinary. The only surviving London monument to the Nazis is the gravestone of Giro the terrier, who technically had no political affiliation even though he was owned by the German ambassador. He could probably have been brought over to our side by waving a lamb chop under his nose.

There are still a handful of apparently Nazi symbols knocking about. One is on a plaque outside India House in the Aldwych, but it pre-dates Nazism, coming from a time before it was hijacked by fascists, when it was a Sanskrit symbol for wellbeing. My old leather editions of the *Just So Stories* by Rudyard Kipling are lined with these golden symbols, which were also popular embroidery motifs dating back to the twelfth century.

MOTHER GOOSE'S GRAVE

St Olave's Church is a tiny, almost square medieval church in the City of London damaged badly in the war and restored in the 1950s. If you look above the stone entrance you'll find three grim skulls peering out that even managed to give Charles Dickens the creeps. Skulls were often found on churches, a sign that all flesh is mortal. But in a lighter motif, the pantomime character of Mother Goose is supposed to have been buried here on 14 September 1586, and there's a plaque commemorating the event. However, there's another Mother Goose buried in Boston, Massachusetts, so it's likely that the surname alone gave rise to the legend. Besides, panto never dies.

THE HOTEL DE BOULOGNE'S ENTRANCE

There was once a French hotel in London's Chinatown. Sadly, a mosaic front step is all that's left of it. Number 27 Gerrard Street was built in 1783 but was turned into a hotel in 1874 by a Frenchman named Philippe Ganosse and his English wife. It suffered during the First World War and became a restaurant, remaining there, along with a famous French patisserie and the lovely trumpet shop diagonally opposite, which can still be seen in the romantic comedy *A Touch of Class*. In the 1970s the Chinese colonized the street and now only the step remains. Inside is a rather good value London Chinatown restaurant.

THE SUNKEN BATH OF PRINCESS CAROLINE

I've nearly fallen into this a few times. It's an unprepossessing stepped hole in the ground at the top of Greenwich Park, but it has an interesting history. Princess Caroline of Brunswick (she of the massive hats) made a pretty disastrous marriage with her cousin, the Prince Regent, who favoured his mistress and slandered his wife by spreading rumours that she stank. She responded by retiring to Montagu House in the park and throwing wild parties. He was so incensed that he had the entire house torn down, and all that's left is her sunken bath, proof at least that she bathed. Royals, eh?

THE 1940S LIVING ROOM

Is a living room an object? I think we can count this as one. The Queen's Head in Acton Street, King's Cross, is trapped in a time warp. Although the pub itself is Victorian, its lounge appears to have stopped moving forward in 1940, with the furniture and—most important—the lighting of a wartime boozer.

The room is complete with old board games and a fireplace, but it's not preciously frozen—it just feels natural, as if a time portal had opened up. Raymondo had his birthday drinks there. Sadly no one else turned up, as he gave everyone the wrong date.

If you'd like to spend time in a perfectly preserved 1950s flat, complete with clanging pipes and a gurgling water heater, come and visit me and Alma. She's hardly bought a stick of furniture since the old King died. She's holding out for a grant from the council.

THE BEVIS MARKS ARK

This ark contains Torah scrolls in the centre of the city's remarkable Bevis Marks Synagogue, for a century the centre of the Anglo-Jewish world and the only synagogue in Europe to hold services continuously for over three hundred years (it still does). Thanks to Cromwell, Jewish people were finally allowed to live and worship openly in London from the middle of the seventeenth century. The ark is like the reredos of a church except that the marble is actually fake and made of painted wood.

THE LONDON BRIDGE SEATS

When London Bridge was demolished in 1831, not all of it was lost. A pair of stone alcoves with seats ended up placed in Victoria Park, the East End's green corridor whose entrance is marked by two massive stone dogs, the Dogs of Alcibiades. The London Bridge seats can still be found there. There's another at Guy's Hospital, with a statue of Keats sitting there looking a bit bewildered.

GUY GIBSON'S LOGBOOK

This is the record of the Second World War 'Dambusters' raid, when the RAF's 617 Squadron used Barnes Wallis's bouncing bombs to blow up two dams and disrupt Nazi industry. It used to be kept in the Windsor Castle pub, off the Edgware Road, where memorabilia of the RAF, the Royal Family and, er, the crooner Dickie Henderson could be found.

With the pub's closure, the items in its extraordinary interior have been mysteriously dispersed. There were a number of such logbooks but they very rarely come up on the collectors' market, and Guy Gibson's was unique. Where has it gone? Did it contain hidden coded secrets? Is someone being chased across Europe by assassins? I think I need to get out more.

THE LIBERTY STAIRCASES

Arthur Liberty's luxurious mock-Tudor department store of 1875 is a very peculiar survivor of the department store boom (I still miss Gamages and Marshall & Snelgrove, gone in my admittedly long lifetime). Liberty holds a key place in the Arts and Crafts and art nouveau movements and is constructed from the timbers of two old warships, HMS *Impregnable* and HMS *Hindustan*.

The reason why everyone gets lost in the store is because it was designed that way. Even the staircases were deliberately planned to be confusing, so that customers would experience more of the store than they ever intended. The staircases leading to the first three floors unusually turn anti-clockwise, but the stairs to the next two floors turn clockwise and are narrower. There was once a booklet published called 'How Not to Get Lost in Liberty's.'

QUEEN ELIZABETH'S OAK

Sadly, this tree now lies on its side in Greenwich Park.

Legend has it that Queen Elizabeth I picnicked near the oak. Henry VIII and Anne Boleyn, his second wife and Elizabeth's mother, were also supposed to have danced around the tree during their courting days. That's what monarchs did back then. They were busy dancing around trees instead of getting on with every English person's rightful job and fighting the Spanish. Or better still, duffing up the French.

The tree has been dead for over a century and its hollow trunk was big enough to make a small room, supposedly used to lock up people who misbehaved in the park.

Maybe it's just a dead tree, though. You never can tell in this bloody city.

39

The Spirit of London & Other Stories

ARTHUR BRYANT: I don't know what I'm doing here. It's a lovely day; I could be outside arresting someone.

Built as an ambitious speculation by the Adams brothers, the Adelphi (1768–74) was a separate district of London, right at the edge of the Thames on its north side. Its main terrace was a block of twenty-four unified neoclassical terraced houses, the home of J. M. Barrie and George Bernard Shaw, and the Royal Society of Arts.

Robert Adams was Britain's most sought-after architect and created a glamorously decorative neighbourhood, but he had overreached himself and the properties had to be marked down.

When the Victoria Embankment and its gardens were built in front of it, the Adelphi no longer commanded its riverfront position on the Thames. In 1936 the great terrace was torn down and the houses were replaced by boring offices, although the Savoy Chapel at the back of the Savoy Hotel was spared. The name survives in the old Adelphi Theatre.

There was a club in the vaults at the far end called the Green

Room, rather like a German *bierkeller,* where you had to be a West End performer to gain entrance. They used to let police officers in too, especially if we threatened to nick them.

At the other end of the now-vanished terrace lay another vaulted venue which you can still visit. Gordon's Wine Bar was established in the late nineteenth century and the interior has barely changed. It's candlelit and cobwebby and still so dark inside that you'll bang your head at least once trying to find your way around, but outside there are now tables which have allowed the owner to keep the bar busy and profitable. It's best experienced in winter.

The alleyways crossing the old Adelphi district still slope sharply towards the river, and there seems to have been a reason for this. The embankment was the home of the York Watergate, built in 1626 for George Villiers, 1st Duke of Buckingham. When Nelson's body came home, this is where it was delivered.

With the construction of the embankment the gate ended up landlocked. Now separated some 150 yards from the Thames it once served, the York Watergate became the primary exit from the gardens of York House, one of a number of mansions along the south side of the Strand. After proposals to move it back to the riverfront failed, the original steps were removed, and there it remains marooned today.

| | |

This next bit isn't my field, so we need an expert.

I say expert. I don't trust anything Maggie Armitage tells me but it turns out she was still in the building and happy to talk. She never seems to go home. Anyway, seeing as she has more costume jewellery than the Moulin Rouge, I thought she could tell us about the Cheapside Hoard.

MAGGIE ARMITAGE: I can't understand a word you're saying, Arthur, I've misplaced the spare battery from my hearing aid. It might be down the back of my sofa but I've been afraid to look there since we lost Dame Maude's Malaysian centipede. What are you pointing at? My neck? What's wrong with it? Oh, *jewellery*. I see. Let me find my notes. And my spectacles. And my magnifying glass.

ARTHUR BRYANT: Darling, you're shouting.

MAGGIE ARMITAGE: No, you're whispering. I only shout at politicians.

In 1912, labourers on a building site in Cheapside in the City of London unearthed an ordinary wooden box. Their pickaxes nearly pierced its lid. Inside they found a great trove of jewelled pieces, nearly five hundred of them. They'd lain undisturbed for some three hundred years. They are now in the keeping of the Museum of London and celebrated as the Cheapside Hoard, the greatest single collection of Elizabethan and Stuart jewellery in the world. The pieces are dazzlingly beautiful, intricate and amazing, like the gold watch that's set in a massive Colombian emerald.

There's an agate cameo of Elizabeth I, plus sapphires, diamonds and rubies from India and Sri Lanka, pearls, opals, Byzantine and classical gems that had been in circulation for at least sixteen centuries when the hoard was buried.

What amazes me most is their tiny size and delicacy. You realize, looking at these pendants and necklaces, earrings and brooches, that jewellery was once far more refined than it is now. It was created to display the prowess of the designer's craft. By way of comparison, I took my neck-chain to a man in the Blackstock Road and he tried to fix the clasp with a claw hammer.

The Cheapside Hoard remains the single most important source of our knowledge of the Elizabethan and early Stuart jewellers' trade and, by extension, life and fashion in London society of the era. It makes most modern jewellery look clunky and vulgar.

What did such pieces reveal about the wearers? Primarily, that they were wealthy and could afford plenty of servants. It must have been such a palaver to put on—the endless loops, swirls and twists of fine gold and silver became tangled with any movement. The items had to be arranged in a very precise fashion. Their owners mostly wore them when sitting for portraits. The most recent exhibition of the hoard was filled with paintings and documents that added to the whole picture of high fashion at the time.

The jewels, bracelets and timepieces were all buried under Goldsmith's Row, east of St Paul's Cathedral, at some point between 1640 and 1666, but nobody knows who buried them or why they were never retrieved. Those twenty-six years saw the Civil War, the Great Plague and the Great Fire of London. So we have a mystery, as well. Were they buried for protection by a King's man who then died?

Viewing the hoard makes you feel that London has once again succeeded in tricking you into thinking you've seen something beyond what you've actually seen—a glimpse into a world that's unobscured for a moment, just long enough to reveal an alien way of life. I've spent my life trying to part the veils of the past, and I've realized that a trip to a good museum is still the best way to do it.

ARTHUR BRYANT: It also helps if you've remembered to take your glasses.

MAGGIE ARMITAGE: William Blake said that if the doors of perception were cleansed everything would appear infinite.

ARTHUR BRYANT: Perhaps if your glasses were cleansed everything would appear, full stop. Blake was a man of extraordinary imagination, but I think everyone agrees that his belt didn't go through all the loops. Thank you so much for your input; you'd better get off or you'll miss the last bus.

MAGGIE ARMITAGE: It's lunchtime.

ARTHUR BRYANT: Then stay with me. You can read out a couple of these.

MAGGIE ARMITAGE: Banking? Why do I get the boring one? Are you sure anyone wants to hear about this sort of thing?

ARTHUR BRYANT: No, but I do. They always say write for yourself.

MAGGIE ARMITAGE: But not *just* for yourself, surely.

ARTHUR BRYANT: *Et tu, Brute?*

MAGGIE ARMITAGE: I'll read it, all right? Banking.
London in the mid-eighteenth century was a city on the cusp of becoming the richest and most powerful place on earth. At its epicentre was one family, running the oldest and greatest bank in the world.
It was the bank of the rich and famous, with a client list that included Samuel Pepys, David Garrick, Beau Nash, Lord Byron, Jane Austen, members of the royal family, prime ministers and countless lords and ladies.

It was run by Henry Hoare II, known as Henry the Magnificent, considered to be charismatic, handsome and intelligent (or perhaps just rich).

ARTHUR BRYANT: I've seen portraits of him. Not a natural smiler.

MAGGIE ARMITAGE: He should have been. Not only did he inherit the lion's share of the bank and premises on Fleet Street, but also the family's country estate, Stourhead House in Wiltshire. Ladies considered him to be the finest catch in London. Funny, that.

But there were both personal and national battles to be fought. Henry's first wife died in childbirth; his daughters were preyed upon by fortune-seeking families; there were deceptions, rivalries and heartbreaks.

The massive trading collapse triggered by the South Sea Bubble brought ruin to business and individuals. Insider trading was rife. Henry was forced into daily battles against embezzlement, corruption, incompetence, fraud and outright robbery. Rich clients lived beyond their means and were caught up in outrageous scandals. The bank had government ties and there was a volatile international war to pay for. Looking after the rich, famous and powerful required tact and delicacy.

Henry, his staff and family had to remain calm in the eye of the storm. They lived above the shop, as it were, right inside the counting house. Private and public business were completely intertwined. A bit like our own royal family.

| | |

Up until the 1970s, anyone entering the Admiralty Arch branch of Drummonds private bank would have found themselves in a Victorian hall with a grandfather clock and a choice of quill pens that were sharpened every week. It also housed a museum of animal fossils, and while you were waiting to see the manager you could ask to see the lion and the woolly mammoth. It had been at 49 Charing Cross since 1760 and used to incorporate a military bank.

Drummonds held accounts for King George III and other members of the royal family, including the Queen Mother. Other famous clients included—and I'm just looking at the first few names on this list—Alexander Pope, Benjamin Disraeli, Beau Brummell, Isambard Kingdom Brunel, Lancelot 'Capability' Brown, Josiah Wedgwood and Thomas Gainsborough. It apparently still maintains a specialized department for UK National Lottery winners but the bank isn't private anymore—it's owned by NatWest.

ARTHUR BRYANT: I don't get that kind of service at Barclays on Euston Road. Right, stay with me, I'm about to attempt a segue.

When he was visiting London in 1863, Dostoyevsky had this to say . . .

MAGGIE ARMITAGE: That's not a segue.

ARTHUR BRYANT: Yes, it's going from one thing to another. Dostoyevsky said:

> The populace is much the same anywhere, but there all was so vast, so vivid, that you almost physically felt things which up until then you had only imagined. In London you no longer see the populace. Instead you see a loss of sensibility, systematic, resigned and encouraged . . .
> The streets can hardly accommodate the dense, seething crowd. The mob has not enough room on the pavements and swamps the whole street. All this mass of humanity craves for

> booty and hurls itself at the first comer with shameless cyni-
> cism. Glistening, expensive clothes and semi-rags and sharp dif-
> ferences in age—they are all there.

And that was London in a nutshell. As each new generation of bright young things arrived and more glittering towers were erected, the old tarnished ones were collapsing. Growth and entropy, over and over.

There's a general history of popular leisure places falling into disrepute in London. The Vauxhall Pleasure Gardens became the haunt of whores and thieves; now it has a dismal model village. Hopefully the one gifted to the people of Melbourne for helping us out in the war is nicer. Highbury Barn, a dairy farm-turned-party palace in North London that once stood just up from the Arsenal, slipped from being a cake and ale house to a festive barn holding three thousand diners and half a million lights (and home to 'La Varsoviana,' a dance halfway between a waltz and a polka) to a place of drunken riots. The Highbury Tavern is on a corner of the original site, but the area retains its original name.

From the Thatcher years on, the right to protest or get generally messy in public has been eroded by police surveillance and overreaction. On most weekends there is a march or gathering of some kind taking place in the centre of the capital, and the intention has long been to find a balance between natural boisterousness, organized traditional protest and having a drunken wee in someone's garden without infringing the Human Rights Act. Policing is always controversial but new legislation looks set to further damage public confidence.

The London nature is to rebel a bit, but not too much. The banning of alcohol on the London Underground in 2008 was a cue to hold dinner parties complete with candelabra and flowing wine in the carriages. There were no arrests.

In the eyes of many around the world, London is the home of pipes and umbrellas and fogs. Well, we only get fogs in November now and nobody except me smokes a pipe. London's a multicultural city that would be unrecognizable to Sir Arthur Conan Doyle, except for a few tiny remaining pockets, one being G. Smith & Sons, purveyors of all things tobacco since 1869. It still sells snuff, and since the sad demise of Fribourg & Treyer in the Haymarket, is one of the only remaining traditional tobacconists in Britain.

Meanwhile, W. Martyn in the Broadway, Muswell Hill, is the best-preserved traditional grocery store in London, still run by later generations of the Martyn family. Many of its products are its own, and the interior has barely changed in a century.

In 1830 James Smith founded an umbrella company which is still in business on the corner of Gower Street and New Oxford Street. The shop's Victorian interior and exterior remain unchanged and it's known by every London cabbie as 'the Umbrella Shop.'

| | |

Once, if you asked a cabbie to take you up the post office he might have dropped you off in Cleveland Street, just off Tottenham Court Road. In 1962, while it was still under construction, the Post Office Tower overtook St Paul's Cathedral to become the tallest building in London.

Commissioned by the GPO to support microwave aerials, it would carry telecoms traffic from London to the rest of the country. It replaced a much shorter tower which had been built on the roof of the nearby 'Museum' telephone exchange in the late 1940s, linking London and Birmingham. With so many new tall buildings in the planning stage, the new structure was needed to protect the radio links' lines of sight.

It looked like no building London had ever seen before. Cylindrical (so that it could withstand a nuclear blast), glass, narrow, tall, with an emaciated middle that revealed its core, the Post Office Tower, together with Centre Point, seemed to indicate the way forward for London architecture—bright, optimistic and futuristic.

And then the tower was bombed.

Responsibility fell on the Angry Brigade, an anarchists' collective of eight politically immature students who couldn't even articulate what they wanted (they were ridiculed as 'the slightly cross brigade'). Nobody was hurt, but the restaurant was permanently closed, which was probably a wise decision. Sometimes you had to switch elevators halfway up because the tower was so slender that it moved in the wind. It was an incredibly narrow space full of awkward pinch-points, and difficult to evacuate.

And here's an odd thing. For most of its life it had never technically existed. The tower was covered by the Official Secrets Act, so its address at 60 Cleveland Street could only be referred to as Location 23. It remained non-existent until 1993.

Now, of course, the Shard makes this look like a cocktail stick, but when the revolving restaurant first opened it was considered the coolest place in London for top people to dine. Unfortunately it was run by Butlin's, the holiday camp chain, and the food was terrible. The revolving restaurant made one full rotation every twenty-three minutes, but although it was successful its small size made it unprofitable. The bombing most likely provided a convenient excuse to close it.

Now called the BT Tower, the building became an icon. Centre Point, which has the same rooftop styling on a slightly bigger floor space, never caught the public imagination in the same way. The sixties design could, I suppose, be described as 'Thunderbirds

London'—big red switches, chromium trims, flashing lights, glass and steel panels, swivel chairs. It was a style much frowned upon at the time, but now feels incredibly sexy and retro.

And it will always be the Post Office Tower to me. It turned up in dozens of films and TV dramas, and was memorably knocked over by a giant kitten in *The Goodies*. I like walking past it on a summer's morning, when the electronic message board at its summit reads 'Good Morning London.'

In the year after Jack the Ripper's spree, 1889, the postal service at number 19 Cleveland Street, on the land where the tower now stands, became London's most notorious address. It was discovered that the telegraph boys had been making a little extra cash on the side, moonlighting as prostitutes to wealthy lords and establishment figures.

The scandal sent shockwaves through society, scattering the gentry in all directions—mostly onto boat-trains to the continent—and resulted in criminal charges. Yet the court took a rather surprising attitude, partly vilifying the entitled clients and expressing some sympathy for the innocent youths, who were neither that youthful (they were mostly twenty) nor, like the local guardsmen, terribly innocent. When the judges asked the boys if they would now mend their ways, their spokesman said, 'Probably not. We'd do it if we wasn't being paid, because we rather likes it.'

Further down, at 44 Cleveland Street, stands London's most intact remaining example of a Georgian workhouse. Completed in 1778, it's been in constant occupation ever since. Part of the site became a parish burial ground and has never been deconsecrated. Documents suggest there are thousands of human remains buried there, going down twenty feet. It's not a very prepossessing building, though, and the battle to keep property developers from it has been lost. Only the building's shell will remain as more upmarket flats go in and the diggers smash deep into the paupers' graveyard without considering the fate of the dead.

Charles Dickens's relationship with the building lasted most of his life, starting in 1815 and continuing until at least 1866. It turns out that for years the author lived less than ten doors from the workhouse. It seems likely that the story of Oliver Twist was first conceived when Dickens lived in the street, and that the workhouse was the original institution featured in the novel. We know he was living there in 1830; at eighteen, he gave number 10 Norfolk Street—the street name changed—as his address when he signed for a reader's ticket at the British Museum Reading Room.

Dickens had a calling card printed for himself, giving his occupation as 'Short-Hand Writer.' He had famously grown up impoverished, a child factory worker, and I imagine he didn't relish sharing personal details of his upbringing after he became famous.

40

The Wrong-Way-Round Church & Other Stories

ARTHUR BRYANT: The Temple Church used to be a hidden gem. Now it is just a gem.

The late-twelfth-century basilica is located between Fleet Street and the Thames, built by and for the Knights Templar as part of their English headquarters. The knights, in their white tunics with red crosses, answered only to the Pope. There's not a lot left of the original stonework, but we shouldn't exercise ourselves too much about that. It was heavily damaged during the Second World War, but has been sensitively restored.

It has a circular nave, which is unusual enough, but its pews also go the wrong way, being traverse, and it has interior grotesques running all the way around it. The Round Church was consecrated in 1185 by the Patriarch of Jerusalem. It was designed to recall the holiest place in the Crusaders' world: the circular Church of the Holy Sepulchre in Jerusalem, built on the site where Christ was supposedly crucified. In the penitential cell, Walter le Bacheler, Grand Preceptor of Ireland, was starved to death for disobedience. That's organized religion for you.

There are nine effigies of medieval knights arranged on the floor of the church, which featured in a popular novel, *The Da Vinci Code* by Mr Dan Brown, the renowned typist. The church always has one or two visitors who are there because of its association with the book and the film. As a result of noisy tourists entering for purposes other than worship, the church now charges a fee for entry.

Thanks for that, Mr Brown.

In modern times, two Inns of Court share the church. The Inner and Middle Temple have some of the most striking architecture and peaceful gardens to be found in any modern city, and are usually quiet. They look so private that you think you can't walk through them, but in fact they're open to the public.

| | |

Wilton's—now this *is* a hidden London gem, a unique building and a bugger to find when you're in a hurry and the show's about to start. It comprises a mid-nineteenth-century grand music hall attached to an eighteenth-century terrace of three houses and a pub, originally an alehouse dating from 1743 or earlier. It's off the East End's Cable Street, under the wing of the Docklands Light Railway, then down an alleyway. Keep your hand on your tuppence if you visit after dark.

John Wilton bought the business in 1850 and opened his 'Magnificent New Music Hall' in 1859. He kitted it out with fancy mirrors, chandeliers and decorative paintwork, and for the next thirty years hosted London's most famous performers. The audience sang along to 'The Boy I Love Is Up in the Gallery' and loved Champagne Charlie, the singer whose story was filmed in 1944. Wartime audiences couldn't get their hands on champagne, so this was the next-best thing.

Wilton's survived the slum clearance schemes of the 1960s and was given a Grade II* listing in 1971. It reopened as a theatre and concert hall in 1997. Most of London's music halls were not so lucky, as property developers colluded with councils to make fortunes. Down came the history-filled halls you can glimpse in James Mason's 1969 time-capsule documentary.

Instead of getting the gold-and-red-wallpaper treatment most theatres get when they're fixed up, Wilton's was restored in shabby-chic style with exposed brick and sanded paintwork, which is much cosier. It's now the home of variety, opera, pop, comedy, fringe plays and art events.

MEERA MANGESHKAR: So, Mr Bryant is looking for London's 'hidden gems,' eh?

I told him I'd do this particular one because the only thing he knows about India comes in a foil box with a poppadom. And it's not hidden, it's an incredibly popular place of worship, as he'd know if he got his arse out to a few places that aren't in Zone One.

The Shri Swaminarayan Mandir Temple is known as the Mandir or the Neasden Temple, and it's a really unexpected building. It's Britain's first authentic Hindu temple, built entirely from limestone and marble using traditional methods. It's huge and white and ornate and in Neasden, off the disgusting North Circular Road. A masterpiece of Indian stonework and craftsmanship, it has towering white pinnacles, smooth domes and marble pillars, all based on ancient Vedic principles of art and architecture. It has an intricately carved teak and oak *haveli*, like a veranda, and is one of the biggest Hindu temples outside India.

There are never any tourists there when we go. Well, they're the ones missing out. It's a dazzling experience, and everyone is very welcoming. There's a permanent exhibition on Hinduism next to it, and attendants are happy to explain anything you don't understand. I took Colin there on a date and at first he was fed up because he wanted to go and see a Marvel movie, but I explained that he's marrying into a Hindu family so he'd better bloody know something about it. Then he got interested and had a good time, especially when he found the Indian café in the car park.

My mum's OK with him marrying me now that he's learned the proper way to make *chai*. But generally she's horrified by the way Londoners have adopted some Indian customs. Holi at the end of March has moved from a religious context into the main-stream. Now it's a monetized event with an all-day pass including bags of paint powder, limitless booze and DJs. And she says that if chicken tikka masala is still the UK's most popular Indian dish, what's the point in cooking anything subtler for them?

JOHN MAY: London may be most famous for its churches, the-atres and public houses, but people rarely talk about its mosques. Historically, London has a strong connection with the Islamic faith.

The London Central Mosque stands at the edge of Regent's Park near the top of Baker Street. One of the best things about it is the spectacular view inside. The floor-to-ceiling windows over-look mature trees which fill the interior with a view of greenery. It's well worth a visit and everyone is very welcoming.

The mosque was founded during the Second World War in recognition of the British Empire's substantial Muslim popula-tion and their support for the Allies during the war.

Churchill's War Cabinet requisitioned the site and King George VI opened an Islamic cultural centre. A new mosque was the crowning touch, but it was delayed for decades by planning ob-jections and irregularities. The finished building can hold five thousand worshippers and was given as an unconditional gift to the UK Muslim community. The land was donated in return for a site in Cairo for an Anglican cathedral.

Finally opened in 1978, it added a golden dome to the London skyline, much to the horror of certain addle-pated politicians who felt it wasn't English.

There had been calls to build a mosque in Central London from 1900 onwards, and the Fazi Mosque, or Grace Mosque, opened in 1926 in Southfields, Wandsworth. London now has more mosques than any other country in Europe except Turkey. The one nearest the PCU is in a converted Victorian pub. The difference with these adapted mosques is that they reuse old buildings rather than being raised as separate new structures, and are almost invisible on high streets—although there's one with a shiny new spire in Brick Lane.

Arthur, are you going to do your Q&A now?

ARTHUR BRYANT: I will if I can find the questions. I had them in my hand a minute ago.

JOHN MAY: You also had a bacon roll in your hand a minute ago.

ARTHUR BRYANT: Did I? Don't sit on anything. I'll soldier on.

Obviously, as a leading expert in street-level London I'm asked all sorts of questions by the general public, the most usual one being, 'Why are you following me?' We left a public question box by the entrance to the PCU for a while but had some very rude suggestions. I thought we could put this on our website, except it turns out we don't have one. Apparently there's a security risk.

JOHN MAY: Yes. It's you.

ARTHUR BRYANT: This is from a Mrs L. Wilberforce of King's Cross, who asks: *What's inside the Marble Arch?*

Most large arches in London have rooms big enough to have dinner in. The rooms inside the Marble Arch were used by the police until the late 1950s and London's smallest police station was in the Wellington Arch.

Marble Arch was built to celebrate the victories of the Napoleonic Wars, and was modelled on the Arch of Constantine in ancient Rome. It was designed by John Nash in 1828 as a triumphal entrance to Buckingham Palace, but it didn't work in that spot. Nash's original design for George IV included all kinds of decorative friezes and statues. Then the King died and everything went wrong. The Prime Minister, the Duke of Wellington, fired Nash when he saw the bills and hired a cheaper architect, Edward Blore, to finish off the work.

The statues and friezes were all done and the arch just had to be assembled. But the disgruntled Nash wouldn't tell Blore how everything fitted together. Blore knew there was a military side and a naval side, with battle scenes and the words 'Waterloo' and 'Trafalgar' set at either end, but the rest of the pieces were just sitting there like bits of an Airfix kit without any instructions.

So he chucked away all the extraneous parts. The stripped-back, sculpture-free and now rather characterless arch was finished in 1833. But there's a mistake on its immense marble sides. The naval side has a portrait of Wellington on the top and the military side has a portrait of Nelson; they should be the other way around.

And where did all the stone decorations go? Some ended up in the main courtyard of Buckingham Palace. Some went to the entrance of the National Gallery. Many were altered. Winged angels lost their wings and Britannia got turned into Minerva, Goddess of Wisdom—you can still see her near the National Gallery roof. Another bit ended up as an elevated plant pot on the Euston Road.

The arch was moved to form a grand entrance to Hyde Park. It stayed there for fifty years until a new road scheme cut around it, stranding it away from the park. So the poor Marble Arch ended up stuck near Oxford Street and the arse-end of Edgware Road, drenched in traffic fumes and isolated from any purpose.

| | |

Mr P. Langford of Kilburn asks: *What were the ladies and gentlemen in lab coats doing in the window of a building on Great Portland Street?*

I can answer this from personal experience. They were drinking tea and spitting it out. Dressed in their white lab coats, the tea-tasters stood in a row in the window doing this all day long until the mid-nineties. I think they may have belonged to the UK Tea & Infusions Association. The tea trade used to play an annual cricket match with the wine trade, and supplied the coats for the umpires.

It takes seven years to train as a tea-buyer and blender. Like wine-tasters, tea experts must be able to pinpoint the tea's exact origin. At the testing station, six grams of tea were brewed for exactly six minutes, making it twice the strength of your usual cuppa. Tests fall into four categories: sparkle, colour, body and zing. Sounds like a 1970s disco dance troupe.

| | |

Somebody whose name I can't read because I've got onion chutney on it asks: *Which is the oldest park in London?*

That would be at Finsbury Circus, the peculiarly cut-off area of Central London hardly anyone seems to know about unless you live there. The circular garden was an Iron Age burial ground and its latest incarnation dates back to 1606, when it was confusingly called Moorfields. There's still a bowling club there and a clubhouse that serves Pimm's. In 1784 it was the site of London's first hot-air balloon flight.

| | |

Mrs J. Harris of Huddersfield wants to know: *Where can I find an outdoor statue of Elizabeth 1?*

Until recently there was only one and it was at the guild church of St Dunstan-in-the-West in Fleet Street. You could only visit it on Tuesdays for some weird reason, or for recitals on Wednesday lunchtimes. It's the only statue of Queen Elizabeth I carved in her lifetime. There's also a clock flanked by our old friends Gog and Magog, as well as statues of King Lud, the city's rebuilder, and his sons. All the statues were originally in Ludgate, as was the legendary pub the King Lud, which survived until 2005. Now there's a new statue of QEI in Little Dean's Yard, Westminster School, which is like a regular school but for poshos. It was unveiled by her descendant, QEII.

| | |

I asked PCU staff to chuck in some questions, as it turns out that most of the public's questions were unprintable, not to mention rhetorical and anatomically unfeasible. This one's from Colin: *Where in London can you find a still-functioning water wheel?*

At Morden Hall Park, a five-minute walk from Morden tube station. This former estate had a school for young gentlemen, but was sold in the 1870s to a tobacco-seller.

The wheel used to be part of a snuff mill, grinding tobacco until 1922. The mill is powered by the River Wandle and is now owned by the National Trust. There's a rose garden and marshy meadowlands, and there are often art exhibitions and other events held here. It doesn't feel like London at all, more like part of rural Surrey, and is a home to herons and kingfishers.

| | |

This one's from Janice: *Where can you see a statue of Peter Pan?*

Obviously, there's the famous one in Kensington Gardens which has rabbits on it, and mice (they get everywhere). But there's another one, rather nicer in my opinion, and it's outside the entrance to the Great Ormond Street Hospital, near Bloomsbury's Foundling Hospital. J. M. Barrie famously left all the royalties and performing rights for *Peter Pan* to the hospital, which has a Barrie wing and a Peter Pan ward.

| | |

John, I can tell this is from you. *Where did Samuel Pepys watch the Great Fire of London from, and can you still go there?*

In his diary, Pepys says he watched London burning from 'a small alehouse on Bankside.' Actually, he started watching it from a boat on the Thames but got rained on by drops of fire, so he retreated to the south side.

I'm pretty sure his alehouse stood where the Anchor pub now stands. The inn hosted a literary club whose members included Dr Johnson and Boswell, Sir Joshua Reynolds and David Garrick. It was rebuilt after two more fires, and is still a great spot to sit with a pint on a winter's morning, when it's not full of tourists taking pictures of the beer pumps, floorboards, sausages, their feet, etc.

| | |

This is from Meera, typically awkward. I had to have it explained to me. *Where can I see Diagon Alley and the Leaky Cauldron?*

I haven't read *Harry Potter* because my idea of a boarding school is more like the one in *Tom Brown's Schooldays*, but I know that one of the locations in the books is based on Leadenhall Market.

Leadenhall was built on the site of a Roman forum and was once larger than Trafalgar Square. It was covered after the Great Fire and continued with great success as a meat and poultry market whose oldest goose (aged thirty-eight) was buried on the site, happily before Alma could freeze it and cook it.

Nobody lives in the area now so there's not much of a market left, but the building has been restored to its brightly coloured Victorian splendour and comes as quite a shock to anyone who wanders into it without warning.

41

The Needle & Other Stories

ARTHUR BRYANT: Cleopatra's Needle is in a very visible spot on the Embankment. It's flanked with benches overlooking the Thames which are held up by pairs of winged sphinxes. This isn't the only bit of Egyptology in London—in Canonbury there's an entire row of houses with sphinxes outside. But the London needle is an oddity. I say 'London' because there are three, the other two are in Paris and New York.

They were originally erected in the Egyptian city of Heliopolis on the orders of Thutmosis III, around 1450 BCE. The London one was presented to the city by Egypt in commemoration of two victorious battles: that of Lord Nelson at the Nile and of Sir Ralph Abercromby at Alexandria. But we wouldn't pay to have it shipped here, so it stayed in Egypt for fifty-eight years, until public subscription paid to have it transported. That should tell you all you need to know about British politics.

The needle had been encased in a protective iron cylinder and when a storm arose the needle rolled. Six crew members were lost—they're named today on a bronze plaque attached to the foot of the needle's mounting stone. After many further adventures it eventually found its way here. A more easily moveable wooden replica was manufactured so that we could decide where to put it. The Houses of Parliament didn't want it outside their front door, so it went on the Victoria Embankment. I feel any other country would have been grateful to receive such a wonderful gift but we were more like, 'Did you keep the receipt?'

On the erection of the obelisk in 1878 a time capsule was concealed in the front part of the pedestal. It contained: a set of twelve photographs of the best-looking English women of the day, a box of hairpins, a box of cigars, several tobacco pipes, a set of imperial weights, a baby's bottle, some children's toys, a shilling razor, a hydraulic jack and some samples of cable, a three-inch bronze model of the monument, a complete set of British coins, a rupee to show our attachment to India, a portrait of Queen Victoria, a written history of the strange tale of the transport of the monument, plans on vellum, a translation of the inscriptions, copies of the Bible in several languages, a copy of *Whitaker's Almanack,* a Bradshaw's railway guide, a map of London and copies of ten daily newspapers.

In other words, a random selection of typical British tat that no one else could possibly want. I found more items of value clearing out my auntie's council flat, but that was because she was keeping a few things safe for her husband until he came out.

Cleopatra's Needle is flanked by two faux-Egyptian sphinxes cast from bronze. These bear hieroglyphic inscriptions that say 'netjer nefer men-kheper-re di ankh' ('the good god, Thuthmosis III given life'). The sphinxes appear to be looking at the needle rather than guarding it. This is because they were installed backwards by mistake. During the First World War, on 4 September 1917, a German bomb landed near the needle. The damage was never repaired and is clearly visible in the form of shrapnel holes on the right-hand sphinx.

It's curious to me that against its domestic London setting of tall plane trees and soft grey skies the obelisk is less impressive than it would have been at home. It barely seems out of place, just another overlooked London folly on the banks of the Thames.

When it saw the London and Paris obelisks, New York wanted one too, and suggested it should have one for the purpose of increasing trade. Previous experience made the arduous task of transporting it rather easier this time, and it went into Central Park in a Masonic ceremony. In 2010 the Egyptians threatened to take it back because acid rain was ruining the hieroglyphics.

A poem from Alfred Tennyson is told from the point of view of the obelisk.

> *Here, I that stood in On beside the flow*
> *Of sacred Nile, three thousand years ago!—*
> *A Pharaoh, kingliest of his kingly race,*
> *First shaped, and carved, and set me in my place.*
> *A Caesar of a punier dynasty*
> *Thence haled me toward the Mediterranean sea,*
> *Whence your own citizens, for their renown,*
> *Through strange seas drew me to your monster town.*
> *I have seen the four great empires disappear.*
> *I was when London was not. I am here.*

I've never rated him much, either.

I keep talking about the Victorians in this guide because they left such a lasting impression on the city. For many visitors to London, Victoria is the first part of the metropolis they see—God help them. It's as if its component elements have been shaken in a cup and thrown together, some neoclassical buildings here, a bit of 1920s monumentalism there, glued together with a new shopping centre and a few theatres that got lost on their way to the West End.

As an area—I hesitate to say 'neighbourhood'—Victoria always had something of a disreputable atmosphere, despite the fact that the Queen lives there.* Railway lines and wide roads segmented the community, preventing it from cohering and developing. Despite the fact that its backstreets hid some surprising residential architecture it always felt—and still feels—transient.

In the early seventeenth century the Stag Brewery stood on Victoria Street with attached properties that once were part of St James's Palace. Music halls sprang up to amuse the local population—and slums crowded in. The brewery closed down in 1959 and was demolished, but Stag Place and a pub called the Stag remained until recent times.

The area's music hall history left it with two major theatres. The Victoria Palace Theatre has been on its present site since 1832. It was originally known as Moy's Music Hall and was most famous for a gilded statue of Anna Pavlova which stood above it. In 1939 this was removed and 'lost.'

Comedian Norman Wisdom slept near the statue of Marshal Foch in Grosvenor Gardens when his parents split up at the age of nine. He worked as an errand boy in Artillery Mansions on Victoria Street, which was then a grand hotel. Clearly child labour was not a problem in those days. Then on 15 September 1940 (Battle of Britain Day), something extraordinary happened above Victoria.

A Hawker Hurricane (one of ours) sky-rammed a Dornier Do

---

* The story goes that when the Queen Mother was told by a Beatle that they'd recorded in Victoria, she replied, 'Oh, that's near us.'

17 bomber (one of theirs) which was supposedly about to target Buckingham Palace. Both aircraft crashed within the city area. They were the only two aircraft to do so during the entire war.

The German bomber fell to earth in the forecourt of Victoria Station. The Hurricane ploughed into the junction of Buckingham Palace Road and Ebury Bridge, burying itself twelve feet beneath the road. Its pilot, Raymond Holmes of 504 Squadron based at Hendon, parachuted from the aircraft, landing on the rooftops of Hugh Street, and was taken to the nearby Orange Brewery as a hero. In 2004, parts of the Hurricane were unearthed from beneath the tarmac and made their way back to Hendon.

Modern Victoria is a transit area trapped between two much nicer neighbourhoods. The station is actually two stations joined together, the Chatham and Dover station of 1862 and the Brighton and South Coast station of 1860. Each frontage competed to be the most ornate. In the atmospheric era of the steam train it was here that Algernon was found in a handbag in *The Importance of Being Earnest*. On its platforms, the soldiers of the First World War said goodbye to their sweethearts as they headed to the Western Front, many never to return.

As ugly glass boxes went up around it, poor Victoria Station fell into disrepair. It was not that the area lacked character; it had the character of someone you'd never want to meet. By now the Stag had become a peculiar concrete theatre pub one critic described looking like 'a gay Wetherspoon's,' wedged under a flyover. The two beautiful working theatres sat surrounded by decades of rubble and dirt. A building like a bright crimson fin went up and won an award, becoming the recipient of the Carbuncle Cup, annually given to the ugliest building in the United Kingdom.

London is peppered with such problematic spots. Pimlico was regarded as traditionally working class after the war, which strikes me as odd considering its closest neighbour is the Houses of Parliament and some properties have incredible views of Big Ben. The reason for its status was that Churchill Gardens in Pimlico became an inner-city regeneration project building homes for all classes. Pimlico is now only for the wealthy.

But that's the way it goes. Notting Hill was inhabited by the disenfranchised, then the entitled. Camden Town was home to some of London's more interesting penniless musicians and artists, but when the local council turned its market into a tourist attraction it raised the property prices and lost its mojo to edgier Shoreditch, which in turn surrendered to Dalston. The London boroughs are very competitive. Clerkenwell, according to its local newspaper, describes its neighbourhood as 'What Hoxton wants to be when it grows up and gets a job.' Which is why I prefer Hoxton.

Soho, once so industrious and creative, the home of tailors, film producers, musicians, artists and writers, is now largely given over to short-lease restaurants. Calm Fitzrovia, formerly the home of the clothing trade, has watched its family businesses move out. Formerly run-down Whitechapel has become a hotbed of art and fusion cuisine. The invisible geographical atmospheres fluctuate around the city like swamp gases, raising some up, dropping others and avoiding certain areas that never seem to change. Of these I would include Kilburn, Barnsbury, Lisson Grove, De Beauvoir Town and a hundred smaller city wards few outsiders have ever heard of.

| | |

Vauxhall didn't turn out the way it was supposed to, either.

Everyone assumed that because it was so close to the Houses

of Parliament it would be the next hot property area. Vauxhall Bridge opened in 1816 and charged a high toll for crossing it—up to half a crown for a coach and horses. But instead of grand mansions being built, factories were quick to move in—and then the Millbank Prison opened, which put everyone off.

The bridge became London's first tramway crossing, taking the workers to their jobs, so Vauxhall ended up very different to how it was intended. Industry stayed and a more ruffianly air settled over the neighbourhood.

The Vauxhall Pleasure Gardens at New Spring Gardens Walk were attended by everyone from cross-dressing 'ladies' of fashion to the Turkish ambassador. The season tickets were medallions made of silver that were designed to be worn around the neck, and the 'life membership' ticket was a glamorous stamped medal of pure gold.

The gardens reached the height of their popularity in the early 1800s, with twenty thousand visiting on one night in 1826. Their winning formula combined music, illuminated fountains, fireworks and light refreshments in an Edenic atmosphere. There were genteel areas, decorative amphitheatres where orchestras played and visitors promenaded in their finery, and 'dark walks' where couples could enjoy each other's company in some privacy. This combination took some policing and the owners employed their own coppers, probably the first private police force in London. The first modern professional force, Sir Robert Peel's 'Peelers,' weren't formed until 1829 and are still giving units like ours grief.

One well-known visitor to the gardens was Casanova. His memoirs record his friend telling him:

> It was one evening when I was at Vauxhall, and I offered her
> twenty guineas if she would come and take a little walk with me in

a dark alley. She said she would come if I gave her the money in advance, which I was fool enough to do. She went with me, but as soon as we were alone she ran away.

So while Casanova may have been a great lover, his mates were mugs.

Growing competition from early music halls and other public entertainments caused the proprietors to become increasingly innovative and offer a wider range of attractions, such as tumblers, tightrope-walkers and lion-tamers. The gardens became particularly famous for balloon ascents. In 1817, one thousand soldiers re-enacted the Battle of Waterloo while young couples held assignations on its crossed paths.

Inevitably the place acquired a dodgy reputation, and a number of brothels became well established in the surrounding streets, including ones at the charmingly named 'Sluts Hole' in Fitzalan Street. One visitor told the owner that 'he should be a better customer . . . if there were more nightingales and fewer strumpets.' Ironically, the advent of the railways killed off the gardens and they closed in 1859.

The idea had been to provide a sensory Elysium for those worn down by the dissonance of the London streets. Instead, like most early London attractions, the gardens became a rip-off haunted by pickpockets, whores and 'demi-reps' (female escorts who provided company for bored lads). The attractions became ever more dubious and even the ham in the sandwiches became so expensive and see-through that the term 'Vauxhally' became an everyday expression meaning extreme thinness.

The Pleasure Gardens are still there in Vauxhall, although they're back to their original name of Spring Gardens. The area is no longer filled with thousands of candlelit globes, but it's a pleasant if somewhat bare space. Vauxhall remains a rather overlooked neighbourhood, which is surprising given its location so close to London's centre of political power.

What's odd is that the residual atmosphere in each neighbourhood clings on. A ghost trace remains, its knotted, incomplete memories linking the past to the present.

42

Beer & Other Stories

Aʀᴛʜᴜʀ Bʀʏᴀɴᴛ: I feel once again the time has come to talk about booze. At this point a quenching ale would go down a treat. It's going to get complicated very quickly, so if you're a teetotaller you might want to skip this section and good riddance to you.

ALE
Stands for mild ale, reddish-brown in colour, the staple drink of the public bar, when there were such things. It is mixed with bitter (mild-and-bitter), Burton (old-and-mild), strong ale or stout. The belief of overseas visitors that English beer was weak arose from a confusion of terminology in which 'ale' was requested, being different from and lighter than beer.

BABYCHAM
During the Second World War few women ventured into pubs for fear of being morally judged. So when a company

making strong pear cider came up to London and asked an
advertising agency how to sell their product, they suggested
diluting it and putting it in tiny champagne bottles labelled
'Champagne Perry.' They added the slogan 'I'd love a
Babycham.' They reasoned that women would then know
what to ask for when they went back into a pub, and they
were right. Babycham had its own special little champagne
glass and always came with a maraschino cherry on a
stick—oh, how sophisticated.

BASS
Pale ale, once Britain's biggest-selling beer, probably because
it's rather bland, from the Bass Brewery in Burton-upon-
Trent.

BEER
Includes all malt liquors and sometimes stout. If you ask for
'a beer' in a pub you should traditionally be served bitter.

BINDER
The second-to-last drink, usually a short after several beers,
the progression being: 'Have one with me,' 'the other half'
(or 'wet the other eye'), 'the odd,' 'a final,' 'a binder' and 'one
for the road.' I'd never heard of this progression until my
friend Harry Prayer told me about it, but he's an expert—i.e.,
a functioning alcoholic.

BITTER
Strong, hoppy beer drunk mainly in the shires these days.

BLACK VELVET

Champagne and stout; once fashionable, though still popular with the elbow-patch-and-wellingtons brigade as a morning pick-me-up.

BOTTLE & JUG

A bar reserved for people to take away. Bottles were charged for (up to threepence a quart), so it was important to bring them back. Many people brought their own earthenware jugs.

BROWN ALE

A bottled beer more like a Burton than a bitter. Each brewery makes its own.

BURTON

A draught beer darker and sweeter than bitter, originally named after the brewery. B&B is bitter and Burton, not to be confused with BBW, Bass Barley Wine, which is a powerfully strong beer. Burton is considered a winter drink and not kept in hot weather. 'Gone for a Burton' is Second World War RAF slang for going missing, and may or may not be connected with the drink. Let me know when you start to fall asleep.

DOG'S NOSE

Beer with a drop of gin in it.

DRAUGHT

Beer, stout, cider, etc. served from the cask without first being bottled. Cheaper and less gassy than bottled beer. Varies widely from brewery to brewery.

FOUR ALE BAR

Pubs were divided into PUBLIC (working-class), SALOON (middle-class), PRIVATE (compartment between Public and Saloon) and SNUG (semi-private compartment within pub). There was also the LADIES' BAR (unaccompanied women) and CHILDREN'S ROOM (mothers and kids, now gone).

HALF AND HALF

Ale and porter mixed together. Coming back in popularity.

HEAD

A beer should come with a little bit of a foamy head but not too much. Of course, if you're in a French bar they'll pour you a tiny doll's-house-sized beer comprising four inches of foam and an inch of booze.

IPA

There are many general pale ales but India Pale Ale was brewed in the UK for exportation to troops based in India. It was actually improved by being stored on a long ocean voyage, which deepened its hoppiness.

LAGER

An iced Northern European beer that became ubiquitous after the 1970s, when British brewers started manufacturing their own. Looked down upon by craft ale enthusiasts.

MOTHER-IN-LAW

Stout and bitter. I suspect the name is derogatory.

PORTER

Stout blended with a mix of other drained-off beers, once popular with Covent Garden porters. It was cheap and plentiful, and is now available again after half a century of unpopularity. Several bottles of porter were found in a 131-year-old shipwrecked vessel and the drink was faithfully re-created.

PONY

Smaller measure than a half-pint (usually a gill), taken as a gesture of goodwill when the drinker doesn't want any more.

POT BOY

A person, usually not a boy at all but an extremely old man who goes around a pub collecting all the empties in exchange for a libation. You don't see them in town anymore. Perhaps the breweries decided that the best way to encourage a new generation of patrons was not by having a smelly old senior interrupting their conversations with 'Oi, 'ave you finished wiv that?'

RED BIDDY

A drink made of cheap red wine fortified with spirits. Nicknamed 'lunatics' broth.' Popular with ladies of a certain age who wish to mask their occasionally excessive temperaments.

ROUND

Americans don't generally buy everyone else in their circle a drink. Not getting your round in is considered a punishable offence in the UK. It doesn't matter if you're only staying for one—you have to make the offer. A polite refusal is always followed by the phrase, 'Are you sure?,' which is in turn followed by a longing look at the glass and a sigh. 'Oh, go on then. One for the road.'

SCOTCH ALE
Nothing to do with whisky but a Younger's Brewery bottled or draught ale.

SCOTCH EGG
A cold hard-boiled egg wrapped in sausage meat and bread-crumbs that may count as a 'substantial meal' required by the government to accompany the drinking of alcohol in pubs, as opposed to nuts or crisps, which are not substantial. This is appropriate revenge on the company Golden Wonder, who in the 1970s encouraged working mothers to replace vegetables in children's meals with crisps.

SEAL
To 'break the seal' is to head off for the first beer pee of the evening, presaging several more visits.

SHANDY
Beer and ginger beer or beer and lemonade, drunk in hot weather.

STOUT
Dark beer (like Guinness) that can be drunk on its own or mixed with mild or bitter, drunk with oysters in the past, or in the present down at Borough Market.

STRAIGHT GLASS

Nobody wants beer in a dimple mug; it makes you look like a character from a wartime film. And you certainly don't want a territory-marking provincial tankard. There's something about drinking beer from pewter that sets your teeth on edge.

WALLOP

Mild ale, usually ordered by darts players in pubs. Clearly fattening.

Don't forget to conclude your order with 'and a packet of crisps.' There can only be one response to the question of flavour. Salt 'n' Vinegar. Nothing else is acceptable. Worst crisp flavour: 'Smoked Paprika, Porcini and Garlic Butter.' It's a potato, for heaven's sake.

Obviously the above are all beer references. You could do what I saw a pair of very sweet American tourists do in a tiny local pub behind Harley Street and try to order a chocolate martini, but you'd most likely be laughed at (as indeed they were, by me, the barmaid and everyone else).

To go with your fine ale you'll need a traditional pub snack: pork scratchings, pork pies, sausages, pickled onions, pickled eggs and gherkins. In an earlier era you'd have been able to choose from pickled whelks, pies, sheep's trotters, jugs of prawns, oysters, mussels and sardines. Anything, in fact, that could be eaten with the hands. Oysters were the poor man's food, plentiful from the ropes in the Thames, usually to be found in beef pies.

I know what you're about to ask: 'You have made me thirsty now. Where can I access such fine beery comestibles in London?'

Follow me.

43

Saucy Minxes & Other Stories

ARTHUR BRYANT: Here follows a fine selection of London ale-houses chosen by an expert. Mr Harry Prayer knows a thing or two about drinking, although nothing at all about paying for it.

HARRY PRAYER: Mr Bryant calls me a gentleman of the road, but I tell him I'm a Harry Ramp, a paraffin, a Terence—a tramp—and that I have no issue with that nomenclature. I'm educated but no gentleman and I'm homeless because I choose to be, the sky is my roof and I sing Ho! for the open road. I do not accept payment without offering useful advice in return and have never threatened to be sick over the outdoor diners in Covent Garden if they didn't give me five quid, unlike some of my fellow itinerants.

Having said that, if I could touch you for a deep-sea diver—better make that a tenner—we'll embark on a little drinking session. The trick to a good sesh is looking sober and, in my case, fresh enough to be served.

Obviously I could have included some of the more famous London pubs I have been thrown out of, like Holborn's Cittie of Yorke or Southwark's George Inn, or Ye Olde Cheshire Cheese off Fleet Street, rebuilt in 1667, home of potty-mouthed Polly the parrot, who imitated the sound of champagne corks popping so much that she became an ex-parrot. But I haven't. The best part of my lifestyle is not having to do what's expected of me.

So let's start here.

THE BLACKFRIAR

Blackfriars was named after the black habits worn by Dominican friars who once inhabited the area. The historic art nouveau Grade II* listed pub that now stands on the foundations of the priory was built in 1875. Henry VIII's court also sat on the site to dissolve his marriage to Catherine of Aragon.

The pub was designed by an architect, H. Fuller-Clark, and sculptors Henry Poole and Frederick T. Callcott, all committed to the free-thinking designs of the Arts and Crafts Movement. Its triangular shape is down to the network of alleyways that cut around it until late into the twentieth century.

Jolly drunken friars appear everywhere in the pub in sculptures, mosaics and reliefs. The little alcoves glitter darkly in black and brown, and are surrounded by improving mottoes. Like so many other felicitous buildings in London, this astonishing little building was saved from demolition by a campaign led by the indefatigable Sir John Betjeman.

I used to busk in the outside area, but now it's full of tour guides who throw things at me.

THE NEWMAN ARMS

You can't visit it because it's currently shut. The Rathbone Street pub dates back to 1730 and was a total ledge. Even though it's gone (hopefully only temporarily) this little bit of Fitzrovia is still atmospheric and overlooked. George Orwell supposedly based his proles' pub from 1984 on it, and the director Michael Powell killed his career by making the 1960 film *Peeping Tom* all around it. But in doing so he immortalized this lovely little corner of London, which once housed many of London's old picture libraries. In his film the windows of the surrounding houses are filled with ladies of the night in complicated corsetry, lit in sultry hues.

The Newman Arms was a funny pub, part hipster, part rough, with a belt-straining winter treat of a pie menu and a gloomy tilted alleyway incorporated at the side. It was used by the Middlesex's hospital porters, and gentlemen of a certain age still potter past expecting to see saucy minxes plying their trade.

I was known in the Newman Arms. Not in a good way.

THE JERUSALEM TAVERN

I used to think this pub was a fake, but I've changed my mind. The Jerusalem Tavern at number 55 Britton St, Farringdon, looks venerable but is relatively new—except that it's not. Allow me to explain.

The fourteenth-century Knights Hospitaller's Priory of St John was burned down during the Peasants' Revolt in 1381, but a Jerusalem Tavern always remained near it. The priory's last remnant is St John's Gate.

The pub had been a townhouse in 1720, was then converted into a watchmaker's a hundred years later, and finally a coffee house. A shop front was added, and suddenly it was the perfect ancient pub, christened in 1996. Why ancient? Because it was the fourth such tavern at this spot to honour its attachment to the priory. If you're going to create a pub, follow the line of its history. So while it may have moved fractionally from where it was, it's spiritually authentic.

There's a wood-flanked seating area in the 'shop window' and, up a short flight of steps, a tiny gallery. The traditional tavern atmosphere is enhanced by bare floorboards, scrubbed tables and low lighting, which I tend to favour. By the time you read this the place may well have changed its appearance again, but it will live on.

THE OLD DOCTOR BUTLER'S HEAD

Dr Butler was a fraud. The court physician to King James I failed to qualify at Cambridge and practised some pretty outrageous 'cures.' For epilepsy he would fire a brace of pistols near his unsuspecting patient's face to scare the condition from them. In cases of the plague, he'd plunge the poor soul into ice-cold water. Another treatment was to drop patients through a trapdoor on London Bridge into the Thames.

His total lack of qualifications did not prevent the 'Doctor' from becoming the King's quack, or from selling his popular medicinal ale. This was available only from taverns which displayed Dr Butler's head on their signs. The last one remaining is in Moorgate. The original pub was destroyed in the Great Fire of London in 1666, but was rebuilt. The wooden façade looks authentic but is probably Victorian, certainly older than the mock-Tudor buildings opposite. But the alleyway in which workers carouse of an evening is heavy in hoppy atmosphere. I perform my sand dance here on warm summer evenings and find punters can be surprisingly generous before they beat a hasty retreat.

THE TIPPERARY

Wherever you find monks you find ale; they brew it.

The Tipperary in Fleet Street used to be called the Boar's Head. It was built in 1605 with stones taken from the White Friars monastery—stones that allowed it to survive unharmed in the raging inferno of the Great Fire of London. The Tipperary claims to be the first Irish pub outside Ireland and the first to sell Guinness in England. It claims a lot of things.

It's certainly an historic site, occupied initially by the thirteenth-century White Friars monastery, then a sixteenth-century tavern at the sign of the 'Bolt-in-Tun,' later to be a busy coaching inn. The 'Boar's Head' name was adopted in 1605 or 1883, depending on whose account you read. And almost everything you read about it is blarney.

The original pub was demolished and rebuilt in the late nineteenth century by Mooney's. The boozer you see before you today is late Victorian, with a battered mosaic floor and two glass panels advertising Irish whiskey and stout. It's very small but has friendly staff; they hardly ever chuck me out.

WARD'S IRISH HOUSE, PICCADILLY CIRCUS

This atmospheric (i.e., smelly) wrought-iron wonder has gone now, sadly. Its surly staff served Guinness and oysters and it was usually pretty quiet. There were gloomy little rooms off the main bar, with names like Leinster and Ulster. But here's the thing: it was almost directly underneath Eros in Piccadilly Circus. More proof that you can be at the centre of everything and find yourself in the calm eye of the hurricane.

Sadly the truth about Ward's mysterious staircase into the

netherworld has a prosaic origin. It began as an underground toilet, possibly linked to the cinema next door.

THE VIADUCT TAVERN

A number of public houses supposedly had tunnels linking them to the Tower of London, including one from the Tiger Tavern, now blocked off. Elizabeth I, clearly the queen of underground tunnels, appears to have dashed all over the place under London, probably to neck a swift half with the Earl of Essex. Nell Gwyn is associated with at least five London pubs and connecting tunnels, including the Nell of Old Drury and the Red Lion in Crown Passage. Unfortunately it's a load of bollocks.

Which brings me to the Viaduct Tavern, a still-impressive corner pub facing its famous namesake, Holborn Viaduct. Queen Victoria opened it in 1869—the viaduct, that is, not the pub, although they both opened in the same year. But the tunnel-thing in the pub basement is not part of the Old Bailey opposite, nor is it connected to Newgate Prison. The pub's tunnel is simply a cellar. A tour can be arranged by appointment but there are no prisoners' cells. It's still evocative and stinkily Victorian, though. Mr Bryant drags his poor punters down there and threatens to leave them if they get too lippy.

The pub has a large curved frontage with some original features. On one wall, three paintings of wistful maidens represent agriculture, banking and the arts. The 'arts' figure was attacked (some say shot, others bayoneted) by a drunken First World War soldier, and she still bears the scar.

There are gilded and silvered mirrors and decorated glass. At the back of the bar is a manager's stall, a sort of office booth, made from carved hardwood and intricately engraved glass panels. The ornate ceiling is made from beaten copper and is supported by cast-iron pillars.

WILLIAMSON'S TAVERN

In the Square Mile, City pubs all seem to get grand ideas and turn themselves into taverns.

Despite the legends about this being the City's oldest surviving watering hole since the Great Fire, most of it only dates from the 1930s. But it did emerge, phoenix-like, from the ruins of the Great Fire. Tucked in Groveland Court off an alley from Bow Lane, it's two interlinked bars. The smaller boasts the most uncomfortable bench I've ever planted my arse on. Oh, and there are ghosts. At least one long-serving barmaid flatly refuses to do evening shifts. It's said that police dog patrols have the devil's own job persuading their canine chums to venture anywhere near the place.

So much for the nonsense. The true part is that it's constructed over Roman ruins which survive some five metres down. And it was once the official residence of the Mayor of London. King William and Queen Mary liked the place so much that they provided it with the iron gates outside. A gentleman called Robert Williamson turned it into a formal public house in 1739.

The bar is supposed to contain an ancient stone that marks the dead centre of the old City. I once went in search of it and asked the barmaid if she had seen an ancient circular stone. She told me to take a look under the rug, and there it was, the heart of London—not very impressive, but nice to know it's there all the same. It's typical that a piece of ancient London history gets an old rug thrown over it.

THE PROSPECT OF WHITBY

The Prospect of Whitby is London's oldest riverside pub—the pub site on Wapping Wall dates back to 1520. The original flagstone floor survives and the pub also has a rare pewter-topped bar, as well as old barrels and ships' masts built into the structure.

The pub was frequented by lightermen, watermen and others who made their living on the river and at sea, and also quite a few smugglers, thieves and pirates. The most famous customers include Charles Dickens, Samuel Pepys and the artists Whistler and Turner.

It used to be called the Pelican, but was also known as the Devil's Tavern. Sir Hugh Willoughby sailed from here in 1533 in a disastrous attempt to discover the North-East Passage to China. 'Hanging' Judge Jeffreys was another punter. He lived nearby and kept a mock gallows outside his window, commemorating his sadistic calling. He was chased by anti-Royalists into the nearby Town of Ramsgate pub, captured and taken to the Tower. According to legend, criminals could be tied up to the posts at low tide and left there to drown because the foreshore was under the jurisdiction of the Admiralty.

THE SEVEN STARS

This is the sort of incredibly old public house you pop into on a winter's afternoon and end up staying in for five hours. At least, I do. How old is it? When renovations had to be made the clues it revealed confirmed a date of 1602, just before the end of Elizabeth I's reign. Shakespeare was working up the road, so he might well have popped in for a pint.

It's a tiny place, lined with film posters for British courtroom thrillers, and is used by those in the legal profession along with 'litigants, reporters, LSE students, church musicians and West End show brass sections.' The landlady is the ebullient 'Alewife for the Ages,' Roxy Beaujolais, and the pub cat is a ruff-wearing paralegal moggy called Tom Paine.

Situated behind the law courts, the Seven Stars is one of the few Holborn buildings that survived the Great Fire. Beaujolais is a chef and connoisseur of the good life, and keeps the pub open seven days a week, which is a rare thing in the City of London these days.

It's all wonderfully eccentric. It saddens me that the major breweries, who only see profit and turnover, never realize that the way to ensure a pub's longevity is to keep its character, or if character is lacking, to imbue it with some. The Seven Stars is not for the casual passer-by. It's for people who like a drink.

THE PINEAPPLE

North London's Kentish Town has always been the home of penniless artists, writers, ruffians, mountebanks and charlatans, not to mention stoners, loners and ladies of slender means. But over the years it has lost many of its pubs. The Jolly Anglers became a Nando's and the Crimea was carved into flats. The Pineapple was due to fall to rapacious developers who reckoned without its formidable residents' committee.

At the eleventh hour the council listed the pub's old bar, which meant that no one could move it, and the developers got cold feet. The pub was returned to its former glory as a neighbourhood watering hole. First they threw out all the druggy Old Etonians who'd invaded it, then they restored the events that had been held there for a century, including the annual Easter Bonnet parade and race-day outings. It soon attracted celebrities, who could be found propping up the bar in true egalitarian fashion. A real London boozer, in fact.

In certain areas you can date the streets by looking at pub names. Many can be placed in the middle of the nineteenth century, around the time Mr Bryant must have been born.

BRADLEY'S SPANISH BAR

I know what you're wondering. Where can I find London's smallest pub toilet?

There used to be a Spanish quarter in Hanway Street, behind Oxford Street, but the sticky-carpeted Costa Dorada Flamenco Bar has gone and now only Bradley's is left. It's a miniscule pub with a toilet that nobody with more than a thirty-four-inch waistline is likely to get into (or, more worryingly, out of) but it's a joy. The bar that is, not the khazi. Favouring shabby over chic, its drinkers take over the entire street in the summer months. They used to do the world's biggest home-made Scotch eggs there, smothered in spicy gravy.

THE ANGEL, ST GILES

Here's something many Londoners have walked past without thinking about. Next to the Angel pub in the now all-but-destroyed neighbourhood of St Giles, at the base of Tottenham Court Road, is a lychgate, a roofed gateway to a churchyard that would once have been used at burials for resting the coffin until the clergyman arrived.

This one is a rather grubby Palladian stone arch with a depiction of the Last Judgement carved on it. The tableau used to be made of wood, but was replaced with a stone carving in 1800. It always disturbed my old mother when she had to pass it on the way to the off-licence for a miniature. You can still see the wooden version in St Giles-in-the-Fields behind it, not that anyone bothers. Londoners have a dismissive attitude to their own history.

The Angel pub next door used to be called the Bowl, and was another stop for condemned prisoners on their way to be hanged at Tyburn in Marble Arch, so they could look upon the Last Judgement and think about their fate. Or get sloshed. The pub still has partitions, decorative ceilings and several cosy neo-Georgian rooms. I sometimes go there for a cleansing ale or three with Coatsleeve Charlie when he's out on bail—er, back from his holidays.

THE DOG AND DUCK

My final choice has to be Soho's old duck-hunters' pub, for the fantastic tilework, what feels like the world's smallest bar, the dismissiveness of its staff, the incredibly unnegotiable staircase and the weird thought that George Orwell and Madonna both drank there.

I I I

I could stay and tell you tales of establishments I have been barred from, but I'm due to give an organ recital at the Blue Posts. Admittedly it's a mouth organ recital, but today I seem to have misplaced my instrument and must make do with a comb and toilet paper. I shall be performing Bach's Toccata and Fugue in D Minor followed by those music hall favourites, 'Any Old Iron' and 'Don't Buy Any Seafood, Mother, Dad's Coming Home With Crabs.'

44

Safety for the Dead & Other Stories

ARTHUR BRYANT: I'm holding up a . . . well, it's supposed to be a police notebook. I'm meant to file witness reports and aperçus about miscreants in it, but instead I fill it with bits of useless information that stick to me as I walk about the London streets. I thought today I'd give you a few jottings from it, a bit of pot luck that might inspire you. Some of this text wasn't very readable so I had to guess. Other bits had sherbet lemons stuck to them, so I apologize in advance.

On the first page: 'We need bleach.'

Hang on, other end.

JOHN MAY: Your trifocals.

ARTHUR BRYANT: I'm what?

JOHN MAY: You're sitting on them.

ARTHUR BRYANT: So I am. Thank you, that's better.

St Bride's is the so-called 'wedding cake' church because its steeple inspired the famous multi-tiered marital confectionery. It's still known to some as the Printers' Cathedral. Tucked behind Fleet Street, it stands on a pagan site dedicated to Brigit, the Celtic Goddess of Healing, Fire and Childbirth.

For two thousand years the spot has been a place of worship, and for the past five hundred it has been the spiritual home of journalists. Samuel Pepys, no mean reporter himself, was born just outside it, and later bribed the gravedigger of St Bride's to shift up his corpses so that his brother John could be buried in the churchyard.

Only the font survived the Great Fire of London. There's meant to be an odd little spot by Farringdon Road that's kept unbuilt upon to mark the site of the church's cholera pit, but I've never found it. Ludgate Circus has been so messed around that I'm not entirely sure what's left, and nobody else is either.

The Square Mile has very few residents now, let alone parishioners. Sometimes there are piano recitals going on inside the church without an audience, which is a shame when you consider the bustling street a few yards from its door.

St Bride's had a secret: a vault, hidden until the Blitz bombs revealed it, which had been closed off since the plague caused it to be sealed.

Until well into the nineteenth century resurrectionists were making up to fourteen pounds on each body they snatched. People sought 'safety for the dead' and inventors produced an iron coffin with a flange that engaged with spring clips in the lid. As was common in times of plague (in this case the 1854 cholera epidemic) some were covered with protective foil. Iron coffins took much longer to disintegrate than wooden ones, so higher burial fees were charged—the result was the end of the fad for iron coffins. You can see them in the crypt.

It was believed that if you were buried near the centre of the church you stood a better chance of getting into heaven, and gravediggers had to be bribed to find spaces. Many of the bodies found here dated back to the earlier Great Plague of 1665.

St Bride's churchyard is raised above the surrounding alleys because it's stuffed full of ancient corpses. Like so many religious sites in London, it overlooks the local pub. The Old Bell has been a licensed tavern for more than three hundred years. Built by Sir Christopher Wren, it housed his masons while they were rebuilding St Bride's after the Great Fire. Because you really want a drunk stonemason working on your building.

| | |

St Katherine Cree in Aldgate is the only church in the City of London that still rings its church bells of a Sunday morning, but it has another claim to fame; in 1643, Sir John Gayer, a London merchant, was travelling in Arabia and was confronted by a lion. He knelt before it and it left him unharmed. Details are sketchy. Did it just wander into his tent? Anyway, he was grateful for his deliverance and bequeathed two hundred pounds at his death to provide a yearly sermon to mark the event. He's also buried at the church. The Lion Sermon is still preached at 1 P.M. on 16 October (or the nearest Thursday) every year.

| | |

The Tudor gateway to St Bartholomew-the-Great in Smithfield had long been sealed up until a German Zeppelin bomb blew away the plaster and stone in 1916. The revealed gatehouse was restored and serves as a reminder of the only bomb for which we can be grateful.

| | |

These next few pages from my notebook have curry sauce on them, so bear with me.

People don't notice that there's a little garden at the centre of Smithfield Market. It has a statue dating from 1873 of a young woman who's meant to represent fertility. In 1924 the market superintendent found a gold ring and soldered it on her wedding finger after deciding that if she was going to produce babies she should be married. The last time I was there I couldn't quite see if she was still wearing it because I'm a bit too short.

| | |

Cuckold's Point in Rotherhithe is on a sharp bend of the Thames near the church of St Mary's Church and the south side's Angel pub, which has a balcony built out over the water. The name comes from a post with a pair of horns on it that marked the starting point of the riotous Horn Fair, a carnival that went from this point to Greenwich. Carnivalesque events are still held on the nearby green.

But there's confusion about the name; traditionally a cuckold is a cheated-upon husband, but it also referred to the God of Winter being cuckolded by the incoming season. The story gets more complex when we consider that the Green Man, a priapic Horned God, is strongly associated with the area. He's a creature made of branches and leaves and represents rebirth, but he belongs in my follow-up volume, *Old Bryant's Folk Tales of England*. I'm joking. I don't go beyond the end of the Central Line.

According to tradition, the Horn Fair was started after King John seduced the wife of a local miller, cuckolding him. King John gave the miller all the land from Rotherhithe to Charlton as recompense. ('Sorry I shagged your missus, have Woolwich.') Cuckolding is also connected to the rutting of stags, so it may be that this was simply a good place to catch deer.

There is still a cave at the edge of Blackheath Common called the Point on the carnival procession route that supposedly has a carving of the Horned God at its entrance. It was sealed up in 1905 and remains unopened, so I can't verify the claim.

Horns remain a symbol of sexual power, and the English expression 'getting the horn' is still very much in use. I've written something after this about matadors. It's probably rude as it's in code, but I've lost the code key.

| | |

Hang on, there's a bit of a jump here.

Parliament.

It's open to all British residents. They usually have a variety of programmes and events taking place. Guided tours bring visitors into both the Commons and Lords chambers and Westminster Hall, as well as up the Clock Tower.

You can attend debates in both Houses and watch committee hearings, which will sap your will to live. When our beloved Police Commissioner held a Meet 'n' Greet with her platoons of plods from all corners of London it was a chance for me to chuck down free booze on the river terrace at the MPs' expense and hear a couple of speeches.

Entering the building is as complicated as passing through US customs, and involves metal detectors and having your picture taken for a badge. After the spectacle of Westminster Hall, St Stephen's Hall and the central open square, you might re-enter through a far less sumptuous part that takes you past endless meeting rooms where people seem to be drinking themselves into oblivion. It will amaze you how many people there are inside these claustrophobic wood-panelled chambers.

The smell of institutional meals can be overpowering. Waiters deliver endless plates along cream-painted corridors, adding to the feeling that you're wandering through a care home.

If you're tempted to attend a speech, might I suggest you don't? What you'll get are some stitched-together aphorisms, snippets of Latin, jingoistic nonsense, delusional predictions, contradictory statements and a bit of nasty-minded *Schadenfreude* about the EU. In other words, Jacob Rees-Mogg. Perhaps there's something about being in the Houses of Parliament that encourages the tyranny of the soap box—in which case, heaven help our under-attended debating chambers. Nice building, shame about the smell of cabbage.

| | |

You often expect to find an ultra-modern room lurking inside a Victorian or Georgian exterior in London, but how many examples are there of the reverse?

I can think of a couple. The exterior of the Lyric Theatre, Hammersmith, may look like a 1970s car park, yet behind its walls is a gorgeously plush red-and-gold Victorian theatre.

Even more surprising, although not normally open to the public, is the Committee Room inside Richard Rogers's ultra-eighties Lloyd's building. It was built for the 2nd Earl of Shelburne by Robert Adam in 1763. Having made its way from Bowood House in Wiltshire to the Square Mile, it remains a true time warp tucked behind glass and steel. The building also houses the Lutine Bell, salvaged from the wrecked British warship, hung in the insurance office of Lloyd's and traditionally rung before announcements of ships overdue or lost at sea.

The most truly wondrous interiors of London buildings tend to be hidden from view, but can sometimes be accessed on open days. They include:

Lloyd's Register (formerly 'of Shipping') on Fenchurch Street, filled with marble processional spaces.

The Masonic Temple, Andaz London Liverpool Street Hotel, built on the site of the first Bethlem (Bedlam) Hospital.

The Criterion restaurant, in Piccadilly Circus, with its sumptuous golden ceiling.

The Supreme Court in Parliament Square, which contains the prison gateway to Tothill Fields Bridewell, creepily inscribed 'For such as will Beg, and Live Idle . . .'

The Clermont Club, Berkeley Square, which has an outrageously theatrical staircase leading to one of the finest rooms in London, its geometrical ceiling inset with grisaille paintings. The property was not allowed to have buildings spoiling its garden's view of Berkeley Square, and remains that way today.

Middle Temple Hall, construction of which began in 1562, with a double hammerbeam ceiling that makes it feel built upside down, in a building which has survived since the reign of Elizabeth I. It contains Sir Francis Drake's 'cupboard,' probably carved from the hatch cover of the *Golden Hind,* and it was here that *Twelfth Night* was performed for Elizabeth I. One of the hall's stained-glass windows has two curious names: Josephus Jekyll and Robertus Hyde. As Robert Louis Stevenson was known to have big nights out in Middle Temple it seems safe to assume he lifted those names for his characters.

What fascinates me is that all these places are united by a common factor: they're exactly how their users expect them to look. The lushness of a theatre. The elegance of a restaurant. The permanence of a bank. And the craftsmanship of an engine house:

Sir Joseph Bazalgette's Crossness Pumping Station in Bexley is a cathedral of sewage treatment, from its humbug-striped chimney to its elaborate interior tracery of green, gold and red ironwork. You'd instinctively trust the workers who designed and built it.

Things are different now. My coffee shop looks like a Norwegian log cabin, my lunchtime café is modelled on a Brazilian favela and my bank looks like an optician's.

45

Sore Throats & Other Stories

ARTHUR BRYANT: I know nothing about popular music after Cilla Black (and I certainly didn't learn much from her), so, John, you have more highbrow musical tastes. Perhaps you'd do the honours?

JOHN MAY: I wouldn't say highbrow, Arthur, but I do like a bit of *musique concrète* every now and again.

ARTHUR BRYANT: You mean someone wading through a flute orchestra with a sledgehammer? Dear God.

JOHN MAY: Discordant 'raw' sound experiments began in the 1940s with the French.

ARTHUR BRYANT: I might have known.

JOHN MAY: I suppose you could argue that punk was part of this movement. But specifically *London* punk was not quite the working-class rallying cry against the monarchy and the rich that it pretended to be. Rather, it was rooted in a classic middle-class desire to make money from mischief.

Far more based around clothes and attitude than actual music, which no one had bothered to learn or understand, punk in London was largely set in motion by Vivienne Westwood's streetwear shop SEX in the King's Road.

The shop was owned by the talented fashion designer and her partner Malcom McLaren—they were creating costumes for films like *Mahler*, and McLaren often quoted his grandmother saying 'To be bad is good, because to be good is simply boring.' Although Westwood described herself as working class, McLaren's background was resolutely middle-class and factory-owning. Eventually Westwood became a dame and something of a national treasure. She lives in an eighteenth-century house that belonged to the mother of Captain Cook.

Like the beatniks before them, many of the early punks were middle-class dropouts eager to be noticed, and this tiny movement was helped by the formation of the Sex Pistols, which allowed them to manufacture outrage through the tabloid press. They were also supported by kids who would charge tourists five pounds to have their photographs taken. How did they come to choose mohawks as the archetypal punk fashion look?

Well, one explanation comes from 1712, when a gang of marauding posh boys caused trouble in London.

It was said they were rebelling against the status quo, which was putting pressure on them to conform to a moral code. They were called the Mohocks, and had modelled themselves on the visiting Iroquois chiefs who had recently dined with royalty in London. Native Americans had yet to be romanticized as 'noble savages' and were thought to be childlike and uncivilized. The Mohocks capitalized on this fear, attacking pedestrians at night, running through sedan chairs with swords and causing panic. Although rewards were posted nobody ever claimed them. The Mohocks were rich and well connected, and their friends didn't need the reward money.

The gang was supposedly later revived as Mohawks in 1771, although this is disputed. It would be interesting to know if Westwood (whose historical knowledge is amply apparent from many of her extraordinary designs) had knowingly tapped into this fashion for rebellion. For a while the King's Road, Chelsea, became the bleeding heart of punk.

ARTHUR BRYANT: How revolting. I have to say, though, that I rather admire the Mohocks. Lords in sedan chairs used to allow their chairmen to whip people's hands and feet to get them out of the way, so the Mohocks were perhaps within their rights to strike back.

Now, what do you think is the centre of London? Eros? St Paul's? That stone under Harry Prayer's pub rug? Leicester Square (God help us)? In fact, there is a centre and we know this because it's clearly marked.

The brass plaque in the pavement behind the statue of Charles I in Trafalgar Square is the site of the original Charing Cross. It's not where we think it is, i.e., outside the station under the fancifully reimagined Eleanor Cross, which was put up in 1865. I warned you this would happen a lot.

There used to be a small area of high ground in the Thames marshes called Thorney Island. It's where Westminster is now, and there was a monastery on it. In a time when monarchs were called things like Herbert the Unpleasant—

JOHN MAY: I don't think there was a Herbert the Unpleasant, Arthur.

ARTHUR BRYANT: I'm extemporizing. Edward the Confessor lasted twenty-three years on the throne, had some very modernist pennies printed with his image and added Westminster Abbey to Thorney Island. However, the city merchants didn't want to go all the way over there to hear the latest mercantile gossip, so they agreed to meet at a halfway point.

The plaque marks the exact mid-distance between the old city and the new seat of government, making it the centre of two Londons. Anyone working within six miles of this was entitled to London weighting pay—and we could perhaps take this as a measure of what made a true Londoner.

In *Sketches by Boz* (1836), Charles Dickens—

JOHN MAY: So you're doing Dickens now.

ARTHUR BRYANT: No, fairgrounds.

Dickens was a frequenter of the Greenwich Fair for years. He described it as 'a sort of spring-rash: a three days' fever, which cools the blood for six months afterwards.'

He said people arrived by every mode of transport—'Cabs, hackney-coaches, "shay" carts, coal-waggons, stages, omnibuses, sociables, gigs, donkey-chaises.' Hawkers and sharps haunted the park and its surrounding area.

The big pastime in the park was 'tumbling.' 'The principal amusement is to drag young ladies up the steep hill which leads to the Observatory, and then drag them down again, at the very top of their speed, greatly to the derangement of their curls and bonnet-caps, and much to the edification of lookers-on from below.' Clearly they were more easily entertained in those days.

Greenwich Fair was closed down in 1857. It had become too crowded—visitor numbers were in excess of two hundred thousand—and too debauched for the locals.

Gone now are the naval pensioners who'd tell hair-raising tales and offer peeks through their telescopes of the Isle of Dogs gibbet, where rotting pirate corpses would hang. Gone, too, is the notorious Crown and Anchor dancing-booth, in which cross-dressing and all kinds of transgressive carrying-on would take place; and Richardson's, a travelling theatre where, according to Dickens, 'you have a melodrama (with three murders and a ghost), a pantomime, a comic song, an overture and some incidental music, all done in five-and-twenty minutes.' It's time they brought that back.

JOHN MAY: I'm finding this a little hard to follow, Arthur.

ARTHUR BRYANT: These are my notes. They're in no particular order.

JOHN MAY: Clearly.

| | |

Now, if you call this next place 'the Harry Potter Hotel' you'll get the benefit of my stick across your shins. One hundred and fifty million was spent on the restoration of the three-hundred-room Midland Grand Hotel. It originally opened in 1873 after Sir George Gilbert Scott, the architect behind the Albert Memorial and the Foreign Office, won a Midland Railway Company competition to design a hotel next to its railway station.

There's still no disguising the fact that for all its space it's an oddly claustrophobic building. There's very little outside space—we are above a railway station, after all—and it feels like a lost Gothic world. The atrium is spectacular, with a curved ceiling that echoes the great station roof, elaborately sculpted girders and painted alcoves.

The most dazzling sight, though, is the great staircase, a serpentine and seemingly unsupported climb that winds up to a vaulted green-and-gold ceiling.

The sheer amount of decoration is staggering—here is Victorian decorative design at its zenith, fiercely colourful, over-wrought, hysterical even, classically themed, painted and frescoed and papered with intricate patterns and colours that somehow never clash because everything does. The Ladies' Smoking Room is particularly elaborate. Its current name is the St Pancras Renaissance London Hotel.

JOHN MAY: To me it always feels rather distant and grand, a little chilly and unwelcoming.

ARTHUR BRYANT: Perhaps that's what makes it so typically Victorian.

I was in Columbia Road Flower Market recently. One of the officers at Bethnal Green Police Station was getting married and I wanted to pick her up some love-lies-bleeding.*

Columbia Road began as a pathway along which sheep were driven to the slaughterhouses at Smithfield. It had several identities over the centuries, but was finally named in honour of Baroness Burdett-Coutts, the first woman to be made a peer in her own right, and a remarkable philanthropist.

In the 1860s, at a cost of two hundred thousand pounds, she built Columbia Market, a grand Gothic building for poor East Enders. It was a place where they could shop cheaply, and contained four hundred stores, but it failed because it had no rail connection. This Victorian cathedral of retail wonders gradually turned into a shabby ghost of itself. It was let out as workshops but was finally torn down in the 1950s.

There was no one to save it. The market building was in the wrong place and too ornate a folly ever to succeed, so it was de-

---

* In the Victorian language of flowers it means 'hopelessness.'

molished and replaced with cheap housing. Had it been saved, it would now be one of London's treasures.

The parade of Victorian shops there today was built to service the population of the nearby Jesus Hospital Estate. Apart from providing all the necessities of life, many shops were given over to upholstery. Timber yards peppered the area until the late twentieth century.

The flower market began as a Saturday trading market, but as the Jewish population grew a Sunday market was established. Plants were brought by handcart from nearby gardens in Hackney and Islington. Pitches were claimed on the day by the blowing of a whistle. The area went into a decline in the 1970s and demolition was suggested, but the locals fought back and saved the area.

Now the narrow streets are filled to bursting point on Sunday mornings. However, London has a way of dealing with this and quickly sprouts new markets in less well-known backstreets. So the market thrives, just in a different form.

The inexhaustible Burdett-Coutts teamed up with Charles Dickens to create what must have been London's first gated community, Holly Village in Swain's Lane, Highgate. It's one of the most peculiar developments in London, comprising a series of twelve small cottages, finished in 1865 in a highly ornate Gothic style. The entrance has two female statues, one with a lamb and one a dove. Together the cottages—which must be very dark inside, judging by the size of their windows—form a unique readybuilt stage set for a costume drama. They very rarely come up for sale these days. Funny, that.

| | |

For its size, London is one of the greenest cities in the world. It's helped by the appalling weather, which keeps everything nice and damp. We plant flowers in bits of waste-ground, allotments and window boxes, but we also plant in more out-of-the-way spots.

The one-and-a-half-acre rooftop gardens in Kensington are the largest in Europe. The spectacularly ornate gardens were laid out between 1936 and 1938 by landscape architect Ralph Hancock on the instructions of Barkers, the Kensington department store giant that constructed the building around 1932. The gardens boast four flamingos, a running stream with bridge, manicured lawns and a Spanish terrace based on the Alhambra in Granada.

Ultra-cool Biba expanded into the store below until 1975, but they didn't have the stock to keep it running. Above them, the gardens thrived and were listed as a Grade II* site by Historic England in 1998.

There are over thirty different species of trees in its woodlands, including trees from over sixty years ago, despite having only a metre of soil in which to grow. It all looks particularly nice in the snow. The gardens featured regularly in Michael Moorcock's Jerry Cornelius books. At the time of writing the gardens are closed after disputes with the landlords.

| | |

All you can say about London Fields is that it's an open green space with some unnecessarily prominent toilets. It's in an unlovely part of Hackney, but there's a gem of a market nearby.

London markets evolve very quickly from local beginnings, like the one in Islington's Chapel Street, to overblown tourist traps, like the ones in Camden. Broadway Market has the balance right, although some Hackneyistas are moaning about gentrification, as if their credibility is somehow being damaged by the arrival of a bread shop.

The market has a mix of organic stalls, fishmongers, a good pub, a jellied-eel shop, a bookstore, an ironmonger's and not too many ironic gift-places. But on a freezing Saturday morning recently it also had some tiresome French accordionists and someone playing a harp, so the rot's set in.

London markets are no longer places where fake antiques sit beside pub mirrors and piles of mismatched shoes. Now they're largely about food and are becoming too similar to each other. Although they seem over-keen to flog you something called a bao bun,* they remain places where people talk to one another. I could do without the ranting Jesus bloke with the dog on a bit of string who always follows me through Chapel Market, but sadly you can't arrest someone just for being annoying anymore.

| | |

If you had a sore throat at the start of February (who didn't?) you could have ditched the Night Nurse and whipped over to St Etheldreda's Church, Ely Place, a tiny cul-de-sac that still has a beadle's lodge. St Etheldreda is the patron saint of throat ailments. Here, you'll find a fragment of the blessed one's hand in the jewelled chest to the right of the altar. Get your throat as close to it as you can and be healed.

The blessing, which takes the form of a pair of crossed candles placed around the throat, occurs at the church each February.

St Blaise's protection of those with oesophageal troubles apparently comes from a legend that when he was on the way to his own execution a boy was brought to him with a fishbone stuck in his throat. The child was about to die when St Blaise 'healed' him in an act that was probably not much harder than unbunging a sock from a spin dryer. Because St Blaise is also the patron saint of wool.

This, you understand, is why I'm not religious.

---

* A food item that looks and tastes like a bath sponge.

46

Miasmas & Other Stories

Arthur Bryant: I just collared Fraternity DuCaine in the corridor outside and asked him to pick a London subject, and he's chosen his home town.

Fraternity DuCaine: I live in Brixton in South London, which has been around a very long time. In the eleventh century it was known as Brixistane, meaning 'the Stone of Brihtsige.' Stones were set down to mark crossings where villagers could meet and argue things out.

Brixton's status jumped when the railway linked it to the centre of the city, allowing wealthy Victorians to settle into grand new houses. It was suddenly the fashionable middle-class place to live, perfectly poised between town and country.

London's first purpose-built department store was the Bon Marché and opened in 1877. It guaranteed to open every order and dispatch the goods within one hour. Eleven years later, Electric Avenue became the first London street to be lit by electricity. The villas grew grander, but in the first half of the next century

Brixton's fortunes sank when the middle classes moved further out. You can see the same pattern occurring again and again all over London.

The grand houses were subdivided into flats, then rooms, and proved popular lodgings for theatricals, which started Brixton's connection with the arts. At the age of twenty Vincent van Gogh lived in Brixton, and drew the house where he lodged.

Although there had been a Black population in London since Elizabethan times, the *Windrush* generation brought a fresh influx of life as West Indian families settled in Brixton after the war. As the first visibly different neighbourhood, it provoked ire from red-faced colonels who feared a loss of 'Englishness,' and faced plenty of serious challenges before finding its place as an integrated community. Brixton's snaking covered market is no longer local but international, and is unique in London.

MEERA MANGESHKAR: I heard there used to be a big dance club in Brixton called the Fridge. It was where the New Romantic movement started. Did you ever get there?

FRATERNITY DUCAINE: Just before it shut in 2010. They opened another bar called the Oven. So you could go to the Oven next to the Fridge.

My folks were affected by the Brixton riots of the early 1980s. The Met's 'stop and search' powers were being disproportionately used against Black people, who took to the streets in protest. A government report found damning evidence that the rules were being abused, and this eventually resulted in changes to the law. So sometimes rioting works.

MEERA MANGESHKAR: Says one of London's top law enforcement officers.

FRATERNITY DUCAINE: You have to see it from both sides, Meera.

ARTHUR BRYANT: Our next guest speaker is Dante August, one of the curators at the Museum of London. He knows a lot about fog.

DANTE AUGUST: At the Museum of London we have all kinds of artefacts marking centuries of events, but how do you mark a miasma? When TV dramas set themselves in the London of the past there's usually one thing they fail to convey: the sheer murkiness of the metropolis. Londoners had long since believed that disease lurked in the miasma, and if the ill humours of the air could just be prevented from wafting across the nice neighbourhoods, the rich would be protected.

Pollution is nothing new to London. From the beginning of the seventeenth century it lay in a cloud across the city, the result of sea coal being burned in factories. London sits in a basin, so the fumes were held in. They stank and left a sepia tinge of soot on everything they touched. Washing left outside changed colour in minutes.

They couldn't get rid of it but managed to name it; a 'London particular' could change colour throughout the day, from amber and pea-green to purple and lurid crimson. It was moist, thick, full of bad smells and could choke you to death. And it was so heavy with filth—some estimated 340,000 pieces of soot per cubic inch of air—that Londoners were breathing very little else.

In November the city was hardly ever without its lights on, but, even so, people fell into the river or were knocked down. It was the month of suicides. The world moved more slowly, sound was muffled and crime rose. The American method of 'sandbagging,' with a cloth truncheon full of sand, became a popular form of mugging. It left no marks and made no noise, and the victim could be abandoned to lie in the fog undiscovered.

To combat the gloom, bright tiles and red brick became popular and made buildings more visible. Homes and public houses looked cosy and inviting. Monet led the charge to come to paint the phenomenon. Curls of sulphur crept into theatres and shops. Entire neighbourhoods vanished. When a particular cloud parted it revealed scenes of London life as if in tableaux, and swallowed them up just as quickly again.

Due to the natural layout of London, fog could lie forty miles in every direction from Charing Cross.

Gas lights and 'the new electricity' made London more atmospheric, a warm glow reflecting down from the cloud ceiling. An updated version of the link boy appeared, who used an electric torch to guide others through the fog rather than a flambeau. As the city warmed, the fogs began to abate, but after the Second World War they returned in a pernicious new form: smogs.

On 5 December 1952, the Great Smog* lasted for four days. It slipped through windows and down chimneys until it was difficult to tell if you were inside or out. The fog stopped traffic and choked cattle to death at Smithfield Market. At Sadler's Wells, performances were halted because nobody could breathe or see anything. Near the Thames visibility dropped to nil. Cars crashed into pillar boxes, cats fell out of trees and residents got lost in their own front gardens. Four years later the Clean Air Act came into force.

Now there's a lot more clear air in London and very little darkness. The city has never understood how to handle a day of full sunshine. Luckily, it doesn't happen very often.

* Smoke/fog.

ARTHUR BRYANT: Sir Arthur Conan Doyle got good mileage out of the London particular. Wasn't his consulting detective forever creeping about in the murk disguised as a one-legged mariner or something? I always thought I was living in a foggy city anyway, until I had my cataracts done.

JOHN MAY: I don't have the same deep attachment you have to London, Arthur. I'd happily live on the Mediterranean coast. London is emphatically not a sunny city. The 'invisible rain' we talk about, which can't be seen falling but which makes the streets wet, is never far away.

There's probably no house in London that's completely dry. Even with global warming we're still a city of mists, rain and coolness, without being very cold. Girls in scrappy tops stand outside pubs with men in shorts, chatting in the lightly sifting rain. London's weather is rarely noticeable enough to make you change plans.

Watching the sixties spy film *The Ipcress File* on TV, I was struck by the sooty blackness of uncleaned post-war buildings. They've either been restored or replaced now, but a penumbral cloak of soft rainfall can return them to other ages despite the invention of central heating and power-sprays. It can make the city appear timeless.

Over winter the pavements turn slick with algae. The side of the old brick King's Cross Station often develops a thick coating of emerald moss. Green shoots grow between even the most used paving stones throughout the year.

While London weather makes you think about taking a sweater, country weather is positively vengeful. For me, rural locations have too much atmosphere and not enough people. I cast envious glances at Southern Europe but I stay here for the Unit's sake, for Arthur. Not for London, where people stare in amazement whenever they see a pale patch of sunlight on the pavement.

ARTHUR BRYANT: You raised a good point there, John, just before you started waxing lyrical. When you look at a London street, how much do you really see of the past? Buildings come and go, and the biggest changes are wrought by a neighbourhood's fluctuating fortunes.

But some buildings return again and again.

47

A Giant Gorilla &
Other Stories

ARTHUR BRYANT: I was thinking about the Theatre Royal, Drury Lane.

JOHN MAY: As you do.

ARTHUR BRYANT: It's the fourth theatre on the same spot. It was built in 1812 and looks largely the same today as then. But in earlier times it existed in the heart of London's fruit and vegetable market, and was surrounded by porters, flower-sellers and carts. The show with the biggest box office in 1958 was *My Fair Lady*, set in Covent Garden market itself, a simulacrum of its location. The market closed and the porters went with it, turning George Bernard Shaw's story of a social experiment into something more like a fable of lost London.

And I suppose at first glance Piccadilly Circus looks the same as it always did, except that now Eros, the statue in the centre of the circus, isn't central anymore. It has been relocated to the lower side in a pedestrianized area.

Westminster Abbey looks more or less the same, except that it has ten new statues over the door, including one of Martin Luther King, Jr., and there's now a stained-glass window of Oscar Wilde.

The Pool of London was never a place, just a crowded area of the river between London Bridge and Tower Bridge. After the docks closed in the 1970s the river traffic entirely vanished, leaving behind no memory of London's rowdiest maritime corner. The riverside cranes have now moved inland to construct buildings.

Harrods looked like a very ordinary grocery store in 1874. The fact that it managed to fulfil its Christmas orders despite burning down helped to secure its reputation. It was rebuilt in the terracotta tiles that still cover its frontage, and the look its new building established has remained ever since.

These buildings and places are all, in essence, the same as they were. Why? The one thing that can't change is London's topography, shaped by its hills, inlets and rivers. As to which buildings survived it's largely been a matter of luck, and whether the prevailing economic attitude favours destruction or rescue.

It seems typical to me that we can't figure out where the names of our country or our capital city came from. There's certainly a strong Welsh influence in both. Just how many other names for London are there? Why do we know so little about our own past? Ask the average Londoner what they know about the city in which they live and their lack of knowledge will appall you. Well, it appalls me, anyway.

But then my friends tend to know far too much about certain subjects. To make the right historical connections you must traverse a minefield. It's a bit like those people who set out to uncover the identity of Jack the Ripper and get lost in the back-doubles of its mythology. London mythologizes itself. Look back and before you know it you'll be immersed in tales of druids and sun cults. Search for Caesar's encampment in London and you'll find yourself right opposite the headquarters of the Peculiar Crimes Unit in King's Cross. When no evidence of the past is left for us to see, all we can do is turn to the myths. Luckily it's a city built on stories, and those remain waiting for us to discover them.

John, there are just a few of my notes left. You could help me out.

JOHN MAY: Must I, Arthur? I've got a date tonight.

ARTHUR BRYANT: At your age. As my old man used to say, you can't get much of a spark off an old flint.

JOHN MAY: What does that mean?

ARTHUR BRYANT: I've absolutely no idea. Look, I'll do this one, you do the next one.

Until the 1970s most of Britain's daily newspapers were put together in Fleet Street. When I walked along its pavements I felt the vibration of the mighty printing presses beneath my boots. I could smell hot ink and paper, and watch the copyboys hurtling around with still-warm issues bundled in their arms. The printers shouted above the rhythmic hammering of machinery. The editors and journalists drank hard in the surrounding pubs, returning to their desks to write up stories while they were half-cut. They worked best when they were slightly less than sober.

The writer Edgar Wallace has a plaque on a corner of the street with a lovely sentiment expressed on it. 'He knew wealth &

poverty, yet had walked with kings & kept his bearing. Of his talents he gave lavishly to authorship—but to Fleet Street he gave his heart.'

Tucked into the back of Temple near the law courts is the Edgar Wallace, a traditional pub in an alley crowded with lawyers. Its shelves are still filled with his books.

I wonder if Londoners remember who Wallace was. The English crime writer, journalist, novelist, screenwriter and playwright wrote 175 novels. His *Edgar Wallace Mysteries* used to run on the lower halves of double bills in British cinemas. Forty-seven of them were released between 1960 and 1965. They always featured men in raincoats loitering in stairwells.

Altogether over 160 films were made of his novels, more than any other British author. In the 1920s, one of Wallace's publishers claimed that a quarter of all books read in England were written by him.

He is best remembered today as the co-creator of *King Kong,* writing the early screenplay and story for the movie as well as the short story 'King Kong,' which was published in 1933. The dozens of other characters he created are now forgotten, but the pub that bears his name lives on.

Newspapers had been born in the coffee shops of the mid-seventeenth century; items of comment and gossip were written down and passed around. These pieces developed into newsletters and were printed in Fleet Street. William Caxton's apprentice, Wynkyn de Worde, had moved his printing press there in 1500, so the associations ran deep.

I remember how the area's hacks and printers always drank together up and down the street. The legendary El Vino's was converted from a hall of mirrors and opened as a wine bar in 1879. Its original owner became Lord Mayor in 1924.

When the setting of metal type was replaced with its digital equivalent, the printers left *en masse* and the editors were glad to see them go. The radicalized print chapels had deliberately reduced productivity for years. But one of their pubs, the Old Bell, is still popular. The worn wooden floor undulates and customers perch on the triangular oak stools. The back door leads into the tranquillity of St Bride's Church courtyard, while leaded-glass windows face out onto Fleet Street.

St Bride's itself remains the spiritual home of British journalism. Wynkyn de Worde had modernized English printing, and was buried here in 1535. At number 71 Fleet Street, the former HQ of *Punch* magazine, Thomas Hood's sentimental poem 'The Song of the Shirt' was engraved on the wall in English and French because it tripled the circulation of *Punch* when they ran it.

John, here's one for you.

JOHN MAY: This is a bit of an odd one. A London Underground tube station that is not a 'closed ghost station,' but rather a 'doesn't exist at all' station. West Ashfield is used most days and provides an essential service, but in fact it is situated halfway up an office block in West Kensington.

Its purpose? To train staff about how to use their stations. In addition to looking like a tube station it also behaves like one. When a train is due to arrive, although no physical train appears, the platform rumbles, speakers drown out conversations and there is a fan in the corner simulating the wind that heralds a train's arrival. It has a control room, *trompe l'oeil* views and even a newspaper stand. Presumably it'll soon be replaced by a VR headset.

ARTHUR BRYANT: Thank God I don't need to know what that is.

Now this.

It was the world's first tunnel under a navigable river. And it's still there.

Running between Rotherhithe and Wapping, the Thames Tunnel was designed by Marc Brunel and is one of the greatest engineering feats of the nineteenth century. 'The Great Bore'—not Raymondo—finally opened to the public in 1843 after eighteen years of construction, and featured the first 'underwater' shopping arcade with a parade of sixty shops selling souvenirs and knick-knackery. Every year a fancy fair was held in the tunnel. The exhibits included panoramas, side shows and scientific demonstrations.

In November 1827 Marc's son, Isambard Kingdom Brunel, organized a lavish banquet in the tunnel to help convince people that it was safe. Victorians called the tunnel the eighth wonder of the world, but—and by now you know where I'm going with this—fortunes fell and it became notorious for prostitutes and brigands. 'Tunnel thieves' lurked in the arches and mugged passers-by.

In 1865 it was bought by the East London Railway Company. In the twenty-first century the grand entrance hall to the tunnel is once more accessible to the public.

JOHN MAY: London is a strangely severe city. Just as pensioners over-prune their back gardens, we don't care much for frills and fripperies (you only have to compare the park benches in Paris and London to see the difference) and from Blackheath to Regent's Park we're drawn to barren open spaces.

The bare-looking Paternoster Square, next to St Paul's, was named after the priests who chanted the opening line of the Lord's Prayer as they walked behind the cathedral. Right up until the Second World War it was filled with bookshops and stalls, as it had been since medieval times, but the Blitz took care of that.

The square languished, ugly and unloved, for decades.

When Prince Charles intervened to soften the proposed plans

for the square (which were horrible enough by anyone's standards), hands were thrown up at the old boy's interference. The square now exists in a kind of limbo, a slap of Italian Renaissance here, a dash of brutalism there, no books and, more insultingly, a bench shaped like one.

ARTHUR BRYANT: What the square needs are the rows of bookstalls that adorned it for so many decades. A bookseller friend tells me that the young haven't acquired the arcane habit of collecting old books. More worryingly, they don't know what to do when they enter his shop. They stare at the spines, poke the odd volume but don't take them down from the shelves, as if they were untouchable alien objects.

JOHN MAY: I'm not especially nostalgic, Arthur, but I have to agree with you on this point. Once London provided what its residents needed: furniture stores in residential neighbourhoods, artists' suppliers in the streets where artists lived, stationery shops and ironmongers and glassware stores. When I walk through the streets around the Bank of England now I see nothing but deserted offices and lonely-looking coffee joints with bored staff. At least Paternoster Square still provides rear views of Temple Bar and St Paul's Cathedral.

ARTHUR BRYANT: Just a couple more. This one concerns the grubby mock-Greek temple of St Pancras New Church. It's right on the hellish Euston Road and is barely noticed by commuters heading to work. They should look up from their walkie-phones occasionally because it looks less like a place of worship than Dracula's townhouse. The bloody thing has *ramparts*, although the embellishments look vaguely Incan, and the front doors are the tallest I've ever seen on a church. Anyway, there's a peculiar story attached to the place. Supposedly, when the four enormous stone young ladies, great draped caryatids destined for the exterior, were delivered, it was found that they were too tall to fit into their allotted spaces. The statues had been provided in sections (they're *very* big), so the sculptor suggested leaving out the midriffs to make them fit, which is why they seem such a strange shape.

JOHN MAY: Clearly the body images of the past are far removed from our own.

ARTHUR BRYANT: Spoken like a true North London liberal. John, can you name three places in Central London that aren't in London at all?

JOHN MAY: Is this some kind of trick question?

ARTHUR BRYANT: A trick? *Moi?* Heaven forfend. The first one is Pickering Place. A darkly polished, very neat square in St James's down an alleyway, it was among the last places in London to be used for fighting duels, popular because lookouts could be posted at the end of the passage. However, it has a bigger claim to fame: it was briefly part of America. Before Texas joined the US it was represented for one year by the Texan Embassy here. Not everything from Texas is huge. Pickering Place is the smallest square in London.

The second one is Ye Old Mitre of 1546, a well-concealed pub in the little yard of Ely Place just off Hatton Garden. It's replete with the kind of gloomy panelling and poky nooks and crannies you'd hope for. If you don't spot the sign on the lamppost in Hatton Garden pointing into the alleyway, you'll walk straight past it. Until recently it was not part of London but in ancient Cambridgeshire, so the City of London Police had no jurisdiction there.

JOHN MAY: Why did it count as being in Cambridge?

ARTHUR BRYANT: Because until the late twentieth century its land belonged to the Bishops of Ely. It was subject to different by-laws, but there's no evidence that criminals avoided arrest by claiming sanctuary in another county. The boundary lines have now been redrawn so that the pub is back in London.

The last one is Savoy Court off the Strand, leading to the Savoy Hotel. It's London's only American street because you have to drive on the right. Technically it's not a public thoroughfare but on private land belonging to the hotel, and required a special Act of Parliament to create. When chauffeured in a horse-drawn carriage a passenger would sit behind the driver. By approaching the hotel on the right-hand side, the chauffeur or the hotel's doorman was able to open the door without walking around the vehicle, allowing the passenger to quickly alight and walk straight into the hotel.

Janice wants to do one more bit. Take it away, Janice.

48

Majestic Merchandise & Other Stories

JANICE LONGBRIGHT: I suffer from flat feet. It seems I've spent the whole of my working life schlepping up and down the Via Trinobantina.

That was the Roman name for the great road between Essex and Hampshire that became Oxford Street. But before it was taken over by giant screens of anorexic girls and trainers that look like children's toy cars, it was even weirder.

The London Dolphinarium was at 65 Oxford Street and featured star attraction dolphins Bonnie and Clyde, splashing about in the narrow basement. It was cruel, smelly and unhygienic, and disappeared in 1973 after only two years of business. I think everyone sensed it was a horrible thing to do to a dolphin.

Oxford Street's compensations were its cinemas, of which I counted at least ten, including the great arthouse Academy Cinema, which was run by old ladies and made its own posters out of woodcuts. It had a no-smoking policy years before a ban came in and was surrounded in black velvet drapes, like a funeral parlour that showed Fellini films.

Studios Seven and Eight were a pair of conjoined cinemas at Oxford Circus—I've no idea what happened to studios one to six—and were less beloved but just as atmospheric. Until the late seventies there was a huge multi-coloured neon fountain spouting up the front of the building that had become a London landmark. The balcony had rows of single seats 'for ladies who do not wish to be disturbed.' There were a lot of wandering hands in cinemas in those days. It never bothered me because I had a fork in my handbag.

London's all-night cinemas were more like armpits than fleapits. Their horsehair seats were split, their floors were sticky and they smelled of tramps' feet. There was a half-hearted attempt to ban smoking back then. They'd sternly announce, 'The seats on the RIGHT-hand side of this cinema are reserved for smokers only.'

I remember blokes pulling in punters to play three-card monte on the pavement and odd little auction shops run by geezers with megaphones. Once Oxford Street had been filled with smashing department stores and theatres, but they had trouble finding quality clientele. The problem was the location; the street had been constructed between the Tyburn gallows at Hyde Park Corner and the old St Giles rookery, a notorious slum that started roughly where Centre Point is now.

Oxford Street really copped it during the war, and was bombed again by the IRA. More recently the Crossrail project took out whole city blocks, leaving a piecemeal mess of chain stores, few of which could compete with online services. You still have to venture into the West End if you're looking for a fuller-figure panty girdle in turquoise satin. I imagine.

When Harry Selfridge was still at his flagship store he had golf pros giving lessons, footballers making personal appearances, the BBC on the roof broadcasting, book readings, cookery demonstrations, fashion shows, cultural and scientific exhibitions. John Logie Baird unveiled his television there in 1926.

Today Westminster Council still refuses to close the street to traffic. Developers think that blingier stores will bring back kids with too much money, but whenever they've gathered here in the past they've tended to stab each other, and the Met gets to clear up the mess.

Why is there no café culture? 'Health and safety,' apparently. Why isn't there a museum about the street's rich history? Museums don't make property developers rich.

You can still go to Oxford Street for cheap knickers but not a lot else.

ARTHUR BRYANT: Sickly dolphins and cheap knickers? Isn't there anything nice you can say about the place?

JANICE LONGBRIGHT: I once bought a half-litre bottle of Chanel for five quid off a barrow-boy.

ARTHUR BRYANT: There you are—a bargain.

JANICE LONGBRIGHT: It smelled of paint stripper and brought the backs of my knees out in a rash.

ARTHUR BRYANT: I know a good shop, but it's not in Oxford Street. The next time you take a stroll past Buckingham Palace, you might think of it as one. In the nicest possible way, the royal family sells tradition and ceremony to the world's visitors, and doing so doesn't make it any less real or unique.

HRH likes a tipple so it makes perfect sense that the Queen should start selling Buckingham Palace gin, described thusly:

'Lemon verbena, hawthorn berries and mulberry leaves are among the 12 botanicals hand-picked for the gin in the Gardens at Buckingham Palace.' I'm not quite sure why *Gardens* gets a capital letter but I suppose when you're royal you can punctuate how you like. There's a mulberry tree that was planted at the time of James I and forty-five different types of mulberry tree in the grounds, which is a lot of gin.

Speaking of which, the Buckingham Palace Garden, thirty-nine lush acres lying behind high spiked walls, magically screens out the street pollution and noise to provide an oasis of calm in the centre of the city. And you can visit it in the summer. After a bit of a dust-up with the more annoying members of the royal family, there was no chance of me ever getting invited to one of HRH's garden parties, so John and I faked—

JOHN MAY: We didn't fake anything, Arthur. We applied for passes from the Met.

ARTHUR BRYANT: Which Coatsleeve Charlie printed up for us.

We got into the garden, the only large Central London park I'd never been inside, and checked the grounds, pretending to look for a cat burglar.

The garden provides a habitat for thirty species of breeding bird, including some rare natives and over 325 species of wild-flower.

The back of Buckingham Palace is a bit less attractive than the front, but warmer. At dusk the amber stone glows. There's a broad terrace for entertaining—the Queen hosts parties for people from all walks of life, apparently not including anyone from the PCU. The lawns are elegantly striped and the lake has islands, fed from the Serpentine overflow in Hyde Park or the Tyburn, depending on which of the security guards you talk to.

One of them told me that no scenes in *The Crown* were ever filmed there. She said that almost everything in the series was subtly wrong, which gave them all a good laugh.

The garden is venerable and outrageously picturesque. There's even a perfect view of the Angel of Peace on her chariot on the Wellington Arch, raised as a smack in the eye for Napoleon.

The garden is also home to the enormous Waterloo Vase, standing alone on a pedestal in a clearing. It was chosen by Napoleon and hewn from a single fifteen-foot block of marble. It nearly fell through the floor of the National Gallery, so it ended up here in the woods instead.

The garden was inspired by the work of Lancelot 'Capability' Brown, designed to be 'long-grass' and free-flowing instead of rigid and formal and dull, like French gardens. You can easily imagine the young princesses Elizabeth and Margaret playing in the summerhouse and holding picnics on the lawn. The Queen loves the vista because she can see it from her rooms.

HRH's home-made gin is available in the pop-up Buckingham Palace shop, but how about handbag biscuits? These are emergency shortbread biscuits that one keeps in one's handbag in case one is suddenly offered tea with nary a decent biscuit in sight. There's a healthy cheekiness in this, the same kind that allowed the Queen to jump out of a plane at the Olympics, which I still think she was very brave to do.

I was looking for something I could buy Alma in the shop and naturally didn't want to spend too much money on her, but there were a surprising number of budget items there, including tiaras and pyjamas with corgis on. The Queen also does dolly mixtures and jelly babies, assuming that in some part of the world it's still 1952.

How about some guardsman socks, Buckingham Palace oven gloves or the world's ugliest teapot for just under six hundred quid? Fair play to Her Maj, she's largely financing herself these days and doing a great job of it. Until recently she remained in Buckingham Palace from Monday to Friday and was there much more often than any of us realized, a benign presence.

I notice there's an absence of Prince Charles–related tat beyond some birthday celebration chargers, which are different to phone chargers. As for Prince Andrew, it was probably too risky finding anything for him to endorse.

Critics reckon the rot set in when the younger members of the Firm appeared on the embarrassing TV show *It's a Royal Knock-out!* in 1987, but I like this side of the royal family. They may be able to trace their bloodlines back hundreds of years but they're not averse to flogging the Buckingham Palace state coach fridge magnet if they have to. One does belong to a nation of shopkeepers, after all.

JOHN MAY: The Proms or, to give them their full title, the Henry Wood Promenade Concerts are an eight-week summer season of daily concerts held annually, predominantly in the Royal Albert Hall.

The Proms are, of course, a Good Thing, bringing wonderful music arranged in imaginative programmes at affordable prices. They're currently run by the BBC, who stick their name in front of them, until they lose the rights that is, when they'll probably become the Kentucky Fried Chicken Henry Wood Promenade Concerts. However, the Last Night of the Proms has evolved into a Bad Thing, for two reasons.

The first, to do with the ticketing, goes back to the construction of the Royal Albert Hall. Promming (promenading) tickets are priced the same as for that season's concerts, but seated tickets are more expensive. To pre-book a seat it is necessary to have bought tickets for at least five other concerts in the season. However, 1,276 permanent seats in the 5,272-capacity venue were leased to 330 individuals for 999 years to help pay for the building, and owners are allowed to optimize their returns by reselling their tickets.

This means that online tickets for the Last Night sell for thousands, with members of the public excluded unless they're very rich indeed. Looking at the audiences you'd also conclude they're also very old and very white.

Some people's perception of the Proms is undoubtedly based on the Last Night, although this is very different from the other concerts. It usually takes place on the second Saturday in September. The playlist is pretty simple: the first half has some variety; the second half doesn't. It usually includes 'Serenade to Music' by Vaughan Williams, a bit of jolly Donizetti, a Latin American medley, 'Land of Hope and Glory,' the *Fantasia on British Sea-Songs* arranged by Henry Wood, 'Rule, Britannia!,' 'Jerusalem,' the National Anthem and 'Auld Lang Syne.'

It descends into an excuse for exuberant and extremely creepy displays of patriotism. Union Jacks are waved by the Prommers, especially during 'Rule, Britannia!' Flags, balloons and party poppers are all welcomed—although John Drummond discouraged this 'extraneous noise' during his tenure as director. The event is peppered with knowing little rituals, such as wiping imaginary sweat from the bust of Sir Henry Wood, and the giving of a speech.

It was a well-intentioned event that somehow became a distorted vision of lost Empire, Brexit writ large, old Tories and young fogeys overexciting themselves in a celebration of non-existent superiority that blindly waves two fingers at Europe, attended by patriots terrified of losing a royal head on the five-pound note yet happy to own second homes in France.

ARTHUR BRYANT: Don't hold back, John. Say what you mean.

JOHN MAY: Sorry about that.

49

The Endless Charivari &
Other Stories

JANICE LONGBRIGHT: The old boys have given me this bit to talk about my London obsessions on the condition that I don't mention vintage boxed Playtex brassieres.

For a while I was stationed in West London near the West London Air Terminal, which operated from 1957 to 1974. You could leave your flight baggage there and they'd take it to the plane for you. Even better was the Imperial Airways Empire Terminal in Victoria, which opened in 1939. The building is an art deco masterpiece with a ten-storey central clock tower and a gorgeous Egyptian-looking sculpture by Eric Broadbent called *Speed Wings over the World*.

The terminal's location was picked because the Air Ministry insisted that Southampton had to be used as a base for flying boats, and the site backed onto the Southern Railway station. A special train consisting almost entirely of first-class Pullman carriages took passengers to the flying boats from Southampton Water. They were delivered onward to Africa, India, the Far East and Australia the next day. What a civilized way to travel. I was born out of my time, I swear.

Another overlooked place I've always liked in that part of London is a row of artists' houses called St Paul's Studios, with their unusual high-domed curving windows. Their only disadvantage is being on the traffic-clogged Talgarth Road.

Further along is the even more neglected Olympia, the grand exhibition centre built as an agricultural hall in 1886. The Victorians loved stuff like that. Both Oswald Mosley's British Union of Fascists and Nigel Farage's Brexit Party held rallies there, but it always makes me think of Fanny Cradock.

OK, a bit of a leap there but let me explain. Her real name was Phyllis Nan Sortain 'Primrose' Pechey, and she was a familiar face on tiny black-and-white television screens in the 1950s. Her parents, Bijou and Archibald—I swear I'm not making this up—were usually bankrupt so the gravel-voiced Fanny tried various menial jobs before entering the restaurant trade, hailing Escoffier as a saviour of British cookery. She and her monocle-wearing fourth husband Major Johnnie had a *Daily Telegraph* column in which they probably appeared quite normal. Then they started turning theatres into restaurants.

In the early 1950s, Fanny would come onstage and cook vast dishes that would then be served to the audience (at this time there were hardly any houses with television sets, remember). Soon she was feeding hundreds of people at every performance. She and the Major became famous for an appalling-looking roast turkey, complete with stuffed head, tail feathers and wings. With fake French accents, they performed as a drunken hen-pecked husband and domineering wife, roles they took to like ducks to an oven.

They dropped the comedy accents but the roles stayed. Fanny

came over as a monster, snapping her fingers in the faces of assistants, nagging Johnnie, smashing around her pots and pans, chucking refined white sugar and pounds of butter over everything. As she aged she painted her eyebrows further and further up her forehead, somehow managing to look like a cross between Danny La Rue and Boris Karloff.

The public loved her. The nation went Fanny-mad. She was always saying 'This won't break your budget' in the most condescending fashion. Her food was hideously garish; she was fond of vegetable dyes in Festival of Britain colours and cocktail sticks shoved through maraschino cherries.

As her fame grew she appeared in the vast Olympia building, which is what made me think of her. An insight into how a copper's mind works. She continued cooking on television and at live events, carrying on right through Johnnie's heart attack and a variety of terrified assistants, also finding time to write awful romantic novels. Famous for a catchphrase that may not have existed—'May all your doughnuts turn out like Fanny's'—she continued until career disaster finally struck.

In 1976 a housewife living in Devon won the 'Cook of the Realm' competition, leading to the BBC selecting her to organize a banquet attended by key political figures. The BBC filmed Fanny advising on the menu. Cradock fake-vomited at the selection and humiliated the housewife on live television, telling her, 'You're among professionals now, dear.'

The public instantly turned on her. Fanny wrote a letter of apology but her contract was cancelled, fans felt betrayed and she was forced to retire. I imagine she was a fairly horrible human being (she walked off set after discovering that Danny La Rue was a drag queen, although I can't imagine how on earth she failed to notice), but her clown-coloured cookery was frighteningly influential. She also worked for the British Gas Council, so she only promoted gas ovens, which was why my mother refused to brew tea on an electric hob.

That's our national cuisine taken care of. What about our national drink?

ARTHUR BRYANT: Beer.

JANICE LONGBRIGHT: Tea.

To understand its importance you have to see it as a ritual deeply embedded in our culture, like going to church once was. Mr Bryant no longer asks me to make him tea, as he grew tired of being scalded.

Nobody knows how many cups of tea the British drink a year. The figure leaps about in the billions. If the British are so obsessed with tea why are there no hip tea shops, only coffee bars? Coffees can be poshed up with complex rituals, from the patterning of froth to the ordering of 'soy decaf flat white, side of hot milk and a twist' variety. Coffee is egalitarian and seems younger and cooler somehow, even though it isn't, and when it's bad can be very bad indeed. London's working-class caffs always served fantastic tea and appalling instant coffee.

Inevitably there are matters of class and gender involved. Tea was mother's calming drink, and the workman's break; 'builder's tea' always comes in a mug. Flavoured teas allowed supermarkets to sell dinky silken pouches to the middle classes, but teabags are inherently common. Loose tea has a richer flavour, 'puts hairs on your chest' and makes grouts, for which you need a teapot and somewhere to empty it. Mr B. emptied his out of the window until he soaked his downstairs neighbour once too often and got a shovel through his letterbox. Tea refreshes and calms and is relatively good for you, but has a bourgeois image. We all drink buckets of the stuff.

How you respond to an offer of tea is also a signifier of who you are. Visitors say, 'Only if you're having one.' Dads say, 'I'm gasping,' 'I'm spitting feathers' and 'Anyone for a cuppa?' Grandmothers foist it on you on hot days, insisting that it cools you down. Tea is also a fantastic device for setting up scenes in books now that people no longer tap out cigarettes and offer them around, but smoke furtively alone out of toilet windows. I asked Meera what she hated most about the job and she said, 'The tea. Everyone you visit offers you one. I'm Indian. I don't want any more bloody tea.'

Throughout its infamous roles in Britain's past—from its key trading position in the Chinese Opium War, when we used it to enslave a populace, to the Boston Tea Party—tea remained ubiquitous and cheap.

After the heavy bombardment of Southern England began, a government unit offering psychological help was set up to aid those bombed out of their homes, but neighbourhood communities were said to be so strong that few were convinced to use it. The standard response was, 'I'll be all right once I've had a nice cup of tea and a sit down.'

In my favourite wartime film, *Brief Encounter*, Celia Johnson says she feels sick at the railway station, but we all know she nearly threw herself under a train. Her gossipy but well-meaning friend Dolly is instantly on the case. A nice cup of tea bucks them up, along with a tot of brandy. But the real counterpoint of the film is the ease with which the tea lady and her porter flirt; they're working-class and not held back by social guilt. Tea ladies and charladies were the salt of the earth, and could always be relied on for a brew. Tea defined radio plays for decades; the endless rattling of all those cups!

In Japan, the tea ceremony is about ritual and control and sitting on your ankles for an hour and a half. Our more mundane ceremonies pass unnoticed, probably because they mostly involve custard creams.

Scientists have found that the catechins (antioxidants) in green tea extract increase the body's ability to burn fat as fuel, which accounts for improved muscle endurance. Drinking tea can help reduce the risk of heart attack and has other fine properties, from protecting teeth to boosting the immune system. And tea without milk has no calories.

Tea traditions are indicators of social class; do you have high tea or a tea break? That's why tea shops have an image problem. Who should they appeal to? Coffee is more socially fluid, but in the UK tea remains the queen of beverages.

JOHN MAY: So, after all that we're back in the Strand, at the Twinings tea shop.

JANICE LONGBRIGHT: You can never escape your roots, John. You might circle the globe but in my experience you end up living a few miles from where you were born.

JOHN MAY: That used to be true, Janice, but now Britons settle up to one hundred miles from where they were born. My attitude towards London changes all the time. I found this quote which explains how I feel; it's by Percy Bysshe Shelley:

Hell is a city much like London—
A populous and smoky city;
There are all sorts of people undone,
And there is little or no fun done;
Small justice shown, and still less pity.

JANICE LONGBRIGHT: A bit dark, John.

JOHN MAY: I'm not quite as misty-eyed as my old friend. There's a country to see beyond the capital, and a whole world beyond that. I'm too old now to experience much of it, so I need to at least be clear about where I live. What I learned about London from Arthur is that it's still Roman and was transformed by four things: the Reformation, transport, war and late capitalism.

JANICE LONGBRIGHT: And Londoners?

JOHN MAY: They have a fondness for ceremonies, processions, rebellions, drunkenness, ridicule and holding dinners inside anything they've built. It's said that fourteen people had dinner on top of Nelson's Column. Arthur, come over here. What's your final word on London?

ARTHUR BRYANT: *Punch* magazine, remember that? It ran from 1841 to 1992. It came up earlier in the bit about Thomas Hood on Fleet Street.

JOHN MAY: *Punch* was funny for a while and then became dreadful. There are probably still some back issues in my dentist's waiting room. What about it?

ARTHUR BRYANT: It was subtitled *The London Charivari*. A charivari was a paganistic procession full of fools who played rough music on kettles, pots and pans and teased everyone around them. Sometimes they were naked and covered in treacle and feathers. They danced through London and played the hornpipe and held mock trials. London was always a carnival: disrespectful, bawdy, riotous. Mr Punch himself summed it up when, after killing the Devil, he said, 'Now we can all do as we like!'

JOHN MAY: And that's how you see London, is it?

ARTHUR BRYANT: Not entirely, but I see traces of mischief and misbehaviour everywhere, from our whinnying press to our capering politicians. They used to say that when London laughed, the whole world laughed. They didn't mention that it would also take all your money. I'm guessing more Londoners died poor than rich. What does it mean to you, Janice?

JANICE LONGBRIGHT: London? I had plenty of time to think about it, walking around on my mother's beat and then on my own. I'd say this. What you see isn't what's there. And what's not there is what you feel.

ARTHUR BRYANT: Hm. I never thought that what's not there wasn't what I couldn't see. I don't think we've ever had this conversation before.

JOHN MAY: That's because, like many of the conversations you seem to enjoy, it doesn't entirely make sense.

ARTHUR BRYANT: Your Shelley quote intrigues me, John. So, which is true? Are we in a carnival or in hell?

JOHN MAY: I would say both in equal measure. And we can't leave either of them because this is home, and that's the struggle we face as we age and the ties bind us ever more tightly.

ARTHUR BRYANT: I have a last little bit about London to add.

JOHN MAY: Dear fellow, of course you do.

ARTHUR BRYANT: Let's take stock of where we are; in a small northern country in a medium-sized city built around a switch-back river. Thanks to its maritime power and the fact that it set the world's time zones it became very rich, like Venice and Constantinople once had been, although that wealth has lately been consolidated to make the rich richer. Time and geography allow its bankers to work for around seventeen hours a day, so more money can be made.

London is a lot nearer the Arctic than most of us realize. We're on the same latitude as the tip of Alaska, on a par with parts of Belgium, Poland and the Czech Republic. This was always a winter city, lit by bonfire embers. Time and again it collapsed, scythed down by the Grim Reaper, only to be pulled back on its feet by the young, who know no better. The city cuts jigs with the Devil, whirling on through the years like a ragged duchess who can't tell that the musicians went home long ago.

It's not the city I grew up in and it won't be yours. As we increasingly look to the Far East, London, like other European cities, is slipping into irrelevance, just another quaint ancient town tethered by its history.

We think of ourselves as connected and informed. Yet a recent national poll found that of two thousand randomly selected adults, a stonking 59 percent couldn't name the last prime minister. That's about the same ratio as in the late eighteenth century. The widening wealth gap means that leisure and choice are only for those with time and money. We under-represent Black and working-class residents. We under-represent women. We must continue to learn from our immigrant population, and respect their work and their lives. We all have common points of interest. Luckily the inspiration lies right beneath our feet.

Despite their shocking underfunding, the arts keep London alive. America has wealthier museums and galleries; we have to think on our feet to survive.

London is one of the few European cities without an Old Quarter. It had constant change forced on it for centuries, starting with separation from Europe in the Ice Age, through the Romans and the Normans and the Great Fire and the Industrial Revolution, from the wars to the banking revolution and the effects of the pandemic. Paradoxically, because of this rolling programme of change it didn't appear to change that much at all.

Those who built London thought about it in the long term. Here's a good example.

Westminster Hall dates from 1393 and has the largest timber roof in northern Europe. When it needed restoring in 1913 a lot of the wood needed replacing. But where do you find such giant trees? It turned out that the original timbers came from Wadhurst in Sussex. The estate's owners realized that new wood would be needed in about 520 years' time so they planted a stand of oaks for that specific purpose. By 1913 they were ready to be cut and used, and the hall was repaired. By comparison, the City of London's new skyscrapers are reckoned to have a shelf life of about fifteen years.

London's pace of change accelerates but we remain Londoners because London is also a psychological and—dare one say—a spiritual state.

We don't make London; London makes us. We carry around the linguistic and behavioural baggage of past generations. We only need to be here for five minutes before we're standing our ground while apologizing for being in the way. And London re-

flects us back, especially in our writing. This is a speech from a
dying hero:

> *Farewell, all you good boys in merry London!*
> *Ne'er shall we more upon Shrove Tuesday meet,*
> *And pluck down houses of iniquity . . .*
> *   I shall never more*
> *Hold open, while another pumps both legs . . .*
>
> *I die! fly, fly, my soul, to Grocers' Hall!*

That's from *The Knight of the Burning Pestle* (literally, 'The Boy
with the Sore Dick'), first performed in 1607. The play was written by the twenty-three-year-old Francis Beaumont and was the
first to make its heroes rudely working-class, and to break the
fourth wall, involving the audience. Those were rebellious, licentious, appalling times and the young playwright reflected this.
Four hundred years later it was performed on the same spot and
it seemed that nothing much had changed.

But for my closing thought on London, I'd echo Virginia Woolf
and ask: 'What are you going to meet if you turn this corner?'

In the countryside the answer to that question would be: 'Another tree and possibly a dead mole.' But in London, as in life itself, you can never know what joys and tragedies wait around the
corner.

JANICE LONGBRIGHT: I think I'd better buy you boys a beer.

ARTHUR BRYANT: I should be the one to get them in, as a thank
you for giving up your spare time.

Oh, Raymondo, there you are! We've been waiting for ages!
What on earth are you wearing?

RAYMOND LAND: Hello, all. I got this in Chapel Market. It's a sheepskin jacket.

ARTHUR BRYANT: Surely you're supposed to take the sheep out of it first. I thought you were going to come in and do a piece about, oh, Clarice Cliff or something.

RAYMOND LAND: I was all ready to give a talk about my Clarice Cliff tableware collection. I dressed up especially. Then you never called.

ARTHUR BRYANT: I'm sure I left a message.

RAYMOND LAND: I don't have voicemail.

ARTHUR BRYANT: Oh, that is a shame. Anyway, it was days ago. We've finished now.

RAYMOND LAND: But you were recording here just a minute ago. I heard you through the door.

ARTHUR BRYANT: No, no, I had the wireless on. You're imagining things again.

RAYMOND LAND: Now, look here, I know what you're trying to do—

ARTHUR BRYANT: Has your memory been a little rusty lately?

RAYMOND LAND: Well, yes, a bit—

ARTHUR BRYANT: Have things been going 'missing'?

RAYMOND LAND: Yes, but only because you keep hiding them.

ARTHUR BRYANT: I don't hide things from you. Why would I do that? It's all in your mind.

RAYMOND LAND: There's nothing in my mind. Why are you always trying to imply that I'm—

ARTHUR BRYANT: Don't you see? It's not me. It's you. You're not well.

RAYMOND LAND: I'm perfectly fine.

ARTHUR BRYANT: That's what they always say.

RAYMOND LAND: Don't keep waving your fingers about in front of my eyes!

ARTHUR BRYANT: Oh, this isn't working. Are you coming with us to the Scottish Stores, then?

RAYMOND LAND: Are you inviting me?

ARTHUR BRYANT: Well, of course we are. You know how much we value your earnest contributions over a quenching libation.

RAYMOND LAND: You didn't invite me last time we were kicked out of the PCU building.

ARTHUR BRYANT: Which time was that? You'll have to be more specific. Er, you do have the company float on you?

RAYMOND LAND: I have a credit card.

ARTHUR BRYANT: Any upper limit? I'd better look after it for you. It'll save time if you just give me your wallet. What's this? An unsigned M&S card?

RAYMOND LAND: I haven't used it yet.

ARTHUR BRYANT: You ought to be careful; there are thieves about. I'll take care of it for you, I need some new underpants. Off you go. I'll see you over there. John, look after him, make sure he doesn't try to get away.

| | |

There, I've given them all the slip. It's just us now. Come closer.

I just wanted to say.

London.

According to the playwright Ben Jonson it was the city of bawds and roysters, claret-wine and oysters. To me it is just home, where I am on the inside looking out instead of somewhere outside looking in. It's my city, not yours. Which is to say that I see it in a certain way that you do not, and vice versa.

I have no fantasies involving a comatose retirement on the Isle of Wight like poor old Raymondo. I have no intention of leaving this grubby, exhausting, maddening city.

London is like a greedy old landlady. She didn't ask me to come, didn't invite me to stay and won't miss me when I've left.

And that suits me fine.

MR BRYANT'S RECOMMENDED
LONDON READING

All the Tiny Moments Blazing by Jed Pope

The Annals of London by John Richardson

Arthur Mee's London by Arthur Mee

City of Laughter by Vic Gatrell

Criminal London by Mark Herber

Curiocity by Henry Elliot & Matt Lloyd-Rose

Dirty Old London by Lee Jackson

The Five by Hallie Rubenhold

The Folklore of London by Antony Clayton

Hidden Treasures of London by Michael McNay

High Buildings Low Morals by Rob Baker

London: A History in Verse, edited by Mark Ford

London As It Might Have Been by Felix Barker & Ralph Hyde

London at War by Philip Ziegler

London: The Autobiography, edited by Jon E. Lewis

London: The Biography by Peter Ackroyd

London: City of Cities by Phil Baker

London: City of Words by David Caddy & Westrow Cooper

London Film Location Guide by Simon R. H. James

London Fog by Christine L. Corton

London Folk Tales by Helen East

London's Grand Guignol by Richard J. Hand & Michael Wilson

London in the Sixties by Rainer Metzger

London Is Stranger than Fiction by Peter Jackson

London Lore by Steve Stroud

London's Oddities by Vicky Wilson

The London We Have Lost by Richard Tames

London's West End by Rohan McWilliam

London: The Wicked City by Fergus Linnane

London in the Nineteenth Century by Jerry White

Lost London by Philip Davies

A Lust for Window Sills by Harry Mount

Medical London by Richard Barnett

The Moving Metropolis, edited by Sheila Taylor

Murder, Mayhem and Music Hall by Barry Anthony

Nairn's London by Ian Nairn

Old & New London by Edward Walford (these six volumes form
    a quintessential portrait of Victorian London)

Piccadilly by Stephen Hoare

The Secret Lore of London by John Matthews with Caroline Wise

Shaping London by Terry Farrell

Underground London by Stephen Smith

Vanishing London by Paul Joseph

Victorian and Edwardian London by Sir John Betjeman

The Worst Street in London by Fiona Rule

Acknowledgements

All of Mr Bryant's recommended books were used in the creation of this volume, and too many more to name or even recall. When I delivered my 'book about London with a twist' to my agent, James Wills, he said delightedly, 'Oh, it's a Bryant & May book, just without the murder plot!' I would like to thank my erstwhile editor, the ever-enthusiastic Simon Taylor, with whom I've worked on every Bryant & May novel and who knows as much about the old boys as I do. A big thank-you is also due to Kate Samano and Richenda Todd for sorting the lingo, and to Mandy Little for her wise advice. Finally, a big group hug to everyone who has shown me that there's always more to London: Martin, John, Sally, Suzi, Maggie, Roger, Darrell and Deborah.

ABOUT THE AUTHOR

CHRISTOPHER FOWLER is the multiple award-winning author of almost fifty novels and short-story collections, including the Bryant & May mysteries. His other novels include *Roofworld, Spanky, The Sand Men* and *Hot Water*. He has also written two acclaimed memoirs, *Paperboy* (winner of the Green Carnation Prize) and *Film Freak*. In 2015 he won the CWA 'Dagger in the Library' for his body of work. He lives in London and Barcelona.

christopherfowler.co.uk
Twitter: @Peculiar

ABOUT THE TYPE

This book was set in Dante, a typeface designed by Giovanni Mardersteig (1892–1977). Conceived as a private type for the Officina Bodoni in Verona, Italy, Dante was originally cut only for hand composition by Charles Malin, the famous Parisian punch cutter, between 1946 and 1952. Its first use was in an edition of Boccaccio's Trattatello in laude di Dante that appeared in 1954. The Monotype Corporation's version of Dante followed in 1957. Though modeled on the Aldine type used for Pietro Cardinal Bembo's treatise De Aetna in 1495, Dante is a thoroughly modern interpretation of that venerable face.